FLASH, GHOST, GONE

A GHOST PHOTOGRAPHER MYSTERY

FELICITY GREEN

Print ISBN: 978-3-911238-10-6

CHAPTER ONE

A misty veil still clung to some of the old tombstones in the Fairwyck graveyard at three in the afternoon. Mist could really hang on tight on dreary November days in the Cotswolds.

It didn't impact my mood, though—not today.

Even though I'd just finished an exhausting day cleaning vacation rentals, I had a spring in my step as I hurried up the gravel path, my Nikon D40 slung at my side. Honestly, I was just glad I had a job. As a single mom of two clawing my way back from total financial annihilation, I needed it.

Before moving back to Fairwyck—where I'd lived until I was nine—I hadn't worked a day in my life. Many considered becoming a cleaning lady a huge step down from wealthy Connecticut housewife. But I was simply happy to be able to pay the bills. I'd nearly given up working for Judith Winters's letting agency after going into business with a friend. We had fixed up the local theater and had big dreams—dreams that had nearly crashed down on us. I'd almost lost everything again. By some miracle, we pulled through. We're still running Ghost Light

Theatre, just on a much smaller scale than originally planned.

I'd been able to get my cleaning job back—working fifty percent in both jobs—and I was glad for it. Truth be told, I kind of liked cleaning. But my good mood today wasn't because I'd gotten high off cleaning products. I'm not that into it.

A project I'd been working on—one that involved my special talent—was coming to fruition. At least, I hoped so. I tried not to think too hard about how spectacularly wrong it could all go.

I had to admit I was proud of myself. I'd come a long way from the girl who was terrified of her own ability. People may think it's exciting to communicate with beings from beyond, but let me tell you: Seeing ghosts in every picture you take is scary as hell. Especially when you're an eight-year-old who has just discovered photography as her favorite hobby. Those beings don't always look like people. And even when they do, it's deeply unsettling to realize they're all around you—you just can't see them.

One could be right next to you, staring at you, this very moment.

But yes, I'd come a long way since my mother ran away to the US with me, forbidding me to ever take a picture again. I have since embraced my paranormal skill as a gift —one that enables me to help people. It connected me with relatives who have equally unique abilities, and we learned to support each other. I was still reluctant to call myself a witch, but my great-aunt Gina and cousin Emerald kept insisting that's what we Seven women were.

Speaking of whom, I spotted Gina standing next to an open grave, uncharacteristically dressed in black. She usually wore colorful caftans, but this was a somber, funeral-like affair, and she was here for her friend Marjorie. I was glad she'd had the forethought to dress appropriately. To call my aunt eccentric would be putting it mildly.

Gina waved in greeting. As she stepped aside, I noticed someone in a detective-sergeant jacket standing beside her.

My heart skipped a beat. Okay—so I was particularly chipper this November day because I knew I'd be seeing my boyfriend, Jamie Rees.

Yes, I called him my boyfriend—even though we were both in our forties. It had taken us a while to get to this point, but since I'd finally committed to our relationship, I used that word in connection with his name as often as I could.

Jamie was talking to the groundskeeper and a forensic officer. When he spotted me, he paused mid-sentence to give me a dazzling smile.

I ran a quick hand over my long dark hair to make sure it wasn't in its usual bird's-nest state. I'd pulled it into a ponytail this morning and dragged a brush through it before coming here. I'd even swiped on a little lip gloss. Since embracing life as a jeans-and-T-shirt girl—no longer expected to look like a wealthy high-society lady—this counted as making an effort.

When I reached his side, Jamie leaned in and whispered into my ear, "Don't ask how many forms I had to beg Farrow to sign. Let's just say I'm his paperwork slave for a month."

I laughed and kissed his cheek. "Thank you. If this works out, you'll be a hero."

He raised a brow, alarm flickering in his chocolate-brown eyes. "If this works out? You said you're sure. I'll be in hot water with my boss if—"

"Don't worry," I cut him off, giving him another quick kiss. "I'm sure."

I sounded confident, but there was a nervous flutter in my stomach.

Jamie had almost lost his job because of me before. His boss, DI Farrow, and I weren't exactly friends, and he would gladly take any opportunity to make me look bad. We'd…bent the truth more than once under the guise of historical research. If I wasn't right about this, I wouldn't be the only one embarrassing myself—I'd drag Jamie down with me.

My eyes went to Marjorie Keane, who stood on Gina's other side. I greeted her with an encouraging smile, but the older woman was wrapped in grief, clutching a photograph of her father.

I'd examined that very photograph on numerous occasions—just to make sure the ghost I'd photographed in this section of the Fairwyck graveyard really was him. Every detail, from his hooded eyes to the thin mustache to the big silver ring gleaming on his finger, was burned into my memory, even though I could only glimpse a corner of the framed photo in Marjorie's hands.

The workers had already unearthed the coffin. As soon as I arrived, they proceeded to open the lid.

I hurriedly removed the lens cap on my Nikon and focused.

Lifting the camera, I took a shaky breath.

Everyone around me gasped as the coffin opened and the remains were revealed.

There was nothing left but bones and scraps of clothing after all these years. Ordinarily, we'd have had to wait for the forensic examination to prove my claim: that even though a different name was carved into the gravestone, the man buried here was, in fact, John Keane—Marjorie's father.

But this time, we were spared that painful wait. And I was so relieved to be proven right, right here, right now. I could feel Jamie's relief wafting off him. But I was mainly glad for Marjorie.

"The ring!" she croaked, tears of joy streaming down her face. Gina wrapped her arm around her.

There, on one bony finger, was the silver ring with the distinctive Celtic pattern—the same ring John Keane wore in the photograph.

"So he didn't run," Marjorie sobbed. "He didn't abandon us."

"No," Gina murmured, holding her close. "He was here all along."

It was as if the shame that had shadowed Marjorie's family for decades lifted in an instant.

Suddenly I wondered why on earth I'd ever been reluctant to embrace my gift. I could help people in such a major way.

Okay, so in this case, Gina helped too.

As the resident psychic, half the town had used her tarot-reading services—even if nobody liked to admit it. Marjorie was her friend, and for years Gina had sensed that Marjorie's father was close. It had been a difficult subject, since Marjorie never wanted to talk about him.

As a soldier in World War II, he had been reported missing. His family—after getting confirmation that he hadn't died in action and exhausting their searches—had long believed he'd abandoned them.

Gina had been convinced he had passed and that he'd stayed close to Fairwyck. She'd asked me to help.

My first thought was to do research, but Marjorie's family had already done all that. Some of the men who served with John Keane were buried here. I'd come to the graveyard to see if any ghosts still lingered near the military graves—maybe one could tell me what happened to him. It was a long shot, but communicating with ghosts was my jam. How else could I help?

I can't say photographing the graveyard was a walk in the park.

The old Liv would have been far too terrified. But after helping a few murder victims, I'd learned that feeling uncomfortable was a small price to pay to bring peace to lost souls. And, honestly, I'd gotten myself into far worse situations than being surrounded by scary ghosts in a cemetery.

I'd brought Marjorie's photo with me, hoping one of the soldiers who fought at John's side could recognize him.

Imagine my surprise when one of the ghosts looked exactly like the man in the picture—right down to the distinctive ring.

Previously, I'd gotten very creative in trying to communicate with ghosts. But this time, I didn't need to paint letters or coax a message out of them. The ghost of John Keane pointing at a grave marked with someone else's name was enough for me to unravel the mystery.

The soldier supposedly buried in this grave had been the same age as John. Back home, I'd managed to get hold of a picture of him. They looked remarkably alike, and they'd served in the same infantry division. I imagine in the aftermath of battle—with so many dead—mistakes happened. The deceased would have been identified by their uniforms, but if bodies were badly burned or damaged…

John Keane's body had been shipped home and buried by the loved ones of his comrade in this grave.

I'd been reasonably certain, but convincing the authorities had been another matter entirely.

I had to fabricate evidence, and it wouldn't have been possible without Jamie's help.

Looking at Marjorie, I reached for Jamie's hand and gave it a squeeze.

He gave me a loving smile.

He hadn't always been comfortable with my gift. But the way he'd come through for me in my quest told me he truly believed in me—and accepted that my strange supernatural abilities were part of who I was.

Jamie turned back to confer with the groundskeeper, and Gina was comforting Marjorie, who had turned away from the grave.

I lifted my camera and took a photograph. Then I glanced at the display.

The ghost of John Keane stood beside his grave. In earlier photos, he had looked miserable. His big, sad eyes reminded me so much of Marjorie when she'd first told me about her father. That small flicker of hope in his expression had been almost identical to hers too. She had never truly believed he would abandon his family.

And John had stayed close all these years, never giving up hope that one day the terrible mix-up would be discovered.

I took another picture. This time, John looked less substantial—his outline frayed around the edges, as though he were dissolving.

Holding my breath, I clicked again. A bright spot of light appeared in the frame.

I heard Marjorie gasp behind me and realized the light was visible—not just through my camera. It wasn't as intense to the naked eye, but there was definitely a glow… and more than that, a sudden feeling of peaceful silence.

Even Jamie, the coroner, and the groundskeeper and his workers fell quiet.

The click of my shutter broke the hush as I took one more photo. There was only the faintest trace of John Keane now, disappearing into the light.

I didn't need to show them the picture. I didn't need to say that the fallen soldier was now at peace.

Everyone around the grave knew.

Marjorie's tears were still flowing, but now she was smiling.

I was in awe myself. It wasn't the first time I'd witnessed a ghost crossing over—but it was the first time I'd captured it so clearly.

Gina no longer needed to prop Marjorie up, and Marjorie went to speak with the police about the next steps. I caught pieces of their conversation: the ring might be enough to sway the family, but of course DNA testing would be necessary to confirm that the wrong man had been buried here.

My great-aunt came over and slipped an arm around my shoulder. "Well done, Liv. If it weren't for you, John Keane might have haunted this graveyard for eternity."

I blushed and waved off the praise. "You were the one who sensed he was still here. It was a team effort."

"We Seven women need to stick together. That's how it's always been. Separating only brings trouble."

A shadow crossed her face.

Of course, I immediately thought of my own mother —still living in the US. She had spent years pretending her ability didn't exist and had renounced it completely. According to Gina, my mother had never been comfortable with her gift of precognition. But since I'd moved back to Fairwyck and she'd reconnected with her family, Mom had finally admitted the truth—to us and to herself.

Still...I had the strong sense that Gina wasn't talking about my mother.

There weren't many Seven witches left: Gina, Emerald, my mother, me, my children—oh, and Ethel, in a way. Even if she had been reincarnated as a cat.

Gina wrapped her black shawl tighter around herself, as though she felt a sudden chill.

Staring at the grave, she murmured more to herself than to me, "Secrets don't stay buried forever, Liv. There isn't a hole deep enough. Why do you think ghosts linger? They can't move on until the truth is discovered."

A shiver ran down my spine.

When it came to secrets, there was only one thing pressing on my mind.

A couple of months ago, during the opening night of *Twelfth Night* at the theater, I'd thought I'd seen Steven.

My fugitive husband.

The man who had completely destroyed my life.

Steven and I had been high school sweethearts. We'd married right after college—where I'd earned a degree in arts administration that I'd never used until reopening the theater with Ellie. Steven had been very successful in his job—investment something-or-other. Or so I believed.

In reality, he'd been running a Ponzi scheme. He'd scammed our friends in the gated Connecticut community where I'd felt so secure. He took out loans, remortgaged our house, dragged us deep into debt…

Our perfect life had been nothing but a house of cards.

It all collapsed when he ran off with the money—and his secretary, who he'd been having an affair with.

I'd had no part in his crimes. But I still blamed myself. I hadn't paid attention to our finances, hadn't asked questions, had happily turned a blind eye to anything unpleasant. Avoidance was something I'd always been good at—especially after years of ignoring my gift.

After I'd sold everything, and once the police had cleared me, the kids and I were left with nothing but the clothes on our backs. We moved in with my mother in Florida—though that was never going to last.

Luckily, Aunt Ethel had left me her cottage in her will. That's how we ended up in Fairwyck, where I slowly pieced our lives back together—messy and imperfect as they were.

But we were happy here. We belonged.

As much as I could never fully understand—let alone forgive—what Steven did to us…in a strange way, it led me to the path I was meant to be on. To a life where I could finally be myself.

I never expected to see him again—unless the police caught him. And even then he'd be locked up in the US, far away from me.

But that night, I saw him. Right there on the theater balcony.

It had to have been a ghost. Or a hallucination.

He'd never appeared again. Not once in all these months.

And I'd never told anyone. Some secrets needed to stay in the dark.

I was so lost in thought that I jumped when Gina spoke. "Don't you have to go?"

"What?"

"Didn't you say you needed to pick up the kids from school?"

I glanced at my watch. "Oh—shoot. I really have to dash!"

Gina patted my arm, and I waved toward Jamie, pointing at my wrist. I'd told him earlier that I wanted to take Blake and Audrey out for ice cream before heading to the theater tonight.

Being a single mom with two jobs required a lot of juggling—but I was determined to make it work.

I headed down the gravel path, lifting my camera and snapping photos more out of habit than anything.

There were always ghosts in the graveyard, and I wanted to get used to it. Slowly but surely, I was learning to be curious rather than terrified by the images I captured.

Glancing at the display as I walked along the path curving between the graves, my suspicions were confirmed. A cluster of figures appeared in the photos. They could easily have been mistaken for living people…if I hadn't just seen with my own eyes that the only living souls in this cemetery were back by the Keane grave.

I suppressed a shiver. I still wasn't *really* used to it. The idea of a dead entity breathing down my neck without me knowing—unless I happened to take a photograph—still creeped me out.

I took a deep breath, trying to imagine the ghosts here with me. I've always had a vivid imagination, and using the photo as a reference, I could picture them easily enough. Oddly, that calmed me. They belonged here. Many likely needed help, but this was their resting place, their history.

One day, I might come back and help them move into the light. I felt a sense of responsibility—so really, if I was being truthful, I had three jobs.

Smiling, I focused on one of the imagined ghosts—an elderly lady in a colorful housecoat patterned like something straight out of the seventies.

She turned her head and smiled back.

I flinched—and reminded myself it was just my imagination, guided by the photo I'd taken. A little creeped out again, I lowered the camera.

That was when I noticed a figure—a handsome, middle-aged man with blond hair—half-hidden behind a grave marker. I only caught his profile before he vanished.

I froze.

He looked an awful lot like Steven.

I shook my head and checked the display. There was the woman in the housecoat—but no Steven. No blond-haired ghost. Nothing.

My imagination must have been running away with me.

Still, I peeked behind the tall gravestone where I thought the man had disappeared.

Of course, there was no one there. Not Steven. Not any ghost.

I breathed a shaky sigh of relief and hurried to the car, anxious about getting to the kids' school in time for pickup.

I must have hallucinated Steven too.

He was a ghost from my past—

One I most certainly, definitely, did not want to bring into the light.

CHAPTER TWO

Even though I had convinced myself during the night that I'd merely imagined seeing Steven, I was tempted to tell the cat about it when we were alone in the cottage the next evening.

First of all, I was bursting to tell someone. Anyone. Clearly, Steven was still in my head for one reason or another. Maybe it had to do with my new relationship with Jamie.

As I washed up the dinner dishes, I tried to examine my emotions. The only thing I could honestly say was that I felt good about Jamie and me. Definitely not like a cheating wife. If you'd asked me right then, I'd have said I felt no loyalty to Steven whatsoever.

There must have been something buried deep in my subconscious, though. Maybe I could ask the therapist Blake and Audrey were seeing. She was a child therapist, but she might be able to point me in the right direction or recommend someone. Then again, she wasn't all that familiar with Steven or my past—the kids saw her because they'd been dragged into the recent criminal investigations I'd been forced to go through.

Maybe my children had told the therapist about their father and what he'd done—or she might have heard about it some other way.

The Cotswold village gossip mill had been doing its job even before I got here. Everyone knew about Steven and my sordid past by the time I moved in, mainly thanks to DI Farrow, who had an ax to grind with my mother. He'd transferred his hatred onto me, and he'd been determined to get me one way or another, since the FBI wasn't capable of nailing me for Steven's crimes.

It was embarrassing, to say the least.

I had been cleared by the FBI—I definitely hadn't known about the Ponzi scheme. But people had asked themselves how I could have been so blithely ignorant. I didn't blame them when they looked at me funny. Sticking my head in the sand and not noticing what was going on was still a source of deep-seated shame.

A year ago, when I'd found myself in a similar situation —being too busy to notice that my business partner, Ellie Bullwart, had gotten us into hot water financially—I'd been forced to face that pattern all over again.

"Hmm," I said out loud, almost dropping the plate I was drying, lost in thought.

Ethel the cat, who was napping on one of the kitchen chairs, opened one eye sleepily.

"Maybe I'm on to something there, Ethel," I murmured, quickly putting the plate away. I searched my memory. I'd been very diligent in all financial matters, taking good care of the books—in our business and at home. I hadn't even been shopping in months, putting the pennies away for a rainy day. I'd looked after the kids' expenses too. We'd been living frugally, I'd been working hard, and I'd made sure we weren't in over our heads with the theater—like we'd been with the Cirencester Curtain Callers.

I was even starting to feel comfortable with my gift. No reason to feel ashamed or to put on blinders anymore.

Groaning with frustration at not being able to figure out why I kept seeing Steven, I turned around.

Ethel was now watching me expectantly. Her golden eyes shone with concern.

I sat down next to her and stroked her marmalade fur. "Oh, Ethel," I said, scratching the tuft of white hair behind her ear. As a living human, Ethel had had a Mallen streak—a white lock in her otherwise ginger hair. The similarities between my great-aunt and the cat had been our first clue that they were, in fact, one and the same.

"I'd love nothing more than to tell you what's bothering me. Really, I want to confide in you."

Ethel meowed, as if to say, *Then why don't you?*

I hesitated, then said, "Sorry, I can't. This just has to stay secret."

The reason I couldn't confide in Ethel was my youngest child, Audrey. Her unique witchy ability was talking to animals. She was able to communicate with Ethel—something I really envied her for. Ethel had been my godmother, and we'd had a special bond when I was a small child. Unfortunately, I'd forgotten all about that. After moving to the US with my mother, I'd suppressed all my memories of Fairwyck and our family, along with the memory of the horrible ghost photo.

When Steven had destroyed our lives, I'd moved back here because my dearly departed great-aunt had left her cottage to me. It had been a lifesaver, and I'd realized far too late that I'd missed the chance to truly know Aunt Ethel.

I'd always planned to reconnect with her. At first, I'd been overjoyed at the opportunity to communicate with the cat. There were just two problems. My ten-year-old daughter had to act as interpreter, and Ethel wasn't just my aunt in cat form—she really was a cat too. Sometimes she was more Ethel, with her thoughts and memories, but I never really knew when that would be.

If I told Ethel about Steven, could I count on her not to tell Audrey? I didn't want my youngest to hear about this under any circumstances. She'd been a real daddy's girl and had had more trouble believing in Steven's dirty deeds than anyone. If she heard I might have seen him, she could get it into her head that he'd come back for her, after all. I didn't want her hopes raised. She'd come such a long way—settling into her school, fitting in so well with the theater group in Meckham… I didn't want her to regress.

That was the big problem with Ethel: I didn't know what I could trust her with. But I also couldn't tell her I was worried about trusting her, in case she was fully sentient in that moment and I actually could trust her. Oh boy. Having a cat as a great-aunt sure was complicated.

Oh, and yes, there was another problem: I was just so busy.

That thought reminded me I really needed to hurry up. I checked my watch and jumped up from the chair. "Shoot, I need to get the dishes done. Gina will be here in five minutes."

There was definitely an expression of reproach in Ethel's eyes. I didn't know if it was because I hadn't told her my secrets or because she didn't approve of my hectic schedule and the fact that I had to leave the children in someone else's care again.

I covered my guilty conscience with a big smile. "Blake and Audrey are at Anthony's right now, but they'll be coming home in a minute. Esme and I are going to Emerald's book club at the library, and Gina is looking after the kids."

Esme was a colleague at WLA who'd become a good

friend since moving in next door. Her son, Anthony, who was sixteen—just like Blake—had in turn become my eldest's best friend.

Esme and I looked after each other's children regularly, and we often did things together, but I was particularly happy about this rare treat of adult time.

Technically, Blake and Anthony were old enough to babysit Audrey, but I didn't like to leave the kids alone after everything that had happened since moving to Fairwyck. "You know Gina loves spending time with the children," I said aloud, finishing my thought, as if I owed Ethel an explanation.

But the cat had already closed her eyes again, her furry head resting on her front paws.

I sighed, but I had no time to wallow, because—speak of the devil—the kids came in through the back door.

My great-aunt arrived not a moment later, stepping through the front door. Today she wore her customary colorful caftan, along with a ton of jingly bead necklaces and bracelets.

She plunked her bag onto the couch. "Hello, everyone! I brought the cards. An unusual deck—look."

The kids, including Anthony, crowded around Gina.

I tried not to let my displeasure show. The children—Blake in particular—were fascinated by Gina's tarot cards. Blake loved drawing, and they were very interested in the designs. But we'd had instances where the children had taken a card spread far too seriously. I was always worried Gina would freak them out with her readings.

I'd experienced Gina's abilities myself when she hypnotized me and took me back to past memories to help investigate a case, so I didn't doubt her when she claimed to be a powerful witch. I also wasn't skeptical about precognition, as such. But I couldn't help thinking tarot cards were a bit like horoscopes when it came to predicting the future—generic and open to interpretation. I just didn't want my children getting hung up on the super-natural.

I was slipping my shoes on when Gina called after me, bracelets clinking like tiny warning bells. "Wait, Liv—I meant to warn you. I did a spread for you earlier, and I drew The Moon."

I tried not to groan, but of course Audrey and Blake instantly looked concerned. Exactly what I didn't want. "Gina, please. I really don't have time for this—"

"The Moon appears when something is hidden in the dark," she continued, eyes widening as if she were seeing it again. "It means someone is watching from the shadows. And what's coming…isn't what you think it is."

"Great. Love that for me," I muttered, forcing a cheerful smile for the kids. "But I really do have to go."

"Liv—" she reached a hand out, worry creasing her face.

"We'll talk about it tomorrow." I cut her off, stepping out the door before she could add more spooky drama.

Outside, I shut the door, leaned my head against it, and exhaled. Being part of a psychic family could be absolutely exhausting.

I straightened, ready to reclaim my night, but when I looked up, the moon hung low and dull in the cloudy sky—exactly the kind of moon that made you feel like some-thing lurked just out of sight.

A chill skittered down my spine.

"Thanks, Gina," I whispered bitterly. "Can't I just have one regular girls' night out?"

CHAPTER THREE

By the time I reached the cottage next door to pick up Esme, I had mostly shaken off the chill Gina's warning had left in my bones. I told myself I wasn't going to let a tarot card ruin my evening. A girls' night out was exactly what I needed.

Esme and I walked to the library—a cozy cottage next to the church, where the parson would have lived once upon a time. It was chilly, and our breath puffed in the dark November air as we made our way there in quick steps, chatting as we went. Nothing in Fairwyck was far enough away to really need a car. Emerald always kept a few bottles of wine chilled for book club, and since Esme and I fully intended to take advantage of that, we'd decided to walk—even though we were running a little late.

When we got to the library, everyone was already there.

My cousin Emerald, a willowy, nerdy-looking young woman with a beautiful face behind big glasses, was already pouring the wine.

Ellie Bullwart, my friend and business partner, smiled and waved in my direction. Michelle, the Fairwyck shop cashier and resident village gossip, was talking Ellie's ear off, so I didn't go over. Michelle was nice enough, but she could drone on, and I didn't want her latching on to me. She had her back to me and didn't see me as I passed behind her to grab a glass from the table.

I did hear her mention Marjorie Keane, so I assumed they were talking about the exhumation. I *really* didn't want to talk to her if that was the topic of conversation. Ellie knew about my supernatural talent—although we'd been far too busy at the theater to talk about my little side project at the graveyard. Now I was glad she didn't know I'd been involved. Ellie was a dear, but she was also quite chatty, and Michelle had a way of getting the truth out of people.

Michelle had always been suspicious of Gina and Emerald and their…let's call it otherness. In fact, she'd warned me about my relatives when I first moved here. She'd always liked me, though, and she'd put aside her reservations about Emerald in order to join the book club. I knew it was only a matter of time before Michelle caught wind of my gift and realized I was just as witchy as my relatives.

It shouldn't have bothered me—I'd accepted my supernatural side, so if others couldn't, that was their problem. But I supposed everyone wanted to be liked. After a lifetime of being a people pleaser, I didn't relish the thought of a friend turning on me because I was as weird as the rest of my psychic family.

I grabbed a second glass for Esme and went back to Emerald.

My cousin was still holding the bottle of wine, but she'd apparently forgotten to pour. Her lips were pressed together, and she was staring at her shoes. She clearly didn't seem comfortable with whatever Judith Winters, my boss at WLA, had just asked her.

I looked at Esme, who'd been standing next to them, with raised eyebrows.

"Awkward," she mouthed.

Judith, a stunning blond who looked like Anna Nicole Smith in her heyday, seemed oblivious to Emerald's reaction. "So anyway, I saw him there, and I wondered if he'd ever taken you. If he does, say hello to the chef if she's there. I helped her out when she got started, after tasting her pies. The pork, apple, and cider one is my favorite. Do give it a try if you're there. Emerald? Is everything okay?"

Judith finally seemed to notice Emerald's strange reaction.

Emerald pushed the bottle into my hand. "Yes, of course. Uh, I…have to check on something. I'll be right back."

My cousin almost ran off, nearly tripping over her own feet in her haste to get away.

Judith looked at us. "Was it something I said?"

Esme said, "I don't think so. You were talking about that restaurant your friend opened, right?"

Judith nodded. "Why would that upset her?"

"But you said something about *him* taking her there," I put in. "I only caught the tail end of the conversation. Who is him?"

"Oh—Emerald's boyfriend, Alaric Hatherleigh."

I sloshed the wine I'd been pouring. "Emerald has a boyfriend? Why didn't I know about that?"

Michelle rushed over, pulling a wad of tissues from her bag. She bent down to wipe the spilled wine off the floor.

"Dr. Hatherleigh," she said, "isn't Emerald's boyfriend."

Ellie joined us, just in time to hear Michelle's words.

"I thought they went out on a few dates," Judith said.

"Yes, but then he stopped calling," Michelle said. "Poor thing. I heard she was quite smitten. They would have made a nice couple, even though he's quite a bit older than her. A librarian and a historian." She shook her head in dismay. "I'm sure she had her hopes up. She's not getting any younger."

"She just turned thirty-five," I said, a little outraged. "Maybe it just wasn't right, and she doesn't need to settle. Why didn't I know about this, though?"

"I had no idea she was dating either," Ellie said. Esme also shrugged.

"I only knew because I'm acquainted with Alaric through some charity events," Judith said. She was a wealthy businesswoman and moved in different circles than the rest of us.

"Still. I'm her cousin. Looks like this Dr. Hatherleigh broke her heart. Let's not mention him in front of her again—and I'm going to check on her."

I found Emerald in her office, blowing her nose, looking as if she'd just been crying.

"Are you okay, Em?" I asked. I put the wineglass down on the desk and gave her a hug. "I heard you had your heart broken by some historian chap, and I didn't even know."

She shook her head and stepped out of the embrace. "No, actually, I didn't want to see him anymore. I'd been taken with him at first, but there was something odd about him. I just don't want to talk about him, you know? It's embarrassing."

"I'm sure it's not. Dating is complicated." I thought about Jamie and me. We'd come a long way, but the first year of our acquaintance had certainly been bumpy. "But we can drop the subject of your personal life. Let's talk about the book. That's why we're here!"

I grabbed my wineglass and noticed a large old coin on Emerald's desk. It had an unusual design, like something from Gina's tarot cards. "Oh, what's that?"

Emerald turned, saw the coin, and frowned. "Oh, nothing. Come on, let's get back to the others and discuss that book already."

We went back into the main room, where chairs had been set up. The others had already taken their places, and I gave them a meaningful glance—*remember, we're not talking about Emerald's beau.*

Michelle looked as if she were about to say something, but Esme cut her off. "So," she said, tossing her beaded braids over her shoulder, "what did everyone think about the book?"

It had been her turn to pick a book this week, and she'd chosen a Jamaican-born writer—someone with the same heritage as her. We all had something to say about it—even me, despite being too busy to finish it. I still planned on reading to the end, especially since everyone was raving about it.

We talked for an hour, and then Emerald ended the discussion for this week. She turned to Michelle. "We're all dying to know which book you picked!"

It was Michelle's first time choosing a book. We already knew everyone else's taste, but no one had a clue what Michelle might be interested in. She was a middle-aged lady who loved to gossip, so I was expecting something lighthearted. Women's fiction, most likely—maybe a thriller or a mystery?

Michelle pulled a bag from under her chair. "I have the perfect book for us."

She passed the books around. Confusion spread across Ellie's and Esme's faces. Judith scrunched her nose, and Emerald flushed bright red.

I was the last to take my copy. I saw it was nonfiction, featuring a handsome gray-haired man on the cover.

Oh no. Surely Michelle hadn't bought a book by that historian Emerald had dated.

But the name was different…not Alaric Hatherleigh, but Malcolm Drake.

Dr. Malcolm Drake. The name tickled my memory.

"Um, Michelle, that's not usually the type of book we read here," Judith said. "We tend to pick fiction. Not always something literary, but this…"

Michelle didn't seem bothered by Judith's grimace. "It's nice to mix it up once in a while. And since he's a celebrity, staying locally, making an episode of his show in Fairwyck—"

"I'm not sure you can call a ghost hunter a celebrity," Judith interrupted.

"He *is* famous, and his show has great ratings," Michelle said, unperturbed.

Now I was catching on. "Oh! It's that guy who wanted to make a documentary at Aunt Gina's inn!"

"He *is* making it," Michelle corrected. "He's there right now. This is his memoir. I just love his TV show. My favorite episode was the one with the nunnery. All those poor nuns who were walled in—they led Malcolm Drake to the right place, and he opened up the walls! There were whole skeletons in there…"

I looked at Emerald questioningly. Gina had mentioned Drake—she was a huge fan too. She'd giggled like a schoolgirl when telling me he'd contacted her. Totally a woman with a crush.

With the whole Marjorie Keane business, we hadn't talked about it again. I never thought she would actually invite Drake to stay at the inn. Surely she wouldn't want that kind of public attention.

The Sacred Salmon Inn had been built in the twelfth century. It was so haunted, the rooms upstairs were uninhabitable—or so Gina claimed. She preferred spending time in the old tavern downstairs. Even that was too creepy for my liking, and I always chose the Victorian annex when

I visited. That's where Gina and Emerald's bedrooms, their living room, and Gina's parlor were located.

Gina had asked me to take photos upstairs so I could "meet" her spectral roommates, but so far I'd refused. I got chills just thinking about that haunted inn. It was far worse than a graveyard!

I would never have guessed she'd invite a television ghost hunter to stay there.

We endured Michelle's enthusiasm about the show until Emerald finally wrapped up the meeting and gently herded everyone toward the door. I pulled her aside. "Is it true? About this ghost hunter show?"

Emerald rolled her eyes. "I don't like it either. But my mother is totally enamored with the guy. I'm afraid the episode is going to poke fun at her."

"I'll go over there tomorrow and check him out," I said.

"Good. Maybe you can talk some sense into her." Emerald sighed.

I said my goodbyes and walked home with Esme.

"Do you watch *Ghost Hunter UK*?" she asked.

I shivered inside my cheap Primark coat. I seldom missed the fancy clothing I used to wear, but a good winter coat would have been nice during this damp, windy Cotswold November.

"Umm…I once flipped to an episode and watched for a bit. Drake and his producers know how to tell a story and make it suspenseful, even though not a lot happens. Very few people can see ghosts, and even though Drake calls himself a paranormal investigator, I don't think he has the gift. He's more of an academic. He knew a lot about the historic building they were investigating for a supposed poltergeist."

Esme pulled a face. "I don't care for scary stuff. Gives me nightmares."

I shrugged. "They make it look scary with effects and music and dramatic cuts. But there isn't anything truly scary—at least not from what I've seen. Nothing compared to what's really out there."

Esme shoved me playfully. "Thanks a lot. It's creepy enough out here—in the dark, with the mist, narrow shadowy lanes, and only every other streetlight working."

I looked around. "It does have a certain atmosphere." Fairwyck's old cobblestone alleys and antique streetlights fit the spooky mood perfectly. I grinned and pulled my camera from my bag. "Should I check if there are any ghosts around?"

Esme scolded me theatrically, but I couldn't imagine her being genuinely frightened. She was a tall, confident woman who had raised two kids on her own after kicking her abusive husband to the curb. I respected her deeply and figured she could handle anything.

Laughing, I snapped a few photos to tease her. I glanced at the display. "You're in luck. No ghosts in the near vicinity."

Esme clutched her chest in mock relief. "No ghosts in Fairwyck? Do you think Drake will come up empty-handed and just make something up at your aunt's inn?"

I frowned, humor fading. I still hadn't fully wrapped my head around Gina inviting a television ghost hunter into that haunted place. What had she been thinking?

I shook my head. "I really hope Drake doesn't have paranormal abilities and that they fake everything. Who knows what the fallout for my aunt would be. And I definitely don't want Fairwyck on the map of ghost-hunter tourism."

Esme shrugged. "Some people find that exciting, it seems."

"I have enough excitement." I yawned. "My life has changed so much. There's a lot to learn and get used to. A bit of equilibrium would be nice. I wouldn't mind things staying exactly as they are right now."

"I'd say the same if I were dating a hunky police sergeant." Esme laughed as we reached her cottage. "Good night. Send Anthony around back, will you?"

Our gardens backed onto each other, so that was the quickest route. "Will do. 'Night!"

I turned toward my own cottage and realized I'd left the lens cap off the camera. I was so used to the strap around my neck that I barely noticed the weight anymore.

I lifted the camera to fix it. It had gone into sleep mode, and when I woke it to turn it off, the display lit up with the last photo. I hadn't lied to Esme—just a quiet Fairwyck alley at night. There weren't any ghosts where we'd been walking, though there was a man in the shadow of an awning ahead of us. He wore an old-fashioned cloak—he could have been a monk. Perhaps a very old ghost, then, and he certainly wasn't bothering us.

But wait…

I squinted and pulled the camera closer to my eyes. There was a figure—peering from behind a building. As if he were watching us. Or hiding from us.

It was impossible to make out features, but something about the outline felt familiar.

A cold shiver raced down my spine.

I rubbed my tired eyes and shook my head. Was I imagining things? No—there was someone in the photo.

Maybe it was a ghost. So what?

I shook off the unsettling dread and turned the camera off, tucking it into my bag.

It was late, I was tired, and I wasn't even sure who or what I'd seen.

This was one mystery that could stay in the dark.

My footsteps crunched on the gravel as I neared the cottage.

Suddenly, a shadow by the door moved.

I shook my head again—my imagination had been working overtime lately.

Bed. I just needed my bed.

A figure stepped out of the shadows, and I stifled a scream.

"Hello, Liv. Good to see you."

I had to be dreaming. Or losing my sanity. Because this couldn't be happening.

"Steven?!"

CHAPTER FOUR

"What are you doing here?" I hissed.

I pinched myself. I rubbed my eyes again.

He'd even tried to hug me—but as soon as he'd touched me, I'd shoved him away.

I wasn't dreaming. This was real.

My fugitive criminal husband was truly here, in front of my cottage.

I probably hadn't been hallucinating back in January either. And I really had seen him in that ghost vision…and in the photo.

Was he stalking me?

I couldn't think about that now. I couldn't even process this.

I needed to get inside. Gina was waiting for me. Anthony needed to go home. And the children…

Oh god. The children.

How would they react to their father suddenly turning up? After we'd built a whole new life here?

No—absolutely not. They could not see him.

"I need to talk to you," Steven said quietly.

"No. You need to leave," I snapped, my voice icy.

"Please. It's important. I…I made a terrible mistake, and—"

I lifted a hand, cutting him off. "Leave."

I turned toward the door.

"I'm not leaving until we talk, Liv. I'm coming inside."

I spun back. "No." I struggled to keep my voice under control. "My great-aunt is in there. Nobody can see you here." I took a deep breath. "Okay. We can talk. Briefly. But only after Gina leaves and the kids are in bed. I don't want anyone to know you're here."

"Fine," Steven said.

"Wait here for a few minutes. Anthony—my neighbor's son—is going to walk home through the back yard any second. Once he's gone, you can go around the cottage and wait in the garden." I almost warned him about the ever-present sheep dung—we had no sheep, but the dung still somehow existed—but decided he deserved to step in it.

"Once the kids are asleep and the coast is clear, I'll come outside," I said.

Steven nodded.

I slipped inside, moving through the living room in a kind of fog. I chatted with Gina and the kids on autopilot. They had to notice something was off, but maybe they assumed I'd had too much wine.

Anthony left. Blake and Audrey went upstairs to get ready for bed.

Normally, I would have asked Gina about that ghost-hunter show and whether she really wanted a whole film crew invading her haunted inn, given…everything. But I couldn't think about that right now. And, honestly, it was her business.

I thanked her for babysitting and said goodnight, cutting her off when she wanted to talk about that moon card again. Boy, she'd been right on the mark with that one. After she left, I nervously peeked out the living-room window toward the garden.

No sign of Steven.

I started to doubt myself.

Had I really seen him just now?

Why would he come here?

How would he even know where we lived?

Maybe I'd been hallucinating—or seeing ghosts? Had Steven died and was now haunting me? But that made even less sense. His ghost would be less likely to find me in England.

Maybe I shouldn't have had those two generous glasses of wine. I wasn't much of a drinker, even though I'd felt completely in control. Maybe I was stressed. Two jobs, a supernatural side gig, a new boyfriend, raising two kids alone…maybe I was simply cracking.

I decided to check on Blake and Audrey, then look outside one more time. If there was no Steven, I'd take a mental health day tomorrow. No cleaning shift, just theater admin work…which Ellie could probably cover. I'd sleep in, maybe splurge on a massage. That sounded heavenly.

I said goodnight to Blake and Audrey, tucked up in their beds reading. It was late, so I told them to turn off the lights in ten minutes.

Back downstairs, I made a calming herbal tea and forced myself to drink it before opening the back door.

The garden was pitch dark. The moon was hiding behind clouds, and there were no lights from the empty rental cottage across the garden or from Esme's place—her house was already dark.

I stepped out, shivering in my cardigan, my breath shallow as I peered into the blackness.

Silence.

"Steven?" I whispered.

"Yes," a loud voice said right next to my ear.

I let out a strangled scream, jumped sideways, and—
my foot landed in something squishy.

The smell hit me instantly. "Shit."

"Liv." Steven chuckled. "I've never known you to swear
like that."

"No," I snapped. "I stepped in shit. Sheep dung."

"Oh. Yes, that explains the smell."

"Shhh…" I hissed, glancing up at the dark windows.
The kids' bedrooms were in the attic. Their lights were out,
and it was too cold for open windows—but what if they
heard us? What if they looked outside?

We couldn't stay here. But I also couldn't allow Steven
inside, risking the kids wandering down for a drink of
water or to ask me something.

I couldn't deal with the emotional fallout. I could barely
deal with the practical implications of him being here.

If you'd asked me yesterday, I would have sworn I'd
never speak to Steven again if he ever turned up. He'd lied
to me for years—maybe our entire marriage. Whatever
explanation he spun now was surely going to be as manip-
ulative and worthless as the last.

But I never imagined he would show up here—in
England. In every scenario I'd ever mentally rehearsed, he
was arrested by the FBI, awaiting trial somewhere far
across the ocean. I'd have months to prepare, maybe only
see him under strict supervision, surreally distant—just
another lifetime away.

This was nothing like that. This was raw, immediate.
And I was utterly out of my depth.

I couldn't just send him away and risk him lurking
around. Someone might see him. Or worse—he might try
to contact the kids.

I had to find out what he wanted.

Why he was here.

How long he'd been here.

Because now I had to assume it really had been him in January at the theater…and at the graveyard today…and in that photo.

Not a hallucination.

Not a ghost.

Not guilt, tormenting me…

Steven. Alive. And back in my life.

If Steven really had been in England for months, that begged a question. Why wasn't he hiding on some tropical island with no extradition treaty? And where was the floozy secretary—his partner in crime?

No. The truth was, I wanted to talk to him. I needed answers.

But where?

I looked around the dark, dung-strewn garden in a panic. This definitely wasn't the place. And I wasn't letting him into my house. Esme's cottage was out of the question —I wasn't dragging anyone else into this until I knew what Steven was doing here. Same for the theater, since Ellie could be there.

Then an idea hit me.

"Wait here a sec. Don't go anywhere."

I slipped back inside, leaving my shoes outside the door, and grabbed the key to the rental cottage from the cleaning supplies cabinet.

When the kids and I had moved in, the cottage next door had been occupied by Phyllis Bishop—Matilda Rutherford's childhood best friend. Matilda, Phyllis, and my great-aunt Ethel had once been inseparable. Until a man came between them, of course. Phyllis had loved Stanley, but he'd married Matilda. Bitterness, years of silence, the whole tragic soap-opera saga.

When Matilda was murdered, Phyllis became my

number-one suspect. But she'd actually witnessed the real killer…and ended up dead herself shortly after.

Phyllis had left the cottage to her only relative: Judith Winters. Yes—the very same Judith who was now my boss at WLA.

The Cotswolds were prime holiday territory for the wealthy, and Judith made a mint converting homes into high-end rentals. She'd refurbished Phyllis's cottage beautifully. Because I lived next door, it was often on my cleaning schedule, and I kept a spare key for emergency access.

It was empty right now—perfect for a clandestine conversation.

I didn't bother changing my shoes. I knew I'd step in more mystery dung along the way anyway.

"Follow me," I whispered, flicking on my phone's flashlight.

A satisfying squelch and a muttered curse behind me told me karma had taken care of at least one small injustice.

I climbed over the low fence as gracefully as I could manage—why I even cared, I didn't know. Years of conditioning, probably. For most of my life, Steven had been the person I'd wanted to look nice for and be nice to.

Life had changed. I had changed. Yet, after only ten minutes with him—without even looking into his eyes properly—I was suddenly flustered.

I hated that.

I unlocked the cottage's back door, telling myself to ease up on the self-judgment. Of course I was rattled. This was the man I'd loved. The man I had entrusted with our future. The man who had shattered everything without a word of explanation. And now he was standing here, invading the new life I'd built.

Feeling out of sorts was a normal reaction.

"Shoes off," I told him sharply. I toed off my own shoes and stepped inside.

I locked the door behind us and led him into the living room, turning on only the one lamp facing the street on the opposite side of my property—so no light would show from my garden or Esme's windows. If anyone saw a light in an empty holiday rental, they might call the police. And then DI Farrow would show up, find me with Steven, and he'd have exactly the ammunition he'd always wanted.

That reminded me: the criminal activities. I had so many questions.

How long had he been running the scheme?

Was everything I'd been told by the investigators true?

I needed him to take responsibility—to face the consequences of his actions—for the sake of our children. They deserved closure.

But the moment I looked at him…my throat closed up.

Maybe we should have stayed in the dark.

Steven hadn't changed at all. Shouldn't a fugitive look stressed? Ragged? Guilty?

Instead, he looked like he hadn't missed a day at the gym. Unfairly muscular for a man our age. Most of our friends had gone soft. I'd gained twenty pounds over the years. Normal aging.

But Steven? Of course not.

He looked better than ever. Defined jawline, just enough lines around his eyes to make him look distinguished, full head of blond hair, without a hint of gray.

I'd once assumed those highlights came from secret salon visits, but apparently I'd been wrong. Unless he'd been touching up his roots between hiding spots.

And those blue eyes…the same mischievous twinkle Audrey had inherited—the one that had always melted me before I even realized it was happening.

Steven didn't notice my speechlessness. He was busy taking in the stylish living room with irritating curiosity.

"Wow," he said, looking around. "Why do you live in that dinky, run-down place next door if you own this? Are you refurbishing?"

"I don't own it," I finally managed to choke out. "I clean it."

Steven blinked at me, as if waiting for the punchline. "Nah. I heard you inherited your great-aunt's place. You've always been lucky, haven't you?" He winked.

Heat rushed up my neck. "Aunt Ethel left me her cottage when she learned we were destitute and the kids and I had nowhere to go. And yes, I count myself lucky— because otherwise we'd have been homeless. And that cottage is the dump next door."

"Oh. Bummer," he said, barely listening. "But why are you cleaning this place?"

"I work as a cleaner," I snapped. "It's a holiday rental. My job."

Steven laughed and dropped into the armchair. "You? Scrubbing toilets? Come on. Do you even know how?"

I was fully fuming now, forcing my words out between my teeth. "Is that funny to you? How else did you think I would provide for our children after you left us penniless?"

"Wow. Calm down," he said, still grinning as if I'd told a joke. "I didn't think you were serious, that's all. You have a degree, you're whip-smart, you're extremely capable. And besides—" He waved vaguely at me. "You don't look like you're starving."

My mouth dropped. "I—wow—just…wow."

I drew a very slow breath. "What do you want, Steven? Did you come here to insult me? To rub salt in the wounds? Wasn't what you did enough?"

He stood, hands raised. "No, Livvie, baby, you've got it

all wrong. I didn't come here to make you mad. That wasn't an insult—it was a compliment."

He stepped closer, eyes raking over my jeans and T-shirt. I wrapped my cardigan tightly around me.

"You look incredible," he murmured. "You know how much I've always loved your curves."

"Oh really?" I said, backing away. "Then why replace me with that stick-insect secretary?"

Steven's face crumpled. His eyes went wide and mournful—his old, reliable weapon. "That was a huge mistake. She seduced me. Caught me at a vulnerable moment when things weren't working out financially. I couldn't talk to you—I was embarrassed. I'm your husband, your provider…and I'd failed. She took advantage when I confided in her. She had this huge crush and —she blackmailed me into leaving with her when I had to run."

He sounded very contrite. It made me furious.

"Oh, you poor, innocent man," I mocked. "Did she also force you to scam and lie to all our friends? Was that her idea too?"

He didn't rise to the bait. His voice softened, pleading. "No. That part was all me. But you have to believe me, Livvie, it didn't start that way. I had real opportunities. Real investments. I believed in them. And in the beginning, everything was working. Then the market collapsed. Money was lost. I thought I could fix it—I wanted to fix it, for everyone. Then it spiraled, and suddenly it was too late to admit the truth."

I crossed my arms tightly against my ribs. "Something doesn't add up. The police told me you walked away with a sizable profit."

"Well, yes!" he said, as if that were obvious. "Of course I set money aside for us, baby! I didn't want to let everyone down, but I never forgot you and the girls. Whatever happened, I never touched the profits I saved for our family."

"What absolute bullshit," I snapped—too loudly. I lowered my voice again, shaking. "It wasn't for us—it was for you. You ran off with it and left us with nothing. With less than nothing. Debt. We had to sell everything. So don't you dare—"

"Liv, I had to," he insisted. "They'd have confiscated it all. I had to protect what was left so we'd be fine, long term. I'm sorry you ended up in a bit of a pickle…"

He reached out, as if to pull me into an embrace. The familiar strength of his hands on my shoulders almost short-circuited my anger—but only for a second. I shoved him away.

"A pickle? Seriously? Is that why you're here—to hand over the money you stole? Two years later? Because we don't want it. We don't want you. We're doing perfectly fine without you."

The look of pity that slid over his face made me stop short.

"Oh, baby," he murmured sadly. "You're not, though. You're a cleaner. My children are living in a dump. That's not the life you're supposed to live."

An eerie calm washed over me.

"You don't know us anymore, Steven. You don't know me. We've changed. We had to—because of what you did. But it turned out to be a blessing. We're living our best lives. I'm living exactly the life I was meant to live."

I meant it.

And he knew it.

For the first time, he really looked at me.

"Yes," he said softly. "I can see that."

My treacherous heart fluttered—and I hated it.

Steven had always had that effect on me. Ever since high school. That one adoring look and I'd forgive forgotten pickups, flirty texts to other women, trips to Vegas instead of family weekends…all those red flags I'd trained myself not to see.

But this wasn't a minor mistake. He had destroyed our lives. I shouldn't even entertain the idea of forgiveness.

And yet my body insisted on remembering him.

"What do you want from me, Steven?" I barked.

"I want to get to know the new you, Liv." His voice trembled. "Leaving you and the girls was the biggest mistake of my life. I want you to take me back."

CHAPTER FIVE

I stared at Steven, utterly stunned.

Of all the things I had imagined him saying if I ever saw him again, that was nowhere on the list.

Inside, I was screaming *No. No. Absolutely not.*

So why wasn't I saying it out loud? What was wrong with me?

At least I didn't say yes. At least I got out, "You need to go, Steven."

I moved toward the living-room door.

"No—wait." He reached toward me. "Please tell me you'll at least think about it. If not for you, then for the girls."

That comment made rage boil up so hot inside me that I was almost grateful for it.

I spun back around. "Don't you dare bring them into this. You're the parent who left. You abandoned your children in the worst possible way. You do not get to shift the responsibility onto me now."

Steven lifted both hands in surrender. "No, no—of course not. I take full responsibility. I made a mistake. I admit that, babe. I'll do anything to fix this and make things right with the girls. That's all I meant."

I glared, arms folded tight across my chest. I wanted to scream that it was far too late. That I didn't care.

But the truth was a little more complicated.

I certainly wasn't taking him back.

But he was their father. If there was even the faintest chance to repair part of the damage he'd done, was I allowed to deny them that?

"What does that look like?" I asked stiffly.

His brow creased. "What?"

"Repairing your mistake. What's your plan?"

"Well, I want to talk to them. Explain. Apologize."

"You want to meet secretly with them while you're a fugitive?" I shot back. "Turn our kids into accessories after the fact?"

Steven stared at me, genuinely shocked. "That's a bit dramatic, don't you think? I'm not a murderer. I didn't hold hostages or rob a bank. A father talking to his children is hardly—"

"A white-collar crime is still a crime, Steven," I hissed. "You are still a wanted criminal. What message does it send to your children if you hide from the law?"

His silence said everything.

"If you want to explain yourself to the kids," I said, voice low and steady, "you have to turn yourself in."

He looked wounded. "You want me to rot in prison for years? Far away from all of you? Please don't tell me you hate me that much, Liv. Leaving was a mistake. I still love you. I want you back. Is it a crime to want your family?"

Tears shot into my eyes. I stepped back. "Stop. I don't want to hear this. If you want a chance at repairing anything with us, you'll take full responsibility. Otherwise—"

"I'll think about it," he cut in quickly. "If…if that means I can see the children."

"I'll have to think about it too." I turned toward the door. "In the meantime, you need to go. And if you contact me again, make sure nobody—"

"I don't have anywhere to go, Liv."

I froze, then slowly shook my head. "That can't be true. I saw you at the theater months ago."

He stepped into my path in the dark corridor. "Yes. But that situation isn't…working anymore."

"You must have been staying somewhere," I insisted.

"Not really. I've been…roughing it." His voice was small, ashamed.

"In this weather?" I asked incredulously. He didn't smell or look like a man sleeping outdoors.

"Not on the street." He gave a humorless laugh. "I'm not a bum."

"Then what are you saying?" My patience snapped. I needed out of this cottage, out of this conversation. Preferably under a blanket with a family-sized bag of M&Ms.

He stared at me hopefully. "I was hoping I could stay with you?"

"With my kids? In my home?" I gaped at him. "You really thought I'd forgive you, just like that?"

He didn't answer—just stood too close, breathing my air, reminding me of a life I'd fought to leave behind.

I shoved past him. "You can stay here. For one night."

"Here?" He looked around the stylish living room. "I suppose it's not too bad."

"Turn the lights off," I ordered. "No one can see you here. Don't leave the cottage. Wait until I come to you tomorrow."

I marched toward the door.

"Bring breakfast!" he called after me cheerfully, as if we'd just scheduled a brunch date.

By the time I crossed my garden, tears blurred everything. I told myself they were tears of rage.

But I knew better.

I steeled myself before stepping inside—if the kids heard me crying, I'd have to explain everything. And I wasn't ready for that. I had to be strong for them.

I locked the back door and grabbed the M&Ms from the cupboard, already tearing into the bag when a strange scratching noise sliced into my thoughts.

A sharp, unpleasant sound—like nails on a chalkboard.

The kitchen light spilled just enough glow into the living area to see the outline of a cat near the old fireplace. Ethel.

We'd never used the fireplace. It was a gaping dark cavity in the wall, covered by a decorative screen I'd bought to hide it. But now the screen was pushed aside.

Ethel was a big cat—but strong enough to move that? Maybe one of the kids had nudged it by accident.

I stepped closer and switched on the living-room lamp.

Yes, it was Ethel. Almost inside the fireplace.

"Ethel?" I whispered. "What are you doing?"

She froze, like a child caught doing something forbidden.

Cats were impossible to sneak up on, but she had been so intent on her mission, she hadn't heard me come in.

"Do you have a mouse?" I asked, frowning.

She lay down, blinking up at me as if trying to soothe my nerves.

It was very strange behavior.

I crouched beside her and stroked her marmalade fur. "I wish I could talk to you," I murmured. "But you talk to Audrey, so…"

That's when I noticed the scratch on the floor—fresh grooves extending out from under Ethel's body, leading toward the dark inside of the fireplace.

"What's that?" I whispered.

Whoever had shoved the screen aside must have scraped the floor…

Or Ethel might have done it herself, and now she was lying there, trying to cover the evidence.

The trouble was, our familiar wasn't just a human mind trapped in a cat. She was also a cat. Sometimes Aunt Ethel surfaced clearly. Other times she was…simply Ethel the cat.

Only Audrey ever knew which side she was speaking to.

But Audrey was ten—not exactly the ideal mediator for deep conversations with my resurrected godmother.

At first, I'd been thrilled by the possibility of reconnecting with Ethel. As a child, I'd suppressed every memory of Fairwyck, including those of her—the love she'd given me, the bond we'd shared. There was so much I wanted to say to her.

Just…not through my child.

I nudged Ethel gently. "It's fine. It's just a scratch. I'm not worried about this old floor—there are plenty of scratches al—"

Ethel stood up, and my eyes widened.

This wasn't just a scratch. It was an entire pattern carved into the wood.

"Did you do this?" My mind flashed back to the screeching sound I'd heard—claws against the floorboards.

"Why would you do that?"

I shifted so more light spilled across the markings.

Symbols.

A row of symbols.

They reminded me of something from a horror movie —sigils. Witchcraft sigils.

I stared down at Ethel.

Supposedly, my great-aunt hadn't had a gift—abilities

sometimes skipped a generation. But Gina had always been convinced Ethel was hiding one. I had hoped, secretly, that reconnecting with her would help me figure out what that ability was.

Yet in the past year and a half, there had never been a moment for that sort of conversation—to my immense frustration.

"Is this…is this your gift?" I murmured.

Ethel only stared back at me with those ancient golden eyes.

I sighed and stood again, groaning as my hip flexors protested. A reminder that I should really exercise more than once a decade.

Ethel butted her head against the decorative screen, nudging it toward the sigils.

"All right, all right." I grabbed the screen and slid it back into place, hiding the pattern. "We're putting a pin in this. But I will get to the bottom of it."

I collected my M&Ms and a bottle of water, then trudged upstairs.

In my bedroom, I set everything on the nightstand and changed into pajamas.

I needed to talk to someone—desperately. The cat was not cutting it.

Jamie was out of the question. He was a police officer; asking him to keep my confidence in this matter would be huge conflict of interest—and an extremely selfish thing to do.

Gina was preoccupied with that ghost hunter. Emerald was busy having her heart bruised by some historian.

Esme was too close to the kids—and I couldn't risk anything leaking to them, not until I figured out what to do.

I huffed a bitter laugh. I'd just scolded Steven for dumping this decision on me—insisting it was his responsi-

bility to fix his relationship with the children. And yet…
here I was, shouldering it anyway.

Because of course I had to. I was the parent who'd
stayed.

I wanted Steven gone, never to return—that was the
truth.

But this wasn't just about me. It wasn't even about me
and Steven as a couple. I had Jamie now. I was happy. Any
flutter Steven stirred up would pass—it had to.

But did I have the right to deprive my children of the
chance to mend something broken? Just because it was
inconvenient…and terrifying…and painful for me?

My throat tightened.

Finally, I grabbed my phone and texted Ellie.

She would understand—at least a little. She'd escaped
a toxic relationship with Jason, a man capable of violence
and cruelty. She had rebuilt her life after him—after their
shared business, their shared dreams.

It was late; I didn't want to wake her. And I definitely
didn't want to write anything that could incriminate me. If
the police found out I'd willingly concealed a fugitive…

So I kept it vague:

*Random question, I know. Something has come up that made me
wonder… Would you ever take Jason back? If he had changed?*

Her reply arrived almost instantly.

And it made me turn off my phone, crawl into bed,
and tear open the M&Ms like they might save my life.

*Monsters don't change at their core. They might transform into
something else, but only to find new ways to hurt you. So no. I have
zero intention of letting the past repeat itself. I'm moving forward.*

CHAPTER SIX

The next morning, after seeing the kids off to school, I drove straight to the Sacred Salmon Inn. Steven could wait for his breakfast. And his redemption. And…well, everything else.

I was no closer to a decision after a restless night, and I wasn't ready to face him again.

I needed advice from someone I trusted. Someone with actual supernatural qualifications. Like…someone who could see into the future.

Who better than Great-Aunt Gina?

At first, after moving back to Fairwyck and being ambushed by relatives I hadn't even known existed, I was deeply suspicious of both her and Emerald—particularly since their very first visit had come with a doom-and-gloom tarot reading.

But I couldn't have embraced my special talent if it wasn't for Gina and Emerald. I'd come to rely on them. My skepticism and mistrust of Gina's psychic abilities, which included putting someone in a hypnotic trance to better examine a past memory, had been laid to rest. She'd been a great help when I'd had to investigate murderous incidents in the past.

If anyone could guide me through this mess, it was her. I had to be extremely careful who I told about Steven, but I knew I could trust Gina.

The Sacred Salmon sat where it always had: crookedly beside the narrow country lane just outside Fairwyck, half-hidden by tangled hedgerows and the slow creep of the woods. The place looked as if it had slouched there for centuries, growing more uneven and more determined with every passing decade.

No surprise Drake had chosen it for his show. The inn practically oozed paranormal ambience.

Someone had already beaten me to my usual parking spot—a pale yellow Volkswagen Beetle hugged right up against the building. I muttered under my breath, pulled up onto the verge, and nearly toppled into the drainage ditch when I opened my door. Brambles snagged at my coat as if to say welcome back.

The inn itself…well, "historic" was the polite term.

From the outside, the inn looked…let's stick with inter-esting. One section still had the original medieval timber frame, the beams dark and bowed, the plaster between them a mottled patchwork of gray and brown. The rest of the building appeared to be a long experiment in stonework completed by various owners with wildly differing skill levels and no shared understanding of what a straight line was. The old painted sign—the salmon swollen and slightly tragic—creaked slowly in the wind.

Ivy and climbing roses had taken advantage of centuries of neglect. They didn't decorate the building so much as clutch it. The greenery looked like it was the main thing keeping the walls upright.

The old inn certainly didn't look like it was habitable, and I was glad Gina and Emerald didn't live there. Gina, especially, still loved the tavern downstairs and had meals there, but even for her, the rooms upstairs were too haunted.

There was an annex that provided a much more comfortable living space for my relatives.

Built in the Victorian period, it had aged, sure, but in a gentler way. The paint was weathered, the windows a little cloudy, but the structure itself was sound. A small porch with climbing roses, carefully trimmed, unlike the chaos elsewhere, framed the door. It didn't match the medieval inn at all—its right angles and modest sense of order only emphasized how lopsided the original building was.

I stepped to the annex door and lifted the Green Man knocker. His carved wooden face regarded me with the same amused, mildly disapproving look he always had.

No answer.

I knocked again, louder. Nothing. The house swallowed the sound.

Gina was always home. Always. And today of all days—

My gaze drifted back to the yellow Beetle. That had to be Dr. Malcolm Drake's. If Gina wasn't in the annex, then she must be with him in the inn.

I'd expect more vehicles if his film crew was here, but perhaps they hadn't arrived yet. Maybe Drake was scouting locations. Or maybe Gina was giving him the grand ghost tour.

I drew a breath and headed toward the old building— the part of the inn that looked like the setting of a fairy tale where children definitely did not make it out of the woods.

The Sacred Salmon's original entrance was on the far side from where I'd parked. During my first visit, Gina had taken me through the annex's connecting door. If I couldn't get in through the annex, I'd have to try the medieval entry.

But when I reached the old door, I froze.

The boards sealing it shut were gone.

I knocked and called Gina's name again. No answer.

Heart thudding, I pushed against the heavy door. It swung open with a mournful groan.

Inside, the taproom stood almost exactly as I remembered it.

A lone lamp burned on one of the slab tables, casting a small puddle of honey-colored light. Another weak bulb glowed behind the bar, outlining shapes rather than illuminating them. The rest of the room dissolved into dark corners and deeper shadows. Ceiling beams vanished into blackness overhead.

The stone walls retained the same damp chill. The benches and tables looked hacked from trees that would have been offended by the craftsmanship. The enormous fireplace yawned like a gateway into somewhere much less welcoming.

It smelled of stale ale, old woodsmoke…and something else. Something ancient.

My fingers tightened around the padded weight of the Nikon inside my bag.

Gina had suggested more than once that I bring a camera here. "Take pictures of our housemates," she'd said with the breezy cheer of a woman immune to terror.

Back then, I'd barely believed ghosts were real.

Now, I knew better.

"Gina?" I called. My voice sounded too small.

The staircase to the upper rooms sat at the far end of the taproom, its banister worn smooth from centuries of hands. I remembered the first time I'd been here, when Gina had told me that no one slept upstairs because the activity was too strong. "Badly haunted" she'd said, in that serene tone of hers. Back then, the idea had seemed more like a campfire story than a warning. Now, after everything that had happened since returning to Fairwyck, I understood exactly what she'd meant.

I took a step toward the stairs. The temperature dropped—sharply, unmistakably. The hairs on my arms lifted beneath my sleeves.

"All right," I whispered. "Everyone just…stay calm. I'm only looking for my aunt."

Each step upward thickened the air, as if I were climbing through layers of history. Layers of disappointment. Layers of spirits who refused to move on.

If I took the camera out here, I wouldn't capture one or two ghosts.

I'd see every single one who had ever refused to leave.

And there was something else—something that scared me more than any other place I'd ever taken my spirit photographs. I couldn't quite put my finger on it or explain it, but I felt it deep in my core.

"Gina?" My voice echoed faintly down the narrow hallway at the top. "Are you up here?"

No answer.

Only the cold digging deeper into my bones.

At the top of the stairs loomed a heavy door. I hesitated.

I had been working hard to get comfortable with ghosts —visiting cemeteries, talking to spirits, even helping them move on. But this place…this place still terrified me. It brought me right back to childhood—sitting alone in my bedroom, staring at a photo that showed a ghost woman I couldn't see in real life. Realizing spirits could be standing right beside me while I slept.

I swallowed back the fear. I wasn't here to take pictures, let alone communicate with dead residents. I just needed to find Gina.

I pushed the door open.

I'd barely stepped into the corridor when I heard Gina's laughter—bright and fluttery, bizarrely cheerful in the heavy stillness. Relief loosened my shoulders. At least she was here.

I rounded the corner and nearly ran straight into Emerald. She carried a stack of boxes so tall it swallowed her face. The top box wobbled dangerously.

"Oh! Sorry." I caught it before it toppled. "Here, let me take a few."

I lifted two of them—wires, camera equipment, something metallic clanking inside.

"Thanks," Emerald muttered, wiping sweat from her brow with her wrist. Her cheeks were flushed.

"Dr. Drake?" she called out, her voice hoarse. "Where do you want these now?"

She leaned toward me and whispered, "He keeps changing his mind about what room has the best energy."

"Just set them here," said a rich, smooth voice behind us. "Yes…I think this spot will do nicely."

Dr. Malcolm Drake stepped into view—tall, a little stooped, silver hair artfully disheveled, tweed jacket and burgundy waistcoat completing the "distinguished academic investigating ancient curses" look. He peered over his slipping spectacles with delighted focus—as though he were inspecting priceless relics rather than dusty, haunted rooms.

And behind him was Gina.

My great-aunt was glowing.

Hands clasped beneath her chin, eyes shining, posture suddenly shy and girlish. She looked like a sixteen-year-old meeting her celebrity crush backstage.

"Liv, darling!" she breathed. "Isn't this marvelous?"

"What's…marvelous," I said, glancing around at the

icy corridor, "is that these rooms haven't collapsed under the weight of their own history."

"Oh, they're wonderfully preserved," Dr. Drake enthused. "No intrusive modernization. It allows the spirits to retain their—shall we say—spiritual integrity. Central heating, plaster, new wiring—terribly disruptive."

Emerald muttered under her breath, "Also disruptive to not freezing to death. But okay."

My gaze drifted to a thick extension cord snaking from under a door frame, running toward the annex.

"You…ran power up here?" I asked.

"Oh yes," Drake said proudly. "Drilled straight through the stone between Ms. Seven's bedroom and one of the guest rooms. Remarkable masonry—nearly broke my bit."

He looked extraordinarily pleased with himself, as though he'd conquered Everest rather than vandalized our notoriously haunted inn.

"Don't you have a production crew for that sort of thing?" I asked.

"They'll come later, to shoot the B-roll. One mustn't crowd a location at first." He rocked on his heels. "I set up the cameras and sensors alone. Ghosts dislike large groups —very shy creatures. Pardon the pun." He chuckled at his own joke.

Gina rested a hand on his arm, looking ready to swoon. "Isn't he just wonderful, Liv? And to think, he's filming one of his marvelous episodes right here. In my inn!" She squealed.

I stared at the peeling wallpaper and the sagging, dust-choked bed behind him. The cold pressed so tightly against my skin, it felt like the dead breathing down my neck. I could feel them hovering. Watching.

If I so much as opened my camera bag, the screen would be crowded with faces.

And yet here this man was, delighted, unbothered,

opening doors no one should open lightly. My aunt was clearly so taken by him that she hadn't thought this through.

"Yes," I said slowly, my skin prickling, "I can see why you'd think that. But are you sure, Gina, that this is a good idea? This will bring a lot of…attention. Is that what you want?"

I looked at her in her colorful caftan, an array of gemstone necklaces and bracelets, her blond hair piled high to add a few inches to her small height. She looked like the stereotypical cooky psychic.

Dr. Drake might be genuinely excited about discovering ghosts in this haunted inn—but I knew how these sorts of TV shows worked. I'd seen episodes. Drake might have control over filming, but clever editors would put it all together. Editors who answered to producers whose main concern was ratings.

And if they could play up the weirdness of a local psychic woman for national entertainment, they would.

Yes, most people in Fairwyck already knew Gina and Emerald were…different. She was already a bit of an outsider here. But it was a contained kind of outsider. The villagers might whisper, but nearly all of them had secretly consulted her at least once—cards read, charms blessed, problems solved. There was a balance. A quiet acceptance.

And while I'd come to embrace my own abilities, I wasn't exactly eager to have my name added to Fairwyck's Witchy Watchlist. I didn't want to become "the other one." Not when I had worked so hard to build a life here. To fit in. To make sure my kids felt like part of the community rather than the strange American imports with baggage.

I worried this TV show would blow up that delicate balance. Turn curiosity into ridicule. Make things awkward and uncomfortable for all of us.

But Gina just waved my concern away—not really hearing me at all. She only had eyes for Dr. Drake.

I turned to Emerald.

"She thinks it'll help business," my cousin murmured. She shrugged. "And honestly…I can use the distraction."

The tired, sad flicker in her green eyes stopped me from pushing further. Even if I could convince Emerald to try to talk sense into her mother…it was already too late.

This place was wired, and Drake was planting roots.

And honestly? He did look perfectly at home in the most haunted building in England.

Which said a lot.

A thought nudged the back of my mind.

This would have been an ideal hiding place for Steven.

No one would come looking here.

Every suspicious noise would be blamed on ghosts.

But Drake had spoiled that.

"How long are you planning to stay?" I asked.

Drake brightened. "That depends entirely on the spirits. I'll remain as long as needed—until they feel comfortable revealing themselves."

"He can stay as long as he likes," Gina beamed.

I nodded, trying to hide my dark amusement. Drake sounded as though he were filming a nature documentary, and the ghosts were shy woodland creatures.

He might be an expert on history and folklore, but he wasn't actually psychic.

If he were, he'd know the spirits here were not timid.

They were restless.

Powerful.

Ready.

And they would likely scare him right out of this inn.

The floorboards creaked under my toes. Dust and mold clogged the air. Darkness pooled in every corner.

I turned my face away from the others to hide a smirk.

Yes—this would be an excellent place for Steven to hide once Drake inevitably fled.

CHAPTER SEVEN

I hadn't been able to confide in Gina or Emerald about my dilemma, but the drive home still left me marginally calmer.

Having Steven next door in Judith Winters's cottage was bad enough. Letting him stay another night? Risky didn't even cover it.

Judith was under no obligation to tell me when someone booked the place. Usually she did, because I was her go-to cleaner for that cottage—and if it had stood empty for a few days, like now, she'd want me to freshen it up. But since I only worked part time, a last-minute booking could easily mean Esme or one of the other cleaners got called instead.

There was an obvious option: throw Steven out and stop dragging out a decision I didn't want to make.

But I needed more time—and a clear head. And maybe more chocolate.

I picked up baked goods from the village shop and carefully avoided the topic of Malcolm Drake with Michelle. The woman was perfectly pleasant but had a habit of disabling the till's product scanner whenever a juicy bit of gossip needed coaxing out. She already knew Drake was filming at the inn, but I wasn't going to provide extra fodder for Fairwyck's rumor mill. The less I said, the better.

Who knew—maybe Drake's footage would never even make it to TV. Maybe this was all dramatic fuss over nothing, and peace and quiet would soon reign in Fairwyck again.

With those positive thoughts and the promise of fresh croissants, I stepped into my cottage—

—and dropped the bag with a scream.

A man stood in my kitchen.

I scrambled backward, slamming directly into the already closed door.

"Ouch!"

The stranger turned. Bathrobe—my bathrobe—ending near the top of strong, annoyingly familiar thighs. A towel turban on his head. A mug in his hand.

Steven.

"There you are!" he said brightly, taking a leisurely sip of coffee.

"What…what are you doing here?" Speech finally returned. "Are you insane? I told you to stay hidden next door!"

"There was no food and, more importantly, no coffee." He lifted his mug as though this were irrefutable logic.

I rushed to the living-room window and yanked the blinds shut. "What if someone saw you? Esme could have looked out her kitchen window! She'd have seen you stroll right across the gardens!"

"I was very careful," Steven assured me. "I've been on the run for a while, so I've had lots of practice."

I shot him a glare, then quickly looked away—because staring meant noticing the robe and…legs. And remembering the fact that I had always loved Steven's legs.

"You took a shower in my bathroom?" I hissed.

"Well, as long as I was here." He shrugged. "Bit cramped, though. Remember the walk-in shower back home? The massage jets? And what we used to get up to in there?"

He waggled his eyebrows.

He should have looked ridiculous—mauve terry cloth robe two sizes too small, towel-turbaned hair—but somehow he didn't. Infuriating.

I focused hard on anger. "Yes, I remember. And I remember selling that house after you left us penniless. After you remortgaged it for your Ponzi scheme. After we had to pay off debts with whatever scraps were left. The kids and I lived in my mother's one-room apartment in Florida with her. That's the shower I remember."

"Really? Oh, I bet the girls loved Florida. Beach life! They probably didn't even notice the tight quarters."

He plucked the bag of croissants from where it had fallen. "Mmm. Croissants."

He sat down at the table—my table—which he had already set using things from my cupboards.

"Don't say 'girls,'" I said, sinking into a chair across from him. "It's not accurate anymore."

Steven blinked at me over a mouthful of pastry.

"When we first moved here, Bianca told me they didn't feel like a girl—or a boy. They are nonbinary. They call themself Blake now."

He stared for a beat, then resumed chewing. "You're pulling my leg."

"I'm not."

"Oh. That explains Blake. I was confused yesterday, but we had...other things to talk about." He dismissed it with a flick of his hand. "It's probably a phase. I'll talk to her about it."

"You will not," I snapped. "This isn't your business

anymore—not until you face the consequences of your actions."

"Fine. I'll play along for now." He said it like we were humoring a toddler with dress-up preferences. "We'll tackle it later."

I clenched my jaw so hard it hurt. His assumption—that everything would fall neatly into place and we'd reunite as a happy little fugitive family—was infuriating.

"No," I said coldly. "You're not talking to the children."

"What?" Hurt flashed across his face. "Liv, I miss them. I need to see them."

A headache throbbed behind my eyes. "Listen, Steven—"

My phone buzzed in my pocket. Jamie.

Oh no.

I'd completely forgotten we were supposed to meet for coffee before my cleaning shift.

"Shoot." I jabbed the answer button. I put a finger to my lips—*be quiet*—while Steven happily munched croissant number two.

"Hey," I said, forcing casual cheer.

"Hey," Jamie replied. "You running late? I already ordered your coffee. It's getting cold."

Guilt stabbed deep.

"Jamie, I'm really sorry. Something came up."

"Oh." His disappointment was obvious. With his shifts and my scattered work schedule, we'd barely had any evenings together this week. This coffee date mattered.

"I'm sorry. I'll explain later, okay?"

"So you're not coming at all? Do you want to meet later—after your shift—for a quick drink?"

"Um…" Panic flared. I wasn't ready to face Jamie. Not until I figured out what to do about Steven. Besides, I did not have a poker face. My expression would probably tell him right away I was hiding a felon in my kitchen.

"I can't. It's…something with the kids."

"Okay." Jamie didn't believe me—of course he didn't. Which only confirmed that I absolutely could not see him again until Steven had either vanished or turned himself in. Jamie was far too good at reading me, and far too honorable not to report a wanted fugitive.

"If you need anything—or if I can help—just tell me," he said.

"I will," I chirped, too cheerfully. "Thanks, bye!"

I hung up before he could say another word.

Steven was watching me, curiosity stitched across his face.

"Who was that?"

"A friend." I stuffed a croissant into my mouth—not because I wanted it, but to block any further questions. Luckily for me, Steven was nowhere near as perceptive as Jamie.

"Listen," I said, swallowing hard. "I have to get ready for work." In truth, I would be leaving absurdly early, but I needed to get away from him before my brain liquefied.

"So here's what's going to happen. You get dressed. I'll check whether the coast is clear next door—Esme and Anthony should both be out. You go back to the rental cottage and stay there. Take food if you need it. I'll subtly confirm with my boss that no one is booked for tonight. Then we'll meet later and talk more."

I scanned the cottage anxiously. The front door opened straight into the living room. If Blake or Audrey came home early…if Esme popped in with a misdelivered parcel…if Gina wandered over mid–Malcolm Drake swoon…

Steven really needed to get out of here.

"…not possible right now," Steven said.

"What?" My attention snapped back to him.

"I can't get dressed. I threw all my clothes in your

washer. I don't have anything else on me. Not even underwear."

My eyes widened. "You're stark naked under that robe?"

"Yep."

I pinched the bridge of my nose. "Why did you do that? I don't exactly have spare menswear lying around."

"I only own one set of clothes," he said lightly. "I figured shower time was laundry time."

I stared. He had escaped with millions—had crossed an ocean somehow—had been around Fairwyck for months—and he didn't even have a second pair of underwear? His story had more holes than my bath sponge.

"You've been around since January," I said. "I've seen you—at the theater, at the graveyard. You don't look like a man who's worn the same outfit for months. So where have you been staying?"

"With a friend. But I can't stay there anymore." He shrugged. "It's not close. I have some things in a safe place too—but again, not nearby. I've been in and out of Fairwyck. And the more I saw you, the more I realized how much I need you. I want to stay with you, Liv."

He reached for my hand. I snatched it away.

"What friend?" I pressed. "And what about your secretary? Was she staying there too?"

"I told you—she forced me to take her. I got rid of her as soon as I could. It cost me a pretty penny, but don't worry—there's still enough left for us."

"That. Is. Not. What I'm worried about." I stood up, heat prickling behind my eyes. "I'm worried someone will see you here, and you'll get arrested, and I'll be dragged down with you, and the children will be left with no one."

Steven smiled indulgently. "Oh, babe, you've always had such a big imagination. That's not going to happen. You worry too much."

My mouth fell open. "I…worry…too much?" I sputtered. "I already lived that situation!"

"Did you really think I'd leave you forever? That I wouldn't find you the moment it was safe? Do you mistrust me that much?"

That nearly knocked the breath from my lungs. The audacity. I rubbed my temples hard. The headache was blooming into a full migraine.

"I have to go," I said, voice tight. "Here's what you're going to do. Go upstairs. Wait in my bedroom. When your clothes are dry, check the front garden to make sure Esme's car is gone, then get back to the cottage. And stay there. I'll come over tonight, and we'll talk."

He agreed—eagerly, too easily. That unsettled me.

Five minutes later, I was alone in my car, lungs expanding properly for the first time since coming home from Gina's. The pressure in my forehead eased the moment I pulled away.

A few hours to think, really think, was exactly what I needed. I grabbed a to-go coffee in Meckham—thank goodness Jamie was already gone—walked a bit, then started my shift. While working, I casually checked in with Judith—under the guise of scheduling—and learned the cottage next door wouldn't need cleaning for another three days. A new booking was coming eventually, but Steven was safe at least until tomorrow. And if Dr. Drake needed another night…well, that bought even more time.

By late afternoon, I had a plan.

For the kids' sake, Steven would get a chance.

Not a free pass. Not forgiveness.

A chance.

I'd help him hire a lawyer. He'd turn himself in properly. But before that, he could speak to Blake and Audrey—after I'd prepared them, and only if they wanted to.

Reasonable. Controlled. Responsible.

I almost felt proud of myself.

I stepped through my front door in a positive frame of mind.

Audrey skidded into the kitchen, eyes bright, hair flying, and launched herself at me.

"Mom! Guess what?" she squealed.

My stomach dropped.

"Daddy's back!"

CHAPTER EIGHT

My eyes darted between the three of them.

Audrey—wrapped around Steven's arm like a jungle-gym koala, grinning wide enough to split her cheeks,

Steven—beaming as if this were the happy family reunion he'd always planned, and

Blake—leaning against the counter, arms folded, eyes narrowed.

"What are you doing here?" My voice came out high and sharp. Too sharp. I sucked in a few breaths and tried again, gentler—but only marginally. "Steven, we agreed you'd go back to the cottage next door and wait."

Steven didn't look remotely guilty.

"You said I should wait until your neighbor's car was gone so I could cross the gardens unseen. When I checked, it was there. I laid down on the couch for a little nap..." His smile was shameless. "And when I woke up, the kids were home. I'm glad I waited—another night without seeing them would've killed me."

I could feel anger pulsing under my skin. I had explicitly told him to wait. I wanted to talk to the kids first—

prepare them. And he'd simply waltzed right through my boundaries.

Again.

A terrible, tempting thought popped up: Call Jamie. Or Farrow. Let the police deal with this.

But then I saw Audrey's face.

I wasn't sure I'd ever seen her that happy.

She had clung to the belief that her dad would come back for us—because she was nine when everything collapsed, and nine-year-olds don't understand Ponzi schemes or extradition laws. For a long time, I feared she blamed me—that I'd refused to go with him. That the life she'd lost was somehow my fault.

And when we first moved to England, she had blamed me. Oh, had she ever. Spoiled, miserable, furious—she'd treated her classmates like employees and me like the jailer who stole her old life.

But slowly…with friends, with theater, with survival… she'd become grounded again. Happy, even.

The one thing she still didn't have was a father.

And seeing her now, eyes sparkling, arms around Steven…

I couldn't take that joy away from her.

I also—if I was being brutally honest—didn't want her to hate me for it.

I let out a long breath.

"Okay. I would've preferred to speak to you privately first, Steven. But since you're here—and the kids are here —let's all sit down and talk." I forced a smile. "I'll make tea."

Steven laughed.

"Tea? A year and a half back in your homeland, and you've gone full Brit. No thanks—I'll have a coffee."

I simply turned on the coffeemaker and fixed myself a

calming chamomile-lavender blend. I needed my nerves intact.

"You okay?" I muttered to Blake, who still hadn't moved from the counter.

They shook their head stiffly.

"We only just got home. Audrey's been glued to him since."

"She's excited," I whispered. "He'll want to talk to you too."

Another shake. Jaw clenched.

I set my mug on the table and motioned for everyone to sit. Audrey dragged Steven over like a prize she'd just won.

"Come on, Bianca," Steven coaxed, smiling too wide. "I know you must have lots of questions."

"It's Blake," they replied flatly, but they sat.

Steven waved it off. "Give your old dad a little time to get used to that. Probably, by the time I figure it out, you'll be a girl again." He laughed at his joke.

"You could've had time to get used to it if you'd been here," Blake said, their face a mask. "And I'm not changing my mind."

"You'll always be my little girl," he said, reaching for their hand.

They pulled away.

Blake didn't waste another second. "Where have you been, Dad?"

Thank god someone said it aloud.

Steven gave the same vague dodge he'd given me. "Oh, here and there. With friends."

Audrey, soft and trusting, looked up at him. "But why did you leave, Daddy?"

He stroked her hair. "Something went wrong with my business. The government would've taken all our money. I had to protect our future—protect us—so I took it before they could."

Blake snorted so hard, it was practically a scream.

Did he really believe that? Or did he just like the sound of that story?

I swallowed hard. It was time for the truth—or at least enough of it to keep my children safe.

"While we're on the subject," I said carefully, "you both need to understand that your father is still wanted by the police. There's an active warrant. So you cannot tell anyone he's here. If people find out, we could all get in a lot of trouble."

Steven shot me a warning look. "You didn't have to say it so harshly."

Audrey's face crumpled. Tears sprang to her eyes. Steven wrapped his arms around her.

And just like that, I was the villain again.

"Well, I'm sorry, but it's true," I snapped, hating myself for both the tone and the necessity. "This is exactly why I wanted to talk to you two first, and to Steven separately—"

"You wanted to keep us from seeing Dad?" Audrey's voice cracked like she was breaking right down the middle.

I pressed my palms against my eyes, heat stinging behind my lids.

"No. It's just…complicated. Dad stole a lot of people's money, and the police are looking for him. He's on the run. And there's nothing I can do about that."

It came out more childish than I intended—but it was the truth.

"But he's come back to sort all of this out…haven't you, Dad?" Audrey asked, small and hopeful.

"Of course," Steven said, pulling her close. "But your mother is right—you can't tell anyone I'm here. Not yet. The police wouldn't understand, and they'd take me away from you."

"So you're going to turn yourself in?" Blake demanded. "You'll go to prison."

"No!" Audrey shrieked. "Dad's not going to prison! That's awful—why would you even say that?"

I took a long sip of chamomile tea and wished—desperately—that I'd added a dash of something much stronger.

Steven lifted his palms as though calming a startled deer. "Nobody is throwing me in prison. Let's not leap to the worst-case scenario. My lawyers will try to prevent that, and there's a whole process first—trials, arguments—lots of steps."

"But you *are* planning to turn yourself in," I said, unable to keep the steel from my voice. "Because I'm not willing to entertain any kind of…family reunion…if you don't—"

"Yes, Liv. I have a lawyer." Steven flashed a reassuring smile. "Everything will work out."

"How can you say that?" Blake burst out. They stood so fast, the chair clattered to the floor. "You cheated people—my friends' parents. Mom struggled because of you. And now you come back after a year and a half and pretend everything's fine? Lawyers won't magically erase what you did. You ran. You didn't face it. That makes everything worse. And even if you could fix it, should you? You can't undo the past, Dad!"

The last word cracked in the air before they spun and stormed upstairs.

Steven blinked after them, stunned. "Jesus. Teenage mood swings, huh? Should I go talk to her?"

"No. Let them cool off," I said, though secretly, I was proud. Blake had voiced everything I'd swallowed. "And that's not just *teenage mood*. You need to hear what they said."

Steven sat again, shoulders drooping. His expression softened, eyes glistening just a little.

"I know I can't change the past. If I could, I'd do a whole lot differently. But I am going to do everything in my power to put this right. To make this family whole again. I'm not just going to let them throw me into a cell and rot. I already missed too much…and I regret that more than you know."

As furious as I was…I believed him.

Then his face brightened, switching moods with whiplash speed as he turned to Audrey.

"So, what's new with you, Audrey-baby?"

"I'm not a baby anymore," she said, pretending to be offended. "That's what's new."

"Of course not." He gently tapped her arm. "So—boyfriend?"

"Ew, Dad!" The disgust was real this time. I couldn't help laughing a little too, despite myself.

"Actually," I said quickly, "Audrey's doing wonderfully. She's in a theater group. She even went to theater camp over the summer."

Steven perked up. "I always knew you were talented. Remember when you were a Pilgrim in the Thanksgiving play?"

Audrey wrinkled her nose. "I was the Pilgrim's wife. I had like two lines. I just had to stand there and look nice."

"Well, you did a great job," Steven said.

"This is different. We do real plays. Not baby stuff." She tossed her blond hair, then giggled. "It's really fun."

"I'm glad," he said warmly. "Anything else new?"

Audrey hesitated—then turned to me. "We all discovered our special talents. Didn't we, Mom?"

I choked on my tea. "Oh—hmm—yes, well. That's… something we can share with Dad another time."

"Why? Dad will want to know," Audrey said, brow scrunched.

"Um—" I began, at the same moment Steven frowned. "What?"

"Mom takes special pictures," Audrey said eagerly. "Pictures with—"

"Yes," I cut in, standing abruptly. "My great-aunt Ethel left me her camera. A family heirloom. I've picked up photography." I dug the Nikon from my bag and plastered on a smile. "Pretty cool, right?"

Steven barely glanced at it. "I've never seen you take a photograph in your life."

"Not just any pictures, Dad," Audrey insisted—

A sharp *Mrrrow!* interrupted her.

Saved by the cat!

"And Ethel left me something else," I said quickly. "A cat."

I opened the door. Ethel strutted in—ginger fur, white-tipped tail held high.

One look at Steven and she hissed, arched, and bolted through the living room and up the stairs.

"She doesn't like me," Steven said, eyebrows raised.

"I just need to tell her who you are," Audrey said confidently. "And Mom said it wrong—Great-Aunt Ethel didn't leave us the cat. She *is* the cat. And I can talk to her. Isn't that cool?"

Steven's eyebrows went higher. "It's nice to feel close to a pet, I guess..."

"No, I mean it," Audrey insisted, leaning forward. "That's our special talent. We're witches. All of us—Mom, Blake, Aunt Gina, Emerald, me. It's in the Seven bloodline. Ethel had a gift too, so she came back as a cat. Everyone has a gift! Mom takes pictures of ghosts, Gina is psychic, Emerald talks to books, Blake can draw what's in people's heads—and I can talk to animals!"

Her pride radiated.

I held my breath.

Please don't crush her. Please don't crush her.

For once in your life, Steven…

Just. Say. The right thing.

Steven laughed. "Oh, honey—what an imagination. You almost had me there! You're right, you're a marvelous actress."

Audrey frowned, confused. "No, that wasn't—"

"Audrey, sweetie," I interrupted before the situation imploded, "can you check on Blake for me? I know you're excited your dad is here, but it's a lot for everyone. Let me talk to him for a moment, okay? He'll still be here tomorrow—we just need to get him next door where he'll be safe. We don't want anyone to accidentally see him."

Amazingly, she nodded. "Okay." She gave Steven a fierce hug. "But Dad will still be here tomorrow, right? So we can talk more?"

"Yes," I said—because at least that much I could promise. "Tomorrow morning. I'll make sure of it."

"Okay! Bye, Dad!"

"Bye, honey."

She ran upstairs, bright as a sunrise. Steven watched her go, and I could practically feel my heart twist itself into knots. If he crushed her soul again…

"You know how devastated she'll be if you leave again," I said quietly.

"I don't plan to," Steven replied, turning back to me, taking both my hands. "That's why I'm here. I want to be with you."

"It's not that easy."

"Why not? I mean—you didn't stop loving me. You didn't stop believing in me, did you?"

That did it. He always twisted it around—as if his

betrayal was somehow about my reaction to it. I stepped back.

"Steven, for the kids' sake, I'm giving you the benefit of the—"

The doorbell rang.

I jolted like a guilty burglar. Steven did too—real panic in his eyes for the first time. Proof he wasn't as casual about the situation as he pretended.

I shoved him toward the back door. "Go. Across the garden. Quickly—before Esme or Anthony sees you."

"Will you come over later?" he whispered—breath warm, familiar, disorienting.

The bell rang again. Then *knock, knock, knock.*

"Liv? It's me—Jamie!"

My heart went into full stampede mode.

"I'll talk to you tomorrow," I hissed, pushing Steven through the open door. "Stay in the cottage tonight. Do not leave. Let me figure this out."

He opened his mouth—I shut the door on him before he could add anything else to my already melting brain.

I sprinted to the front door, plastered on what I hoped resembled a normal face, and opened it.

"Jamie—hi!"

"You look…warm," he said, brow furrowing as he touched my forehead.

"Yes, actually," I stammered, stepping back. "I think I'm coming down with something. You probably shouldn't get too close."

"That's why you didn't want to meet earlier?" His disappointment was a physical thing. "Why didn't you just tell me?"

"Oh, you know me," I babbled. "Didn't want to jinx it. If I say I'm sick, it becomes real. And I don't have time to be sick."

"Liv," he said gently, "you need to look after yourself."

He moved to step inside. "And as your boyfriend, I get to look after you when you're ill."

"No, no—seriously." I ushered him back like a feral raccoon. "I am a terrible patient. Truly. I prefer to suffer alone. A good night's sleep, and I'll be fine. There's nothing for you to do."

He studied me—I prayed my face kept its secrets.

"Okay," he said slowly. "If you're sure."

"I am." I ushered him out the door, smiling too brightly. "Thank you for checking on me—that's very sweet."

"Of course. I'll come back tomorrow—"

"Just…not too early," I said quickly. "Sleep is the best medicine."

A tiny frown, then a nod. "Okay. Feel better."

"Thanks," I said, and shut the door before he saw the panic behind my eyes.

I sagged against the wood, then stumbled into the kitchen and downed the rest of my tea. At this rate, I'd need a gallon of chamomile and about ten lavender fields.

Why did Steven have to show up now? Why not call? Or write? Or send a carrier pigeon? Why drop a bomb into the middle of the life I'd barely managed to piece back together?

Everything felt precarious. One wobble away from catastrophe.

It was only one more night. One.

I couldn't keep this from Jamie any longer than that. It just wasn't right.

I straightened my shoulders. I needed to hold it together. For the kids.

Upstairs, I tried talking to Blake, but they were still bristling.

"I hope you don't actually buy his lies," they muttered, refusing to meet my eyes.

That about summed up the situation: one child who'd hate me if I didn't give Steven a chance, and one who'd hate me if I did.

I changed into pajamas and crawled under the covers, praying unconsciousness would bring clarity.

It didn't.

At 6:30 a.m., my phone rang.

Gina.

I fumbled in the dark. "What is it?"

"Liv, can you come to the inn?" She sounded frantic. "Something terrible has happened."

Suddenly, I was wide awake. "What's wrong?"

"It's Dr. Drake," she whispered. "He's disappeared."

CHAPTER NINE

I was making the kids' breakfasts and packing lunches while on the phone with Ellie.

"I'm really sorry, but I can't come to the theater this morning. I know we planned to go over the books, but something's happened at Gina's—"

"Is it about Dr. Drake disappearing?"

I froze mid–butter swipe. "What? How do you know about that?"

"The man is famous, Liv! A ghost hunter filming in a haunted inn vanishes? Tabloids practically beg for that kind of story."

I stared at the clock. It wasn't even seven thirty.

Gina had noticed something was wrong around five. A strange noise had woken her—loud enough to get her and Emerald out of bed and upstairs into the inn to investigate. Everything up there was unchanged. Except Dr. Drake wasn't in his room. Or anywhere else.

All of his belongings were untouched—wallet, phone, jacket. His yellow Beetle was still outside.

They had checked the building, calling his name. Nothing.

Then his phone rang while they were holding it—his producer. Drake was supposed to check in regularly, and when he hadn't, they'd searched the remote camera feeds. The one above the stairs proved he hadn't left that way. So they checked the feed in his room.

He was visible until 4:43 a.m.

Then a short glitch. Seconds. When the picture returned…he was gone.

Vanished. Without leaving the room.

The production company was still scrubbing through footage, trying to find anything they might have missed. Meanwhile, Gina and Emerald had searched the entire property again before finally calling me, frantic.

I'd promised I'd be there the moment the kids left for school. I'd wanted Dr. Drake to be gone today—but not like this!

"I can't believe they'd already alert reporters," I muttered. "Cheap marketing ploy. *Ghost hunter disappears!* They don't know if this is something awful or totally harmless—but the tabloids won't care."

"I don't know that they have," Ellie said. "But I'm sure they will. And Michelle at the shop already knows about it. Her…boyfriend works at the police station, remember?"

I blinked. "Boyfriend?"

Michelle was pushing sixty—somehow the word felt illegal. "Wait—the guy she's been talking about? George? I thought he was a janitor."

"He is. At the police station in Gloucester."

"Oh." Of course. Jamie and DI Farrow also worked for the Gloucestershire Police. If Drake had truly disappeared, they'd almost certainly be called to investigate.

And if gossip had reached Michelle? Then half of Fairwyck probably already had the headline queued up in their minds.

"If Michelle's talking"—I groaned—"it might as well

be in the tabloids already. The whole Cotswolds will know by lunch."

"Probably," Ellie agreed. "The production team will want to control the narrative."

"Yeah, yeah—I've seen *Scandal*," I muttered, in a very foul mood.

The last thing I needed was the Sacred Salmon swarming with reporters—and police.

"Listen, I've got to go," I said as the kids stumbled downstairs in sleepy chaos. "We'll talk tomorrow, okay?"

"Sure. He has to be hiding somewhere," Ellie said. "Probably part of the show. You'll find him."

"I hope so. Bye."

I hung up and greeted Blake and Audrey, sliding scrambled eggs onto plates like a short-order chef on deadline.

"Did you talk to Dad yet?" Audrey asked, bright-eyed. Blake rolled their eyes.

"No. It's only seven thirty, and I'm pretty busy," I said.

"But you'll do that while we're at school, right? Sort out the lawyer stuff?" Audrey chirped.

"Probably. But something's come up—I need to go to Gina's this morning. So finish up, okay?"

"Is Gina all right?" Blake asked, frowning.

"Oh, yes. It's about that ghost-hunter show they're filming. Just…weirdness." I cleared my throat. "And Audrey—remember, you cannot tell anyone about your dad. Not a soul. If anyone finds out he's here, he will get arrested. It's serious."

"I know, Mom," she said, chewing toast. "I'm almost eleven. I understand."

"Just making sure—it's important." I kissed Audrey's head and dashed upstairs to brush my teeth and pull myself together.

By the time I returned, the kids were finishing breakfast and bickering.

"What's going on?"

"Blake says I shouldn't have told Dad about my special talent," Audrey huffed. "They said he can't be trusted. But that's not true…right, Mom?"

Oh, terrific. Conflict before eight a.m.

"To be honest," I said carefully, "I was…running a little interference yesterday. I don't think it's a good idea either."

"But—"

"There's just a lot to sort out. Your dad isn't a Seven. He's not from here. He doesn't understand—"

"Loads of people who aren't Sevens know," Audrey argued. "Jamie does. Esme and Anthony do. So why shouldn't Dad?"

Because I didn't trust him. Because I didn't even know who he was anymore. Because telling him would make everything real—and dangerous—and impossible to take back.

"It's probably a bit much for him right now," I said instead. "He just came back. We need to go slowly with… all the new information."

"It's part of who I am," Audrey insisted, chin lifting stubbornly. "I want Dad to know. You're always saying how brave Bianca is about being—"

"It's Blake," Blake snapped, springing up. Their sister's jab had landed exactly where she'd aimed it.

Audrey folded her arms. "Dad still calls you Bianca. Why shouldn't I?"

Blake's face flushed scarlet. "You know—"

"Children," I cut in, sharper than I meant. "Stop. Blake, please go get your things. I'll talk to your sister."

They gave me a stiff nod and disappeared upstairs.

I drew a long breath. Then another.

The truth—which I hated admitting even to myself—was that Audrey wasn't completely wrong. She should be able to share her identity with her father. She should be proud of her gift.

But doing so meant revealing everything. Including the fact that I could photograph the dead.

I'd come so far in accepting my ability. In using it to help instead of fearing it. I'd told the people closest to me. I'd built friendships. A life.

But I still didn't want people like Michelle looking at me like I'd grown a second head.

I'd finally found somewhere I belonged. Somewhere my kids belonged.

I didn't want to become Fairwyck's newest curiosity.

And Steven…Steven would never get it. Audrey had spoken from her heart—and he'd laughed it off. If I'd have insisted, he'd have assumed I'd lost my mind. He'd pity me. And worse—he'd pity them.

A terrible thought lurched into my chest: If this story did hit the press—a ghost hunter vanishing on camera—reporters would descend like vultures. And they would sniff out everything connected to the inn.

Gina's "quirky" psychic business would become witch-craft headlines. The Seven legacy would be national gossip. Our gifts—out in the open.

The whole world would know.

And Steven would have to believe it. Whether he liked it or not.

That scared me more than anything.

Not because of me—my ego could take the hit—but because if he rejected the kids now, especially after they'd opened themselves up so vulnerably…

There wouldn't be any repairing that. Ever.

I let out a shaky sigh and checked the clock. "All right —time to catch the bus. We'll talk more later, okay?"

Audrey nodded, though her eyes remained troubled.

I grabbed my coat and bag and hovered impatiently by the front door, waiting for them to leave so I could get straight to the Sacred Salmon.

I had to find Dr. Drake. And fast.

Before the media descended.

Before the village started whispering.

Before anyone discovered Steven.

Before anyone uncovered the truth about the Sevens.

Before I became the woman hiding a fugitive husband—witch and criminal accomplice rolled into one disastrous headline.

The clock was ticking.

CHAPTER TEN

"Oh my god, Liv—I'm so glad you're here."

Gina looked pale and oddly fragile as she opened the door. She pulled me into a hug. "I hope you brought your camera. We must contact the ghosts. They're probably important witnesses. I told DI Farrow they should be questioned if he wants to find out what happened to poor Dr. Drake, but he refuses to take me seriously…"

Oh no.

DI Farrow was already here—and Gina had told him I could communicate with ghosts? She knew better. The man already thought I was strange and had tried to pin multiple murders on me. The last thing I needed was to become his supernatural consultant.

"Can I come in?" I asked, when she still didn't open the door properly. "Where's Emerald?"

"She's with Jamie and DI Farrow in the inn," Gina said. "She said I should put my feet up and drink my tea, but how can I sit still? I'm dreadfully worried about Dr. Drake. He's such a lovely man. I will never forgive myself if something happened to him in my inn."

Her hand clutched at her chest, and she wavered on her feet.

I slipped through the gap in the door and placed a steadying hand on her back. "Really, Aunt Gina, you mustn't get worked up. Let's go to the parlor and sit down."

She gave me a shaky smile, then said in a loud voice, "Of course. Liv is coming through to the parlor!"

I shot her a worried side glance. She wasn't the youngest anymore, and this whole incident seemed to be making her behave in even more unusual ways than she normally did. I might have to talk to Emerald about it.

The annex was as eccentric as Gina—like stepping into a Victorian curiosity shop.

Heavy drapes, antique furniture of wildly differing heights, and shelves overflowing with charms, crystals, old books, and the sorts of witchy artifacts that immediately made outsiders assume you were summoning demons for breakfast. Most newcomers stared so hard their eyes watered.

I'd once joked they could charge admission and call it a private museum. Or that choosing a chair was like starring in a fairy-tale trial—pick wrong, and you'd end up child-sized with your feet dangling three feet above the floor.

And if you weren't invited into this room, you might be taken into the adjacent one, full of tarot cards, herbs, and spiritual paraphernalia—Gina's reading room.

God help us when the reporters arrive, flashed through my mind. They wouldn't need Gina to say a word—one look around would be headline enough.

There was a teapot on the coffee table, and I poured the still-steaming liquid into the empty cup. "Please rest, Aunt Gina. I'll go next door and see what I can do."

Her gemstone-studded fingers curled around my wrist.

"Thank you, dear." Her voice rose again. "Head straight to the inn, Liv!"

I flinched and wondered if there was something wrong with her hearing. But then she resumed talking in a much softer voice. "Now that I know you're here with your camera, I feel so much better."

I forced a smile.

There was no way I was pulling out that camera in front of DI Farrow.

At the door, I hesitated. Gina was alone—maybe I should tell her about Steven right now. The secret felt too big, too heavy to keep contained.

But she was lying back, eyes closing. Beltane, her familiar, had hopped up beside her, purring as Gina stroked her fur. The cat cracked one green eye at me—*Don't you dare disturb her with mortal drama.*

Message received.

I slipped through the connecting door between annex and inn and stepped into the taproom.

"Hello?" I called. The thick stairwell door muffled most noise, as I'd already learned yesterday.

I climbed the stairs and entered the corridor.

"Liv? Is that you?" Jamie's voice answered.

My gaze flicked toward the camera mounted above the door. A tiny red light glowed.

"Is that still recording?" I asked as Jamie and Emerald appeared.

"Yes," Emerald said, hugging me tightly. "I replaced the batteries per the production team's instructions. I thought keeping surveillance going was a good idea— though some people think it's unnecessary."

She shot Jamie a pointed glare.

He lifted his hands. "Hey, not my call."

Unease prickled at me. "Not necessary? Do the police know where Dr. Drake is?"

Before either could answer, a familiar voice boomed from the ghost hunter's room. "Is that the infamous Ms. Grantham?"

Oh joy.

Jamie gestured for us to join them.

"Yes, it's me. Good morning, Detective Inspector," I said through a stretched-thin polite smile.

Farrow nodded stiffly. He was in his sixties, barely reached my shoulder, and—much to my irritation—twirled his mustache as though auditioning for the role of Poirot.

"Why is it," he mused, rocking back on his heels, "that whenever a crime occurs in this village, you're somehow involved?"

I stiffened. "This is my great-aunt's home, as you well know. She called me because she was upset. Hardly a criminal conspiracy."

He clasped his hands behind his back. "She also insisted she summoned you not merely to comfort her, but to investigate. Ghosts, she said." His lip curled. "And for reasons beyond me, she believes you're competent to assist. Considering your track record—and my repeated warnings to stop meddling in police matters—I am astonished."

I clenched my jaw. *Deep breaths.*

"You must have misunderstood her. She wants me to take photos for the ghost hunters—documentation of how the place looks before and after Dr. Drake stayed here and…well…vanished."

Farrow narrowed his eyes. "Why? How involved is she with the production of this ridiculous TV show? Is she being paid? It wouldn't be the first time a stunt was staged to boost ratings. Falsifying evidence to mislead police is a criminal offense, and if I—"

"Oh my god, no!" Emerald snapped. "You saw my mother. She's terrified. She would never—"

Farrow turned his beady glare on her. "Really? Isn't

performing for money exactly what she does? And if this episode draws attention, so too will her…business. Convenient marketing, as the kids say."

"You cannot be serious," Emerald hissed. "A man disappeared. This isn't a stunt. My mother has nothing to do with it."

Jamie stepped between them. "Okay, let's not start a fight. We don't actually think Dr. Drake faked his disappearance for ratings…do we, boss? He doesn't need to—he's already on top. And from everything we've heard, he's obsessed with the supernatural as research, not entertainment. He barely acknowledges the show. His producer said he seems to use it just to fund his experiments. He's so focused, he forgets everything else."

"Hmm." Farrow twirled his mustache, enjoying himself far more than the situation warranted. "It never hurts to keep all avenues open. But yes—his agent confirmed Drake has pulled stunts like this before."

"He's vanished from a haunted location before?" I asked, incredulous. "Phone, wallet, equipment left behind —just gone—and then comes waltzing back?"

"I don't know the details," Farrow said breezily. "But he has abandoned sets to chase other haunted sites. He's gone missing for days, following—what did he call it?—'the research.' Hyperfocused. Not great with communication."

"But his car is still here," I pressed. "And the cameras —Gina said they never show him leaving."

Farrow waved a dismissive hand. "Someone could have picked him up. And there was a glitch in the feed. There might have been one at the door camera too. This wasn't exactly a professional installation." He gestured at the hacked-together hub beneath the drilled hole. "Bluetooth. Batteries. Hardly reliable."

He wasn't wrong—Drake's engineering looked like something out of a YouTube tutorial. Still…

"So what are you doing to investigate?" I asked. "Checking camera footage yourselves? Looking at his phone—any calls or messages last night—"

"You clearly watch too many detective shows, Ms. Grantham," Farrow cut in, his voice condescending. "This isn't fiction. We don't have the resources for that kind of meddling. And getting information from phones requires warrants, paperwork—time. We'll wait. Most likely, the problem will solve itself. Dr. Drake will return, and everyone will praise the Gloucestershire Police for not wasting manpower."

"You're just going to wait?" I tried not to shriek. "What about his belongings? His specialized equipment?" I pointed at the array of ghost-hunting gadgets, including a handheld EMF meter I recognized from part of an episode I'd caught once.

"He can collect it when he comes back."

"Right. Because surely he's off researching a more interesting ghost," I said brightly, my laugh skittering into hysteria. "This inn is dreadfully dull."

Emerald stared at me like I'd declared the Earth flat. "Don't you think we should leave the cameras running? To…observe things?"

Jamie backed her up. "Also, just in case it does become a police matter. Better to preserve the scene, right? We could take his phone, let our techs check logs and missed calls—it would quickly prove he left voluntarily, and then the media frenzy will die down."

Farrow sighed. "Fine. But leave everything else as it is."

He stepped toward the door.

I said, "But do we truly need the cameras on? Seems a waste of batteries to film empty rooms."

He shrugged again. "Your call." Then his gaze speared me. "And a word of advice, Ms. Grantham—do not muddy things up again. Comfort your aunt, but do not"—

he air-quoted—"'investigate.' Ms. Seven, show us out. This place is a maze."

Jamie gave me an apologetic look—clearly sorry we couldn't talk privately. "Are you feeling better?" he mouthed.

I nodded and barely attempted a smile back.

Honestly, I was relieved he was leaving. My face had never been good at lying.

I stayed back so I wouldn't have to talk to him. I really wanted to tell him about Steven. As my partner, he should know.

Now that the others were gone, the chill crept back into my bones.

The air felt thick, charged.

Despite myself, I lifted my camera.

I snapped the hub.

The equipment.

The makeshift cot.

The sagging antique bed.

Bare furnishings.

The tall mirror with the ornate carved frame—

I froze.

Had that mirror been here yesterday?

I couldn't remember.

I swallowed hard, refusing to look at the screen.

Cowardly? Maybe.

Smart? Absolutely. I preferred to face whatever was lurking after I got home—with coffee in hand, the doors locked, and every light blazing.

Or maybe not at all. Maybe Farrow would, by some miracle, be right for once. Drake might turn up. I could even move Steven in here. And leave well enough alone as far as the ghosts.

But deep down, I knew exactly what I was doing—slipping back into old habits. Ignoring my instincts, plastering on a smile, and burying my head in the sand.

And honestly—when had Farrow ever been right about a single investigation I'd been involved in?

I let out a wry laugh as I fled the haunted inn. The ghosts were one thing—but relying on Farrow? Terrifying.

CHAPTER ELEVEN

I headed back into the annex to check on Gina.

Emerald was with her, having just seen the officers out.

Gina yelped, then cried out, "Liv!"

Emerald smiled at me as she dashed out of the room. "Let me make a fresh pot of tea and find some cups for you and me," she said breathlessly.

"Thanks." My gaze drifted to the table. "Oh—you already have an extra cup," I noted, spotting two matching gold-rimmed teacups and saucers.

"Must be from earlier," Emerald mumbled, hurrying past me, almost knocking me over in the process.

I frowned, steadying myself on the back of an armchair. I could have sworn only one cup had been there when I poured Gina tea before going over to the inn.

Gina had a hand clasped over her mouth as she peered around me nervously.

My aunt and cousin still seemed really rattled by Drake's disappearance. Trying to put Gina's mind at ease, I said, "DI Farrow is convinced Dr. Drake just… left, Aunt Gina." I sat gingerly on an antique chair whose spindly legs looked one wrong shift away from collapse. "So you don't need to worry. Apparently, it's his usual MO—and the cameras probably just glitched."

I had Gina's full attention now. She shook her head firmly. "And what was that strange loud noise?"

"Probably a car outside," I suggested. "Someone must have picked him up."

"It came from the inn," she insisted, pressing her hand over her heart. "Right beyond my bedroom wall. I appreciate you trying to calm me, darling, but I know what I heard. I've had a dreadful feeling in my chest ever since. And I asked the cards. They're never wrong."

"No," I said, forcing patience, "but they didn't show you exactly what happened, did they? You always say they're open to interpretation."

I really needed there to be a rational answer—one that meant the inn would soon be empty, and this sudden spotlight on Fairwyck would disappear.

Emerald returned with a tea tray holding a fresh pot and two cups and set it down with a sharper clink than necessary.

"Why are you so insistent Farrow is right?" she asked, arms crossed tight. "You know there are other explanations —less…logical ones. And I thought you trusted my mother's instincts by now."

"You make it sound like I'm siding with Farrow against you," I said, stung. Emerald almost never snapped like this. "It's not about trust. It's about the most likely scenario. If Drake has a history of wandering off when he finds another location, or—"

Emerald cut me off. "Oh, do you think there's a more haunted or promising location than the inn?"

"And Dr. Drake was very excited," Gina murmured. "This was his rabbit hole. Yes, he gets obsessed—maybe so obsessed he lets people down. But this place was the obsession."

"With respect, Aunt Gina, you only just met him," I said gently. "You don't really know what he might do."

"I feel like I know him rather well," she sniffed, cheeks flushing.

"What's up with you, Liv?" Emerald shot back, glaring over the teapot. "I never thought I'd see the day you'd take Farrow's side."

"I—I'm not!" My voice cracked at the accusation. I found Emerald's reaction to be completely over the top. "I just want Drake to be okay. Like you do. I didn't realize this was about taking sides. And honestly, you sound a little…confrontational."

"Girls, please," Gina soothed, patting Emerald's knee. "Like Liv said, we all just want to make sure poor Malcolm is all right."

I took a sip of the scalding-hot tea.

"But the police aren't investigating," Emerald countered. "They're convinced he walked out on his own. So it does matter whose theory we support. If we go with Farrow's…nothing will be done."

"Don't worry. Liv is going to investigate," Gina said confidently, as though she'd just assigned me homework.

"Um…I'm not sure how I—"

"You'll ask the ghosts," Gina said matter-of-factly. "They must have seen something."

"Well, I did take photos in Drake's room," I offered, trying to restore peace.

Gina clapped once, delighted. "Wonderful."

"Which reminds me," I said. "There's a mirror in there I don't remember seeing yesterday. Big, old, ornate. Did Drake move it?"

"Yes," Gina said thoughtfully. "He must've dragged it

from another room…though I don't recall ever seeing it before. But then—I haven't ventured upstairs in ages."

"He might have brought it with him," Emerald suggested. "For scrying. Trying to communicate with the ghosts himself."

"Maybe…" Gina said, unconvinced. "But that tiny car of his was packed to the roof. I don't see how the mirror would've fit—not with the cameras and cables and gadgets. And I was there when he unloaded everything."

"Did the mirror show anything unusual in your photos?" Emerald asked. "A ghost attached to it, maybe?"

"I haven't looked yet," I admitted, fingers brushing my camera through the fabric of my bag. "I'd rather review them at home—light on, coffee in hand—before I get too close to whatever's lurking in there."

I took a breath. "Which brings me to my question. Yes, I was hoping Farrow's theory would pan out." I kept my tone neutral—no need to poke the angry witch. "Because, logically, what else could cause someone to literally vanish?"

"Something not logical," Emerald said pointedly. "Something supernatural."

"Yes, but…what?" I persisted. "You've lived here forever. This place is supposed to be the most haunted inn in England. And you"—I nodded toward Gina—"say the ghosts are helpful, that their energy supports your work. You've never suggested they're malicious. So what kind of supernatural event could make a man disappear?"

Gina and Emerald exchanged a look.

A secretive one.

And the twisted feeling in my stomach grew cold. I downed the rest of my tea, as if the hot liquid could be a remedy.

"I've never had the feeling there's anything evil in the inn," Gina said slowly.

"We've never been afraid of anything here," Emerald agreed. "Though…sometimes the energy gets intense. Intense enough that I need a break."

I remembered Gina telling me Emerald sometimes moved out for a while—though I'd never really thought through what that meant.

"But ghosts are unpredictable," Gina continued. "The spirit realm is unpredictable. There's rarely a clear line between good and bad. It's called the shadow realm for a reason." She gave me a meaningful little smile. "We've left the ghosts next door alone for years. Dr. Drake is a hunter —he confronts entities for a living. He probes aggressively. Maybe he pushed too far. Spirits linger for a reason, Liv. Something traumatic holds them here. You help them resolve that. You approach with compassion. But digging up what's buried—however necessary—can cause upheaval. Stir things up. Malcolm, in his eagerness, might have pushed too hard."

I stared at her, stunned. "If you knew that, why did you let him stay here and stir things up in the first place? Why poke the hornet's nest?"

Gina's face brightened with unapologetic delight. "Because I love his show. I couldn't let this opportunity pass me by. And sometimes a little upheaval is precisely what's needed. The cards said it was time."

"Time for what?" I asked.

They exchanged another secretive look.

A spike of disappointment stabbed through me. Trust had been the foundation between us these past eighteen months—and now? It felt like there were things they weren't saying. That they knew more than they were telling me.

Or maybe Gina was just trying to justify her choice, shaken by what had happened to Drake.

I sighed and pushed to my feet. "Well, all we can do

now is hope he turns up. And if Farrow is right, it'll be a relief. Just a scare. And a reminder that maybe the ghosts should be left alone. The production team ought to pack up the equipment and go. The cameras should definitely come down—nothing good comes from them staying on." I aimed the last part toward Emerald but avoided her eyes.

"We'll know if he turns up quickly," she said tightly. "Or if he needs help. That's why the cameras stay."

I didn't have the energy to argue. I reached for my teacup to take it to the kitchen.

"Oh—no need," Emerald said quickly, practically snatching it from my hands. "I'll take the whole tray."

"There's still plenty in the pot," I pointed out, frowning. "It's no trouble."

"No, really," she insisted. Then she shot Gina a look—sharp, meaningful.

Gina hopped up at once. "Yes, leave it to Emmy." Her hand settled on my back, gently steering me toward the door. "If you must be off, we won't keep you. Thank you for coming, darling."

"Of course," I said, dazed by the sudden dismissal. "I'll check the photos, make a plan, and come back later to… communicate with the ghosts."

"Yes—but phone first," Emerald said.

"Sure." They'd never needed me to announce a visit before. I tried not to let it bother me. Probably they just wanted to update me first if there was news.

"And call us if you hear anything," Gina added.

"Yes, yes," I murmured. She'd already opened the door.

"Okay, bye—"

But it clicked shut behind me before I'd even finished.

I stood blinking at the painted wood. Something was definitely off. For the past year and a half, they had been my rock—trusted allies. And suddenly there was distance. Secrecy. A barrier drawn. And I was left on the wrong side.

What were they hiding? And why?

I headed across the yard toward my car, passing Drake's yellow Beetle. It struck me again—how absurd it was to think he'd walked away and left everything behind. His wallet. Phone. Car. Equipment.

It didn't look like he'd left at all.

Unless he'd gone on foot…into Fairwyck? The villagers would've noticed. Into the surrounding countryside, then? The inn backed straight onto fields and woods…

What if he'd panicked—fled—and gotten hurt? A twisted ankle, a fall down an embankment? Farrow was wrong to wait. Someone should be searching.

I checked the time. I needed to get home. Steven could not be trusted to stay hidden for long.

But the thought of finding Drake and ending this mess before it spiraled further was too tempting.

Five minutes. A quick look. Just in case.

So I headed across the field toward the tree line.

Two hours later, I emerged scratched, exhausted, and empty-handed. No sign of Malcolm Drake—no trail, no dropped equipment, not even a footprint. Just mud on my boots and a rip in my trousers where a thornbush had attacked me.

I reached my car, careful to avoid toppling into the ditch again, and tossed my bag onto the passenger seat. I stretched, back aching.

The inn loomed against the slate-gray sky—crooked, ancient, watching. A shiver crawled up my spine.

Movement flickered behind one of the upstairs windows.

I squinted. A figure stood half-hidden by the old lace curtains. Shorter than Emerald. Squarer build. A head full of dark curls. Not Gina—her hair was teased and bottle-blond. Not Drake—wrong height, wrong posture.

A woman, then.

But no other cars were around.

I stared harder. Blinked.

The figure vanished.

Had I actually seen someone? Or was my mind playing tricks?

There was another possibility—one that sat directly between the rational and the absurd.

It might not have been a living person at all.

It could have been a ghost.

CHAPTER TWELVE

The woman in the window had spooked me, and when I got home, I didn't even look at the pictures on my camera.

I grabbed some food, double-checked that Esme wasn't around, then slipped over to the cottage next door.

Steven was watching TV with the curtains drawn, clearly bored out of his skull. He lit up at the sight of me—and the bag of food.

When I asked whether he'd contacted his lawyer, he pulled out an ancient flip phone—definitely a burner—and checked the blank screen. "Still waiting for a call back."

"Okay." I didn't want to get into everything again until I had a legal opinion. Turning himself in was nonnegotiable. And I wasn't pretending when I told him I was going back home, because I needed a nap. Between the early wake-up call and the hours stumbling around the woods, I was exhausted.

Steven looked disappointed. "I'm getting a bit lonely here, babe. What am I supposed to do all day?"

"I'm figuring it out, all right?" I snapped. "This isn't easy for any of us, and I have other problems too. You can't expect to slide neatly back into our lives. You dropped in unannounced and completely unexpected. I need time to process and figure stuff out."

Steven held up his hands. "All right, all right. I get that. But you said yourself—it's risky for me to stay here."

I rubbed my eyes. "Yes. That reminds me. I got a message from my boss asking me to get the cottage ready for the renters who are arriving tomorrow afternoon. You can only stay here one more night. I'm working on a plan to get you somewhere safer, to buy us time to sort this out. Or you can look for different accommodations yourself, if that doesn't suit you." My voice was tight.

He gave me puppy-dog eyes. "I don't want to be elsewhere. I want to be with you and the girls."

"Children," I corrected automatically.

"Whatever. I want to be with my family."

I pressed my palms over my eyes, bone-deep tired. "We're going to have to see about that. Now please stay here and keep your head down. Let me work on this."

I didn't look back as I walked out.

At home, I went straight to my bedroom, peeled off my torn trousers, and slid under the covers. Despite the storm of worries ping-ponging around my brain, I must have fallen asleep instantly—because the next thing I knew, Blake's voice cut through my dreams.

"Mom, wake up."

I jerked upright and squinted at the alarm clock. I'd slept for hours. The kids were home from school.

"Are you all right?" Blake asked, brown eyes wide with concern.

"Yes, I was just really tired. I'll take a shower and start dinner."

After cooking, doing homework, and cleaning up, I sent the kids upstairs. I was done with Audrey's nonstop pleading to see her father.

"I'm sorry, but I need to sort out the legal stuff first. I don't want to drag you into any trouble because we harbored a fugitive."

Audrey opened her mouth to argue, but I cut her off. "You are not to go over there or talk to him. That's final."

Eyes filling with tears, she stomped upstairs behind her sibling.

"You can watch something or read, but lights out at eight," I called after them.

Perfect. Another day of Steven, another disappointment waiting to happen. The sooner this ended the better, for Audrey's sake.

I called Jamie to ask for an update on Drake.

"No sign of him yet," he said. "Nobody's heard from him."

I hadn't expected good news—Gina and Emerald would have called—but I'd hoped Jamie might have something.

"You're still going with Farrow's theory?" I asked.

"For now."

"Shouldn't you do more? Track his phone records, at least?"

Jamie hesitated. "I probably shouldn't tell you this, but…we did. No calls or texts. The only outgoing ones were to his production team—just like the producer said."

"So he definitely wasn't picked up, was he?"

"We haven't checked whether he contacted someone online—social media, forums. That'll be harder. And his laptop's still at the inn."

"Then shouldn't you process the crime scene before it's contaminated? Clear out Drake's stuff in case any of it is evidence?"

"Crime scene? We don't know that it is one. There's no sign of a struggle. You saw the room—Emerald and Gina searched the whole inn. Nothing indicates foul play. Sure, the laptop might be useful. But the rest? What evidence could we possibly collect?"

"Then the production company should just clear it all out. Why leave the cameras running? Whatever happened to Drake—and clearly something did—surely it's in bad taste to keep filming."

"That's up to the production company. Why do you care so much about Drake's stuff?"

"I don't," I said too defensively. "I don't want attention on the inn. Or on my family. If anyone had asked me, I would've told them that filming *Ghost Hunter UK* here was a terrible idea. Now it's going to be even worse. I just want this shut down as fast as possible."

"Attention on your family's psychic abilities, you mean?"

"Yes," I muttered, annoyed.

"You seem stressed. I'm sure it'll be fine and sort itself out. Why don't I come over with a bottle of wine? I'll give you a nice relaxing neck massage—"

"No!"

"...Hmm?"

"I mean—tonight's not good. I'm helping Blake cram for a test they haven't studied for."

"Oh. What subject? Maybe I can help."

"That's all right. Thanks, though. I've gotta go. Talk to you tomorrow!" I hung up.

Jamie had accidentally given me an idea. I wanted to go back to the inn and get Drake's laptop. It had all the recorded videos on it—and possibly his internet search history. Maybe I could speed things up a bit.

I dashed upstairs to tell the kids I'd be popping over to Gina's for a short while.

Audrey barely grunted in reply, but Blake was in charge anyway. "I should be back within half an hour," I said to them. "Just make sure Audrey doesn't get any bright ideas and wander next door."

Downstairs, I grabbed my bag and keys and drove back to the inn.

It was dark—but the almost-full moon lit everything in stark silver. The inn looked even spookier in that light, its Victorian annex like a pale, crooked limb stretching out.

Gina had asked me to investigate. I hadn't looked at the photos yet, but I figured gathering real evidence would be a better place to start. No need to tell Gina I wasn't planning on interrogating ghostly witnesses just yet.

To my surprise, I had to ring the doorbell and knock at least ten times before Gina finally answered. And she didn't remove the security chain—just cracked the door barely wide enough for one blue eye.

"Yes?" she whispered.

"It's me, Gina!" I said, more exasperated than I meant to sound. "I want to go into the inn, remember?"

"Oh dear. Sorry, honey, but I don't think that's a good idea right now."

"What? Why?" My heart dropped. She had asked me to help earlier. And she'd never barred me entry to her home before.

"It just isn't. Why don't you come back tomorrow, hmm?"

"Did you hear anything from the police or the production crew about Drake?" I pressed, refusing to be dismissed so easily.

"No. I have to go. I…have a client. Bye."

She shut the door.

I just stood there, stunned. I called Emerald—but she didn't pick up.

Lost in thought, I circled the inn back toward my car.

Maybe Gina really did have a client. Maybe it was the woman with the dark curls I'd seen at the window earlier.

But why would a client be in the inn? Gina always saw them in the annex. And I'd seen that woman hours ago.

I paused by the front entrance—the one that had been boarded up. New nail heads gleamed from the old slats. Someone had put them back up in a hurry. Gina? The police? I could probably pry them off again without much trouble…if I had the right tool.

Probably not wise to break in right after being turned away.

But maybe later—once Gina and Emerald were asleep—I could slip inside, run upstairs, grab the laptop, and slip out again. Quick. Silent. Done.

No biggie.

Except the thought of entering a severely haunted building at night—a building where someone had *vanished*—made my skin crawl with goose bumps and my lungs forget how to function.

I told myself I was being ridiculous.

Get in. Grab laptop. Get out.

Worth it. I could know by tomorrow morning what had happened to Dr. Drake.

What could possibly go wrong?

CHAPTER THIRTEEN

The country lane looked different in the middle of the night—emptier, narrower, as if the hedges had crept closer since sunset. I parked far enough down the road that the car wouldn't be spotted if Gina or Emerald looked out their windows, but that meant walking the rest of the way in darkness. My flashlight stayed off. I gripped it so tightly my knuckles ached.

The Sacred Salmon Inn emerged, hunched against the moonlight. With the clouds shifting, its angles looked even more wrong. One wall leaned so crookedly, I couldn't believe the timber frame still held it up. As my imagination sprinted ahead of me, I caught myself wondering if something supernatural—something alive—kept it standing. The ivy didn't help, clinging to the stone like black veins feeding a rotten heart.

I pulled my collar up. A building itself can't be evil, I told myself. Spirits, yes. Buildings, no.

I'd seen what trauma could twist a spirit into. The theater ghost hadn't been born vengeful—she had been trapped by the injustice of her death. I'd helped her find the truth and let go, freeing everyone else from her curse. If anything dark lurked here, I'd help it too…eventually.

But not tonight. Tonight I'd just go in, grab Drake's laptop, get out.

That's all the courage I could muster.

The hanging sign with the grotesque salmon swayed soundlessly on its rusted chain. Beneath it, the original entrance hid behind the boards I'd seen hastily nailed up earlier. Maybe Drake had needed them open to drag his equipment inside…and then they'd boarded it back up. Or it maybe it had been done after the disappearance of the TV host.

I took the small claw hammer from my tote, praying each pop of metal on wood wouldn't echo down the lane. One nail, then another, then the stubborn one at the top. The planks loosened with a soft groan. I caught them before they fell.

The door yawned open, dark and cold—the room inside full of that heavy pressure I now recognized as spiritual presence, like deep water forcing its chill into my bones.

I slipped inside and closed the door.

My flashlight cut a narrow, shaky beam through the taproom. Heavy tables loomed like sleeping beasts. Shadows clung to the low ceiling beams—blackened with age, and now blackened with…dread.

I tightened my grip on my tote, feeling the Nikon through the fabric. I wasn't taking it out. If I started photographing this place now, I'd end up with enough ghosts for a Halloween flash mob.

I swept the light behind the bar—just to prove there was no monster crouched there. The movement triggered a memory: little me, refusing to step near my bed at night, convinced skeletal hands would shoot out and drag me under. Turned out, the ghosts in my childhood room had been real—quiet, watching—making those imagined hands almost quaint.

A bitter laugh escaped before I could swallow it. It echoed oddly in the empty tavern.

Focus.

The faint scent of stale beer and sweat—centuries old, but somehow still here—mixed with a metallic tang, like old pennies. My pulse ticked faster.

I hurried to the stairs. Each creak sounded far too loud. At the top, I turned off my flashlight and eased the door open. Darkness greeted me, thick and breathless.

I listened.

Nothing.

I stepped into the corridor.

Drake's camera was mounted above the doorway. I hugged the wall, stretched up on my toes, and found the switch. A click—the red recording light died.

Good.

In the darkness, no other tiny red lights glowed. No more cameras pointed at the corridor.

Deep breath.

The creak of the warped floorboards under my boots sounded like cracking bones as I crossed to Drake's room. Another temperature drop kissed my skin—sharp, biting. Ghosts. Lots of them.

Jaw clenched, I switched the flashlight off again, nudged the door open, and reached for the second camera above it. My fingers brushed the switch—

—and the red light flicked on.

I jerked back. Then slid it again. Off. Thank god.

Had it already been off? Had I turned it on by mistake?

No time to unravel that. Move.

Flashlight on, I darted to the wall where the extension

hub was plugged in. One angry yank, and the whole cord came free.

The hum from the equipment disappeared, and silence rushed in, like the room was holding its breath.

No cameras. No recordings.

Now I just had to survive long enough to find that laptop.

The beam of my flashlight slid across the room. For a moment, my heart stopped—there was someone lying on Drake's cot.

I inched closer.

Phew. Just his duffel bag and coat. Someone had neatly piled all his things on the cot. Gina or Emerald must have been in here since Drake vanished. Great—so much for an uncontaminated crime scene. And I was about to make it worse by stealing the laptop.

It sat beside the duffel bag. I grabbed it, then noticed the power cable still plugged in and stuffed that into my tote too. On top of Drake's clothes: a notebook. Of course —old-school field notes. I wedged it in beside the laptop.

Enough. Time to get out.

As I closed the door behind me, movement flickered at the edge of my vision, from the opposite end of the corridor.

I froze. Breath caught.

Probably imagination. Probably.

Then—a rustle. Fabric against wood.

Against every rational command from my brain, I turned right instead of bolting for the stairs.

My voice came out in a scratchy whisper. "Gina? Is that you?"

No response.

"Dr. Drake?"

What if he had come back? Was this all some elaborate

stunt for ratings? If so, he was lucky I didn't hit him with my flashlight.

Anger gave me courage. I swung the beam ahead of me and rounded the sharp bend.

"Dr. Drake, if this is you—enough already. You owe my aunt an explanation. She's beside herself—"

Silence. Just the long, empty corridor. I tried a few doors—some locked, some opening into more neglected rooms like Drake's. No person. No sound.

"Ghosts," I whispered into the dark.

I'd only really seen spirits through my camera before. But Gina always said the lens was just a tool—I was the medium. And I'd felt them before, the graveyard chill, the sense of a presence. Here more than anywhere else. It wasn't impossible that I could experience them without a viewfinder between us.

Still, my legs were done arguing with my nerves. I turned back toward the stairs.

The floorboards shrieked under my boots. If Gina heard me and came to investigate, this whole covert mission would be blown.

Then—another flash. Not movement this time…light. A thin bright line under a door.

I squinted. Yes—there was definitely a light on in there.

The same door I'd tried earlier. It had been locked.

Careful not to brush the moldy wallpaper, I crept closer. My pulse hammered against my ribs. By the layout, this had to be the room facing the woods. The room with the window I'd seen someone watching from.

I tried the handle again. Still locked.

Every instinct screamed run, but my knuckles knocked anyway. "Hello? Is someone in there?"

No answer. I pressed my ear to the wood. A creak. A quiet rustle.

"I can hear you," I called, louder now. "And I see the light under the door. Open up!"

Suddenly—the latch clicked.

The door edged inward.

I stumbled a step back, flashlight jerking up.

A woman stood framed in the glow. Short. Stocky. A wild cloud of dark curls. Eyes dark as coal, glittering with mischief—or danger.

She smiled crookedly.

"Oops. Busted."

CHAPTER FOURTEEN

The woman wore an old-fashioned dress with a full skirt, and she looked so at ease in the ruined inn that, for a heartbeat, I wondered if she was a ghost.

I blinked hard.

No—she was flesh and blood. And something about her was oddly familiar.

"Who…who are you?" I stammered.

"I'm Maggie. A friend of Gina's." Another smile, just a little too bright.

She was attractive—mysterious, even—which made her seem younger at first glance. But in the harsh beam of my flashlight, I noticed fine lines around her eyes and mouth. Probably closer to Gina's age.

"O…kay." I was still stunned. "But what are you doing here?"

"Like I said, I'm staying with her."

"In the old inn?" I asked, incredulous. "Where Dr. Drake just disappeared?"

"Ah, no." She tilted her head, curls shifting. "I'm just

taking a peek around. It's fun, isn't it?" Her eyes sparkled with something I couldn't quite decipher.

"Um…I wouldn't exactly say fun. Most people are terrified of ghosts. This inn is extremely haunted, and there's a missing ghost hunter, so—"

"That's why you're here, isn't it?" Her voice suddenly sharpened. "You're wondering what happened to him."

"Yes," I said defensively. "Aunt Gina asked me to investigate."

"Aha. So you must be on friendly terms with ghosts, if you're creeping around this place at night." She studied me as I scrambled for a reply.

"You're Liv, aren't you?" she went on before I could form words. "Gina's niece who moved here from the States with her children. Into Ethel's cottage?"

I shifted the heavy tote bag on my shoulder. "You… knew Ethel?"

"Of course. Always liked that little cottage of hers." She stepped closer, smile turning speculative. "I only just relocated back to Fairwyck—hence, staying with Gina. I don't suppose you're interested in selling the cottage? I'd happily take it off your hands. It has…nostalgic value."

The whiplash question stole my breath for a moment. "No. It's not for sale. I, um—better get going." I started backing away. "Are you…staying here?"

"Oh, I might take another look around." She shrugged, almost playful. "Find anything interesting? Any…ghosts?"

I made a show of scanning the corridor. "Not that I can see. And definitely no Drake. You?"

She smiled—mysterious, secretive. "Not sure yet. Something may still turn up."

"Right. Well…" My skin was crawling. Leaving a total stranger alone in my aunt's inn felt wrong, even if she did seem to know about me, the cottage, everything. "Good night."

"Night, night," she sang softly. "Don't let the bed bugs bite."

Her chuckle followed me down the stairs. I hurried out of the main entrance, not even bothering to put the boards back up.

Outside, in the cold air, I stood shivering, staring up at the looming structure. The annex was completely dark.

Should I wake Gina? Ask her about this Maggie?

But then I'd have to explain why I'd just broken into the inn in the middle of the night.

I remembered Gina's strange behavior earlier—the extra cup of tea, the way she and Emerald had shooed me out before I could enter the kitchen. Not letting me in when I'd knocked earlier that day. That could easily have been because Maggie was there.

But why hide her? Why act like her presence was some great secret?

I hugged myself as I hurried toward my car. I was hiding someone too, and desperately wishing he would disappear again. Maybe I shouldn't judge.

Still…a tiny, uncomfortable voice in my head whispered that Maggie could somehow be tangled up in Drake's disappearance. I dismissed it immediately. Gina wouldn't have called the police if Maggie were involved. And Emerald certainly wouldn't have insisted on leaving the cameras running if there was foul play.

Back inside my warm car, I rubbed my frozen hands together and dug out my phone from my tote. I typed a quick message to Emerald:

Does Gina have a friend named Maggie?

Back home, I was so relieved to be in a warm, comfortable place devoid of ghostly energy that I made myself a cup of cocoa, wrapped myself in a blanket, curled up on the couch, and savored every sip of the chocolatey goodness. Ethel curled up beside me, purring, and I stroked her soft fur.

I wanted to tell her everything—she'd been such a good sounding board during my last case, a surprising but effective partner in solving it. But I kept quiet. I didn't even know what I would tell her. Why was I so determined to investigate a stranger's disappearance? Yes, it was Gina's inn—but if I started explaining myself to Ethel, I might very well slip and tell her about Steven.

The truth was…I needed to tell someone.

I considered calling Emerald again, but she still hadn't read my message asking about Maggie. Of course she hadn't—she'd be asleep. And she'd been acting so strangely. Whether that had to do with Maggie or with the man who'd broken her heart, I wasn't sure. Either way, I had a strong feeling I shouldn't burden her with this problem.

With a sigh, I set the empty cup on the coffee table and slid Drake's laptop and notebook out of my tote.

At first, I was ecstatic to find a list of passwords tucked inside the notebook. It was one of those refillable leather-bound ones, and in the clear sleeve at the front, Drake had slid a small piece of paper with passwords. He must have thought it was reasonably safe, since he hadn't written login details next to them—but it only took me a couple of tries before I was in. Strike!

I'd pegged Drake as the dusty-library, analog type—the kind of professor who hated technology—but apparently he was tech-savvy enough. Well, I should have guessed that from the way he'd set up the cameras and other equipment.

Unfortunately, he also seemed to be in the habit of regularly deleting his browser history. All I found were a few searches about Fairwyck, the surrounding region, and local folklore. Nothing remotely useful.

Then came the next disappointment: His notebook insert was new. Maybe he used a fresh one for every job. Only two or three pages had any writing at all—and even then, the writing was half symbols, half fragmented English notes. I squinted at his terrible scrawl, but the only words I could make out were *ancient*, *dead*, and *power*. Comforting.

I gave up and turned to the recorded videos. His files were neatly labeled by date and episode number—the previous *Ghost Hunter UK* episodes. I opened the folder with yesterday's date. No episode number yet, just a messy jumble of folders and files.

It took forever to figure out what was what. The folders held feeds from different cameras. If I tried to watch them all, I'd fall asleep on the couch. Nothing happened in most of them anyway. Sometimes Drake drifted into view, fussing with equipment. I recognized the EMF meter once. The eerie glow of his eyes under the night-vision filter made him look like something out of *Paranormal Activity*. And the footage was crystal clear—not grainy like on the show. Maybe they added that later to make things spookier.

Then I noticed something strapped to his head—a camera. A head-cam. A GoPro.

That should have shown exactly what he saw when the glitch happened.

I searched for the footage…but couldn't find it. No head-cam files anywhere. I had a sinking feeling that the answers we needed were in that missing feed.

Eventually I found the folder for the camera in his

room—the one that had the glitch. And yes: One moment Drake was there. The next—gone.

I watched it over and over, frame by frame. Nothing. No shadow. No blur. No clue. The timestamps, the file size—everything looked consistent. If it was doctored, it was expertly done.

There were still dozens of other files, but my eyes were burning. I tried searching again for the head-cam footage—nothing. Instead, I found a folder full of research. I was too tired to dive into it. That would have to wait.

Before I went to bed, I found the producer's name and email address and sent a message:

Hello, I'm Gina Seven's niece. Gina is upset that the police aren't taking Dr. Drake's disappearance seriously. Do you have any updates?

Gina mentioned this morning that Dr. Drake was using a GoPro. Was it recording when he vanished? Do you have access to that footage?

I felt guilty for not checking the photos I'd taken in Drake's room—those potential ghost witnesses—but I couldn't do it tonight. I was exhausted, and seeing what might be lurking in those images would keep me awake for hours.

So I shut the laptop, tucked everything back into my bag, and carried it upstairs. I'd feel safer knowing it wasn't just lying around.

I taped a note to the bathroom door for the kids, explaining that I'd gone to bed late and needed them to get themselves ready in the morning. I set my alarm for just early enough to see them off.

Then I collapsed into bed. As soon as my head hit the pillow, I was out.

Unfortunately, my sleep was anything but restful. I drifted in and out of bizarre nightmares. In one, Steven chased me through the upper floor of the inn—which had somehow become ten times larger than in reality, a maze of twisting corridors and interconnected rooms. Ghosts lurked in every one. I didn't need a camera to see them in the dream: a chambermaid, a child holding a candle. The child terrified me most—because in the dream, I was certain my own children had become ghosts too. They were missing their mother desperately. I ran, desperate to find them before Steven caught up and dragged me into death along with them.

That nightmare kept intersecting with another: Gina laying out tarot cards. The King of Pentacles turned up over and over. It had to symbolize Steven, given Gina's interpretation—material wealth, greed, earthly desires. The golden sphere on the card—the coin—seemed to remind me of something I couldn't fully grasp. I sensed it had to do with Emerald, but whenever I asked, the cards shifted, and I was back in the inn's maze, searching for a ghost.

And then there was Ethel—my dream version of her nudging me insistently, her weight heavy on my chest, her whiskers brushing my lips as she pressed her face against mine. Her fur tickled my nose as I squinted at the cards Gina was trying to show me.

"Can't see the cards, Ethel," I muttered, sputtering— then realized I was awake.

I opened my eyes to a blur of marmalade fur. Ethel really was lying on top of me, pressing her face into mine. "Ethel!"

She was usually only this affectionate with Audrey. I sat up, gently shifting her aside. The numbers on the clock glowed red in the early dimness—an hour before my alarm would go off.

I groaned and flopped back onto the pillow. "Great. You can stay, but I'd really like to get a little more sleep, okay?" I mumbled.

Ethel refused to settle. She headbutted my chin. She kneaded my blanket. She meowed directly into my ear.

Finally, I gave up. "Fine. You win." I threw off the duvet and swung my legs to the floor.

Ethel hopped down as though that had been her goal all along. I crept to the bathroom, snatched down the note I'd left for the kids, and crumpled it. They were still blissfully asleep upstairs. "Why didn't you wake Audrey instead?" I grumbled, but the cat had already bounded down the stairs—no doubt to demand breakfast.

I caught sight of myself in the mirror. Dark circles under tired, amber-colored eyes. Hair like a bird's nest. I ran a brush through it and shoved it into a bun. Concealer could wait for days when I wasn't scrubbing toilets. Then a thought hit me: I had to clean the cottage next door today. Steven needed to vacate it. I'd better go over there as soon as the girls left for school. Avoiding Steven wasn't going to keep him from making trouble.

Though…if he just quietly disappeared again, that would solve one problem. But the idea didn't sit right. This wasn't simply logistics anymore. A decision was looming, and I wasn't ready to face it.

I dabbed on tinted moisturizer and mascara, then pulled a fresh pair of jeans and a caramel-and-gold knit sweater from the closet. Too nice for cleaning shifts, so I grabbed an ancient long-sleeved shirt and a T-shirt to change into later.

The girls' alarms chirped upstairs. I shuffled into the kitchen and started breakfast. Coffee was my first priority. As I measured grounds into the filter, I noticed Ethel at the front door, pawing at the wood.

"Hey—stop that, you'll scratch the door." I stepped closer. "You're very busy this morning, aren't you?"

She meowed sharply and pawed harder.

"You want me to open it?" I whispered.

I could have sworn she nodded.

I unlocked the door and cracked it open. The cold morning air hit me—but no one was there. I nearly closed it again, but I noticed something on the step.

A folded newspaper.

"Huh," I muttered. We didn't get the paper delivered. Had to be a mistake. But Ethel planted both tufted paws on it and meowed insistently.

I bent to pick it up. The local paper—for Fairwyck and a handful of villages on this side of Gloucestershire. The headline screamed:

TV STAR GHOST HUNTER DISAPPEARS IN FAIRWYCK INN

CHAPTER FIFTEEN

I stood there, dumbstruck, staring at the newspaper in my hands.

"Oh no!" I blurted—followed by an expletive I rarely used.

"What is it?" Blake asked.

I jolted—I hadn't heard them come down.

"It's just…the press seems to know what happened at Gina's house."

Blake snatched the paper from me and spread it on the kitchen table as I shut the door. Audrey scooped Ethel into her lap and stroked her absently.

I hurried through packing lunches while giving them a quick explanation of Dr. Drake's show, why he'd been staying at the Sacred Salmon Inn—and how he'd vanished.

"A celebrity was in Fairwyck, and you didn't tell us?" Audrey gasped.

"Well, we had bigger problems."

"How's Dad?" she asked eagerly. "Is he still next door? Can I go say hi before school?"

I set a bowl of cereal in front of her. "No. He's still…

sorting things out. Eat your breakfast. You can maybe see him after school."

Blake poured us coffee. She sipped hers while frowning at the article. "Mom…this mentions Gina by name. And it kind of implies she might've had something to do with it."

"What?" I was at her side so fast I sloshed coffee across the table.

I scanned the article quickly. It didn't blame Gina outright, but it definitely nudged readers in that direction. It claimed locals had always been wary of the Sacred Salmon Inn and its "eccentric owners." It mentioned that Gina worked as a psychic and quoted someone from *Ghost Hunter UK* saying she'd been very eager to land the episode.

"I was there during the meeting and initial viewing," the person said. "She practically threw herself at him. Total kooky-old-woman vibes—fluttery, esoteric, batting her eyelashes. It was embarrassing, honestly."

My heart ached for Gina. Yes, she'd been enthusiastic —she adored Drake's show—but the article twisted it into something ugly, like she'd been chasing fame or money.

"Poor Gina," I murmured. "This is so unfair. Luckily it's only the local rag. It'll blow over."

Blake and I kept reading—until Audrey interrupted us. That was when I noticed she hadn't even touched her cereal.

"Um, Mom? Ethel says it's worse than that. She wants you to turn on the TV."

I blinked at the cat on her lap. Then I marched into the living room.

One press of the remote, and morning-show cheerfulness burst into the room—hosts too bright for this hour, smiling like mannequins. A banner crawled across the bottom:

BREAKING NEWS: TV GHOST HUNTER VANISHES DURING FILMING

I turned up the volume. The kids scrambled onto the couch beside me.

The male host held up the front pages of the national papers.

"The whole nation is worried about a beloved celebrity," he declared with the exact smile hosts use for escaped zoo animals.

The *Guardian*:

PARANORMAL PRESENTER MISSING—QUESTIONS OVER REALITY TV SAFETY PRACTICES

The *Telegraph*:

"HAUNTED SINCE THE 1100s!"—CELEBRITY ACADEMIC DISAPPEARS AT HISTORIC INN

Then the *Daily Mail*:

DR. SPOOK GOES POOF!—TV HUNTER VANISHES IN "MOST HAUNTED" INN

His cohost fanned herself theatrically. "And my personal favorite—" She brandished the *Sun*:

GONE WITH THE SPIRIT!

…and the sub-heading:

GHOST GURU MAY HAVE "ASCENDED," SAY FANS

"Ascended? Where to?" Blake muttered. "The attic?"

A stifled laugh escaped me—more panic than humor.

Then the studio lights dimmed, and the screen behind the hosts changed.

Grainy footage appeared.

The footage I had naïvely emailed the production company about.

"Oh no," I whispered.

It was the view from Drake's head-mounted camera. The Sacred Salmon's hallway, beams sagging, shadows sinking into cracks. His voice echoed, staticky:

"—remarkable energy signature in this room, stronger than anticipated—"

The camera turned as he entered the bedroom I recognized.

A flicker. Static.

Drake jumped, gasped. "It's just the mirror—it's me!"

He'd startled himself, filming his own reflection. Had he dragged that mirror there for dramatic effect? When I'd met him, he'd claimed to be serious about his work—but maybe a bit of theatrics came with the job.

Audrey clutched my arm. "Mom, this is scary."

"Yes—don't look," I yelped, half hysterical. I tried to cover her eyes. Suddenly I wasn't so sure this would stay morning-TV-appropriate.

But nothing monstrous appeared. Of course they wouldn't show that before breakfast.

The footage glitched again—this time longer. A smear of movement. A harsh cut. The image tilted toward the floor.

Then: blackness.

The hosts reappeared, faces arranged into tasteful concern.

"Authorities say there's no evidence of foul play," the woman announced delicately. "But the mystery deepens, as Dr. Drake's personal belongings were found at the scene."

"And," the cohost added, leaning in as though delivering gossip, "Fairwyck residents claim the inn is infamous for supernatural disturbances. Its owner, Gina Seven—"

I froze.

On screen was Gina—caught mid-blink, outside the inn, vulnerable and confused.

"Has long been the subject of rumors," the presenter continued. "Occult rituals, a troubled family history—"

"Oh, for crying out loud," I snapped.

Ethel hissed at the television. Actually hissed.

Audrey stroked her. "She says they're being stupid and mean."

"Well, she's right."

They brought on more so-called locals giving sound bites. My breath caught when Michelle's perfectly judgmental face filled the screen.

"Something's not right with that family," she said primly. "Everyone knows the Sevens mess with paranormal things. Gina earns money from it! I have friends who swear she predicted their futures. Spookily accurate. I'd never set foot inside that inn."

Heat rose up my neck—anger, shame, and fear all tangled together.

Michelle had sat beside Emerald in book club only a few days ago. I'd thought of her as a friend. Disappointment burned hot in my chest—followed by a cold fear that everyone in Fairwyck I'd begun to trust could turn on me and my children just as quickly.

The presenters shifted tone, reading from an official statement. "We can confirm that Dr. Malcolm Drake, host of *Ghost Hunter UK*, has not checked in with the production team as scheduled. There is no indication of foul play. Dr. Drake has previously taken unannounced breaks in pursuit of research leads. We are cooperating fully with local authorities and hope for his safe return."

The male presenter leaned toward the camera with his too-white smile, somehow still managing to look solemn.

"Dr. Drake, if you are out there somewhere and can hear this, please let us know you're safe. Whatever happened, we want you found."

His cohost tilted her head, eyes sparkling with manufactured awe.

"When you say *out there somewhere*, Richard…you mean in the real world, right? Not, you know, in a ghostly realm?"

They cued cheesy spooky music. A slow pan of dramatic faces followed.

"Glad they're having fun," Blake muttered. "It's only a man's life on the line."

"Well," I said weakly, turning off the TV as the show segued into celebrity gossip, "they're right about one thing. If this is all over the news and Drake just ran off, he'll hear it eventually and reach out. At least it would be over."

"And that would spare Gina this mess," Blake added.

I nodded, but the pit in my stomach remained.

"Maybe someone's already seen him." Blake pulled out her phone. "I'll check online—"

Her face drained of color. "Oh no."

"What?" I leaned over her shoulder.

On the screen was a flood of tabloid headlines. The ones I'd already seen—and worse.

GHOST GURU GONE

FEARWYCK FIASCO

INN OF DOOM

And the one that made bile rise in my throat: SPOOKY SHOOT GONE WRONG: WHO IS GINA SEVEN, AND WHY DO PEOPLE DISAPPEAR IN HER INN?

"How has this blown up so fast?" Blake whispered, scrolling.

"And look at this—Reddit." She tapped a thread.

r/GhostHunterUKTV

I freeze-framed every second of the glitch—nothing there. But it's WEIRD. Here's the footage. Have a go, paranormal detectives!

ParaTruth4Real

WAKE UP SHEEPLE—the govt seized the REAL video.

.　.　.

His phone, wallet, AND car were all still there. That's not like him. Usually he leaves a note when he goes walkabout.

He's disappeared randomly three times before. Probably hiding in a hedge writing his next book.

My cousin's neighbor's mate works at a nearby pub—says the inn got boarded up again yesterday…WHY?

I live in Fairwyck. That place is creepy as hell. Owner's a dodgy psychic, everyone knows it.

BELOW THAT WAS A PHOTO OF GINA—TAKEN AT A VILLAGE fair—shielding her eyes from the sun. But to strangers, it looked like she was hiding her face in shame. The floaty scarf, the chunky bracelets, the teased hair…they made her appear like the exact stereotype the tabloids wanted.

"Oh my god," I breathed. "If these people show up here trying to *investigate*…"

"Some of them are probably already in Fairwyck," Blake said grimly. "The place is probably crawling with reporters."

I shot to my feet. "You're right. I need to get over there."

I glanced at the clock. "And you two need to hurry if you want to catch the bus."

I hurried to finish their lunches, shoving them into the kids' school bags as they bounded over to put on their shoes.

"Mom?" Audrey's voice was small. "Do you think Aunt Gina is in danger?"

"No, sweetheart." I forced calm into my voice while grabbing my coat. "The police will have to act now. And Jamie's on duty—he won't let anything happen to her."

I smiled for Audrey's sake.

But inside?

I wasn't sure I believed a single word.

CHAPTER SIXTEEN

What I couldn't tell Audrey—and what gnawed at me during the entire drive to the Sacred Salmon—was that I was terrified of what national reporters swarming Fairwyck would mean for a wanted criminal hiding out here. I could only hope Steven stayed put and didn't do anything stupid.

If anyone caught wind of him, it wouldn't just be the inn and Gina plastered across the morning shows and tabloids—it would be me and the children too.

My overactive imagination was already generating headlines.

COTSWOLDS CON-MAN COVEN? Fugitive Fraudster Holed Up with Local Psychic Clan!

HOCUS BROKUS! Busted Banker Claims Wife "Cast Spell" to Welcome Him Back!

THE REAL HOUSEWIVES OF FAIRWYCK! Broke Mom Reunites with Wanted Husband—Is She In On It?

YANKS FOR NOTHING! American Swindler Hides in "Most Haunted Inn in Britain"—Locals "Not Surprised"

By the time I arrived at Aunt Gina's house, I was in a full hysterical spiral.

But the sight that greeted me shocked the panic right out of my system.

News vans. Satellite dishes. Boom mics. Reporters clustering around the inn like flies on a carcass. I'd expected a few journalists knocking on Gina's door—I'd seen the *Good Morning Britain* clip of her—but clearly Blake's warning hadn't come close to capturing the chaos.

This was next level.

I parked farther down the lane, grabbed my things, and yanked the hood of my coat up so the fake fur trim would hide most of my face. No such luck. As soon as I stepped onto the path, the reporters descended on me.

"Are you a friend of Gina's?"

"Do you know what happened to Dr. Drake?"

"Any insight into what's going on here?"

Flashes went off. Microphones were thrust toward my mouth. I held up a hand to shield my eyes and kept moving.

They blocked the door, though, forming a human barricade. If Jamie hadn't suddenly appeared—my unexpected knight in a navy police jacket—I legitimately might have bolted back to my car.

"You need to stay off the property," he barked at them. "You know the drill."

He took my arm and guided me through the crush. I didn't breathe until the door shut behind us.

Inside, I shoved back my hood and exhaled shakily. "This is insane!"

"I know." Jamie's jaw was clenched so tightly, the words came out through his teeth. "Someone in the production company must've had the bright idea of leaking the GoPro footage early this morning."

Heat flooded my face.

The email.

I had emailed the producer asking about the GoPro recording.

Surely I hadn't given him the idea? I'd only wanted to know what happened to Drake. I had naïvely assumed that everyone else wanted the same.

Had I accidentally thrown gasoline on the fire?

I pressed my lips together. Better not mention it. The last thing I needed was to feed DI Farrow's conviction that I "muddled every case I touched."

"Did they sell it to a news outlet?" I asked, latching onto the most obvious villains. "Surely that's unethical and not—"

"No, they wouldn't be that stupid," Jamie cut in. "It showed up on an internet forum. Untraceable source. Anyone from the production company could've leaked it. And they're already cashing in—old episodes are trending like crazy. If they turn this into an episode, the ratings will be through the roof. That's likely their goal now."

My heart dropped. My fragile hope—that Drake would reappear, the episode would be scrapped, and they'd leave Gina and Fairwyck in peace—evaporated. Of course they'd try to profit from this. Come hell or high water, there'd be an episode.

"So you think this is all some elaborate hoax to boost ratings?" I asked, hearing Farrow's theory echo in my mind.

Jamie shook his head slowly. "No. They'd have staged it better. They'd have leaked the footage immediately, arranged for someone from the crew to check on him and find him missing—a cleaner narrative. Having Gina and Emerald discover it? Too risky. And that noise… Something happened. The production company's just exploiting it after the fact."

I exhaled. "If Drake really went off on one of his

disappearing acts, he'll have to come forward now. If he's anywhere with an internet connection, he can't avoid this."

"We hope so," Jamie said. "That'd be the only good thing to come of this mess."

"How's Gina?"

"Go see her," he said gently. "She'll be glad you're here. She's in the parlor with Emerald."

I stepped past him. "She must be going out of her mind—I can't believe they're invading her privacy like this. I'm surprised she didn't call me this morning. Are you coming too?"

"No. I need to man the front door. I'll go back out on the porch. They're not allowed to step foot on private property, but I've seen them circling. I'm here to make sure nobody gets any bright ideas."

"Thanks. I'm surprised Farrow can spare you."

Jamie gave a wry smile. "He isn't. I'm not on shift yet. I just…put the uniform on early to check on a friend."

"Thank you. You're the best."

My smile was genuine, even though that bittersweet ache flared in my chest. Jamie had a heart of gold. I was so lucky he was my boyfriend—and yet I was keeping secrets from him. It stung.

When I slipped into the parlor, Gina was perched in one of the armchairs. Those chairs always made people look smaller, like something out of Alice in Wonderland, but today she seemed diminished in a way that had nothing to do with the furniture.

She had the local *Gazette* spread across her lap—the same paper Ethel had led me to this morning. So it hadn't been Gina or Emerald who'd left it on my doorstep.

Gina looked up, startled. "Liv—what are you doing here?"

"I woke up to the media circus and wanted to make sure you're all right."

I sat beside her on a spindly stool. "And of course you're not. I can't believe they're invading your privacy like this."

Tears welled in her pale blue eyes. "It's an absolute nightmare, Liv. And the worst part is—Dr. Drake still hasn't turned up. I'm so worried about him."

I took her hands; they were ice cold. "I'm worried about you."

"That's kind of you." She slipped her trembling hands away. "But I wish you wouldn't have come. I don't want your name dragged into this too."

"Nonsense. I'm family. Of course I came."

Her gaze kept darting toward the door. She seemed jittery, almost skittish—but with everything going on, who wouldn't be?

"I had a dream about you reading my cards," I said, hoping to gently steer her mind elsewhere. "And you were on my mind. I couldn't just ignore everything and go about my day."

The mention of a dream snapped her attention to full alert. "What cards?"

"The King of Pentacles—maybe Coins? I don't remember exactly. It had a coin on it..." I watched her eyes sharpen with that psychic intensity she got sometimes and instantly regretted bringing it up. I'd wanted to calm her, not ignite her. "But it doesn't matter. It was just one of many weird dreams."

"Don't say it doesn't matter," Gina chided. "Seven dreams are important. Maybe I should read your cards..."

"Okay," I said, though I wasn't sure it was wise. Still— if it took her mind off the scandal...

I stood, ready to head to the reading room, but Gina was suddenly out of her armchair with surprising speed.

"I'll get the cards—we'll do it here."

"Here?" I blinked. "You never do readings in this room."

"I will today. I'll be back in a jiffy. Don't move!" She practically shoved me back down.

"All right…" I murmured, startled, as she hurried out.

She'd only been gone thirty seconds when someone else slipped into the room.

"Aunt Gina, I know I'm not supposed to roam, but I can't find—"

The petite woman froze mid-whisper.

I stood, staring at her.

It wasn't the stocky older woman in the old-fashioned dress I'd met last night—Maggie. But there was a resemblance. The same dark curls, though this girl's hair framed a softer, heart-shaped face. And her eyes…not Maggie's coal-black, mischievous ones, glittering with secrets.

These were wide, gentle, and unmistakably blue—Gina-blue.

Gina hurried back in with a deck of tarot cards clutched against her chest. "Oh dear," she breathed. "You weren't supposed to meet."

I slowly turned to her, suspicion prickling up my spine. That old defensiveness stirred—the one I thought I'd buried when Gina and Emerald became my safe harbor. It hurt, that sudden flicker of distance—like a door quietly closing between us. I'd trusted Gina and Emerald with my life, with my children…yet here I was again, wondering what they weren't telling me, and why. And did I want to be tangled up in their secrets? Become an outsider right along with them?

"How many people," I asked, "are you hiding in this inn?"

CHAPTER SEVENTEEN

"Hi, I'm Lucy," the softspoken, petite woman said. She had enough of a resemblance to my great-aunt that I instantly clocked her as family. She *had* called Gina "Aunt." But she also looked a little like the woman I'd met last night.

"What's going on here?" I demanded. "Who is this person? And who is the woman hiding in the old inn?"

Gina wrung her hands. "Oh dear, oh dear, oh dear. You weren't supposed to meet her. And Emerald said she'd take care of it."

"Take care of what?" I asked, exasperated.

"Why don't I make us all a nice cup of tea, and we can talk," Lucy said gently, steering Gina back into her armchair with practiced ease.

I sat back down on the spindly stool. Miraculously, it didn't collapse beneath me. Antique or not, the furniture in this house was sturdier than it looked.

"I should probably tell you something," I said, bracing myself. "I went into the inn last night to retrieve Drake's laptop." Because Gina was already giving me a raised-eyebrow look, I added defensively, "The police are sort of sitting on their hands, and you did ask me to investigate, so I figured it was a good idea." I paused. "And while I was there, I ran into Maggie."

Gina's breath hitched.

"I honestly thought she was a ghost at first," I went on. "But she knew things about me—about Ethel's cottage… I believed her when she said she was a friend of yours. I didn't stay to ask more. I just wanted to get out of there, to be honest. I texted Emerald afterward, asking who Maggie was, but she never replied."

Gina rubbed her eyes. "Emmy was supposed to explain everything when the time was right, but…well… She has her own problems right now." She sighed, folding her hands tightly in her lap. Then, softly, she said, "The woman staying in the inn next door is my sister, Maggie. And Lucy is her daughter."

I blinked. "I've never heard of a sister named Maggie."

My mother hadn't exactly been generous with family details—she'd been far more invested in helping me suppress my scary past than sharing anything meaningful. Before moving here, I hadn't even known Gina and Emerald existed.

I was still learning the Seven family tree.

Over the past year and a half, I'd pieced together a good chunk of it. My great-grandmother, Trixie, had my grandmother Phoebe very young, which was why Phoebe's daughter, my mother Calista, was only a little younger than her own aunt, Gina. Emerald and I were a good ten years apart in age. I called her my cousin, even though technically we were one branch further removed. Later, Trixie remarried and had more daughters – Ethel and Gina.

"As far as you ever told me, you had two sisters— Phoebe and Ethel. You never mentioned Maggie."

Gina looked genuinely ashamed. "No. Maggie was… she had some problems. Trixie disinherited her. She left

Fairwyck when she was twenty, and we never heard from her again. We were told not to mention her, and I got so used to it over the years that, well…"

My eyes widened. Just when I'd thought I finally had a grasp on the Seven family…

"Does my mother know she exists?"

"Well, yes, of course. Maggie's only two years older than me, so your mother was there when she…when the thing happened."

"What thing?" I asked—right as Lucy returned, saving Gina from answering.

She set down the tea tray and poured cups with calm efficiency. I gratefully stuffed a cookie into my mouth.

Gina pasted on a brittle smile, glancing toward Lucy. "Best not to rehash the past. We're trying to leave all that where it is and move on."

"I take it you made up with Maggie. Why didn't you tell me?"

"I just didn't know how to explain everything," Gina murmured. "Maggie came to me and said she and Lucy needed a place to stay, that she'd turned over a new leaf long ago and wanted to reunite. I couldn't turn her away. But I thought…well, I thought we should work through our issues privately before I introduced her around."

She looked away, and my heart softened despite my confusion.

I knew how she felt. She couldn't turn her sister away, but she'd wanted time to figure things out. It was exactly how I felt about Steven.

And then there was Lucy. Knowing Gina, she would've been over the moon to discover she had another niece. Whatever Maggie had done, none of it was Lucy's fault. I could only imagine how badly Gina had wanted to get to know her.

"And then Drake came with his episode," Gina continued, "and I couldn't very well say no. It was Maggie who introduced me to him, actually. I thought he'd only stay a night or two, and Maggie and Lucy would keep to their room. They're staying in Emerald's room, and Emmy is bunking with me. Then all this happened…"

She closed her eyes, defeated. "They can't exactly leave now, and everything has gotten away from me terribly…"

I frowned. "But Maggie said she's staying in the inn. Was she there when Drake disappeared?"

"No, no," Gina assured me quickly. "She wasn't then. But after Drake's disappearance… Maggie thought it wouldn't be such a bad idea if someone stayed next door—look after the place, spook anyone who entered uninvited, report immediately if Drake returned."

"My mother thinks it's fun," Lucy said with an apologetic shrug.

That explained the old-fashioned dress and Maggie's theatrical attitude.

Still, something didn't sit right. It had to have been Maggie who'd turned off the camera in Drake's room.

And she'd introduced Gina to him? So Maggie had brought Drake here.

Maybe she was tied to the TV production somehow—maybe she'd orchestrated this whole thing to boost ratings.

"Was she with you yesterday morning? Searching for Drake?" I asked.

"Yes, we helped Aunt Gina and Emerald," Lucy said. "And then we thought it best to keep to ourselves in the annex when the police—and you—came."

The extra teacup, Gina's odd behavior…it all made sense now.

It still stung that they'd felt the need to hide relatives from me, but that wasn't what bothered me most.

Jamie's words echoed in my head.

Perhaps Maggie had been the one pulling the strings the entire time.

Was she being paid? Or was this one long, elaborate revenge plot for being pushed out of the family all those years ago?

And she'd dragged her daughter into it. Lucy seemed innocent enough…but how much did she really know?

A slow burn of anger lit in my chest.

One question wouldn't leave my mind. How could Emerald let this happen?

"Where's Emerald?" I asked sharply.

"Now, now," Lucy soothed, which grated instantly. "No need to be angry with her. Emerald has her own problems to deal with right now. She's off tending to them."

She patted my hand—lightly, patronizingly—which only increased my irritation. She'd known my cousin all of a day or two, and somehow she already knew more about her than I did?

But antagonizing the long-lost relatives didn't seem wise. Not now. Not when I desperately needed to figure out what these two were really after. My gut said it wasn't a warm, fuzzy family reunion.

So I forced a smile.

"When I came to England, I thought I had no one," I said lightly. "I'm still adjusting to…all this." I gestured vaguely. "Never a dull moment, right? But if Gina and Emerald are welcoming you back into the family, then I should too. I'd love to introduce you to Audrey and Blake. I have to get to work now, but maybe we can come for dinner?"

Lucy's expression softened into a knowing smile—as if she could see straight through me—but she nodded. "Sure. I'd love to meet them. I've heard so much already."

I glanced at Gina, whose eyes dropped guiltily.

"Of course, come by," she murmured. "You're always welcome, sweetheart."

The words felt empty, considering it hadn't been true recently, but I brushed the bitter thought aside and stood. "And I trust Maggie will join us here in the annex for dinner? I want to meet her properly."

"Of course," Lucy said. "In fact, she'll insist on it."

"Great. See you later, then."

I slipped out. Jamie was still manning the door.

"Jamie…" I started, then bit my lip. Now was not the time to talk to him about Steven. But I really should. Instead, I told him I'd be back later, and he said he had to head to work soon. He escorted me to my car to shield me from the cameras.

As I drove toward Meckham, to the rental apartment that was first on my schedule for the day, I mentally rehearsed my twofold plan.

First, at dinner tonight, I'd get a better read on my dubious new relatives—with the help of my children.

Blake could quietly check whatever was going on inside Lucy's and Maggie's heads.

And Audrey…well, she could talk to Beltane, Gina's cat. Cats saw everything.

Second, the more complicated part.

I had to get Steven into the inn, if he hadn't sorted everything out with his lawyers by then. He'd have to vacate the cottage next door before the new renters arrived this afternoon. Even keeping him in my house for a few hours was dangerous. The inn would be empty while we were having dinner in the annex—Steven could slip inside, hide in one of the upstairs rooms, and lock himself in. I just needed to convince Maggie to stay put in the annex, so the inn remained empty.

Only one problem: Steven would be hidden once he was in there—but entering was the tricky part.

With reporters swarming the place, he'd basically need an invisibility cloak to pull it off.

CHAPTER EIGHTEEN

While I was cleaning the apartment, I had an epiphany.

What was the next best thing to an invisibility cloak?

Hiding in plain sight.

For a glorious five seconds, I felt brilliant. Then the pendulum swung the other way, and I wondered if this might, in fact, be the dumbest idea I'd ever had. Wasn't there a saying? There's a fine line between genius and insanity.

Still riding the high of my questionable brilliance, I rushed back to Fairwyck, grabbed my cleaning equipment, and headed toward the cottage next door to give it a quick once-over before the guests arrived that afternoon.

I usually took a shortcut through the gardens—going around the long way to the parallel road took forever. But the second I stepped out my back door, Esme's cheerful voice rang out.

"Hey, Liv! Long time no see!"

I flinched so hard I nearly dropped the bucket. Esme

stood a few yards away, winter-proofing her plants, wearing gloves and an easy smile.

Darn!

I needed to get Steven out of the cottage next door and into mine without Esme seeing anything. The last thing I wanted was to drag my best friend into the very messy, very illegal, very Seven-family-adjacent disaster unfolding in my life.

"Yeah," I said weakly. "Been really busy."

She came over to lean on the fence that separated our gardens, gloved hands resting on the weathered wood.

"Your kids are busy too, it seems. They're usually always here. Anthony said something about Blake avoiding him…but I couldn't get anything else out of him. Did something happen between them?"

My stomach sank.

Of course Anthony had noticed.

Ever since coming out as nonbinary at their all-girls school, Blake had gained plenty of admirers, sure—but no one they'd truly connected with until Anthony moved in next door. They were best friends. Practically glued together.

And now Blake was avoiding him for the same reason I'd been avoiding Jamie.

Because Steven was here.

Because Blake was terrified Anthony would immediately sense something was wrong and start asking questions they couldn't answer.

This situation was messing with my life—fine, I could handle that. But seeing it affect my children? Seeing Blake cut off from their one real confidant?

It made my newly hatched "hide Steven in the inn" plan seem suddenly ridiculous. Childish. Maybe even dangerous.

But what was I supposed to do? March Steven to the police station right this second?

I hung my head, letting my hair fall into my face. Sorting out legal trouble—major legal trouble—took time and strategy. I wanted Steven to face the consequences of his actions, absolutely. But for my children's sake, I also needed him to get the best possible deal with the least possible prison time. And if—if—what he'd said was true, and he'd done those stupid, awful things for us…

If only I knew whether I could trust him.

"Liv?" Esme prompted gently.

"Hmm?" I didn't dare look at her. She'd see my troubled expression and ask what was wrong.

"I was saying maybe we could take the kids out this weekend? Do something together?" She sounded like she'd already said it once—and I'd completely missed it.

"Oh. That would be nice, but…I'm really busy. Work, and—"

"I thought things were slow at the theater right now," Esme said, frowning. "You told me you had everything balanced."

"Yes, but…something's come up." I latched on to the safer topic. "And added to that, you must have seen what happened at the inn with Dr. Drake. The reporters are everywhere. It's been horrible for my aunt."

"Oh my gosh, I was going to ask!" Esme exclaimed. "It's all over the news. Is your aunt all right? Some of the things people are saying—acting like she had something to do with the disappearance…"

Her sentence trailed off, waiting for me to fill in the space.

Esme didn't mean anything by it—I knew that. She wasn't like Michelle. She didn't gossip maliciously, wasn't gleeful about scandal. She cared. That was the problem.

Right now, any conversation was a minefield.

Between Steven, the inn, Drake's disappearance, the hidden relatives, and the media circus, my life was one giant pile of cans of worms waiting to be blown open by one wrong comment.

I swallowed hard.

I really did need to avoid my best friend a little longer—just until I could untangle all these messes.

"Anyway, I have to go. Got some cleaning work to do next door." I lifted my cleaning caddy as proof. "But I think I'll go the long way around. The gardens are way too muddy, and I'll only make more work for myself tracking it into the house."

I was rambling. I knew I was rambling. Esme looked mildly alarmed.

"I wouldn't worry about Blake and Anthony," I added quickly. "Blake's just got tons of schoolwork. And actually, this weekend is terrible for getting together—tests, work, everything. Oh, I promised Jamie we'd see each other too. But…uh…I'll be in touch."

I was halfway to my back door by the time I finished tripping over my own excuses. "Talk to you soon!"

Inside, I closed the door and leaned against it, sucking in a shaky breath.

All the relationships I'd built in Fairwyck—the friendships, the trust, the sense of belonging—felt like they were unraveling. And my kids were getting pulled into the mess right along with me.

Something had to give.

Something had to be resolved. Soon.

I couldn't do anything about the reporters—not yet. But I could sort out the disaster with Steven. Hiding him in the inn was way too risky. What had I been thinking? I had to stop all these lies too. They were starting to erode my relationships—and spread like cancer, impacting my loved ones.

I slipped out the front door and slid into my car. I drove slowly past Esme's house, then turned onto the main road, looped around the block, and parked just beyond the rental cottage. From this angle, Esme wouldn't see me—or see Steven being shuffled around like contraband.

I hurried to the front door.

"There you are!" Steven appeared in the hall the moment I stepped inside. "I'm starving. What did you bring?"

His face fell when he saw the cleaning caddy.

"Well, I have to give the cottage a quick once-over—guests are arriving soon, remember?" I pushed past him and opened the hall closet for the vacuum. "You're coming with me next door. We need to take the car, though. My neighbor's in the garden. I have to be quick."

"So I'll be staying with you now?" Steven asked, sounding far too hopeful.

"Only for a few hours—and that's risky enough," I snapped. "But you need to call your lawyers now. You keep calling until you reach them, do you hear me? I want to know their plan. This cannot go on."

I tried to sound firm and controlled, but my voice wobbled, betraying me. Tears stung my eyes. I turned away under the guise of plugging in the vacuum.

Steven followed me into the kitchen, where I set the caddy on the table.

"Relax, babe. Everything's under control. I already got ahold of them. I set up a virtual meeting for tomorrow—with a couple of people from the firm. We'll need to use your laptop, but…"

"That's fine." I cut him off. At least something—finally—was moving forward. "I have a place to stow you tonight. A plan." He'd survive one night at the inn, wouldn't he?

"And now, let me do this," I said, grabbing a spray bottle with trembling fingers. "I need to get you into my cottage before the renters show up. And I still have errands to run before tonight."

A flutter of anxiety twisted in my tummy. Yes, I had errands.

But not normal ones.

I needed to buy Steven a disguise.

And I needed to break into my boyfriend's apartment.

Oh god—my stomach clenched.

One more night of deception, I told myself. One more ruse.

CHAPTER NINETEEN

Well…it wasn't exactly breaking in when I had a key, I told myself a few hours later.

I'd gotten the cottage ready for the renters, managed to shuttle Steven into my house without Esme or anyone else noticing, swung by the costume shop…and now I was in Jamie's apartment, having let myself in with the key he'd given me.

The silence in the bedroom felt accusing as I opened the wardrobe and took out one of his neatly pressed uniforms and a shirt. Jamie was taller and lankier than Steven—who somehow had kept up his fitness routine even while on the run, judging by his muscled arms—but the uniform would have to do. Steven was wearing dressy black leather shoes; those would pass well enough.

When I got home, the kids were already back from school, and Steven was at the kitchen table eating my M&Ms.

I tried very hard not to show how irritated I was. "Hi," I said through gritted teeth. "Making yourself at home?"

"I told him he should stay hidden in your bedroom, Mom," Blake said.

"That's okay." Truthfully, I wasn't comfortable with Steven being in my bedroom either. I plucked the bag of M&Ms out of his hand and shoved it back into the cupboard. That was *my* comfort food. I needed to find a better hiding spot for it.

"I'm glad you're all here," I said. "I have news."

I told the kids about our long-lost relatives suddenly materializing out of nowhere. "The timing is…suspicious, considering what happened with Dr. Drake. So I invited us over for dinner, and we can—"

My gaze flicked to Steven, then away. "Investigate them a little."

"Investigate," Steven laughed. "Look at you—a regular Nancy Drew now, Liv."

"I don't know if that's a good idea, Mom," Blake said. "Why assume any of this is connected to Drake? Isn't it good if Gina reunites with her sister? Shouldn't we support her, especially right now?"

I shook my head, irritated. "Maggie introduced Gina to Drake. There's definitely a connection. And there must be a reason she was disinherited and erased from the family history. She must've done something truly bad. I mean—the Seven family women…we're all a bit strange."

Steven raised an eyebrow. "Aren't you one of the Seven women?"

He popped a yellow peanut M&M into his mouth. Had he emptied part of the bag into his lap?

I ignored him. Blake and Audrey knew what I meant.

"But people can change, right, Mom?" Audrey asked softly. "Sometimes they do bad things, but that doesn't mean they're bad. And they can change."

Her big blue eyes were hopeful. She reached out and took Steven's hand.

Oh no. This wasn't about Maggie at all. This was about her father.

I chose my words carefully. "Yes…some people can change. If they have a good heart and made a terrible mistake—sometimes they truly want to make things right. But there are also people capable of genuinely harmful things. People without any heart at all. Those people don't usually change."

"Oh. Okay." Audrey seemed relieved—because she fully believed her father had a good heart.

I got that. I wanted to believe it too. I'd shared my life with the man, had kids with him. That I'd made that big of a mistake, loving a heartless, egotistical asshole…that I'd wasted half my life loving him…the thought was almost unbearable. It was most likely the reason I clung to everything Steven was telling me now.

"But do you really think Gina's sister is like that?" Blake pressed. "We don't know anything yet. She might be all right."

I threw up my hands. "Okay, fine! You're right. But can you just humor me? Look into her thoughts a bit? For Gina's sake? She's vulnerable right now—we don't want someone taking advantage."

Blake frowned but nodded. "I suppose."

Relief washed through me.

"How is she supposed to look into her thoughts?" Steven asked.

"Blake can draw what people are thinking," Audrey announced brightly.

I sucked in a breath, panic spiking.

But Steven only laughed, ruffled Audrey's hair, and said, "You're great at that game. Maybe you'll be a fantasy writer someday."

I ushered the kids upstairs to change out of their school uniforms.

Then I turned to Steven. "Here. I want you to put these on."

I pulled a brown wig, a fake mustache, and a pair of large sunglasses from my bag.

He stared at them. "You can't be serious."

"Wait, there's more."

I went out to the car and came back with Jamie's police uniform in a bag.

Steven's eyes bulged. "Is that a real uniform? Where did you get it?"

"I borrowed it," I said briskly. "There was an officer at Gina's earlier to keep reporters from trespassing—he's a friend. He had to go to work."

I held up the uniform. "The point is, nobody will look at your face. To them, you're just a police officer entering an active crime scene. They won't question it. They won't photograph it. You'll be…a uniform without a face."

Steven stared at me. "Why the wig and mustache, then?"

"Just a precaution. In case you do end up in someone's photo."

"That's actually quite a clever plan."

He looked at me in a way he hadn't looked at me in at least the last ten years of our marriage—almost… impressed. "But isn't there another way? Couldn't we just go somewhere else? Somewhere remote. You could rent a place, and we could stay there together."

My turn to stare. "No. I'm not sure what you're imagining, but I have work here. A home. A business. Also, you said it's one more night, and tomorrow you'll—"

He held up a hand. "All right, all right, I get it. But your aunt's old inn? Do I really need to hide there?"

"I don't have anywhere else to stash you, Steven," I said, exasperated. "And yes, it's spooky. I'm not sugar-coating that. You'll probably be scared, and we still don't know what happened to Drake—"

Steven let out a hearty laugh. "I'm not scared of

ghosts, Liv. That old geezer was probably miserable in that drafty inn and just walked out. I've seen the news. Didn't have much else to do next door. So trust me—I know how he felt."

I wasn't about to argue with Steven about the existence of ghosts. I certainly wasn't going to tell him about my abilities. That would open a door I wasn't ready to even knock on.

"You'll be fine," I said instead. "You go into the inn, I'll sort out what's going on with Maggie and Lucy, and hopefully the Drake situation will resolve itself. Tomorrow, we meet with your lawyer and go from there. Now put on the uniform. I'm going to change."

I went upstairs, showered quickly, then put back on the jeans and caramel-and-gold knit sweater from this morning —I hadn't bothered changing out of my work shirt earlier.

When I came downstairs, both kids were laughing. Really laughing—Audrey's full belly laugh and Blake's smirk, which absolutely counted.

"What's so fun—?"

Then I saw Steven.

The uniform was straining at the seams, the shirt buttons threatening mutiny, and the wig-mustache-glasses combo made him look like a stripper cop from a budget ladies' night.

I snorted. "Yeah…you have to take the glasses off. It's too much."

"It is getting dark out," Steven admitted, grinning as he set them aside. "Would look suspicious."

"I packed you a change of clothes, toiletries, food, and water." I handed him a duffel bag and talked him through the layout upstairs. "Find a room, stay there, lock it from the inside. There are plenty of locked rooms already—pick one. Drake's cot is probably the most comfortable bed in the building. And don't worry about the cameras. I turned the one above the stairs off, and the camera in Drake's room was already off. Probably Maggie—another point against her." I held up a hand before Audrey could object. "Yes, Audrey, I know, benefit of the doubt. Point is, I doubt the production team is watching anymore."

When Blake confirmed the coast was clear next door, we all piled into the car and drove toward the Sacred Salmon.

It was dark, but the news vans were still there—if anything, more reporters than earlier. I pulled to a stop.

"Shit," I breathed.

"Mom!"

"Liv!" Steven wiggled his eyebrows. "I always pegged you as the *sugar* type."

"Sorry. Don't these people ever sleep?" I muttered. Rain streaked across the windshield, but the reporters remained undeterred, like damp vultures.

"Hang on," Blake said, scrolling through their phone. Then they hit call.

"Hi, this is Michelle Doggery. I run the Fairwyck shop," they said in a shockingly convincing Gloucestershire accent. My eyebrows shot up. Audrey was supposed to be our actor. "Yes, right, you interviewed me earlier. Well— you won't believe this. Malcolm Drake just came into the shop. Yes, I'm sure. He looks really out of it. Maybe drugs? Could be. The man is seeing specters everywhere…"

I slapped a hand over my mouth to keep from bursting out laughing.

It didn't even take five minutes after Blake hung up for the vans to start peeling off.

They'd only needed to fool one TV station. Rumors spread like wildfire—or reporters just chased each other's cars.

"Let's go," Blake said, once most of the caravan had disappeared.

I pulled up to Gina's. Two vans remained, but they were dark—no movement.

"Great," Steven muttered. "So this getup was for nothing?"

I waved a hand. "It'll help if anyone does spot you."

I pointed toward the formerly boarded-up door. "You might be surprised by how chilly it feels in there. But don't hesitate—go straight up the stairs, and—"

"Yes, yes. Don't get too scared." Steven smirked.

He slipped into the rain and went to the door beneath the old sign.

"Famous last words," I muttered, dread curling in my gut.

CHAPTER TWENTY

T he children and I dashed to the annex entrance through the rain. I clutched my big bag—camera, Blake's sketchpad, the usual—tight to my side.

Emerald opened the door and ushered us in. "Hi," she said, looking suitably chagrined. "I hear you've met the lost relatives."

"I can't believe you didn't tell me," I whispered as Blake and Audrey slipped past us down the narrow corridor.

Emerald gave a half-shrug. "Mother didn't want me to. Not until she was sure—"

She broke off when Maggie's voice rang out from the parlor, loud and theatrical.

"I've been so looking forward to meeting you children!"

I touched Emerald's arm before she could move. "Wait. Sure about what? That Maggie really means it when she says she's changed? You two must realize this is too much of a coincidence—"

Emerald pulled free, jaw tight. "I can't do this right now. You have no idea what I've been dealing with, and this is the last—"

"Is this about that guy you've been seeing? Because I would've loved to know—"

Suddenly Lucy was standing beside us. I actually flinched. She was one of those people who moved without a sound—easy to forget she was in the room at all.

"Is everything all right?" she asked gently. "I sense anger again…and disappointment."

Normally, a near-stranger narrating my emotions would have irritated the living daylights out of me—thanks for the unsolicited therapy, random psychic cousin—but instead, a strange, cool calm slid over me. Maybe I was too tired to feel affronted.

Neither Emerald nor I answered her, and we all drifted into the parlor.

A dining table had appeared in the middle of the room —apparently conjured from thin air. Or dragged in from some forgotten corner. For all I knew, it had been folded up behind a chaise somewhere. The room was a jumble of antiques, florals, and odd trinkets; keeping track of furniture in here was like cataloging Wonderland.

Every available chair had been pulled to the table. The chaises and armchairs were pushed back against the walls.

Gina sat at the head of the table, cradling a crystal wineglass. She started to rise, but I motioned her down and leaned in for a half hug.

My children were already seated opposite the woman I recognized from the night before. Tonight, she wore sensible gabardine trousers and a blouse—not the old-fashioned dress I now understood had been her "ghost costume." She looked elegant, really. Compact, but put-together. Her tousled brown curls were piled artfully on her head, and if she dyed them, it was excellent work. Same for the makeup—tasteful, but definitely present. As someone who once spent too much money on facials, I could spot a woman who invested in upkeep.

Maggie was two years older than Gina, yet she didn't look to be in her late sixties. She could pass for ten years younger, easily.

The two sisters couldn't have been more different. Gina—ethereal, hippie, floaty. Maggie—polished, grounded, sharp. Gina's blue eyes often drifted somewhere beyond the room; Maggie's dark ones missed nothing.

"Nice to meet you properly, Liv," Maggie said, extending a hand. Her rings glittered in the candlelight.

"Likewise." I sat beside her. "I'm very curious, since I only learned you existed a few hours ago."

"Oh yes, I'm quite the persona non grata." Maggie let out a hoarse laugh.

"Can I pour you a glass of wine, Liv?" Lucy's soft voice materialized at my elbow, startling me again.

"Oh for heaven's sake, don't sneak up on the poor woman," Maggie scolded lightly.

"Sorry," Lucy murmured.

"It's fine. And yes—I'd love a glass, thank you."

"What would you two like?" Lucy asked Blake and Audrey. They followed her to the kitchen to pick out sodas.

I turned back to Maggie. Time to start digging. "So— what brought you back to Fairwyck after all these years?"

She smiled serenely. "It was time to reconcile with my family—if not for my sake, then Lucy's."

She aimed the smile at Gina, who looked…unsure.

"I did some silly things in my youth," Maggie continued. "We all do, don't we?"

"Oh, I don't know," I said. "If you ask me, I wasn't silly enough when I should have been. It feels like I only started doing silly things after my husband left and I moved here. And honestly, I'm a better person for it."

"I heard about that. Poor girl." Maggie tutted. "Men. We Seven women never had much need for them."

Gina opened her mouth to object, but Maggie waved

her off. "Anyway, I don't mean the kind of silly things that make you better. Quite the opposite. They weren't really silly…more like—"

"Dangerous?" Gina supplied.

"I suppose. Magic is always a little dangerous."

"You almost destroyed the cottage," Gina muttered, not looking at her sister.

"What cottage?" I asked sharply.

"Your cottage." Maggie regarded me with cool curiosity. "I have to say, I'm surprised Ethel left it to you. It's a little…unusual."

"My children and I needed it. We were grateful beyond words." I choked up a little.

"Let's not forget, Liv is Ethel's goddaughter. I don't think it's that surprising. And they take wonderful care of the place," Gina added quickly.

"Do they?" Maggie asked, turning to her sister with a strange note in her voice. "Take care of it properly?"

A flicker of tension passed between them—sharp enough to stop me from pressing the cottage question further.

A moment later, Emerald, Lucy, and the children reentered, carrying steaming dishes, plates, and serving spoons.

We all helped ourselves to chicken, beans, Yorkshire pudding, and gravy.

Maggie complimented Emerald's and Lucy's cooking, and we all readily agreed it was delicious.

"Of course, we're a bit spoiled when it comes to Yorkshire puddings," Maggie added. "They're never as good anywhere else as in Yorkshire. You'd think Lucy would've mastered them by now, after all the years we lived up there."

Lucy turned pink and let her hair fall forward like a curtain.

"Oh, so you've been living up north?" I asked, eager to get any information about Maggie I could.

"Yes, in York," Maggie said. "I moved there when Lucy was a baby."

"Was it work that took you there?" I asked lightly. I wanted to know what Maggie did for a living, but asking outright felt too blunt. She could have married into money, inherited it, or stolen it—who knew?

"Oh, Mother is a rather successful rare-books dealer," Lucy said proudly. "That's what really brought us back to Fairwyck, actually—"

"Lucy, that's quite enough." Maggie cut her off, a sharp edge to her voice, which she then softened into a smile. "I can answer questions about myself, thank you very much."

I felt bad for Lucy, but that tiny sliver of information tightened every suspicion I had. Maggie had business in Fairwyck. A reunion hadn't been her only motive. And if she'd introduced Gina to Drake... What did rare books have to do with a paranormal TV host?

I drifted into my thoughts for too long. When I resurfaced, Maggie had shifted her attention to my children—far too interested in their gifts, asking question after question.

Given that my entire goal tonight was for Blake and Audrey to quietly "read" Maggie and Lucy, I wasn't thrilled she now knew so much about them.

I made a subtle gesture for the kids to stop talking, but Maggie noticed before they did.

"Please excuse my prying, Liv," she said. "I'm always eager to hear about other Seven children's gifts. I never had the pleasure of nurturing a gift in my own daughter."

"What?" I stared at Lucy, who ducked behind her hair again. "You don't possess any magical abilities, Lucy?"

She just shook her head.

"Oh, don't worry," I said. "I suppressed my abilities for years. They didn't come back until we moved to Fairwyck —I was in my forties."

"Yes, but that's different, Liv," Gina added gently. "You had abilities. They were just buried because of your trauma…and because of how your mother handled everything. Lucy never displayed anything at all—or so Maggie tells me." When this made Lucy wilt further, Gina added quickly, "But that doesn't mean anything bad, dear. Your Aunt Ethel didn't have any special abilities either. It happens. But she was still deeply attuned to magic, and I'd wager you are too."

I knew Gina had always suspected Ethel of having some secret ability. I'd never gotten an answer out of the cat myself. Maybe that was intentional—maybe she didn't want me to know.

"Yes, and Aunt Ethel is still magical," Audrey added. "She's a cat now, so… A human without magic couldn't come back as a cat, right?"

Maggie looked up sharply. "Ethel is a cat? Does she still live at the cottage?"

"Yes, and she talks to me," Audrey continued, while I silently begged her to stop. Tonight was supposed to be our fact-finding mission, not the other way around.

"How interesting…" Maggie murmured.

"So what's your magical ability, then, Maggie?" I cut in, redirecting.

"It's not all that different from Emerald's gift, actually," she said, piercing a piece of chicken.

Gina frowned deeply and cleared her throat, but said nothing—just took a long sip of wine.

"Books talk to you?" I asked, confused. That gift had always sounded extremely rare.

"It's not the books themselves," Maggie said. "More like…the authors."

My eyebrows rose. Rare books were usually old. Very old. "The…dead authors?"

"Pretty much." Maggie smiled, unbothered.

Audrey perked up. "Oh! So your gift is more like Mom's. You talk to ghosts."

Maggie looked intrigued. "I thought your mother only photographed them?"

I couldn't believe she had managed, yet again, to turn the conversation back to us.

"Yes, but—" Audrey began, but I cut her off again.

"So you communicate with the ghosts of dead authors? Is that why you're such a successful rare-books dealer? Must be handy, getting information straight from the source."

Before Maggie could answer, there was a loud clatter from Gina's side of the table.

She had dropped her heavy silverware onto her porcelain plate. The plate shattered cleanly in half, gravy spilling like a brown river across the tablecloth as green beans and chicken scattered.

"I'm sorry," she murmured, sounding small.

"Oh, Mom…" Emerald stood. "I'll get a bowl to pick up the pieces—and a cloth."

"No, I'll get it," Maggie said, rising with unsettling briskness. "This is my fault. Poor Gina is worked up because of me. Come, Lucy—don't just sit there. Fetch your aunt a new plate."

They disappeared into the kitchen.

Blake and Audrey stared at their plates, unsure what to do.

I leaned toward Gina and whispered, "Are you all right? What's going on?"

"Maggie doesn't communicate with ghosts, Liv," Gina whispered back. "She raises them."

"What?" I gasped. "Like a necromancer?"

"Yes, I suppose you could call me that," Maggie said calmly—already back in the doorway, wearing rubber gloves and holding a plastic bowl. She bent to collect the shards as if we were discussing nothing more controversial than the gravy recipe.

"I don't actually raise the dead," she went on. "Never have. Not for lack of trying." She shot Gina a pointed look. "And that, understandably, is what my family didn't appreciate. But when you're born with a calling, it's only natural to test your limits."

Gina pursed her lips but said nothing.

"But I've learned control," Maggie continued. "I don't raise the dead. I raise shadows."

"Shadows?" I echoed.

"Books contain pieces of their authors' souls," Maggie said lightly. "Sometimes they even hold remnants of readers—especially the ones who adored them, annotated them, left their thoughts in the margins. Marginalia can hold astonishing power. Handwriting is a fragment of the soul, after all. And ink..." Her eyes glinted. "Ink is the blood of the page."

"Wow, okay. Probably not so much anymore with books written on computers—so it's only rare manuscripts?"

Maggie simply smiled, maddeningly enigmatic.

"So you raise the shadows and ask them questions. To get information about the book—make it more valuable. Smart."

"There's nothing smart about it," Gina said sharply. "It may be relatively harmless, but it still drains the spirits of their souls, doesn't it, Maggie?"

I frowned. "Drains them? How?"

"It's not like when you ask a ghost a question so they can find closure," Gina said. "Necromancy drags a soul back into this realm. It steals energy."

"Just a little bit," Maggie said, waving a dismissive hand. "Like I said, they're only shadows. It just helps with my work. You make money with your paranormal skills too, Gina."

"But I also help people."

"So do I!" Maggie exclaimed. "Don't you think authors want their books to be valuable? Why else would they become writers? They want their words to live on."

"Well, some people are successful antiquarians without raising authors from the dead," Gina muttered. "Like Emerald's beau, for example."

"Mother!" Emerald yelped. "He's not my beau! I told you." She sounded like an embarrassed teenager, not a woman in her thirties.

"I'm sorry, darling, I know I promised not to bring him up," Gina said. "But all I meant was—he seems to be successful in the same line of work as Maggie, and he doesn't rely on—"

"Stop it, Mother!" Emerald jumped to her feet. "Don't talk about him. He's not even an antiquarian, really. It's just a hobby, it turns out. You don't even know him!" She stormed out of the parlor.

Lucy rose immediately. "I'll make sure she's all right," she whispered before following her out.

Silence settled over the table. Everyone stared at the remnants of dinner as if hoping for a distraction.

I cleared my throat. "Who is this man, Aunt Gina? Emerald hasn't told me anything. I only heard at book club that he broke her heart. What happened?"

"His name is Dr. Alaric Hatherleigh," Gina said. "A distinguished gentleman. He runs some sort of book club —not like yours, more scholarly. She met him at the library. He was searching for rare texts, and she helped him find them. Books are the way to Emmy's heart." She twisted her napkin anxiously. "I never met him, that's true, but she was so happy. I was sure they were a good match. The cards were promising too—I drew the Knight of Cups. The Prince Charming card." Her shoulders slumped. "I must have interpreted it wrong. He just stopped calling."

"Oh no!" My heart ached for Emerald. "Why didn't she tell me?"

My aunt patted my hand. "Darling…no one wants to talk heartbreak with a woman who's in a wonderful relationship."

"Oh, do you have a boyfriend, Liv?" Maggie asked.

"Yes," I said, with emotions I'd rather not examine too closely. "Jamie—he's a detective sergeant with the Gloucestershire Police." I cleared my throat. "Speaking of which, he told me they might want to check the inn again tonight. They could come by at any time. I really think it's best you stay out of the old inn, Maggie. No one should be in there."

Maggie regarded me with sly amusement. "I was bored of it anyway. Playing ghost is no fun if none of these cowards dare to sneak in. The British are such rule-followers. I'll bet Americans wouldn't let a simple no-trespassing sign stop them from entering a crime scene. Right, Liv?"

"Um…" If she only knew an American was already inside. "I suppose."

"I'm also looking forward to sleeping in a proper bed again," Maggie added. "Those old, sagging mattresses in the inn were made for people from the Middle Ages. And they were even shorter than me, if you can believe it."

"Mom, can we be excused?" Blake asked. No one had taken another bite in ages. "I'd like to do some sketching."

"Oh?" Maggie arched an eyebrow.

"Just…regular sketching," Blake said quickly. "I do that too, not only supernatural stuff."

"Of course. I'd love to see some of your work."

I handed Blake the sketchbook from my bag. They flipped it open for Maggie to see.

Audrey stood. "I'll look for Beltane. Or dessert."

I gathered a few plates. "Let me help clear up." I followed Gina into the kitchen with the dirty dishes, then said quietly, "Do you mind if I check on Emerald?"

"Go ahead," Gina said.

Instead of searching for Emerald, I slipped through the connecting door into the old taproom. The moment I entered, goose bumps rippled up my arms. After all the talk of necromancy, merely moving through this space felt unnerving. Maggie sleeping upstairs last night—willingly—was a fact I didn't quite know what to do with.

But she'd said she used her abilities only on books. And I hadn't seen a single one in the inn—just peeling wallpaper, shredded curtains, and furniture in various states of collapse.

I hurried upstairs, ignoring the feeling of a hundred unseen eyes tracking me. The cameras were still off.

"Steven?" I hissed.

A door creaked open next to Drake's room. Steven stood there, still in the tight uniform, but with a blanket around his shoulders. He looked pale—and rattled.

"Hey," I whispered. "You should've changed. I need that uniform back."

"I'm not getting undressed in here," he said, darting his gaze around.

I suppressed a smile. "Oh yeah? Why not?"

"Don't you feel it?" He shivered. "Like someone's watching."

"I told you—the inn is haunted," I said smugly. "But I thought you weren't scared of ghosts."

"Well…this place could change anyone's mind."

"If you'd rather not stay here," I said, "then you need to leave Fairwyck tonight."

I looked at him searchingly. I'd suspected Steven had been lying to me—surely he hadn't been roughing it for almost a year, since I'd first spotted him at the Ghost Light Theatre. He just didn't look it. So he had to have been staying somewhere. He had to have had the means not to rely on me for a hiding place. The whole I-don't-have-anywhere-to-go routine had been easy to keep up as long as he was in the nice cottage next to my home, with the added bonus of being close enough to the children to ingratiate himself with them again. Staying in this place—cold, dilapidated, haunted, and alone—was another matter entirely. I'd secretly hoped it would put his claims to the test.

And what I needed from Steven most of all—why I hadn't turned him away despite everything, the danger, my lies and deception—was to know the truth.

Steven shoved a hand through his hair—now sticking up wildly, very unlike him. "No. No. If this is what it takes to prove to you I mean it—that I want you back, that I want us together again—I'll stay."

"Fine." I nodded, feeling a smug little glow of satisfaction I refused to examine too closely.

Steven, shaken. Steven, not in control. Steven, forced to sit with discomfort for once.

Honestly? It was…refreshing.

"Okay," I said lightly. "Your choice."

I left him there—hovering between bravado and terror—and returned to the annex to collect the children.

Dinner hadn't ended harmoniously, but I'd learned a great deal about Maggie. Unfortunately, Maggie had learned a little too much about us as well.

I didn't like the belittling tone she used with her daughter. Though, to be fair, Lucy had a bit of an eerie quality about her too.

The necromancy gift unsettled me, and it was painfully

clear Gina wasn't sure about her sister either. She'd hidden Maggie from us for a reason.

And Lucy had let slip that they'd had another motive for coming to Fairwyck.

But how did any of that connect to Drake's disappearance? Necromancy didn't seem relevant, and rare books even less so.

I was also relieved to finally understand what had been troubling Emerald, though I didn't get the chance to speak to her. She stayed out of sight while we gathered our coats.

Another small mercy: The reporters were gone. Blake's brilliant fake-shopkeeper call had done the trick.

By the time the children and I returned home, I felt—astonishingly—hopeful.

I should have known that feeling was too good to be true.

CHAPTER TWENTY-ONE

The ringing of my phone dragged me out of a blissful, dreamless sleep. With one eye open, I squinted at the glowing red digits on my alarm clock.

Almost time to get up, anyway.

Groaning, I sat up, grabbed my phone, and hit "Answer."

"Yeah?"

"A beautiful good morning to you," Jamie said cheerfully.

My mouth was dry as dust. I really needed to start keeping a glass of water on my nightstand like a functioning adult. I licked my lips—it did nothing.

"Good morning."

"I didn't wake you, did I? Isn't Thursday the day you go to the theater in the morning?"

"Oh. Yes. Right."

I had completely forgotten it was Thursday—and that I'd rescheduled my meeting with Ellie for this morning.

I shut off my alarm, shuffled into the bathroom, squeezed toothpaste onto my toothbrush, and held the phone between shoulder and ear while Jamie kept talking.

"Listen, this may be a strange question, but…did you let yourself into my apartment yesterday?"

I pressed too hard and shot a two-inch ribbon of toothpaste across the sink. "Fff…Flapjacks!"

"What?"

"Oh—nothing. What did you say?"

Jamie repeated his question while I furiously brushed—too much toothpaste, too vigorously. Only after a few seconds did it dawn on me that Jamie couldn't see I was brushing, and therefore my plan to avoid answering was flawed.

"I'm not accusing you or anything," Jamie continued, sounding more uncertain with each passing second. "It's just—one of my uniforms seems to be missing. Nothing else is gone. I'm sorry, I don't know why I even thought—why would you have taken it? Anyway, I should go. Farrow wants me at the inn before I head to the station. Drake still hasn't turned up, and there's pressure from—"

I squeaked, spat out a foam tsunami, and coughed violently.

"Liv? You okay?"

I rinsed, splashed water on my face, and croaked, "You're going there now?"

I put the phone face-down on the sink while I wiped my face, peed, and tried to dress all at once. If Jamie was going to the Sacred Salmon, I had to get there first.

"Um, yes? In a minute. As soon as I finish my coffee."

"Do me a favor, honey?" I shouted from the toilet. "Put some coffee in a thermos for me. I'll meet you outside the inn, okay?"

"Okay…" Jamie said slowly. "I can pick you up if you—"

"No, no. I'll meet you there. Outside."

I flushed, left my pajama pants on the floor like a four-year-old, and washed my hands. Snatching the phone with wet fingers and nearly dropping it, I barreled into my bedroom.

"Why, though?" he asked. "I mean—I miss you too, but—"

"I need to show—give—you something."

I grabbed a random T-shirt and hoodie from a drawer and stepped into my jeans from the night before. Thank god I'd slept in a bralette; no time for bra logistics. Jamie definitely wasn't getting to second base today—scratch that, if this plan went badly, he might never see my underwear again.

"Okay…see you in a bit."

I hung up, yanked off my pajama top, and pulled on the T-shirt and hoodie. Putting on socks while hobbling upstairs to the kids' tiny attic rooms, I barked out instructions.

Once I was sure Blake understood why I needed to leave immediately, I thundered back downstairs, grabbed my bag, shoved my feet into sneakers, and ran out the door with my coat still over my arm.

Esme was about to get into her car just as I reached mine. She waved, then frowned at the sight of my disheveled state. "Are you okay? You look like someone's chasing you."

"It's…Jamie…" I was really out of breath. "Sorry—no time to explain."

I got into the car and drove off.

I definitely broke a few traffic laws on the way to the inn. Worth it—I arrived before Jamie.

I slipped straight into the tavern through the main entrance.

It was daylight, and with everything going on, I was

wholly unconcerned with the usual ghostly ambience. I bolted up the stairs.

"Steven! The police are on the way—hide!"

Drake's door was open. Jamie's police uniform lay abandoned on the floor. I froze. The rest of the room was exactly the same as yesterday: the cot, the mirror, Drake's bag.

A noise outside.

I dashed to the window—Jamie climbing out of his police car.

"Oh no!"

Well, I had told him to meet me outside. Maybe I'd bought a few seconds—

But why hadn't Steven come out?

I didn't dare call again. Jamie was close enough to hear.

Jamie looked up—saw me—and waved.

"For fudge sake!"

I spun in panic, grabbed the uniform, and pressed it to my chest.

Bootsteps—Jamie's—pounded up the stairs. He was fast.

I lunged for the door to Steven's room, cracked it open, peeked in.

Empty.

"Hey, Liv."

I nearly levitated from fright as Jamie appeared behind me.

"Oh! Jamie!"

"I thought we were meeting outside. I have the thermos in the car…"

His gaze dropped to the garments clutched to my chest. He frowned. "Is that…is that my uniform? You did take it? But why didn't you say so…?"

"Um…" I lifted my hands, and the rumpled uniform and shirt nearly slid to the floor.

Jamie caught them reflexively.

They'd been crisp and immaculate when I'd stolen them.

Now they looked like they'd been used as bedding in a barn.

A flicker of anger crossed Jamie's bewildered expression.

I couldn't blame him. Not even a little.

"Um…" I repeated. "The thing is…I…borrowed your uniform. I wanted to get you a tailored suit for Christmas. And…well, I thought I'd take this one, so I'd know your size. I was going to give it to Aunt Gina—because she knows about sewing and taking measurements—and then bring it back to your apartment today. But you caught me."

I let out a flimsy laugh. "So I figured I should return it right away. And then I found out that Beltane—Gina's cat —got hold of it and played with it and, um, dragged it all the way to the inn. If you can believe it. You know how witch familiars are…they do things…nobody knows why. Maybe she has a grudge against you? I don't know. But! Nothing's torn or broken. Just a little…worse for wear."

I plastered on the brightest smile I could manage, praying he bought even a fraction of the avalanche of lies I'd just dumped at his feet.

"I'm really sorry," I added.

Later, I would absolutely have to apologize to Beltane for throwing her under the metaphorical bus.

Jamie wrinkled his nose. "You want to give me a suit for Christmas?"

"Yeeesss."

"But you always say you prefer me dressed casually."

"Usually. But you'd look terrific in a suit. And…I wanted

you to have one for when we go to the…opera. It's always been my dream to go. That's the real present. Opera tickets for New Year's. In London. A whole weekend. Just us. A hotel."

I had heard of "verbal diarrhea" but hadn't understood the term fully until that moment. I only stopped myself by biting the inside of my cheek so hard I tasted blood.

"Oh. I'd love a weekend in London with you," Jamie said softly. His face brightened. "Not sure about the opera or a suit, but you clearly put thought into this. Sorry I ruined the surprise. Still—sounds wonderful."

He bent to kiss me; I managed to kiss him back around the pain of my self-inflicted cheek wound.

Fantastic. Now I would need to actually find money, childcare, and opera tickets for a fictional trip that only existed to cover the fact that I had stolen a police uniform to hide my fugitive husband in a haunted inn.

And that wasn't even the worst part.

The worst part was knowing that soon, when Jamie discovered the truth, this sweet, understanding reaction would be nothing but a memory.

Jamie handed the rumpled uniform back to me. "Could you take this? I need to start another search of the premises." He walked past me toward Steven's room. "I'll begin in here—"

I darted after him. "Do you need help, maybe?"

"Nah. Thanks, love, but Farrow would lose his mind if he knew you came into an active crime scene."

"Right…yes…"

I spun twice, looking for any sign of Steven. There was nowhere—nowhere—for him to hide. The small bed was built into the wall and open underneath. No mattress, just slats. An old washstand and a mirror frame missing its glass. That was it.

"I'll just go grab the thermos from your car and wait downstairs until you're done."

"Okay—if you've got the time."

Jamie looked faintly puzzled—probably wondering why I was lingering at all—but the moment passed. He was in full cop mode, laser-focused on his task.

This task unfortunately included the risk of discovering Steven. And there was nothing I could do now except pray Steven had found some miraculous hiding place.

I slipped out, hurried to Jamie's car, retrieved the thermos, and then sat in my own vehicle drinking coffee I absolutely did not need, waiting through the longest twenty minutes of my life.

When Jamie finally knocked on my window, every instinct screamed at me to floor the gas pedal and escape the country.

Instead, I lowered the window. The mechanism chose that moment to roll down at a glacial pace.

"All done?" I asked. My mouth was still dry, despite the coffee.

"Yeah. Still creepy in there, but nothing new. Funny thing, though—Drake's laptop and notebook are gone."

Sh…ugar.

They were still in my house. Why hadn't I thought of that?

"I told you you should've taken his stuff the other day," I said quickly. "Some reporter probably snuck in. You saw what they were like."

"Hmm. Or Farrow came by and grabbed them earlier."

"What? Why would he? Didn't he send you for that?"

"To do the dirty work—full search, all the corners. He has to be shaking in his boots now. He wrote off Drake's disappearance, and the man still hasn't turned up. Something is clearly wrong. He must know it. He's too proud to admit he was wrong, but now? He'll make sure no stone is left unturned."

"You think?" I mumbled around my thumbnail—currently being bitten to the quick.

Had Farrow found Steven? If he had, surely I'd know…right? Or would he wait, savoring the moment to wield it over me?

If Jamie hadn't found Steven up there…

"…gotta go," Jamie finished.

"What?"

"I need to get to work. Are you okay?"

"Yes! Yes." I forced a smile. "I'm going to talk to Gina and Emerald. Thanks for the coffee. You know they only make tea in there."

I shoved the thermos back at him.

"All right. See you later."

"I put the uniform on your back seat." I let Jamie give me a quick peck through the open window. "Bye."

I waited until he'd fully driven off. Then I flung open my door, launched myself out of the car, and sprinted back into the inn.

"Steven!" I shouted, loud enough to wake every ghost in Gloucestershire. I clattered up the stairs. "Steven, where are you?"

I was tearing through rooms—flinging doors open, slamming them shut, finding nothing—when Emerald burst into the hallway, followed by Gina, Maggie, and Lucy.

By then I was a complete mess: sobbing, frantic, hands shaking.

"Oh—it's you, Liv!" Emerald gasped. "We heard a noise and—what's wrong?"

"Steven's here," I choked out.

They all stared at me.

"Well—he was here. He turned up a few days ago, and

I hid him in the cottage next door, but renters were coming in yesterday, so I had to stash him somewhere else, and I needed time to think, and there's been so much going on, and he's the father of my kids, not that I want him back—I don't—because there's Jamie, and he was sent here this morning to check the inn again, and I got here just in time, but now Steven's not here, and he was here last night, and now I can't find him, and—"

Full verbal diarrhea. I had a bad case of it. Clearly.

I finally sucked in a breath and covered my face.

Emerald blinked slowly. "Your husband, Steven…came to Fairwyck?"

"The one who's on the run from the FBI?" Maggie added.

I sighed. "The one and only."

"Oh, honey," Gina murmured, making a sympathetic face.

"Why would you hide him?" Emerald asked, looking genuinely stunned.

"He swears he wants to make amends," I said helplessly. "And Audrey is so excited her dad's back. I don't know."

Lucy placed a gentle hand on my back. Instead of being creeped out, I felt…calmer. "That must be so confusing," she whispered.

"You have no idea."

All of them—including the relatives I'd met barely twenty-four hours ago—moved in and wrapped their arms around me. And that was it. I burst into full-on, uncontrollable crying for a solid two minutes. Then I hiccuped the last of it out and scrubbed my face.

"Will you help me look for him?"

"Of course," they all said at once.

Together, we combed every inch of the upstairs. Every

dusty corner. Every warped floorboard. Every unsettling shadow.

We ended up back in the hall—tired, baffled, and completely empty-handed.

"Maybe he just left," I said weakly. "I sort of put him to the test, having him stay here. He was freaking ou—"

"Shh." Maggie lifted a hand.

I swallowed my irritation.

But then I heard it too: a soft, rhythmic thump.

Emerald's head tilted. "I hear it as well."

We traced the sound to the room I'd assigned Steven last night.

"There's nothing here," I insisted, exasperated. "It's empty."

But Maggie had already stepped toward the wood paneling beside the bed. "It's coming from behind this."

She ran her fingers along the boards—and then, impossibly, the wall shifted.

We all stared, open-mouthed, as a hidden panel swung aside.

A dark, narrow space lay behind it.

And out of it stumbled Steven—coughing, squinting, and holding one hand up as if the light stabbed his eyes.

"Oh my god," he rasped. "I thought I was going to get stuck in there. Thank god you found me."

CHAPTER TWENTY-TWO

I had a lot of explaining to do about Steven while the ever-helpful Lucy trotted off to fetch flashlights from the annex.

We needed to examine the hidden room properly. It was far too small for a man of Drake's size to have shared with Steven, but there was stuff in there—stuff that might relate to Drake's disappearance.

And honestly? It wasn't outside the realm of possibility that a dead Dr. Drake could be tucked behind a panel somewhere.

"Please—you can't tell anyone Steven's here," I said, my voice cracking. "We'd all get into trouble for harboring a fugitive. And when Farrow realizes I've been hiding Steven for days…and if Jamie finds out I lied to him…"

I dropped my head.

"Who's Jamie?" Steven asked.

"Honey," Gina said gently, patting my arm. "He's your husband. The father of your children. You never had closure. Of course you needed some time. But you should have come to us straight away."

"I didn't want to get you into trouble." My eyes

burned. "You already had enough chaos. This is just…" I snapped my gaze to Steven. "The worst possible timing!"

He held up both hands. "Hey, how was I supposed to know any of this spooky stuff would be going on with your family? I've been watching you from afar and thought you lived in a boring English village. Opening that theater with your friend looked like peak excitement. I didn't expect to wake up in a Simpsons Treehouse of Horrors."

Despite everything, I laughed—and immediately hated that he could still make me do that. Even disheveled, with cobwebs in his golden highlights and dark circles under his eyes, Steven could be maddeningly charming.

I exhaled. "At least we now have a clue. This inn is hiding more than ghosts. There might be more secret rooms—we don't know how many. Drake could be in one of them. Gina, did you know anything about this?"

My aunt shook her head. "Wouldn't Dr. Drake have tried to draw attention to himself? Steven knocked—we would have heard something during the searches for Malcom too."

"Unless another room is more insulated," I said. "Better hidden."

"Let's be realistic," Maggie said. "Secret rooms don't extend into alternate dimensions. If one exists, the walls should tell us. We'd see inconsistencies."

"That's true." I recalled the hidden archive in the theater—how one dressing room had been smaller, with a suspiciously newer wall. "We should check for architectural oddities."

"Then let's look," Maggie said briskly. "The inn's not that big."

We scattered. She was right—technically it wasn't large —but the place was a creepy rabbit warren. It was difficult to judge wall thickness or which rooms adjoined which. Some doors were still locked.

"You really need keys for these, Gina," I said, frustrated, as we reconvened in the corridor just as Lucy returned with flashlights. "We should mark rooms we've searched so we don't double back."

"Like breadcrumbs?" Steven offered, eyebrow raised.

"I—don't know."

A thought tugged at me. Seeing Maggie in the inn window the other night…the tale of Glamis Castle bubbled up from memory.

"There's a legend," I told them. "The owners suspected a secret room in the castle. They had the servants hang a handkerchief out of every reachable window. Then they went outside and counted. Every window showed a signal—except one. That unreachable window marked the hidden room."

"That's clever," Steven said. "But the room I was stuck in didn't even have a window."

Lucy stepped forward and shone her flashlight into the dark opening. "No window," she confirmed. "Just books."

"Books?" I moved beside her and gently took the flashlight, sweeping the beam across the cramped space. "Huh. Interesting. I would've thought the books would have… spoken to Emerald."

That's what had happened with the theater archive.

I turned to Emerald. She stared at the floor, shoulders hunched.

Suspicious. Very suspicious.

I pointed the flashlight at her.

"Emerald?"

Blinded, she threw up a hand. "Hey! Stop that!"

"How could you not know these books were here?" My tone sharpened.

"Not all books talk to me, all right?" she snapped. "Maybe these ones don't have anything to say!"

"Children…" Gina murmured, trying to ease the tension.

I stepped toward the opening, pulse hammering.

"How'd you even end up in there?" I asked Steven as I crouched and slipped one foot into the secret room.

"You yelled that the police were coming, and I panicked," he said. "Tried to shove the bed aside to hide behind it or under it, pressed the wrong panel, and the wall just—opened. I slipped in and closed it behind me. At first I thought, great hiding spot…then it got creepy. Pitch black. I swear I heard someone breathing. But I didn't want to shout with cops around. When you yelled my name, I tried to get out and couldn't find the latch. So I knocked."

By then I was fully inside the room. I had to stoop, or I'd hit my head. I could've curled up in a ball and barely fit.

A small secretaire stood against the wall, books piled on top and strewn around it.

The books looked old—possibly very old—and in surprisingly good condition. The air was dry and stale, which made me think someone once took great care to insulate this room.

My flashlight beam slid across the wall—and my breath caught.

Symbols. Painted sigils I recognized.

The same kind etched around the mirror frame in Drake's room.

And an unpainted rectangle on the wall—exactly the size of that mirror.

"That mirror in Drake's room," I said slowly. "It must've come from here."

I glanced back at the group clustered in the doorway. "Remember? It wasn't there when Drake first set up, Gina."

"What are you thinking?" my aunt asked. "That Drake found this room and moved the mirror? But why?"

"He'd want to capture it on film," Maggie said, leaning in beside me. "This is exactly the sort of discovery he'd crave. Hidden room. Old books. Perfect TV fodder."

I considered that.

"Maybe he planned to reveal the room later," I said. "To make the episode more dramatic…"

Steven frowned. "I thought you said he found it already and took the mirror out."

"Yes." I pushed my hair out of my face. "Drake's TV series looks spontaneous, but of course it isn't. He could've found the room earlier—before he turned the cameras on—and decided he'd rather 'discover' it," I broke out the air quotes, "later—on camera—in some dramatic, climactic moment."

"That would make sense," Maggie said. "But why remove the mirror?"

"The mirror makes a great set piece—spooky, atmospheric." I thought of the footage I'd seen where he'd jumped at his own reflection…or pretended to. "An episode needs pacing. You can't blow all the creepy stuff in one room in the first ten minutes."

"I don't know…" Gina looked troubled. "Dr. Drake struck me as a serious man—rigorous in his scientific approach to hauntings. We were told the TV series is only a means to an end. I don't think he'd stage any of it."

I smiled at her gently. "Maybe it's both. He needs the show to fund his research, so he shapes things for TV without faking his actual findings. And these findings—the sigils, the books—they're real. This room would've thrilled him."

I moved the flashlight toward the secretaire and the stack of books. Ancient leather-bound volumes sat there looking fragile. One slightly newer book caught my eye. I opened it—and my eyes bulged.

Alaric Hatherleigh.

"Emerald," I said, keeping my voice even. "Come in here. You're the book expert. Can you look at these?"

My cousin hesitated, then stepped inside.

Maggie bristled. "Actually, I'm the rare-books expert. Emerald is just a librarian. I should—"

I lifted the flashlight and let its beam hit her squarely in the face. She recoiled instinctively.

"That's all right," I said sweetly. "This is Gina's and Emerald's home. They should see all this first, don't you think?"

"I don't know," Maggie muttered. "If I can be of help identifying—do you mind not shining that right at me?"

"Oh—sorry." I didn't lower it.

I handed the book to Emerald, who went ghostly pale at the sight of the author's name.

Alaric Hatherleigh—*the* Dr. Hatherleigh. The man who had broken her heart.

Unless he was a few centuries old—which, frankly, I no longer considered impossible—someone must have placed the book in this hidden room. And given Emerald's expression, it wasn't her.

If Emerald had known about this room, she would've said something—especially with her book-scrying ability. I'd seen her in a full trance before: eyes glowing green, walking like a sleepwalker toward a "calling" book. She couldn't have hidden a reaction like that. She'd shown none of it here.

Maybe there was some kind of magical insulation that prevented the books from contacting her—the sigils on the wall? But what mattered most to me right now: She hadn't known.

That left only a few options.

Drake, who had definitely been in the room.

Steven, who had also been in the room (but who was unlikely to own arcane manuscripts).

Or Maggie, who had been in the inn last night, was a rare-books expert, and had more motive than anyone to keep the existence of the place to herself.

I didn't know her. She didn't really know me. And I certainly didn't trust her the way I trusted Gina.

Although… Gina had been acting strangely too.

I shifted my flashlight toward my aunt. She looked distraught, wringing her hands.

"Gina, what's wrong?" I stepped out of the cramped space to join her, gently pushing Maggie away from the entrance to get to my aunt.

"What you said about Dr. Drake makes so much sense, Liv."

"Oh—what did I say?"

"That he would have been excited to find this room. He would have wanted to examine these books."

"Well, yes…"

"So it makes no sense—no sense at all—that he would have left this inn voluntarily." Gina's voice trembled. "He would've stayed. He would've shown this discovery to his viewers. He'd have been desperate to study these books."

A cold shiver crept down my spine as her meaning hit me.

Our discovery didn't just cast doubt on Drake leaving.

It made it nearly impossible.

Everything pointed to one terrible truth: Dr. Malcolm Drake had never left the Sacred Salmon Inn.

So where was he?

CHAPTER TWENTY-THREE

I didn't want Maggie examining all the books in the secret room. I still wasn't convinced we could trust her.

But she was a rare-books specialist, and these texts might be connected to Drake's disappearance.

I had to give her something.

I grabbed one of the older tomes and thrust it into her hands. A cloud of dust exploded upward, and Maggie coughed—whether from the dust or from horror at my handling technique, I couldn't tell.

"Careful," she gasped. "We don't know how old these are. They should be handled with gloves—"

"Do you have gloves in your room?" I cut in.

"Well…yes. I always carry my equipment. One never knows when one might come across a treasure—"

"Like this," I finished for her. "Let's go get them so you can start. Emerald and I will meet later at the library to research the symbols."

I turned, pulled the camera from my bag, and snapped photos of all the sigils painted on the walls.

I wanted Emerald to do the research—but I also needed to talk to her about Alaric Hatherleigh.

"I need to stop by the theater first," I told my cousin. "I was supposed to meet Ellie ages ago. I'll come by the library afterward, okay?"

Emerald nodded, still clutching the Hatherleigh book behind her back. Maggie didn't notice—too absorbed in the dusty tome I'd handed her.

"But what are we going to do about Dr. Drake?" Gina asked, clearly rattled.

I tried to sound confident. "We already searched the inn. Something happened to him here, but I think we all know that it must have been something…supernatural. If his disappearance is tied to this room, then researching what we found here is our best shot at finding him."

She still looked doubtful, so I squeezed her hands. "It's what we can do right now. And I promise—I'm on it."

She nodded. "I want to do something too. I feel so useless."

"Try and find the keys to the locked rooms. And run interference with Farrow. Nothing good can come of the police poking around here. If what we suspect is true, DI Farrow isn't going to find Dr. Drake. And don't forget, Steven is hiding here."

Gina agreed. Following Maggie and Lucy out, she asked, "Are you coming?"

I smiled. "Yes. I just need a word with Steven."

Once she was gone, I shut the door to the hidden room.

"Listen," I said to Steven, who still looked dazed. "I need you to stay here and make sure Maggie doesn't sneak back in and…I don't know…remove anything."

I gave him the quick-and-chaotic version of our newly reunited relatives. He only half absorbed it.

"Did you say your aunt and cousin live in an annex that's more modern? Can't I stay there?"

I shook my head. "It's already full—with Maggie and Lucy in Emerald's room. No, you're better off here. Think of yourself as a guard dog. Don't let Maggie snoop."

Steven dragged a hand through his hair. "Okay, but… that Drake guy stayed here and then disappeared. It's gotta be connected to this room, right? He removed the mirror…who knows what happened. Isn't it dangerous for me to stay here?"

I crossed my arms, studying the man I no longer thought of as my husband. He'd always acted superior—even now, even after everything he'd done to us. Seeing him unsettled, for once, was…satisfying.

"Yeah, maybe don't go into the room. And stay away from the mirror. We'll cover it—just in case."

I ducked into the next room, grabbed Drake's coat, and draped it over the mirror. Steven hovered behind me, watching with a dubious expression.

"There," I said. "I'll check in on you later if it helps. I didn't know you were that afraid of ghosts. Thought you didn't believe in them."

"I didn't. But after staying here…who wouldn't?" He gave a strained laugh.

I looked down at my camera, then slid it back into my bag. For the briefest moment, I considered telling Steven about my gift.

"Hey, strange question," he said. "Audrey said something about your cat being your reborn aunt…and that she talks to her. She didn't mean that, right? I mean, she's imaginative, but—this environment—Liv, I worry she's… you know…losing it."

I straightened. "She's not losing anything. And I suggest you talk to her again. It's not my place to explain.

But whatever you do, Steven, take her seriously. The same goes for Blake."

"Of course."

Leaving the inn, I was relieved I hadn't confided in Steven. I liked him a little frightened. It made me feel in control—something I'd rarely felt during our marriage. I still didn't know what I wanted to do about him long term, but I definitely didn't want him freaked out about me.

That reminded me about the meeting with Steven's lawyer. It was supposed to be today, and with everything that had happened, he hadn't brought it up again. Considering the time difference, it might not happen until later tonight. I'd be checking in on him anyway, and we could sort it out then. I made a mental note to bring my laptop, just in case.

I arranged a meeting time with Emerald, then went to the theater to apologize to Ellie for my lateness.

She looked at me with concern. "You look…tired. Are you okay?"

"Oh, it's nothing, just… Jamie needed me really early this morning," I said—the first thing that came to mind— then quickly changed the topic.

Fortunately, nothing major was happening at the moment. We had our check-in, I answered a few emails, and I took a look at the accounts before heading out to squeeze in a quick grocery run.

After Michelle's betrayal, I wasn't ready to face her shop, so I went to the supermarket in Meckham instead.

I picked up milk, bread, dinner ingredients, the usual— and paused at the newspaper rack.

The *Sun* featured a big exclusive with Drake's ex-wife, a psychic, claiming he'd contacted her from the afterlife.

Another tabloid quoted a "close friend," insisting Drake was in hiding.

Several papers were pushing the "tragic genius with many enemies" angle.

The *Guardian*, predictably, focused on unsafe practices at the production company with questionable ethical values.

At least most had moved on from the *Inn of Doom*, as one paper had dubbed Gina's home.

But once their other leads dried up—and Drake still didn't surface—they'd be back.

Probably with a vengeance. We'd better find Dr. Drake before that happened.

I picked up the kids from school—they only had a half day, and I was already nearby. I told them how their father was doing at the inn, made us lunch, and then let them know I'd be meeting Emerald at the library and would see them later.

I decided to walk to the library, taking the opportunity to clear my head a little. By the time I got to the honey-colored building, I wasn't any closer to making my mind up about Maggie, but I had a whole list of questions for Emerald.

Since the library was officially closed this afternoon, I knocked.

Emerald opened the door and led me into her office.

"Would you like a cup of tea?" she asked distractedly, already lowering herself into her desk chair. Her dark-blond hair was scraped into a haphazard bun—messier than usual—and two pencils were stabbed through it like improvised chopsticks. Her glasses had slid halfway down her nose. The desk was buried in books and notes.

"I'll make myself a cup," I said, filling the kettle. "Looks like you've already been hard at work."

"Hmm?" Emerald glanced up.

"You've been busy."

"Oh. Yes."

I kept quiet while the kettle boiled and the tea steeped. Once it was ready, and after adding milk and sugar to both our cups, I shifted a few papers aside to make room on the desk.

"Take a little break for me, would you?" Emerald grumbled, jotting down one more note.

"Em." I waited until she finally looked up. "Before we dive into these symbols, I really want to hear more about Alaric Hatherleigh."

She froze, pen still in hand, but didn't speak.

"Look—I get why you're reluctant. You thought he genuinely cared about you, and when he ghosted you, it hurt. And now it feels even worse, because it looks like he might have used you for information."

Emerald squirmed in her seat and avoided my eyes.

I leaned in. "Well, from one fool to another—you can tell me anything. Been there, done that. I know how it feels."

Her eyes widened. "And now Steven is back! What are you going to do? Do you believe he wants to make amends?"

I shrugged. "I don't know yet. He needs to turn himself in—that's what I told him. He has a meeting with his lawyers scheduled, and I want to hear what the plan is. I don't know *what* to do, to be honest. Part of me thinks I owe him a second chance because of the kids. On the other hand, fool me twice… You know the saying. Anyway, this isn't about me. We have bigger concerns."

"But he can't stay at the inn forever. You'll need to decide—"

"Emerald. Stop evading my question. We're talking about your love life now."

Her shoulders slumped. "There is no love life to speak of." She picked up her tea, leaned back, and blew on it. "Alaric and I met at an event at the Cirencester library.

He's very learned and has a passion for books. We connected over that immediately." A blush crept up her cheeks. "He leads an antiquarian book club."

I immediately wanted to ask how that connected to Maggie's rare-books background, but I didn't interrupt.

"He asked me out, and we went to dinner a few times. He was the perfect gentleman, though in hindsight… He never revealed much about himself. He's older—fifties, I think—and described himself as an Oxford man. He mentioned working in academia, in research. I assumed he still worked for Oxford University, but he never really confirmed it. He had this way of answering questions with more questions."

I scrunched my nose.

"Yes, I know," she said with a sigh. "It sounds irritating —and maybe it would have become so. But at the time, I was too in awe of him." She sipped her tea. "Anyway, he asked a lot about Fairwyck and its history. He was interested in visiting the library, so I invited him here. I was excited." She set the mug down on a stack of yellow legal paper filled with her looping handwriting. "This is my element. I wanted him to see me here. And I was nervous —I hadn't told him about my gift, and it can always… happen. A book might call to me. I was prepared to let it happen. To let him see…me."

She gave a sad little shrug, then straightened and met my eyes. "I'm glad he didn't witness it. He asked me about certain texts. He stayed down here, looking through some books, while I went upstairs. A book called to me, and I grabbed it to add to the stack I was putting together for Alaric. When I brought them down, he took the book— and only had eyes for it."

She sighed. "I'd been standing there, watching him, because I was debating whether to tell him how I'd found it. But when he noticed me looking, he closed the book. He seemed…annoyed. As if I'd been snooping. Which is ridiculous—it was a book from my library. I had literally just handed it to him. Then he gathered the books and said he'd borrow them and bring them back. I tried to make a joke—said he'd need a library card and the librarian's permission first."

"He took them anyway and just left?"

"No." Emerald shook her head. "Honestly, I would've let him take them if he'd reacted normally. But instead he took my joking seriously. Insisted he needed a card. I had to issue one right there. It was so awkward. And then he said he had to go. He wasn't rude. He still kissed me. But… he felt colder. Distant. I felt weird after he left. Like I'd done something wrong."

"Hmm." I drank my tea with her in silence for a moment. "And then you didn't hear back from him?"

"He never brought the books back either. It's been weeks." She pouted. "I sent him a reminder and issued a late fee last week."

"So you did try to contact him."

Emerald flushed. "Yes. I texted him and tried calling. I just…didn't understand. He could've said he wasn't inter-ested anymore. And he should have returned the books."

"So you mailed him the overdue notice," I said slowly, "which means…we have his address."

She jutted her chin out. "I'm not going there. I have some pride left."

"What was the book about?"

Emerald shuffled through her notes. *"Paths of the Ances-tors: Old Roads and Sacred Sites of Gloucestershire."*

"Hmm."

"Yeah, I thought it was about Roman roads and medieval churches. It clearly wasn't."

"When it called to you, what did you hear? What did it…talk about?"

She frowned. "Alaric was interested in ancient things. Really ancient. And the impression I got from the book was…old knowledge. And rituals."

I leaned forward and pointed to her notes. "Did it have these symbols in it?"

"Not that I could see. No—I don't think so. These sigils are about rituals, but not the church kind." Emerald looked up at me, expression tight with worry. "I'm afraid this is about dark magic. And this book"—she lifted the one by Alaric Hatherleigh—"is about that too. This isn't good, Liv. I helped this man. I don't know what with. And somehow it's connected to the inn." Her voice wavered. "Did he know that? That I live there? He never asked. Not once. I swear!"

Tears spilled down her cheeks.

"Oh, Em." I moved some papers aside, hunting for tissues.

I found tissues—but also something else.

The coin. The one with the symbol. The one Alaric had supposedly given her.

I held it up. "He gave this to you?"

Emerald turned beet red. "Actually…he didn't. He dropped it while he was here. I guess I just…wanted something to hold on to. To him."

I examined the symbol on the coin. I'd seen it before—not in the secret room, but recently…

Drake's notebook.

CHAPTER TWENTY-FOUR

With the constant chaos and all the new discoveries, I kept forgetting the things I'd already examined. I'd taken Drake's laptop and notebook, glanced at the camera footage, and skimmed the notebook—but I'd never truly tried to decipher his scribbles. And there were research files on his computer I still hadn't opened.

I told Emerald, "There were these symbols in his notebook. At the time they didn't make any sense to me, but now…they're like the sigils we found in the room. And one of them was this symbol." I held up the coin. "He circled it and added exclamation marks next to it."

"Okay," Emerald said, already gathering her papers. "I think we need to move this research session to your house. Let me pack all this up."

We took her car.

On the way to my cottage, it struck me that there was something else I'd put on the back burner for far too long.

When Emerald reached for the door handle, ready to step out, I touched her arm. "Wait. The kids are in there.

There's something…I haven't looked at yet. I prefer to not have Audrey and Blake around when I do."

I stared out the windshield into the dark, star-scattered sky. Without turning toward my cousin, I continued, "I took photos after Drake disappeared. Of his room. There's never been a right moment to look at them." Finally, I faced her. "The truth is, I was too scared. I'm supposed to embrace my gift, but sometimes…" I let the sentence fall apart.

Emerald, bless her heart, didn't push me. "Want to look at them together?" she asked softly.

I took the camera from my bag.

We huddled together, waiting for the display to light up.

"Here," I said once I'd found the sequence.

Emerald leaned in so close, her hair brushed my shoulder.

I tapped the screen.

The first image bloomed into view—a wide shot of Drake's room. And it was full of figures.

We gasped in unison.

The specters clung to the corners of the room—here a hunched back, there a raised shoulder. None of their faces were clearly visible.

"It's like…they're cowering," Emerald whispered.

I flipped to the next photo—close-ups.

A fragment of silver armor, dripping with water.

Then a woman, crouched, her neck at a wrong, painful angle. Her clasped hands made her look like a praying child. My chest ached at the sight of her. She wasn't threatening—she was terrified.

By the door lingered a man half-merged with shadow, hat brim low, coat black. I'd caught him in a half-profile, his expression anguished, his gaze fixed on the exit. He looked as if he longed to leave but couldn't.

Near the old bed—a faint glow at knee height.

"Can you zoom in?" Emerald breathed.

I tapped the plus button several times. The faint outline of a child appeared—upper body and hands cupping a candle, shielding its light. From what?

The last image was of the mirror—no ghosts anywhere near it. The photo was overexposed, but the light seemed to radiate from the center of the mirror itself, bleaching out the edges. The sigils on the frame were swallowed entirely.

I switched back to the first image.

My mouth went dry. I swallowed and finally voiced what we were both thinking.

"It looks like they're all angled away from the mirror, doesn't it? As if they're trying to get away from it."

"Yes." Emerald hugged her arms. "As if they're terrified of it. Why wouldn't they just leave?"

"They seem trapped. Maybe the mirror is holding them…or pulling them in." My stomach tightened. "This whole time, I've been scared of the ghosts haunting the inn. But it almost looks like…"

I licked my dry lips. "They're the ones being haunted."

Emerald rubbed her arms as though chilled, despite her thick parka, scarf, and hat. "You're right. The bad energy must be coming from the mirror. How did Mother and I never notice that?"

"Well, it must have been locked in that secret room all this time—its energy strong enough to draw ghosts to the inn, but still mostly contained. I already suspected there was some sort of magical ward in place, because the books in that room never called to you. Then Drake took the mirror out. Maybe he even…activated something. We still don't know what the sigils in Alaric's book mean. If I'm right, and Drake brought the book into the room and then forgot it there…"

"Then Drake must be connected to Alaric somehow. Isn't that weird?"

I shrugged. "He could've just had the book. If it deals with the paranormal, Drake would be interested."

"But the sigils on the wall, the mirror—some of them are in Alaric's book. So Alaric is connected to the inn and that room somehow. He never said anything to me about the Sacred Salmon. I thought he only used me to get access to certain texts…but what if it's bigger than that?" Emerald's voice cracked.

"Come on, let's go inside. It's freezing. I'll make cocoa —with marshmallows."

I switched off the camera and climbed out of the car. Emerald followed as I unlocked the door to the cottage.

I dropped my bag on the couch and set a saucepan of milk on the stove.

"There's another connection we need to consider," I said. "Maggie and Lucy turning up out of nowhere. Maggie introduced Drake to Gina—that's why he's filming at the Sacred Salmon in the first place. Maggie was staying in the inn the night before last. She acted surprised about the room, but…how well do we really know her? It could've been an act. The book might even be hers."

Emerald, paging through Drake's notebook on the table, murmured, "Hmm. I don't think so. This is Drake's notebook, right?"

"Yes. I looked at it, but I couldn't really make heads or tails of it." I mixed cocoa and sugar into the milk and stirred.

"He noted down symbols like the ones in Alaric's book," Emerald said. "I think it must have been Drake's copy. It makes sense—he found the room and took the mirror out. He didn't just want it as a spooky set piece for the series. He recognized the sigils from the book. He put the mirror in his room to copy the symbols—to study them."

As I poured the cocoa into our mugs and sprinkled marshmallows on top, I thought about that. "If he was that interested, why go to such lengths to keep it out of the episode? There's no footage—none I've seen. And the production company would've noticed the room. He could have been trapped in there, like Steven. They would've mentioned it regardless. A mysterious room with witchcraft symbols and old books? That would've stirred up more paranormal theories—better PR, even. Drake didn't just avoid getting anything related to that room or the symbols on camera—he actively tried to hide it."

"Hmm. You said he might have wanted to *discover* the room later in the episode."

"Maybe—properly, dramatically. But any earlier glimpses, or him studying the symbols, could've been edited out. No need to make such an effort to keep it off camera. It feels more like he didn't want anyone, including his production team, to know about it."

"In that case, maybe he was scared." Emerald lifted Drake's notebook. "I told you Alaric's book is about dark magic. Drake realized the inn was dangerous, and he—"

"Just ran?" I finished, frowning. "Without taking anything? Without using his car?"

Emerald deflated. "Yes, you're right. That part still doesn't make sense."

I shook my head, frustrated. "We keep going around in circles."

I handed Emerald her mug and sat beside her on the couch.

"I agree it makes sense that Alaric's book belonged to Dr. Drake. But why are you so quick to dismiss my suspicions about Maggie?" I asked. "You have to admit, her presence at the inn while all of this is going on…seems dubious. And Gina doesn't seem sure about her at all."

Emerald sighed. "It's complicated. She's her sister. She wants to believe the best. She wants to be the bigger person. But you're right—after everything that's happened, I think she regrets taking Maggie and Lucy in." She paused. "And I'm not dismissing your suspicions. It's just… I've talked to Lucy a lot, and she seems genuinely gentle. Her desire to reconnect with us feels real."

"Really?" I wrinkled my nose. "You don't find her… creepy?"

"Lucy's not creepy, Mom!" Audrey's voice cut in.

I jumped—both kids were coming downstairs, and I hadn't heard a thing until Audrey's indignant tone hit me.

"Hi, you two." I scrambled to amend myself. "No, no —not creepy. Just…quiet. She always appears out of nowhere, ready to soothe people. It's a little unnerving, that's all."

"That's her gift," Audrey said matter-of-factly. "Beltane says she has a special one."

"Her gift?" Emerald blinked, stepping forward to hug Audrey and Blake. "Maggie says Lucy doesn't have one."

"She doesn't recognize it," Audrey said simply. "Can I have cocoa too, Mom?"

"I'll make some more," I said.

"Nah, I'll do it," Blake said, already heading for the stove. "I like Lucy. I think her mother isn't very nice to her. She doesn't really…see her."

"I think we can all agree on that," Emerald said. "But we all know how complicated mother–daughter relation-ships can be. That doesn't make Maggie a bad person."

"I know," I admitted. "I just wish we could figure out her motives. I wanted Blake to draw what was going on inside her head the other night at dinner, but it didn't work out—Maggie practically interrogated the kids about their gifts. It would've been too obvious."

"Oh, I did draw something," Blake called from the kitchen.

"What? Why didn't you say so?" I blinked in surprise.

"Let me get my sketchpad." Blake finished the cocoa and set two mugs on the kitchen table. Audrey plopped into a chair and immediately began sipping hers.

Blake grabbed their bag, tugged out the sketchpad, and flipped it open. "It's not much—just an impression. I don't know if it'll tell you anything about Maggie."

They held it up.

It was a network of lines—curving, splitting, intersecting. Like a tangle of old roads. Or a maze. Or some kind of map.

"I only had my pencil, but the lines were sort of golden in her head," Blake explained.

I was about to shrug and say it didn't mean much—but then I saw Emerald's expression.

Her eyes were wide. Almost frightened.

"What is it?" I asked. "Do you recognize it?"

Emerald nodded slowly, and when she spoke her voice sounded hollow. "Yes. This was in the library book I gave Alaric. *Paths of the Ancestors*. I think…I think this is what he was looking for."

CHAPTER TWENTY-FIVE

I squeezed my eyes shut.

Another puzzle piece—another twist in Drake's disappearance. There were so many connections now that keeping track of them all felt like trying to hold fog in my hands.

I needed to think.

But a rustling sound snapped my concentration, and I opened my eyes again.

Emerald was putting on her parka.

"Where are you going?" I asked, startled.

"I have to warn my mother," Emerald said, frazzled and pale. "Clearly you were right, and Maggie is involved in all of this." She yanked on her gloves. "Who knows what she's up to—and she's home with my mother right now—"

"Wait!" I jumped up to stop her. "Let's think for a minute. I'm not sure confronting Maggie now is wise. We'd be showing our cards too early—loosely speaking, since we barely have any." I placed a gentle hand on her arm. "If we confront her, she'll just talk her way out of it. And all we'll accomplish is making her more careful in…whatever she's doing. She doesn't strike me as the type to slink away with her tail between her legs at the first hurdle."

Emerald hesitated mid-button. "But what if she's a danger to my mother?"

"I honestly don't think she is," I said softly. "She's her sister. And she's been in your house for days—if she meant harm, it would've happened already. Plus, Lucy's there too, and you all swear she's harmless."

"Yes, I suppose…" Emerald slowly removed her gloves and coat and collapsed back onto the sofa. "Then how do we find out what Maggie is up to?"

I stood, went to the kitchen drawer, rummaged around, and pulled out a notepad and pen. Then I returned to the couch and sat beside her.

The kids—who'd clearly been listening the entire time—brought their cocoa closer and crowded around as I started writing.

"I think we need to keep track of everything connected to Dr. Drake and his disappearance. I keep forgetting important bits. Now we've also got this book Alaric Hatherleigh borrowed…and the golden web Blake saw in Maggie's head." I wrote MIRROR at the top of the page. "I think we need a proper list. Patterns. Connections."

"Wow, you're finally getting the hang of this, Mom," Blake teased, poking my arm. "DI Farrow would be so impressed."

I rolled my eyes and refocused. "Let's start somewhere simple."

I tapped the word mirror. "The mirror wasn't originally in Drake's room. He found the hidden chamber, took the mirror out—probably fascinated by the symbols."

"And he likely recognized them from Alaric's book," Emerald added.

"Exactly." I wrote *mirror symbols* beneath the first heading, then sketched the symbol from the coin. "We need to learn more about the mirror and the sigils. Drake circled one in his notebook—the same as the one on Alaric's coin. It has to be important."

Emerald opened Drake's notebook on the coffee table and leafed through it until she found the circled symbol.

I continued, "Speaking of Alaric Hatherleigh—he courted you to get information about something—"

"What's courted?" Audrey asked, nose scrunched like a curious mouse.

Emerald went pink. I stepped in quickly. "It means he took Emerald out on a few dates. Anyway," I said, redirecting, "he wanted information—the book with the golden web. But he never once asked about your home. Never asked about the Sacred Salmon. Right, Emerald?"

"He never mentioned it," she answered quickly. "He never asked about my family or anything personal. But you're right—the coin symbol and the sigils in his book match the ones Drake drew…" She touched the notebook. "He must be connected to this."

I jotted down *Alaric Hatherleigh*.

"What was the book with the golden web called again?" I asked.

"*Paths of the Ancestors*," Emerald replied, checking her notes to find the subtitle.

"We need to find out more about it," I said, writing the title down.

Blake was already scrolling. "I'm checking online. Maybe there's a summary out there…"

"And then," I continued, "there's Maggie."

Under her name, I began a list:

Necromancer

Performed dark ritual in youth; went wrong

Disinherited by the Seven family

Stayed away for decades, returned just before Drake's disappearance—introduced Gina to Drake

Knows about Paths of the Ancestors—*has golden web pattern in her mind (Blake's drawing)*

Blake spoke up. "I found the title on a couple of rare-book sites, but every listing says sold or not currently available. No summary. It looks like you had the only copy Hatherleigh could get his hands on, Emerald."

"I'm such an idiot for giving it to him," Emerald groaned, eyes watery, cheeks blotchy. "Why did I do that?"

"Hey," I said gently, touching her arm. She was trembling. "You couldn't have known he'd ghost you afterward. And we don't even know what he's done with it—if anything."

"But he must have shown Maggie," Emerald insisted. "She knew the content. And she convinced my mother to let Drake film in the inn. We don't know why or how it's connected, but it can't be a coincidence."

"Hang on," I said, frowning at my notes. "Maggie is a rare-books specialist. We know more copies existed years ago. It's at least possible she owned her own copy. So it doesn't automatically mean Alaric showed it to her."

Emerald nodded slowly. "There's a small possibility. But Alaric told me he runs a book club for antiquarian texts. Maggie being a rare-book specialist is…another point of connection between them. Unless"—she swallowed—"unless Alaric made the whole book club thing up just to justify being interested in older volumes from my library—because he was after that one specific book…"

"They have something else in common," Blake said. They were holding Alaric Hatherleigh's book. "This is clearly some sick, dark stuff. And we heard Maggie was into dark magic too, so…"

I gently plucked the book from their hands. "I'm not sure I want you handling this. In fact, I'd prefer both of you stay away from anything involving dark magic."

Blake waved me off and returned to their phone, but Audrey looked genuinely frightened.

"Can it hurt us, Mom? The book—or the mirror, or the drawings in the inn? Are they dangerous for Aunt Gina and…" Her eyes went wide. "Dad! He's in the inn. And he doesn't know about any of this. He's completely defenseless. Mom—we have to get him out of there!" She jumped up.

"It's okay, sweetheart, it's okay," I said quickly. "We're not going over there right now. There might be reporters again—I don't want you photographed. And we can't warn Maggie yet. Besides…where else would he go?"

"He can stay here," Audrey insisted, hands flapping, still rattled. "We have to make sure he's okay!"

"I'm going to check on him later," I assured her. "But how about I call him now? Would that help?"

She nodded, her panic easing a fraction.

"Come sit with me." I guided her to the kitchen table and pulled out my phone. I'd gotten Steven's burner number earlier. I hit "call" and put him on speaker.

When he answered, I said, "Hey—Audrey really wanted to check on you. She's here with me. You're doing all right, aren't you?"

"Yes, of course," he replied smoothly. He sounded far more relaxed than he had earlier.

"You're still at the inn, right?" I asked, suspicious. With Gina's bottomless hospitality, I half-expected she'd lured him over for tea and biscuits.

"Yes, yes. Still here. But I've had some visitors, so it's not so bad."

"Maggie?" My pulse spiked.

"No—Lucy. She brought me homemade food. Very kind girl. And your aunt checked on me too. We spent a bit of time together playing a game. Quite good fun, actually."

"A…game?"

"Tarot, I believe it's called."

"Tarot's not a game, it's—never mind." The thought of Steven doing tarot with my aunt was bizarre enough to short-circuit my brain. "So you're holding up all right?"

"Yes, yes. The cat is keeping me company too."

"That's Beltane," Audrey said, visibly relieved. "I'm glad she's protecting you, Dad."

He laughed. "Sure."

"See?" I told Audrey. "He's perfectly fine. No need to worry, love. Now let me talk to him alone for a moment." I took the phone off speaker and shooed her back to the living room.

Steven lowered his voice. "Why did Audrey think I need protection—and that a cat could guard me?"

"Ghosts," I said lightly. I wasn't about to tell him anything about black magic or predatory symbols. And frankly, he was getting a little too comfortable. I liked him better when he was spooked—it made the power dynamic feel…finally even.

"Cat familiars help ward spirits off," I added breezily. "Seen any ghosts yet?"

"Uh…not really. But it's spooky as hell up here."

"Anyway," I said, "I forgot to ask what time the meeting with your lawyers is. You need my laptop, right? And I'd like to be—"

"Oh, that's all right. Lucy lent me hers. Everything's set up. It's in five minutes. You won't make it here in time."

"Five minutes?" I blinked at the oven clock. What sort of meeting started at twenty minutes before the hour? But then again, lawyers did love to monetize every spare minute. "I wish you'd told me—we're in the middle of something over here, and—"

"It's actually more like two minutes," he cut in. "I'd better go. Don't worry, I'll tell you all about it tomorrow."

"Well, if you——"

"Bye!" He hung up.

I stared at the phone, frowning. I really didn't appreciate how he'd handled that. Steven knew I wanted details about his legal trouble. And he absolutely needed to give me the law firm's name, a contact person I could verify, and a concrete timeline for turning himself in. If he didn't, I'd contact a lawyer myself.

"Hey, Mom—guess what?" Blake called from the couch.

I walked over. "What is it?"

"I thought I'd check on Alaric Hatherleigh's book too," they said. "But I can't find anything about it online. It doesn't have an ISBN or publisher, and it's nowhere."

"I told Blake it must be self-published," Emerald said.

"Interesting," I mused. "Considering the content…he might only give it to select people. People *in the know*. People with a similar interest in the paranormal."

"You mean Alaric might have given Dr. Drake a copy himself?" Emerald asked.

"Why not?" I picked up the pen and drew a line between *Hatherleigh* and *Drake* in the notebook. "Drake was scholarly—everyone says he lived for his research. It's entirely possible he was part of Alaric's little book club, no? And Maggie, with her rare-book background and her… enthusiasm for black magic…" I drew another line connecting *Maggie* to *Hatherleigh*. "She could easily be part of it too. Maggie introduced Drake to Gina—and no one has yet asked the obvious question: How does a rare-book dealer know a TV ghost hunter well enough to bring him to the Sacred Salmon in the first place?" I connected *Maggie* and *Drake*, completing a neat triangle.

"From the book club!" Emerald breathed, as though she'd discovered the Holy Grail.

I held up a hand. "Maybe. It's only a theory. But look

—Drake had Alaric's dark-magic book." I added another line. "The sigils in that book match the ones on the mirror and in the secret room." More lines. "Alaric wanted *Paths of the Ancestors*. Maggie knew its contents. Maggie raises the shadows of authors; Drake hunts ghosts." Line after line, the page became a tangle of connections.

Finally, I stared down at the web. "One coincidence is nothing. But this many? I think it's safe to say Drake, Hatherleigh, and Maggie are all after something—and whatever it is, it's tied to the inn."

I looked up at Emerald. "Drake has tons of research on his laptop. Something there might help us—or even confirm he knew Alaric."

Emerald pulled the laptop closer. "I'm happy to go through his files. They cross-reference the sigils and Alaric's book anyway. I've already made a little headway."

"Great—but I can help," I said.

"That's okay. You handle the ghosts. That's your specialty, after all."

"My—what ghosts?" I said, a little too quickly.

"The ones in the inn," Emerald replied, as though explaining arithmetic to a toddler.

"Yeah, Mom," Audrey chimed in. "You have to photograph them. Find out why they're so freaked out by that weird mirror."

"And ask if they saw anything," Blake added.

"Yes—my mother told you to interrogate the witnesses," Emerald said, amused.

"Oh. Um. Yes." A cold shiver ran through me at the thought of those terrified figures cowering in the corners of Drake's room. I absolutely did not want to go back there tonight. "I will. But we need more information about the mirror first. It could be dangerous. I'm not messing with it until we know more."

"I'll prioritize identifying the mirror sigils," Emerald promised.

I nodded, relieved. Steven was still at the inn, and even though he now accepted the paranormal, I wasn't ready to perform my…"ghost-thing" in front of him.

"The other thing we need to do," I said, shifting back into business mode, "is get *Paths of the Ancestors* back from Hatherleigh. We need to know what's in it and how it connects to the inn."

I tapped the page decisively. "I know you've tried contacting him—"

Emerald's eyes filled instantly. "I can't face him, Liv." Her voice was barely above a whisper. "I already tried. I was on my way to his house yesterday, but I turned around before I got there."

My children exchanged alarmed glances, clearly confused by the sudden emotion.

"That's fine," I said quickly—too brightly. "I'll handle it. I'll drive over there tomorrow morning and get the book back."

Secretly, I was pleased. It was a clear task I could tackle —one that didn't involve stepping into a haunted inn at night.

"And what can we do, Mom?" Audrey asked.

I blinked at her. "You?"

"Yes," Blake said. "We want to help too."

I chewed my lip, considering. Involving them was dangerous. I hated the thought of dragging them deeper into whatever darkness Maggie and Hatherleigh had stirred up. But they were already entangled—through Maggie, Lucy, their gifts, and the strange family ties holding us all together.

And…there were things they could do.

"All right," I said slowly. "Audrey—why don't you talk to Ethel about Maggie? Maybe she knows more about why

Maggie was banished. Gina never told us much, did she, Emerald? Do you know more?"

My cousin shook her head.

"On it!" Audrey shouted, already sprinting upstairs in search of the cat.

"And you, Blake…maybe talk to Lucy. Ask if she'd like to go out tomorrow after school. She must be stir-crazy stuck in that house. She might open up to you about her mother."

Blake nodded thoughtfully. They were sensitive. Lucy, who didn't even realize she had a gift, just might reveal something around them without meaning to.

Audrey tromped back down the stairs, deflated. "I can't find Ethel."

"She must be out. Try again after school tomorrow, all right?"

Audrey nodded.

"Now," I said, standing and heading to the fridge, "let's figure out dinner. Emerald, you're welcome to stay."

"I should really start on this research," she murmured, flipping through her notes distractedly.

"Which you will. But first you need to eat," I said reasonably, grabbing tomatoes. "Did everyone finish their homework?"

Two guilty faces told me everything.

"Upstairs," I said firmly. "You can get it done before dinner."

They trudged up the stairs.

I paused with a tomato in my hand and exhaled slowly.

For the first time in days, I felt…steady. Not calm—not even close—but steady.

We finally had a plan. Tasks. A direction.

After days of lies, secrets, ghosts, hidden rooms, break-ins, paparazzi, and my fugitive ex-husband living in the world's creepiest B&B, I finally had something resembling control. A fragile structure, yes—but it was something.

I started chopping tomatoes. When I turned around to put them in a salad bowl, Emerald was still hunched over Drake's notebook, surrounded by pages of notes and Alaric's book.

"Find anything?" I asked casually, grabbing mozzarella from the fridge.

"I'm not sure," she murmured.

Something in her tone made the hairs on my arms lift.

I wiped my hands on a tea towel and walked toward her. Emerald didn't look up. Her finger hovered over a page in Alaric's book.

"Here," she said quietly. "This symbol—the one from the coin. And the one Drake circled."

My stomach dipped. "Yes?"

Emerald swallowed. Her voice came out small and strangely flat, as if she wished she hadn't found it at all.

"It's not just a sigil. According to this…it's part of a ritual. A very old one."

"What kind of ritual?" I whispered.

Emerald looked up at me then, eyes wide behind her glasses.

"It's meant to open a door, Liv." She hesitated. "A door for the dead."

CHAPTER TWENTY-SIX

The next morning, I called my boss at WLA, Judith Winters.

I briefly considered pretending to be sick, but lying felt wrong—and unnecessary.

"Judith, a personal matter has come up, and I'd like to take the rest of the week off. If that's not possible, I understand."

"Is this about what happened at the Sacred Salmon?" Judith asked.

"Sort of…and something connected to it."

A quiet pause. Then Judith's voice turned uncharacteristically warm. "I get it. Sometimes family comes first. I appreciate you being straight with me. I have someone who can cover today, at least. Let me get back to you about the weekend."

I breathed out, relieved. "Thanks, Judith. I really appreciate it."

I hesitated. Judith didn't know about my paranormal life. But she did know Alaric Hatherleigh, and with him now tangled in our investigation, I needed whatever scraps of information I could get. The conversation felt like walking into a minefield.

"One more thing," I blurted out before I could lose my nerve—or before she could hang up, because Judith was a busy woman, and I'd stalled too long already. "You said at book club that you know Alaric Hatherleigh—the man Emerald dated a few times. What can you tell me about him?"

"Oh—I don't really know him that well," Judith said. "We run into each other at charity events sometimes. His family is very well off. I'm more acquainted with his sister, Mabel Scarboro. She's a professor of history at Oxford. Quite a formidable woman."

I heard the fond smile in Judith's voice. She admired strong women—and had made it her life's mission to help others escape toxic relationships and stand on their own.

"Alaric has good taste. Very cultured. We talk about restaurants and art, but never anything personal. Although…" She trailed off.

"Yes?" I urged, detecting something juicy.

"I'm not sure I should say," Judith murmured.

"You know he basically ghosted Emerald," I said softly. "It really hurt her. But she was quite smitten and is…well, considering letting him back into her life."

I silently apologized to Emerald for the lie.

Judith's tone cooled instantly. "If he behaved so disrespectfully, I hope she does no such thing. I've heard he's the bad egg of the family, although the Hatherleighs have the money to hide that sort of thing well."

My pulse picked up. "Bad egg how? What did he do?"

"I'm not entirely sure. Something to do with his academic title—I believe it's bought. I think he's employed at Oxford University, but he's not actually a lecturer. Nobody really knows what he does. He also deals with antiquarian books, although it might be more of a passion project.

Rumor has it that his family forbade him from talking about his work in public, or they'd cut him off financially."

"Hmm."

Not useful in the way I'd hoped—and it put a dent in my plan to snoop around Oxford if he didn't truly work there.

"Okay, thanks, Judith. I'll let Emerald know."

"If she needs to talk, she can call me anytime," Judith added.

"She'll appreciate that. Thanks again for being so flexible with my work schedule."

We said goodbye, and I hung up.

I sipped my coffee thoughtfully. My plan for the morning suddenly felt much less solid. I could still try to retrieve the library book from Hatherleigh, but what were the odds he'd just hand it over?

And even though I was grateful Judith was being so understanding, a queasy feeling crept up at the thought of my work once again taking a back seat to an investigation. Historically…that has never ended well.

My spiraling was interrupted by the clatter of feet on the stairs. Blake bounded down, school bag slung over one shoulder.

I stood and handed them their lunch.

"Where's your sister?" I asked, checking the time. "It's almost time to leave."

"She was in your room. Talking to the cat," Blake said dryly.

I stepped to the bottom of the stairs. "Audrey! You'll be late!"

She came down quickly, worry etched across her face.

"What's wrong?" I asked, instantly alert.

"I spoke to Ethel," she said. "About Maggie."

I glanced at the clock again, grabbed her school bag,

stuffed her lunch and water bottle inside. "You spoke to her now? I thought we said after school."

Audrey ignored the question. "Ethel said not to let Maggie into the house, Mom!"

I nearly dropped the backpack. Blake, thankfully, caught it.

"In this house?" I said. "Why would she come here? And why would it matter?"

"I don't know, Mom," Audrey said, distressed. "But you said if I don't come down now, I'll be late!"

Blake helped her into her coat—she was too shaken to manage it herself—and they were already running late.

"Yes, yes—go. Go." I ushered them out.

I threw on my coat, stepped into boots, grabbed my bag with my keys, locked the door, and hurried after them down the path toward the bus stop.

"So Ethel knows about Maggie being back in Fairwyck?" I asked, breath puffing in the cold morning air.

"Yes," Audrey said. "Remember Aunt Gina was here that night you had book club at the library? She said something to Ethel while we were watching a movie. We didn't hear her then, but Ethel told me. Aunt Gina said she wished Ethel were still alive so she could ask her for advice. She could've just asked me to talk to Ethel, Mom! Why didn't she?"

"Well, she didn't want us to know about Maggie yet," I said carefully, choosing my words so the children wouldn't panic. "She didn't want us involved…"

I let the sentence die unfinished—*involved in whatever Maggie was up to* hung unspoken between us.

"Anyway," I continued, "are you sure Ethel meant Maggie shouldn't come into our cottage? Not the inn?"

"No," Audrey said, exasperated. "Our home, Mom. Why would she say that about the inn?"

The bus rounded the corner.

"I don't know, sweetheart. You'll have to ask her again later."

Audrey looked anxious. I pulled her into a quick hug.

"It's okay. Don't worry. Everything's going to be fine. Maggie hasn't come by the cottage at all—she's not going to start today. Maybe Ethel meant something else, or it's a misunderstanding. We'll clear it up."

She gave me a wobbly smile and climbed into the bus after her sibling.

I waved brightly as she found a seat and looked back at me through the window.

The moment the headlights passed, my smile dropped.

I turned and power-walked back home.

Maggie had mentioned our cottage multiple times. At our first meeting, in the inn at night, she'd even asked if it was for sale. At dinner, she'd looked almost affronted by Aunt Gina's comment that we were taking good care of Ethel's place. There had been tension—a ripple I'd ignored.

I'd assumed Maggie simply wanted to return to Fair-wyck. The cottage had been in the Seven family for generations; maybe she felt it was her birthright. Ethel's sister did have more familial claim than I did.

But I never truly believed she wanted to live here. Maggie carried herself like a woman with money—real money, not smoke and mirrors. She was elegant in that effortless way only the wealthy managed. Lucy, too, had understated but expensive clothes, shoes, and jewelry. I couldn't picture either of them happily settling in this crooked, cramped little house with its unreliable heater and drafty windows.

And anyway, I had inherited it fair and square. Even if Maggie wanted it, she had no legal claim.

So why would Ethel be adamant Maggie must never enter?

Back inside, I dropped my bag, shrugged off my coat, and didn't bother removing my shoes before racing upstairs.

Ethel lay curled on my bed exactly where Audrey had left her.

The orange cat blinked up at me, her silky fur warm beneath my hand as I stroked her back.

"All right," I murmured, "what about Maggie? Are we in danger? Is she dangerous?"

Of course, Ethel didn't answer. But her golden eyes darkened, and a sorrowful heaviness settled over her face.

Judith's words about Alaric echoed back—the bad egg of the family. Was Maggie the bad egg of ours?

The idea made my chest hurt. It must be devastating for Gina to face the truth about her sister. And for Ethel— if she still had any human awareness inside that feline form —it had to be just as bad. I understood the impulse to give someone so close a second chance, not wanting to accept their faults. It was the same instinct tugging at me with Steven, no matter how hard I tried to ignore it.

I wanted desperately to know what Maggie had done. But I'd have to wait until Audrey could speak to Ethel again. Or hope Blake learned something from Lucy this afternoon.

I scratched gently along Ethel's spine. "What is it about this cottage, Aunt Ethel?"

She only closed her eyes and tucked her nose under her paws.

Maybe she was just a cat right now. Or maybe she was refusing to say more.

I sighed and headed downstairs.

I grabbed my coat again. Reaching for my notebook on the coffee table, my gaze snagged on the fireplace.

A memory flickered.

I moved the screen aside.

The markings I'd seen Ethel scratch into the floorboards were still there.

My stomach tightened.

I knelt, opened my notebook, and copied the marks to the best of my ability. I erased, redrew, corrected angles—my drawing skills were nowhere near Blake's—but eventually I managed a reasonable reproduction.

They weren't scratches.

They were sigils.

And they resembled the symbols on the mirror, in the secret room, and in Alaric's book.

A chill rolled through me.

I recoiled from the fireplace as Emerald's words from last night surged back. The sigil on the coin, the symbol in Drake's notebook—possibly one he'd copied from the mirror—was tied to a dark ritual meant to open a door for the dead.

Surely this couldn't be the same thing…could it?

The last thing I wanted was that kind of door in my own home. But why on earth would Ethel create one?

My hands suddenly unsteady, I snapped a picture of the page and sent it to Emerald.

Can you figure out what these sigils are? Same style as in Alaric's book?

Then I slid the notebook back into my bag, replaced the fireplace screen, and headed out to the car.

Once inside, I took a breath, opened the notebook again, and flipped past the sigils to the page with the address Emerald had written down—the one Alaric had given for his library card.

I typed it into my phone's GPS.

Before leaving, I cast an uncertain glance back at the cottage and checked my phone, hoping for a reply from Emerald. Nothing yet—she hadn't read my message.

Shaking off a creeping sense of unease, I started driving.

~

I'd expected some gloomy scholar's hideaway—ivy-strangled stone walls, heavy curtains, maybe a gargoyle leering from the roofline.

Instead, I found a pristine modern home in a neat Oxford cul-de-sac, framed by a white picket fence and blooming rosebushes. A welcome mat instructed *Mind the Gap in Your Logic*.

My palms were sweating by the time I rang the bell.

"Here goes nothing," I muttered.

The door swung open to reveal a woman in her sixties with a severe gray bob and the posture of a retired general.

"Yes?" she said, clipped and cool.

"Good morning." I attempted my friendliest smile. "I'm looking for Alaric Hatherleigh."

Her frown deepened. "That's my brother."

So this was the formidable Mabel Scarboro.

"He gave this as his address when he applied for a library card," I explained.

"Yes, he lives with us," she said, a hint of impatience in her tone. "He's not in. Did you want to leave a message?"

"That's very kind, Mrs. ....?"

"Scarboro."

"Mrs. Scarboro. Lovely to meet you. As I said, I'm from the Fairwyck library—"

"And you are?"

"Hmm?"

"Your name?" She regarded me with cool, steel-gray eyes.

"Uh...Liv Grantham." I couldn't come up with a fake

219

name on the spot. When she requested my ID, I was suddenly very glad I hadn't tried.

I rummaged in my bag until I found my ID card and handed it over.

She frowned. "I meant an employee ID."

"Oh." I tried a pleasant smile. "We don't bother with that in Fairwyck. It's a small library—one full-time employee and the rest of us are volunteers." Not entirely a lie; I had volunteered to retrieve an overdue book, after all. A bit more confidently, I added, "We're reviewing overdue loans, and I'm here to retrieve some books Dr. Hatherleigh has had out for…rather a while."

One eyebrow arched.

"Oxford libraries don't send collectors," Mabel said dryly. "Fairwyck, you say?" She returned my ID, and I slipped it back into my bag. "Yes, I recall it now. Quite an adequate library for such a small place. You lot take your books very seriously."

"We do," I said, resisting the urge to laugh nervously. "There's a waiting list for the volumes he borrowed."

She pressed her lips together—clearly a woman who found rule-breaking personally offensive.

"How long overdue?"

"Several weeks."

She shook her head and rolled her eyes. From all accounts, Hatherleigh was an impressive man, but he had nothing on his sister. I was getting severe *my younger brother is such an irresponsible child* vibes. That was clearly the role he played in his family, if the rumors Judith had heard were to be believed.

"Wait here."

She vanished down a set of stairs. I heard muffled grumbling, cupboards opening, drawers banging shut. Finally, she returned with a small stack of books.

"These were in his room. They all have your library's stamp."

The top volume read *Sacred Geometry in Regency Landscape Planning*.

Not exactly bedtime reading, but I prayed *Paths of the Ancestors* was among them.

"Thank you," I said, taking the stack.

"You're welcome. Now if you'll excuse me—I need to get to work."

She grabbed her coat and briefcase, locked the door, and we walked down the drive together.

"Have a nice day," I said.

"You too." She climbed into a gleaming Mercedes and drove away.

I continued to my car, slid into the driver's seat, and placed the books beside me.

And there it was—*Paths of the Ancestors*.

A thrill ran through me as I opened it. The illustration Emerald had mentioned unfolded across the page: golden lines twisting and crisscrossing like Blake's drawing—but beneath them, faint place names etched onto a map.

I snapped several photos, zooming in until the text was legible.

Flipping to the start of the chapter, I found the title—ley lines.

I skimmed while taking more photos.

Ley lines: invisible channels of ancient Earth energy connecting sacred sites, stone circles, burial mounds, Roman roads, old churches —places of power. Used for ritual purposes, navigation, spiritual energy. Modern occultists saw them as conduits amplifying psychic gifts, hauntings, or darker things.

Lovely.

When I finished, I paused, thinking hard, then pulled up Mabel Scarboro's Oxford University profile. Judith had been right—Mabel was a respected historian.

But Alaric?

Not listed anywhere.

I searched again. And again.

Finally, I found him—not as staff, but as a doctoral student. That was…unexpected. And suspicious.

I texted Emerald, attaching the photos:

Something for you to dig into—I'll bring the book later. Also, Alaric lives in his sister's basement. She works at Oxford, but he's only listed as a PhD student. I'm heading to the university to check him out.

I saw her typing back immediately.

The sigils you sent me aren't in Alaric's book. But I found something anyway. They resemble the marks painted in the hidden room at the inn. Liv—I think they're for protection.

Protection.

A cold prickle ran up my spine.

Why, exactly, would our little cottage need protection?

CHAPTER TWENTY-SEVEN

The history department at Oxford looks exactly like you'd imagine: grand old stone, stained-glass stairwells, and students in tweed arguing about Crusader logistics over to-go lattes.

I'd taken more care with my appearance than usual this morning—brushed my hair, put on lipstick, even chose a respectable wrap dress.

A mistake.

Oxford history students dress in varying degrees of professor-chic: cable-knit jumpers in *historically accurate beige* or *monastery gray*, oversized scarves meant to imply tortured genius, leather satchels large enough to smuggle a medieval manuscript, and hair deliberately styled to look as though they'd been up all night arguing about Charlemagne. I thought one or two were wearing lipstick until I realized the stains were from last night's red wine.

Meanwhile, I looked like I was headed to a parent–teacher conference, not an undercover academic sting operation.

I wandered the corridors for a while, peeking into alcoves and scanning notice boards plastered with advertisements for things like fellowships, seminars, and a lecture titled *Death Rituals in Early Medieval Britain.*

Cheerful.

I grabbed a cappuccino at the small department café and was just about to sit down when I spotted Mabel Scarboro rounding the corner, marching purposefully toward the counter. I ducked so fast, I sloshed half the cappuccino over my hand. Students at the next table stared at me as if I were an unusual specimen worthy of cataloging. I waved them off like an embarrassing aunt.

Luckily, Mabel took her beverage to go, and it looked as if I'd acted fast enough—she hadn't spotted me.

I retreated to the bathroom to run my scorched hand under cold water while sipping what was left of my cappuccino. Then I braved the boring brown hallways again.

After hours of useless loitering and asking random students about Alaric—more staring, zero responses—I was ready to give up.

I scanned the study area for one last attempt.

A small knot of students—two men and one severe-looking girl—sat clustered around a table littered with open laptops and too many half-finished coffees. They regarded me the way one might regard a stray terrier begging for scraps.

I squared my shoulders. "Excuse me," I began. "I'm trying to locate Dr. Alaric Hatherleigh."

The three exchanged a look—one of those significant academic looks, a blend of disdain and gossip.

One of the men snorted. "He's not a doctor yet."

The girl lifted the corner of her mouth. "I think he is. He's a mature student—this is his second degree. Or third."

The other man, wearing a blue button-down, crooked tie, and unfashionable sideburns, scoffed. "I'm a mature student. That means I worked before coming back. I don't think Hatherleigh's done an honest day's work in his life. He's more of an…eternal student."

The girl flushed. "He takes his academic pursuits seriously. And if he doesn't need to work, why should he?"

The first man rolled his eyes. "He knows how to charm young, naïve women, that's for sure."

The girl shot him a glare sharp enough to decapitate a medieval king, then stormed off.

Regret flickered over Sideburns's face. "That was unnecessary. You're just annoyed he didn't invite you to his circle."

The other man waved a dismissive hand. "I don't care about his little club. It's just a bunch of self-important people pretending they've discovered some new"—he made aggressive air quotes—"'historic sources.'"

"Some of those sources have been published," Sideburns countered. "Publishing's about who you know. And Hatherleigh cultivates connections."

"Did you read the articles?" the first man asked. "It's all occult nonsense. Not credible scholarship."

Occult.

My pulse quickened.

Before I could ask anything, both men abruptly gathered their things and left, leaving me with more questions and a sinking feeling that this trip might be a colossal waste of time.

I drifted toward a seating area by the window—clusters of chairs, soft chatter, students highlighting textbooks with terrifying intensity.

Maybe someone else knew something?

I was about to approach a pair of students when a breathy voice whispered in my ear. "You're interested in Hatherleigh's circle?"

I turned sharply.

A young woman stood beside me—loose cardigan, long skirt, curls like a nest of thorns, and eyes that were… too knowing.

"Um…yes," I managed. "Do you know something about it? Have you been to one of the meetings?"

She just stared. Unblinking. As if waiting for a signal.

I swallowed, and just as I was about to back away, she murmured, "You've got the sight, haven't you?"

My heart stuttered.

"I—I don't know what you mean—"

She smiled, revealing crooked, yellowish teeth. "I have it too. Hatherleigh likes that. He wants people like us. For the rituals."

My mouth went dry. "Rituals? At his antiquarian club?"

She reached into her bag, tore a scrap from a notepad, scribbled something, and handed it to me.

"This is where we meet. Midnight tonight."

An Oxford address.

She leaned in, her breath a pungent cloud of garlic. "The password is *speculum*."

I recoiled—and not because of her breath.

Because *speculum* meant mirror.

The password to Alaric's occult club was the Latin word for mirror.

My stomach dropped.

I looked up, meaning to ask her more, but she was gone.

Instead, DI Farrow stood directly in front of me, mustache preened to perfection, wearing the smug expression of a man who'd found his favorite chew toy again.

Beside him stood Jamie.

And beside Jamie—

Oh god.

Professor Mabel Scarboro, her expression crisp with indignation.

"Miss Grantham," she said in a voice that could cut glass. "You were at my house this morning—ostensibly to retrieve my brother's overdue books. Yet here you are, following me to my place of work. Are you stalking me? Or is it Alaric you're after?"

My mouth opened. Closed. Opened again.

Jamie lifted his hands, trying to mediate. "Professor, I'm sure there's a reasonable explanation—"

"Oh, I look forward to hearing it," she snapped.

DI Farrow twirled the end of his mustache, far too pleased with himself. "Professor Scarboro contacted me the moment she realized you'd turned up at her residence under false pretenses."

"I did not—" I sputtered.

"She spotted you again, here at Oxford, lurking near her department. Naturally, she grew concerned."

Mabel sniffed. "Detective Inspector Farrow is an acquaintance of mine. We met at the police commissioner's anniversary celebration. When you said Fairwyck, I remembered he's stationed there. I called him. He confirmed you are already known to the Fairwyck police."

Brilliant. Thank you, Farrow.

I forced a brittle smile. "This is all a misunderstanding. I really did retrieve the overdue books—as a volunteer for the library. You can call my cousin Emerald. She asked me to do it when she heard I was going to Oxford anyway."

Jamie frowned. "And you're here because…?"

"I'm meeting a friend," I said quickly.

"A friend?" Jamie repeated, suspicion sharpening his tone. "Here? At Oxford?"

Before I could fabricate a name, a voice behind me chimed sweetly. "She means me."

I nearly jumped.

Yellow-Teeth Girl had reappeared, smiling like a cat watching a mouse.

Jamie blinked. "You two…know each other?"

"Oh yes," she said cheerfully. "We're in the same tarot circle. Very advanced stuff."

She winked at me.

Winked.

Jamie's expression shut down instantly. He absolutely did not believe her. Or me.

Farrow, however, nodded sagely. "Ah yes. The Seven family and their psychic hobbies. It's all over the news."

Mabel's brow furrowed. "Seven? But she said her name was Grantham."

"Oh, that's her married name," Farrow supplied helpfully. "Her maiden name is Seven. She's related to the family who owns the inn where Dr. Drake disappeared. Her husband"—he paused for dramatic effect—"is a criminal fugitive."

For the love of—

But Mabel had seized on something else entirely. "You're related to the inn?" she asked sharply. "That inn?"

I straightened, heat prickling under my collar. "My aunt owns it, yes. Dr. Drake happened to disappear while staying there. My family had nothing to do with it. Everything else is the media sensationalizing the case."

Silence stretched.

Finally, Mabel drew in a long, frosty breath. "Well. If your…friend…confirms your presence here is benign, I have nothing further to say."

Yellow-Teeth Girl nodded solemnly. "Very benign."

With visible reluctance, Farrow let the matter drop. Jamie gave me one more searching, wounded look before turning to leave with the others.

When they were gone, I sagged against the wall.

"Thanks," I whispered.

Yellow-Teeth Girl grinned. "Come to the meeting. Midnight. Hatherleigh will want to meet you. Trust me."

She drifted off, humming to herself.

I left the building and headed for my car.

I felt wrung out, as though I'd narrowly escaped disaster—but also quietly triumphant. My investigation had finally turned up a real lead. And since my stomach was rumbling, I decided I deserved a celebratory lunch.

I stopped at the first decent Italian chain restaurant I spotted and indulged in pizza and tiramisu.

When I got back to my car, my phone rang.

Jamie.

Instantly, I regretted the tiramisu. My stomach lurched.

"Hey, Jamie," I answered, throat tight.

"Liv," he said quietly, "what in heaven's name are you up to?"

I closed my eyes. "What do you mean? Nothing at all. I was just visiting a friend in Oxford—"

"I know you're lying."

CHAPTER TWENTY-EIGHT

My vision blurred.

"What do you mean?" I said weakly.

"About meeting that girl at Oxford University. I don't know why that random person played along, but—"

"Um, no, I really was having a chat with her."

Not a total lie. I hadn't gone there to meet her…but I had talked to her.

Jamie was having none of my half-truths.

"Oh yeah? What's her name?"

"Um…Yell-ahh." The first thing that popped into my head—inspired by the girl's yellow-toothed smile.

"Yeller? Are you kidding me? Like the dog in that old movie?"

Jamie sounded stone-cold.

He had never spoken to me in that tone before. I wriggled in my seat, deeply uneasy.

"No. Yella. It's Polish."

"She didn't sound Polish."

"On her mother's side." I struggled out of my coat, suddenly too hot in the confined space of the car.

"And where do you know this Yella from?"

Boy, he wasn't letting this go.

"Emerald. She introduced us. Yella wanted to show me the university. Blake might want to apply."

"Then why wouldn't Blake come with you?"

"They have school—plus, Oxford is a big deal. I wanted to check it out without pressuring them."

"Okay, but why—"

I had to go on the offensive. Jamie was far too persistent, and at this rate, I'd crack before I wrestled my arm out of this damned sleeve.

"Where do you get off interrogating me?" I snapped, phone wedged between cheek and shoulder as I yanked at one stubborn coat sleeve. "I don't appreciate it. I'm not some suspect in one of your investigations. I already get enough of Farrow treating me like that. I do Emerald a favor by picking up overdue books on my way to Oxford, and then the woman who gave me the books happens to see me there? She immediately assumes she's being stalked —ridiculous! One hysterical phone call later, and you and Farrow have nothing better to do than rush over and accuse me? Shouldn't you be on a real case, finding out what happened to Dr. Drake?"

I finally tore off the coat and hurled it onto the passenger seat with a huff.

Silence.

For a moment, I thought Jamie had hung up. A part of me would've welcomed it—a temporary reprieve from confrontation.

But then he spoke again, softer now.

"I know Farrow's prejudiced where you're concerned. And you know I always defend you when I can. I've risked my job more than once by doing that."

Guilt crashed over me.

He was right. Jamie had risked his job—he'd even been

demoted to desk duty once because he took my side. He hadn't been comfortable with my gift at first, but he'd tried. He'd been supportive. Only a few days ago, he'd helped me cut through red tape so we could exhume Marjorie Keane's father.

And here I was…lying. Not just a little white lie or an *I'll explain the truth later* lie—no, a whole frigging web of lies I'd tangled myself up in. What I'd sworn I'd never forgive Steven for, I was doing to Jamie right now. I felt nothing short of despicable.

"Jamie…" I began, but he didn't let me finish.

"I know when you're lying, Liv. So spare me any more excuses. What I can't understand is why you feel the need to lie to me. I've given you every reason to trust me. And this thing about meeting some friend at Oxford is just the tip of the iceberg."

My throat tightened.

"You've been avoiding me," he continued. "Canceling dates. Pretending to be sick when you clearly weren't. And why did you really take my police uniform? You know impersonating an officer is a criminal offense, right? Your explanation at the inn made no sense. And why did you have to meet me there? Why was the uniform there? This all started with Dr. Drake's disappearance. I just don't understand."

A beat. Then, hesitantly, "Do you have anything to do with this, Liv? Did you do something…really bad? Something you think you can't tell me because I'm the police?"

"Oh my god—no! I swear. How can you think that about me?"

This time, my outrage was real.

"Maybe one of your relatives did something? It's normal to want to protect them, but—"

"Jamie, no! I didn't have anything to do with Drake's

disappearance, and neither did Gina or Emerald. That is God's honest truth!"

"I don't know what to believe anymore." He sounded heartbroken. "I just know you're hiding something from me."

I had no words left. Because he was right—and I didn't want to lie again. Jamie didn't deserve this.

My heart grew very, very heavy.

"Liv?" he asked quietly.

I swallowed. "You're right," I whispered, trying not to cry. "There's something I just...can't tell you. And I'm so sorry."

Another long pause.

"I thought we were past this, Liv. I thought we were finally ready to trust each other and commit to this relationship."

"I did too," I said hoarsely. "We were. I was. I—"

I stopped myself, squeezing my eyelids shut so the tears wouldn't fall.

"This is something else, Jamie. Something I can't talk about. Not yet. Maybe soon you'll understand—"

"No," Jamie said, voice steady but breaking. "I really like you, Liv. In fact...I more than like you. I was falling in love with you. I've given you the benefit of the doubt so many times. I was patient. We were finally on a good path. Our relationship was going somewhere—and now I feel like we're going backward. I want to be with you. But not like this. I have to guard my heart too. It's too much."

He drew in a breath. "I don't think we should do this anymore."

I couldn't speak. I couldn't breathe. I just sat there, staring at nothing. I deserved everything he was throwing at me.

"Liv? Liv—are you still there? I'm sorry."

He hesitated...then hung up.

The moment the line went dead, the tears came. Hot, unstoppable. I sobbed for five solid minutes before fumbling blindly in the glove compartment for tissues. I blew my nose, wiped my face, breathed.

When I could finally trust my voice again, I called Ellie.

"Hey," I said when she picked up. My voice was embarrassingly hoarse from crying.

"Are you okay?" Ellie asked immediately. "You sound…funny."

"No. Um. It's—I'm fine."

"Have you been crying?"

I sighed. "To be honest, yes. It's…something with Jamie."

"Jamie made you cry? What—"

"No. Ugh. Sorry, but I really don't want to talk about it."

I steadied myself. "I just wanted to ask about a lawyer. You got one when you divorced Jason, didn't you? And got a restraining order and all that? Would you recommend them? Can you send me the contact info?"

"Of course." Ellie's voice shifted into careful, friend-on-alert mode. "Why do you need a lawyer?"

"Again, I'm sorry, but I can't answer that right now."

Ellie fell quiet for a moment.

"But it's important," I added softly. "So I'd really appreciate it if you could look up the details and send them to me."

"No worries. I'll send you a text as soon as we hang up."

I exhaled. "Thank you."

"That's what friends are for, Liv. And…I'm here if you need to talk."

"I appreciate it, Ellie."

We said goodbye, and true to her word, my phone pinged with a text from her five minutes later.

I didn't read it—I was already back on the road—but I resolved to contact the lawyer later, once I was home. The situation with Steven needed to be resolved, and clearly I couldn't rely on him to handle it. I needed to take matters into my own hands. I'd make an appointment, and we'd go together. I wanted to hear what his legal options actually were.

And if he didn't like it or refused to go?

I was done harboring him in Fairwyck. He'd have to leave, or I'd call the police.

The thought made me wince, but it had to be done.

I'd just lost my boyfriend over this entire mess. I wasn't letting it spiral further.

But before I dealt with lawyers and fugitives, I needed to go to the library.

When I'd left the restaurant, Emerald had texted me, asking me to stop by.

She'd discovered something in her research.

I know why everyone is so interested in the Sacred Salmon Inn.

CHAPTER TWENTY-NINE

The moment I stepped into the Fairwyck library, I saw Emerald's head pop up from behind a fortress of open books. Her hair was escaping its bun in frantic wisps, like ideas sparking out of her skull.

"There you are!" she blurted. "Liv, I've found something incredible! I think I finally understand why everyone is—"

She stopped. Her expression softened, confusion melting into concern.

"Have you…been crying?"

Of course she noticed. My eyes probably looked like someone had swapped them for two pickled plums.

I sank into the chair opposite her. "A little."

"What happened?" Emerald slid closer, already half-reaching for my hand.

I told her.

All of it.

Meeting Alaric's sister.

Being cornered at Oxford by Farrow, Mabel Scarboro, and Jamie.

The panicked lie about meeting a friend.

Yellow-Teeth Girl swooping in like some unhinged guardian angel to corroborate my story.

And then Jamie calling afterward to brutally call me out on my lies and break up with me.

Emerald's face twisted in sympathy. "Oh, Liv…come here—"

She leaned in for a hug, but fresh tears threatened, hot and humiliating. I gently pushed her away.

"It's okay," I whispered. "Let's…not do this right now. I think I'll feel better if we make progress on all of this. If I can solve this mess, maybe I can talk to Jamie sooner rather than later and explain."

Emerald hesitated but nodded.

I wiped my cheeks with my sleeve. "Besides, the trip wasn't for nothing. The weird girl who helped me? We'd talked before that. She…knows about Hatherleigh's book club. And she invited me to their meeting. Secret address, password, everything."

Emerald blinked. "She invited you? Why?"

"She said she recognized I had…the sight." I grimaced at the term. "Apparently Hatherleigh likes that. She said it's useful for their rituals."

"Rituals," Emerald repeated faintly. Her complexion paled by two shades. "Liv, that could be dangerous."

"I know. But the meeting is tonight. And it might be the only chance we have to understand how Hatherleigh ties into Drake, Maggie, the mirror—everything."

Emerald wrapped her arms around herself. "Then… you should see what I found. Because I think it all connects."

I straightened. "What is it?"

She walked back around the desk and lifted a notebook thick with post-it notes and other scraps of paper.

Her voice trembled with a blend of fear and excitement.

"Remember the sigil I told you about—the one on Alaric's coin? The one Drake copied into his notebook? The one we suspect is etched into the mirror?"

"Yes," I said. "The door to the dead." A shiver ran down my spine just thinking about it.

"Right. I found the original reference." Emerald opened a heavy, leather-bound volume with the reverence of someone cracking open a tomb. "It isn't just a metaphorical door. It's…an actual attempt to create a passage between worlds. A threshold."

My blood iced.

"You can summon the dead through it," Emerald continued quietly. "More specifically—you can draw on their energy. Their souls. Use them for…power."

"Why would anyone want to do that?"

"Power for power's sake is a good enough motive for many," she said. "Control. Have the living and the dead at your disposal to do your bidding."

I swallowed. "Do you remember what Aunt Gina said about Maggie raising shadows? That it drains the spirits? That it takes something from them?"

She nodded.

"That…sounds similar, don't you think? Just on a larger scale."

Emerald winced. "I hate to say it, but…Maggie fits right into this."

I pressed a hand to my forehead. "Okay. And it's somehow connected to the inn. The mirror was there, with the sigil. It seems as if Maggie got Dr. Drake to look for it there, doesn't it?"

Emerald's eyes lit with renewed urgency. She dug through her papers and pulled out several printed pages, including the photos I'd taken of the map in *Paths of the Ancestors*.

"You sent me these maps earlier. The one with the

golden web? I compared it to historical maps of our region. Look."

She laid them out: my blurry phone photos, her enlarged prints, and several old topographical maps that looked as if they'd been rescued from a monastery fire.

"These place names are ancient," Emerald said, tapping at the faded lettering. The ink on the parchment map she'd sourced looked like waterlogged veins, threatening to dissolve if touched too firmly. "And look—here's the River Fair, before the course was redirected in the nineteenth century."

"The river used to run closer to the village?" I asked.

"Much closer. Practically through the lower meadow," she said, tracing a sinuous line where the old flow had once cut through farmland. "This tributary is part of the old Severn system—this whole region was salmon country. Medieval records mention *salmo* and *læx* constantly. But what matters is this—see how the distances on this map are measured from the river's original bank?"

She shifted to the printed photos I'd taken from *Paths of the Ancestors* and laid them beside the historical map.

"And this—this knot of intersecting golden lines," she continued, circling a point where half a dozen luminous strands met. "This is the nexus. And if you compare old field boundaries and early parish records…"

She overlapped the maps until the lines and names aligned.

"…the convergence sits exactly where the Sacred Salmon Inn stands today."

I blinked at the cramped, spidery handwriting on one of the oldest maps. The script was a mix of Latin and Middle English, letters looping into each other.

"*Salmonlondes*," I read slowly, stumbling over the medieval spelling. "Salmon Lands. Was that always the name of the area?"

"Apparently," Emerald said. "It appears in documents from the twelfth century. But here—look at this." She pulled a separate vellum reproduction from the stack. "We always heard the inn was built in the eleventh century. But of course that's not quite right."

"What do you mean?"

"In the eleventh century, nobody was building stone inns here. At best, there might have been a timber hall or a farmstead. This area was listed as *communis terra salmonis*—common salmon land. Communal grazing and fishing rights." She tapped a small marginal note in crabbed Latin: *Hic stat lapis Salmonis ad viam vetustam.*

I squinted. "My Latin is rusty. What does that mean?"

"'Here stands the Salmon stone by the old road.' A waymarker. Probably carved with a fish symbol. Later, this whole area becomes associated with salmon because of the river's abundance—people named anything and everything after it. Salmonlondes, Salmonhus, Salmonhylle." Emerald smiled faintly. "It was basically medieval branding."

"So the inn wasn't the original landmark," I said slowly. "Just…built on the site where earlier salmon-related things already existed."

"Right. And here—look at this next map." She slid over another sheet, slightly newer but still centuries old. "Late twelfth century. After the Normans. Now we see a stone structure marked *Hospicium ad Salmonem.*"

"A hospicium?" I repeated.

"A medieval hostel, guesthouse, or travelers' lodging," she said. "The Normans built lots of stone buildings— priories, hospices, outposts. This was probably a small hospicium connected to a monastic holding. And then, sometime in the late medieval period, it likely became an alehouse. Eventually the inn we know."

The progression sent a prickle down my arms.

"The power was already here," Emerald went on.

"The building changed, but the location didn't. These ley lines"—she tapped the shimmering golden web—"meet right at the point labeled Salmon. Every variant of 'Salmon' on these maps refers to the same general landmark zone."

"And you think Alaric figured this out?"

"I think he devoted half his life to figuring it out." She pointed again at the nexus. "This is what he was hunting."

I studied the maps, trying to reconcile the geography with the village I knew.

"Are you sure about this?" I murmured, frowning.

"I'm not the only one who thinks it," Emerald said. "Alaric's book references an old occult society. He seems to admire it greatly. They discovered all of this too. They must have used the site—possibly before it was ever an inn. Maybe they built the hospicium for cover. They knew it was a powerful ley-line nexus." She tapped the golden knot again. "The society believed this was their seat of power."

"Alaric wanted to find the place," I realized aloud. "He searched for it—and when you located the ley-line map in *Paths of the Ancestors*, he finally confirmed what he suspected. The rituals were done here. Their texts were hidden here. The mirror was hidden here. This is what he was after."

She exhaled shakily. "It aligns perfectly, Liv."

I sat back, stunned.

"So you think he sent Drake here?" I asked slowly. "To investigate? That seems risky. And very public."

"He needed a way in," Emerald said. "An investigation in plain sight. Clever, if you think about it."

"And Maggie?" I whispered. "How does she fit in?"

Emerald closed the book softly, her mouth tightening.

"I don't know," she said. "But something must have gone horribly wrong."

"And if Maggie and Hatherleigh are after the mirror

and the books and everything, why didn't they…just take it? Why is Maggie still playing along? And what about Hatherleigh? Where is he? Why hasn't he shown up at the Sacred Salmon even once?"

"Well," Emerald said, "Maggie was definitely interested in the books. She's better off being on the inside, having access to everything. So it makes sense she'd continue playing along. And…look what happened to Drake after moving the mirror from the secret room to the next room. Perhaps Alaric and his society haven't moved it because it's truly dangerous. That might also be why Alaric is staying away."

We both stared at the pile of ancient maps and occult diagrams.

The air in the library felt chilly.

A cold thought lodged in my chest. If this nexus was real—if the mirror was part of a ritual once performed here—then Gina, Maggie, Lucy…even Steven…might become tangled in forces we barely understood. And every step anyone took upstairs might be tempting fate.

CHAPTER THIRTY

A knock sounded at the library door, brisk and familiar.

Before either of us could react, it opened, and Gina bustled in, cheeks pink from the cold, arms laden with a basket and a paper bag that smelled dangerously good.

"There you are," she said cheerfully. "I thought as much. Emerald, you disappear into books and forget the rest of the world exists."

She set the basket on the edge of the desk and began laying out her haul like she was setting up a picnic blanket: waxed paper, napkins, a thermos, a small bottle of grape juice.

"Mom," Emerald groaned, already scrambling to shove loose papers and ancient-looking folios into neater stacks. "Careful! Some of these are very old."

"So am I," Gina said serenely. "Most of what's old has endured for a reason and is less fragile than you might think."

Emerald rolled her eyes.

"Just admit you haven't eaten," Gina pressed on,

unbudging. Then she added, with a mischievous grin, "I brought cheese scones. Still warm."

I'd devoured a whole pizza and tiramisu for lunch, but my resolve crumbled instantly. "I'll just have one," I said, already reaching.

Emerald shot me a look that said traitor, but she smiled despite herself.

Gina glanced between us. "So. How's the research going?"

Emerald coughed and subtly slid a notebook out of sight. "You know. Okay."

I raised an eyebrow. Gina noticed, of course, but chose to ignore it.

"And how is everyone at the inn?" I asked, forcing my voice to sound casual. "Steven, I mean."

"Oh, he's fine," Gina said lightly, pouring juice into paper cups. "Lucy's been very attentive. She baked him a Battenberg cake."

Emerald winced. "That's ambitious."

"Exactly," Gina said. "Takes some skill. And it looked cute, with that neat pink-and-yellow checkerboard pattern. I think Steven was charmed. They had a long chat. And I checked on him too."

"I heard," I said. "You read his cards."

Gina paused, cup halfway to her lips.

"Yes," she said slowly. "And I actually wanted to talk to you about that."

My stomach tightened. I remembered the dream I'd had a few days ago—Steven chasing me through the inn, and then the tarot card, the King of Pentacles. Gina had said it signified wealth and worldly success. That was what mattered to Steven. That was what had gotten us into this mess.

"You didn't pull the King of Pentacles, by any chance?" I asked carefully.

"No," Gina said. "It was…the Seven of Swords."

That didn't sound good. When I first got to Fairwyck, Gina had drawn the Ten of Swords for me. It was bad. I still had the image of a prone figure stabbed by swords seared into my mind. Any card with too many swords made me uneasy.

I quickly changed my perspective when Gina explained the meaning of that particular card.

"I hate to say it, Liv, but he's still keeping something from you," she said gently. "There's deception there. Dishonesty. Getting away with something. Avoiding responsibility."

I let out a long breath. "I figured."

The whole lawyer business. The vague answers. Even turning up here after all this time. I'd wanted to believe he was trying to make things right—but belief didn't make it true.

"I'll put a stop to it," I said. "One way or another."

Gina nodded, satisfied, and began gathering her things. "Good. Now, I should head back."

"I have to leave too," I said. "Take care of something long overdue. I'll be right out, Gina—I just need a quick word with Emerald."

Once Gina stepped out, I turned to my cousin. "Why didn't you tell her about…all of this?"

Emerald's expression softened. "Because it would break her heart. Owning the inn has been her dream, Liv. She's always believed it was special—and it is. But if she thought it was tied to something…evil?" She shook her head. "And Maggie—Mom wants to believe in her sister. I don't want to take that away from her unless we're absolutely sure."

"Aren't you afraid something could happen?" I asked quietly.

Emerald considered that. "No. Maybe because it's been my home all my life. I can't quite think of it as dangerous."

She hesitated. "And if this gets out—if the press decides *The Inn of Doom* is accurate? None of us could live there anymore."

I nodded. "You're right. We need to be sure."

I hesitated, then added, "I might find out more tonight. At the book club meeting that's most likely *not* a book club meeting."

Emerald went pale. "You're really going?"

"I'm terrified," I admitted. "But yes."

Gina's voice floated back down the hall. "Liv?"

I followed her, taking a bite of my cheese scone. "Delicious," I moaned through a mouthful. "Hey—did Blake meet up with Lucy?"

"Oh yes," Gina said. "They took the bus to Meckham. Wanted to get hot chocolate at the café, walk around a little. Lucy was thrilled."

I smiled with relief, waving at Gina as I got into my car. I didn't want to worry about Blake being inside the inn— the farther away she was, the better.

But with Gina gone, and Blake out with Lucy, that left only Steven and Maggie at the inn.

Steven—who might be lying to me.

Maggie—who might be playing a far deeper game.

And the mirror.

For a moment, I considered going back. Getting him out. Taking control.

Then I remembered his evasions. Gina's warning. The way he'd reinserted himself into my life without truly facing the consequences of his previous actions.

Steven was a grown man. He'd chosen his hiding place.

And if part of me felt a flicker of grim satisfaction knowing he might finally be uncomfortable? Well. Given everything, I decided I could live with that.

I'd just started the car when my phone rang.

Ellie's number flashed on the display.

"Ellie? Thanks for the lawyer info—I'm just on my way home to call them."

"Would you mind stopping by the theater first?" Ellie's voice sounded…odd.

"Um…why?" I said. "I've had a really long day, and I was kind of hoping to—"

"Something important has come up," she cut in. "It won't take long. I just need you to stop by real quick."

"Okay," I said slowly. "I guess so…"

"Great! See you soon!"

"See y—"

She'd already hung up.

"That was weird," I muttered, but I turned the car toward the Ghost Light Theatre—the old playhouse formerly known as the Fairwyck Theatre.

Ellie and I had renamed it after the friendly theater ghost had left a light burning onstage the first time we'd visited the premises.

The building sat on a cobblestone road by the river that ran past our little Cotswold village.

A familiar sense of pride and accomplishment settled over me as I stepped into the lobby, as it always did when I came to work.

I'd majored in arts administration in college, but I'd never actually done anything with the degree. Running a small theater had always been a dream of mine—and when my friend Ellie Bullwart had asked if I wanted to be her business partner and reopen the theater together, I'd agreed, against all reason and logic.

At the time, I'd only just found my feet as a cleaner, earning enough to support my family. The theater was a risky venture. Ellie—who was as enthusiastic as she was optimistic—had convinced me to take on a production by the Cirencester Curtain Callers after their theater flooded, even though we were nowhere near ready. Not with the refurbishment. Not with our partnership.

It was too fast. Too soon.

And then there'd been a murder.

It could have ended in catastrophe, but somehow—with the help of a benefactor—we'd pulled through. We were still putting on productions, and the workload was manageable with my fifty-fifty split.

It had always been Ellie's dream to open a café and bar alongside the theater, serving food and drinks before and after performances. She was still working toward that, but at her own pace now, which I thought was wise. She spent far more time at the theater than I did, focusing on that side of the business.

I walked through the empty auditorium, crossed the stage, and headed into the area behind it where our small office was located.

"Ellie?" I called. "I'm here."

Antigone, the theater cat, emerged from the doorway, meowing indignantly.

I bent down to pet her. Her black fur was always scraggly, and she usually looked a little underfed. Antigone came and went as she pleased, sometimes even staying for days at the former caretaker's cottage down the road. I didn't see her often, so I took the opportunity to greet her properly.

She seemed to enjoy it.

"Liv?" Ellie called.

"Yes—just petting Antigone." I gave the cat one final scratch, then straightened and stepped into the office.

I stopped short.

Esme and Judith were sitting on the couch.

Ellie was perched on the chair behind the desk.

The office was tiny at the best of times, and with me standing in the doorway, the space felt instantly cramped.

"What are you guys doing here?" I asked, genuinely surprised.

Esme was my best friend and neighbor. She worked for Judith too. Ellie knew both of them—Judith had helped her a great deal when she'd finally decided to leave her abusive husband. And she knew Esme through me and Judith. We all saw each other at larger social events and at book club, but apart from that, we didn't really spend time together in this particular constellation.

Ellie vacated the desk chair and gestured toward it. "Why don't you sit down."

She moved to the couch and balanced on the edge next to Judith, smoothing her yellow skirt.

I did as she suggested, suddenly feeling incredibly awkward—as if I were facing a jury. Or an interview panel.

I gave a nervous laugh. "What's going on, guys?"

Esme stared at the floor instead of meeting my eyes. "We're a little worried about you, Liv."

"Yes," Judith said in her usual brisk tone. "Ellie called me earlier because she was concerned. And given that you asked me to take time off for personal reasons—and told me it wasn't just about what your relatives are dealing with at the Sacred Salmon—I put two and two together."

"We decided we should get you here right away and talk," Ellie added.

Judith pursed her pink lips—the same shade as the tailored blazer she wore over a low-cut white blouse—and leaned forward to study me. "Your eyes are puffy. But otherwise I don't see anything. Did you cover it with makeup, or..." She hesitated. "Is the abuse not physical? That can be the worst kind."

Ellie nodded. "That's how it was with Jason. He never laid a hand on me. But he smashed things around us. He was violent. Judith thinks it would only have been a matter of time before he hit me. I'm so grateful I got out—"

I held up a hand. "Hang on. What are you talking about?"

"It's okay, Liv," Esme said gently. "You don't have to pretend. We'd believe you—you must know that. It's often men no one suspects. They seem so nice. So respectable. My husband was the same. A police officer too. Did I ever tell you that? An upstanding citizen. No one believed he'd do something like that to me."

I stared at her, mouth open.

I sometimes forgot what Esme had been through. Many years ago, she'd left her abusive husband with Judith's help—Judith volunteered for a charity that helped women rebuild their lives after situations like that. Esme seemed so self-assured now, such a wonderful mother—her eldest was already living away from home—that it was hard to imagine her as a battered wife.

But now I saw a shadow in her brown eyes that made my chest ache.

I couldn't imagine what she'd endured.

I had witnessed Jason's treatment of Ellie, though. I'd seen firsthand what it took to wrench yourself free from a relationship like that.

My heart swelled with respect for these women.

It occurred to me far too late what they were suggesting.

Ellie was already speaking.

"I reached out to Esme, and she confirmed what I'd been suspecting. You've been isolating yourself. She's hardly seen you, and you keep making excuses when she tries to get together."

"It's a classic sign," Judith said.

"And then I remembered that text you sent me," Ellie went on. "You asked if people could really change. If I'd ever give Jason a second chance. I feel stupid for not understanding what you meant at the time. But my answer still stands. People might change in little ways—but not like that. Not when it comes to abuse. You can't wait for it. You have to protect yourself and get out, before—"

"Guys!" I blurted. "You've got this all wrong."

They froze.

"I was upset earlier because Jamie broke up with me," I said. "So I'm not even in a relationship. Abusive or otherwise."

I immediately regretted the sharpness in my voice. This wasn't something to be glib about.

"I'm sorry," I added quickly. "I'm honestly touched you'd do this for me. But please believe me—Jamie isn't hurting me. He's a good guy."

The three of them looked at me with varying degrees of pity and skepticism.

I huffed. "I know—that's probably exactly what an abused person protecting their partner would say. Someone in denial. I don't know what to say to convince you. But this isn't about Jamie."

Judith studied me with narrowed eyes. Ellie twirled a strand of blond hair around her finger, her forehead creased—clearly undecided. And Esme…the compassion in her brown eyes was almost unbearable.

I desperately wanted to confess. To tell them this was about Steven.

But I couldn't. Not yet.

Exasperated, I got to my feet. "Like I said, I don't think I can convince you. And frankly, I don't have the time. I have something urgent to sort out—something that is connected to all the fuss at the inn. I know you mean well. I hope I can tell you about it soon."

Avoiding Esme's disappointed gaze and Judith's disapproval, I hightailed it out of the office.

Ellie jumped up from the couch and followed me. "Liv, wait—"

I couldn't face her. I couldn't face explaining any more. I moved faster, ignoring her. By the time I reached the auditorium, she was no longer behind me.

She'd given up.

I didn't blame her.

I hadn't even begun to process Jamie breaking up with me—and now it looked like I was damaging more of my relationships on top of that.

It would have been easier to channel all of these feelings into anger. I wanted to. In just a few days, Steven had managed to destabilize almost everything I'd built here over the last year and a half.

And he hadn't even done anything.

He'd simply turned up—and made himself my problem.

It was infuriating. I should be furious.

Anger might have propelled me forward. Fueled me. Given me the momentum to see this through.

But no matter how hard I tried, I couldn't summon it.

Instead, a heavy gray cloud seemed to settle over me.

Maybe because I knew I couldn't put all the blame on Steven. Yes, this was his fault—he'd come here and put me in this position. It was because of him that we'd ended up in Fairwyck in the first place, desperate and penniless.

But I bore responsibility too.

I could have handled things differently. Acted with integrity. Called the police right away. Not spun a web of lies for the people who genuinely cared about me.

I'd wanted to spare my children. Protect them from the fallout. But Steven's actions—those were on him. And shielding my kids from the consequences…that hadn't really been my choice to make.

I'd dragged things out because I didn't want to decide.

And what good had that done?

I'd alienated my friends. And my partner.

That ends today, I resolved as I slid into my car.

I would call the lawyer the moment I got home. Maybe we could get an appointment tomorrow and finally sort this out.

Then I could explain everything—to Jamie. To Esme, Ellie, and Judith. Maybe they'd understand.

Maybe—if I groveled hard enough—Jamie might even consider forgiving me. Not that there was much of a chance of him ever taking me back.

I hadn't realized tears were streaming down my face until I glanced in the rearview mirror while easing out of the narrow parking space.

I wiped them away with my coat sleeve.

There was still some hope.

I could still fix this mess.

CHAPTER THIRTY-ONE

By the time I pulled up outside the cottage, my whole body was protesting.

My head throbbed. My shoulders ached like I'd been carrying something heavy all day—grief, secrets, dread. The idea of staying awake until midnight, then driving back to Oxford to infiltrate a secret occult meeting, felt laughable.

All I wanted was silence. Darkness. Sleep.

For a moment, I just sat there with the engine running, forehead resting against the steering wheel. My body wanted to check out. To slow down. To pretend the world could wait until morning.

Maybe I could lie down for twenty minutes, I thought. Just a short nap. Set an alarm.

I forced myself out of the car and went to the mailbox, fishing out a bundle of envelopes.

My phone rang.

"Blake?" I answered immediately, balancing the phone and the stack of mail while searching for the key in my bag.

"Mom—hi—okay, I don't have much time," they said

in a rush. The background noise told me they were in a public place, maybe the café. "Lucy's in the loo, but I needed to tell you this."

"Tell me what?" I asked, already tense.

"It's about Maggie. Lucy was talking." Blake lowered their voice. "She said Maggie never wanted to come back to Fairwyck. Ever. She used to speak horribly about the family. Said she didn't need them. That she was better off without them."

My grip tightened on the envelopes. "Then why did she come back?"

"That's the thing. Lucy said Maggie changed her tune completely a few months ago. Out of nowhere."

"Why?" I asked. My mind immediately jumped to Alaric. "Did she meet someone?"

"No. She found out Aunt Ethel died."

The words hit like a stone dropped into water.

"That's when she decided to return," Blake continued. "Lucy said Maggie acted like…like something was finally out of the way. Like Gina would forgive her now. Because Gina's always been the soft one. She wrote to her a few times, and Gina wouldn't budge. Until she dangled Drake in front of her nose."

A cold prickle crept up my spine. "Forgive her for what?"

"I don't know," Blake said quickly. "Lucy didn't say. Just…something from the past. Something connected to why Maggie was banished in the first place."

A pause. Muffled movement.

"Mom, I have to go—Lucy's coming back."

"Blake, wait—"

The line went dead.

I stood there for a moment, the late afternoon light slanting across the cottage, my thoughts racing.

Finally, Ethel is out of the way.

The phrase echoed in my head, unbidden.

I unlocked the door and stepped inside.

"Mom!"

Audrey came flying toward me, her face pale and panicked. "There you are! I can't find Ethel!"

"What?" I dropped my bag on the floor and the mail on the kitchen table. "What do you mean, you can't find her?"

"I was supposed to finish talking to her after school, remember?" Audrey said, words tumbling over each other. "About Aunt Maggie. About her not being allowed in our house."

"I remember," I said, shrugging off my coat.

"I couldn't concentrate all day," she went on. "It felt urgent, Mom. Like she was trying to warn me. And now she's gone."

"She was on my bed when I left this morning," I said, forcing myself to stay calm. "I haven't been home since. Did you check everywhere? Under the beds? She sometimes curls up underneath."

"Of course I checked everywhere," Audrey snapped, then immediately looked guilty. "I'm sorry. But she's not here."

"That is odd," I murmured.

Protection sigils. Ethel's warning. The unease I'd felt leaving the cottage this morning. I still had Blake's words in my ear, that Maggie was glad Ethel was dead.

That was the reason Maggie had come back here. She'd figured Ethel would no longer be in her way. Then she'd heard—we'd told her—that Ethel wasn't really gone. That she had come back as a cat.

And now the cat—Ethel—was gone.

"We'll look outside in a minute," I said, trying my very best to keep my tone light. I didn't want to scare Audrey. "She probably slipped out."

There was a loud humming in my ears. I wasn't sure I could keep standing upright, so I sank down onto a kitchen chair. I turned my attention to the mail, needing something ordinary to ground myself. Bank statements. Junk. Flyers.

And then—

An envelope of thick white paper.

My breath caught as I unfolded it. The ink was dark. Handwritten words with weirdly shaped letters, as if someone had purposefully added flourishes to make their writing look different.

I read it once.

Then again.

"Mom?" Audrey said. "What is it?"

She leaned over my shoulder before I could stop her.

We have your cat.

You'll get her back for fifty thousand pounds.

We'll be in touch with details for the exchange.

For a heartbeat, Audrey just stared.

Then she screamed.

CHAPTER THIRTY-TWO

My hands were shaking as I took out my phone. I typed a short message to Emerald—barely coherent, all urgency and fear—and hit send. Then I shoved the phone back into my bag and turned to Audrey.

"Come on," I said, already moving toward the door. "We need to go."

She didn't react. She was curled in on herself on the kitchen chair, sobbing so hard her whole body shook.

I crossed the room in two strides, crouched down, and wrapped an arm around her shoulders. "Shh," I murmured, pulling her gently to her feet. "It's okay. Everything's going to be okay. I'll sort this out."

She clutched at my sleeve. "Ethel—"

"I know who took her," I said, my voice steadier than I felt. Rage had burned through the panic, hot and sharp, giving me something solid to stand on. "I know exactly who did this."

Audrey's crying hitched. She looked up at me, blue eyes even bigger with tears. "You do?"

"Yes." I nodded firmly. "And I'm going to confront her."

I grabbed my bag, didn't bother with my coat, and steered Audrey out the door, scooping up her jacket and draping it around her shoulders as we went.

By the time we got into the car, my exhaustion was completely gone, replaced by a cold, focused fury.

This was Maggie's doing. It had to be.

Her appearance in Fairwyck had been suspicious from the start. Even Gina—the sister who wanted to forgive her—had harbored so much mistrust that she hadn't told me about her at first. Now we'd learned that Ethel's death was the only reason Maggie had come back. She'd been interested in our cottage—had even asked if she could buy it. Ethel the cat had scratched protection marks into the floor by the hearth, had warned Audrey that Maggie shouldn't be allowed inside. Once Maggie had learned that Ethel wasn't really gone, she'd had to make another plan. So she'd taken Ethel away from us—away from the cottage.

I had no idea why Maggie wanted our home. Why Ethel had been adamant about not letting her in. Why Maggie needed Ethel out of the way. But it all fit.

When the country lane curved and I caught my first glimpse of the inn, I already saw the swarm of reporters.

I'd known it was inevitable they'd come back, but I still cursed—why now?

I didn't slow down. I couldn't care about them now. I pulled up right in front of them and got out without a word, Audrey close at my side.

Ignoring their shouted questions, I stormed up to the front door and knocked so hard my knuckles scraped painfully against the wood.

The door opened almost immediately.

Gina stood there, surprise flickering across her face. "Liv, is everything—?"

I brushed past her without stopping.

Maggie was in the parlor.

She was reclining on the chaise longue, perfectly composed, a delicate china teacup in her hand.

Drinking tea.

The sight of it—the calm, the domesticity—nearly made my vision blur with anger.

"You," I said, my voice cutting through the room. "I know what you did."

Maggie looked up slowly, brows lifting. "I beg your pardon?"

"You took my cat," I snapped. "You kidnapped her. You left a ransom note in my house."

Her expression shifted—not guilt, but something closer to irritation. "What on earth are you talking about? I didn't take your cat."

"Oh, don't play innocent with me," I shot back. "I know about your affiliation with Hatherleigh. I know you're involved in all of this. You've been after our cottage from the start. You waited for Ethel to be out of the way to get it. I don't know why—but when you found out Ethel isn't really gone, you…you…took her! How dare you?"

Maggie set her teacup down with exaggerated care. "You're upset," she said coolly. "But you're making wild accusations."

"What's going on?" Emerald's voice came from the doorway. "I got your text, Liv."

She'd arrived quietly, breathless, eyes darting between us. Audrey was crying again, clinging to my arm.

I finally said it out loud, the words tumbling over each other. "Ethel's gone. Someone took her. They left a ransom note. Fifty thousand pounds."

I dropped the envelope—which I'd been clutching the entire time—onto the table.

Emerald's face drained of color. "You think Maggie did this?"

"Yes," I said without hesitation.

"Why?" Emerald asked carefully. "For money? Maggie has money."

I faltered for half a second. It was true.

"The ransom thing must·be a ruse," I said, frustration creeping in. "No one would extort me for money. Everyone in Fairwyck knows I'm broke."

"And excuse me," Maggie put in calmly, almost politely. "Had I taken Ethel—because I want her *out of the way*, as you put it—why would I write a note in the first place? Ransom ruse or not, why draw attention to it? Cats disappear all the time. You might not have noticed for days. You could have assumed any number of explanations."

"I don't know," I shouted, irritation spilling over.

Emerald's gaze sharpened. "You're right—everyone knows you're broke. But you know who isn't?"

"What?" I looked at her with narrowed eyes, absolutely unsure where she was going with this.

"Steven," she said quietly. "Your husband. He famously conned a lot of people out of their money. And he came back to you. Someone could have seen him. This could be opportunistic. Not…all of this." She gestured vaguely, meaning the occult mess we were all drowning in. "I don't think it's connected."

"But no one knows about Steven," I protested.

Emerald hesitated. "We know. Gina knows. Lucy knows. And Esme could have seen him. Blake could have said something to Anthony."

"I completely vouch for Esme," I snapped. My heart squeezed, thinking about the intervention—the way she'd spoken about her husband who had hurt her so deeply. She was my friend. "She would never do something like that. Audrey, you and Blake never told any—"

I broke off, suddenly realizing Audrey wasn't pressed against my side anymore. In fact, she wasn't in the room at all.

Panic surged. "Audrey?"

"She went to the inn," Gina said from the doorway. "She said she wanted to check on her father."

"Oh." I pressed my hands to my temples. My head throbbed. Everything was just too much. I'd completely forgotten about Steven. I needed to see him too—talk to him about the lawyer situation. And if Emerald was right, and this was about Steven's money, then he might know something about it.

"I'd better talk to him too," I said, and explained my thought process to the others.

At the door, I turned back and pointed at Maggie. "You're not off the hook. I still believe you could have done this—and regardless, I have questions for you."

Gina followed me as I made my way through the connecting door into the old tavern. I wrapped my arms around myself; it was very chilly down there.

"You can't really believe Maggie would have done something like that," Gina said nervously. "Her own sister? Kidnap her for money?"

"Not for money," I said. "But Maggie wants something. And this has to be connected. You know it too, Gina. You've felt it in your gut from the start—otherwise you wouldn't have hidden Maggie from us. Everyone says something happened all those years ago when Maggie was disinherited. And it happened at the cottage. You said she almost destroyed it. It had something to do with her necromancy gift. What was it?"

Gina opened her mouth to answer—but was interrupted by Audrey running down the stairs.

There was something wrong with her expression. Too blank. Too stunned.

"Mom," she said in a small, thin voice. "Dad's gone too."

"What?" I said. "You've got to be joking!"

I took the stairs two at a time.

"Steven!" I called as I burst into the corridor. "We need to talk."

Silence.

I checked Drake's room first. Empty. Then the room with the hidden chamber.

He wasn't there.

I ran my fingers along the wall, searching for the right panel, my hands clumsy with dread until I found it and the wall slid open.

The secret room yawned empty before me—except for the books.

"Steven?" My voice wavered despite myself.

Gina, Audrey, and I searched all the rooms again, the strong sense of déjà vu making me feel almost nauseous.

Back in the hidden chamber room, I looked around more thoroughly and found Steven's bag—the toiletries and things I'd given him. There was even some of the Battenberg cake left. The one Lucy had baked for him.

I didn't find Steven's phone, though. Or any other personal items, like his wallet.

What I did find—in lieu of a note, I supposed—was a tarot card.

The Seven of Swords.

Deception.

CHAPTER THIRTY-THREE

"I should have known something like this would happen," I whispered.

I sank down onto the chaise longue in the parlor, as if my legs had simply given up on me.

Gina patted my arm, brisk but gentle. "There, there," she said. "Let me fetch you some nice hot tea. Extra sugar. That's always the right remedy."

The room tilted. Its multitude of colors and patterns blurred and spun together like a deranged kaleidoscope. I squeezed my eyes shut, willing it to stop.

I felt a presence beside me. An arm slipped around my back.

"It's okay, Mom," Blake said softly. "It's all going to be okay."

They and Lucy had come back to Fairwyck, and Emerald had picked them up as the rest of us were searching the inn top to bottom for Steven. I'd known the entire time we wouldn't find him and had eventually convinced everyone to give up and regroup in the parlor.

Eyes still closed, I shook my head. "No. It isn't going to

be all right. This is all my fault. I should have known. I shouldn't have let it come to this."

"Honey, don't blame yourself," Emerald said gently. "You said there was no other place for Steven to hide. You did everything you could. This was your only option. He's an adult. He went along with it."

A bitter laugh tore out of me, sharp and ugly. I opened my eyes.

Emerald sat in the large armchair opposite me, Audrey curled tightly against her, her face pressed into Emerald's shoulder. My daughter's small body shook with quiet sobs. I was relieved Emerald was holding her, because I couldn't—not right now.

There was too much self-loathing in me.

Of course I knew Steven was the real culprit here. I'd always known that. But I could have stopped this. I could have made a decision sooner. I'd told myself I was protecting my children's hearts by giving him a chance—by letting him try to make things right. Instead, my hesitation, my inertia, had cracked those hearts wide open. And what had been the real reason behind my indecision? Probably my bruised ego that couldn't bear to have been wrong about the man I'd loved for over twenty years. Not to mention that I'd enjoyed punishing Steven by sticking him into the most haunted inn in England.

Emerald kept talking, her voice calm, careful. "We don't know what happened yet. There's no reason to assume the worst. Just because Drake hasn't returned in a few days doesn't mean Steven—"

"Don't you get it?" I snapped, cutting her off.

The words burst out before I could soften them.

"This has nothing to do with Drake. There's no paranormal explanation for Steven's disappearance." I shook my head. "With Steven, it's always very…worldly."

I reached for the envelope on the coffee table—the one

I'd dropped earlier during my confrontation with Maggie —and clenched it in my hand.

Then I turned to my great-aunt, who sat very still on one of the antique chairs, her expression unreadable.

"I believe you," I said quietly. "Because I know who took Ethel."

Maggie returned at that moment, followed by Lucy, who was expertly balancing a tea tray in her hands.

"Who?" Gina asked, alarm sharpening her voice. "What do you mean?"

"Isn't it obvious?" I said. "It was Steven. He took Ethel. The ransom note should have clued me in from the start."

Audrey lifted her head.

Her eyes were swollen and red, her lashes clumped with tears. "Mom," she said hoarsely. "Why would you even say that? Dad would never do something like that."

What was left of my heart shattered again—into dust this time.

"Sweetheart," I said, my voice breaking, "I'm so sorry. But you know your father is wanted by the police. He ran a scheme—he pretended to invest people's money. Friends. Neighbors. Family. People who trusted him with their life savings. He took some of that money and hid it away. He took ours too. Loans. The house. Everything. That's why we ended up staying with Grandma. That's why we had nothing—nothing—until Aunt Ethel saved us by leaving me the cottage."

I swallowed hard.

"I tried to protect you from all of that. I tried to keep you from knowing how bad it really was, but—"

"I know all of this, Mom!" Audrey shouted, her voice cracking. "Dad apologized, remember? He said he did it for us. For his family. And he wouldn't just leave us and take Ethel and—" She sobbed. "He wouldn't do what you're saying he did."

I wanted to go to her. To gather her up. But my body wouldn't move. I felt nailed to the floor by the weight of what I was saying.

Emerald pulled Audrey closer, murmuring softly to her, rocking her slightly. I was grateful beyond words.

"Liv," Gina said carefully. "Are you sure? Do you recognize his handwriting?"

I shook my head, holding up the note. "The handwriting is obviously disguised."

"Why would he try to extort money from you?" Gina asked. "You said yourself—he left you penniless."

"He must be desperate," I said. "There were inconsistencies from the start. I didn't push hard enough, but—he showed up with no belongings, claimed he'd been roughing it. Yet he didn't look like someone without access to a bathroom or clean clothes. He claimed he still had money stashed away for us—enough to go on the run together—but then he said he had nowhere else to stay."

My hands twisted together.

"He must have been staying somewhere. Somewhere near Fairwyck. Or at least in England. I saw him months ago—at the Ghost Light Theatre premiere. I thought I'd imagined it. Or worse—that it was a ghost."

I let out a shaky breath. "He admitted he'd been watching me. He saw that I was back on my feet. Maybe he thought being Ellie's partner means I have money. Maybe he thought you had money and gave it to me." I shook my head. "He was disappointed by the cottage. He called it a dump. Maybe he hoped Ethel left cash."

My voice dropped. "I don't know. But something about his story never added up."

Blake surprised me then.

"Even if that's true," they said quietly, "it doesn't mean he was lying about wanting to redeem himself. He said he'd turn himself in. He said he was talking to lawyers."

"I'm sorry," I said softly. "But he was stringing me along. He never followed through. I don't think he ever intended to. He was planning…this." I pointed to the note on the table.

Audrey sprang to her feet.

"I can't believe you have so little faith in Dad!" she screamed. "He would never kidnap our cat. He knows how much Ethel means to us. He'd never do something that cruel."

"I can't imagine it either," Blake added quietly. "He made terrible mistakes. I don't know if I can forgive him. But he's still our dad. His heart's in the right place. He wouldn't do something this malicious."

"I want to believe that too," I said. "I wanted to believe it for a very long time." My voice faltered. "It hurts to accept that you were wrong about someone you loved."

I couldn't look at them.

"A friend once told me," I whispered, "monsters never change."

"Dad's not a monster!" Audrey screamed.

She stood there trembling, her blue eyes blazing, fists clenched at her sides.

"How can you even say that?" she cried. "As if…as if you don't love him anymore."

I stared at her.

It hadn't occurred to me—until that moment—that she believed we might become a family again. That Steven coming back meant something could be fixed.

Understanding dawned on her face.

And then something broke.

She turned and ran.

"Audrey—" I lunged after her.

Blake caught my arm. "I think…I think it's better if I go."

I hesitated, then nodded.

I would have to talk to Audrey later. Many times. If I could fix this at all.

My hands shook as I pulled out my phone.

"Who are you calling?" Emerald asked.

"Steven's burner." I waited. The line went dead immediately. "Number isn't recognized. Just as I thought."

My stomach clenched.

I scrolled, then dialed another number.

"Jamie?" I said when he answered. "There's something I need to tell you."

CHAPTER THIRTY-FOUR

"Liv," Jamie said flatly.

"I need to talk to you."

A pause. A sigh. "I don't think that's a good idea right now. I told you," he said. "I need space."

"This isn't personal," I said quickly. "It's police business."

Another pause. Longer this time.

Then, cool and clipped, "Well. In that case, come to the station."

I glanced at the clock on the mantel. "It's past six o'clock. Are you still there?"

"Yes," he said. "Late shift."

"Okay," I said. "I'm on my way."

He hung up without another word.

I turned back to the others.

"I need to go to Gloucester," I said. "To the police station. I have to report this."

Emerald nodded immediately. "Of course. We'll look after the kids."

"Where are they? Please don't let them go into the inn, okay? I just…" I trailed off. I had a few thoughts about where Drake might be and what had happened to him—crazy, far-out thoughts—but I couldn't follow up on them right now. I didn't have the mental space. "I want to find out what happened to Drake first."

Emerald nodded again. "They're in the kitchen. My mother went to check on them while you were on the phone—wanted to make them some hot chocolate."

"Okay." I picked up the envelope from the coffee table—the ransom note—and tucked it into my bag.

I gave a terse nod in Lucy's and Maggie's direction, then rushed out of the room.

Emerald followed me into the hall. "Are you still going to that meeting in Oxford, Liv?"

I leaned my forehead briefly against the front door. "Oh my god. I don't know if I can still make it. I've never been so tired and overwhelmed in my entire life."

Emerald hesitated. "Do you really think involving the police is a good idea? We could try to find Steven…other ways. You know. The ghosts. That's worked before."

"I will," I said. "I promise. I'll ask them. But I should have reported Steven the moment he turned up. I should never have lied to Jamie. This"—I swallowed—"this is the right thing to do. I need to do it."

Emerald studied me for a moment, then nodded. "Okay."

"If I go to Oxford, I'll be back very late," I said. "Can you do me a favor and stay with the kids at our cottage?" I didn't want them to be alone. I also still had that uneasy feeling about our home. Maggie was here right now, and I no longer believed she had taken Ethel—but still. The protection sigils. Ethel's warning. I'd rather someone was watching over the cottage.

"You don't even need to ask," Emerald said. "I'll take care of them. Don't you worry."

"Thanks," I said with great relief. "Goodbye. Call me if anything comes up."

"I will. See you later." Emerald waved goodbye, but closed the door quickly when the reporters started taking pictures.

I brushed past them and sped away, almost mowing a couple of the pesky vultures down in the process.

The drive to Gloucester passed in a blur of headlights and dark hedgerows.

I rehearsed what I was going to say the entire way. Clear sentences. Facts only. No emotion. No excuses.

By the time I stood in front of Jamie, none of it remained.

He was in uniform. Solid. Familiar. But there was a desk between us—and so much more.

I couldn't get a word out and just handed him the envelope.

He frowned, opened it, read.

Then he looked up.

Surprised.

"I think—" My voice broke. I cleared my throat and tried again. "I think it was Steven."

Jamie blinked. "Your husband Steven?"

I nodded.

"The criminal fugitive husband Steven?" he repeated incredulously.

"Yes."

He stared at me for a long moment.

"He came to Fairwyck," I said, the words tumbling out now. "He said he regretted everything. He promised to turn himself in. I didn't know what to believe. The children—he's their father—I thought maybe—" I stopped, realizing my words were completely incoherent. Furious tears burned my eyes. "I was stupid."

Jamie came around the desk.

He put a hand on my shoulder and pressed a tissue into my palm.

"Go on," he said quietly.

I blew my nose. "He kept talking about lawyers. About sorting things out. And now he's gone. And this—" I gestured helplessly at the envelope. "This happened."

Jamie straightened slowly.

"I'm going to have to tell Farrow," he said.

"I know," I whispered.

He sighed deeply. "We'll get him."

The next two hours were a blur.

Statements. Repeated questions. Dates and timelines. A call patched through to Interpol.

No one seemed particularly interested in my cat.

When I finally voiced that—quietly, miserably—Jamie didn't contradict me.

"They're focused on Steven," he said. "But if he contacts you about the ransom, that's our in. That's how we catch him. And hopefully"—his voice softened—"that's how you'll get Ethel back."

Fresh tears slid down my cheeks.

"I just hope she's all right," I whispered.

Jamie studied me for a long second, then glanced at the clock behind the desk.

"Come on," he said.

"What?"

"I've got a break," he went on. "And you look like you're about to fall over."

"I'm fine," I said automatically.

He snorted. "You haven't eaten, have you?"

I opened my mouth to argue, then closed it again.

I had eaten a lot that day, but it felt like five days merged into one. I was completely drained—and yes, I was starving again.

"Didn't think so." He grabbed his jacket. "There's a

place around the corner that does decent food. Not police-canteen decent. Actual decent."

I checked my watch.

The meeting in Oxford was only a few hours away—and I still needed to drive there.

For a moment, the urgency slipped out of focus, like a word on the tip of my tongue that refused to come back. Yes, we wanted to find out what had happened to Drake. He was connected to Maggie, and Maggie to Hatherleigh—and Hatherleigh to that old occult society. There were the ley lines converging at the inn, the frightening mirror, the books, the sigils…a door to the dead.

On the other hand, I was incredibly worried about my dear cat, who was really my reincarnated aunt. My husband had betrayed and abandoned me for a second time and was trying to blackmail me.

I couldn't have explained my hesitation to Jamie even if I'd wanted to.

I didn't need to—he was already steering me toward the door.

The restaurant was warm and softly lit, the kind of place that smelled like bread and comfort. My body responded before my brain did—my shoulders sagging the moment I sat down.

Jamie ordered for me without asking. Soup. Something solid. Water.

"You look wrecked," he said, not unkindly.

"I feel wrecked," I replied.

For a few minutes, we ate in silence. The kind that wasn't awkward—just tired.

Then a familiar voice cut through the low hum of conversation.

"Oh!"

I looked up.

Marjorie Keane stood beside our table, hands clasped to her chest, eyes bright.

"It is you," she said. "Liv. Detective."

Jamie smiled politely. I froze.

"I just wanted to say again—" Marjorie went on, beaming, "thank you. My father…I can't tell you what it's meant to me. Having him found. Having answers. It's like I can finally breathe again."

She laughed softly, wiping at her eyes.

"All thanks to you two," she added warmly. "My heart warms to see you together—such a lovely couple. You really are a dream team."

The words landed between us like a brick on glass.

When Mrs. Keane said goodbye and left, the silence was louder than before.

"She's right," Jamie said eventually.

"About what?" I asked, though I knew.

"We were a dream team."

I swallowed.

So I told him everything.

Steven. Drake. The mirror. The book club. Hatherleigh. The ley lines. The meeting tonight.

I didn't hold anything back.

When I finished, Jamie leaned back in his chair, exhaling slowly. "Bloody hell," he said. "You always do this, don't you?"

"Do what?"

"Fall into the middle of something enormous," he said, with a crooked smile. "And somehow keep going."

"You think I shouldn't investigate," I said. "Not go to the meeting tonight." I half-hoped he'd agree—stop me from going, tell me I was reckless, echo Farrow admonishing me for inserting myself into cases.

"I think it's dangerous," Jamie said. "And I don't like that."

I hesitated. "You could come with me."

He raised an eyebrow. "Are you serious?"

"We *are* a dream team," I said weakly.

He thought about it. Really thought.

Then he shook his head. "As much as every instinct I have says I should protect you," he said quietly, "this part? This is yours. Your world. Your rules. You and your… witchy relatives."

I smiled despite myself.

"I'll focus on Steven," he went on. "On finding him. That's how we get Ethel back."

The loneliness hit then. Sharp and sudden.

It felt symbolic that we wouldn't do this together, like it somehow mirrored the fracture in our romantic relationship.

"You think I can do this?" I asked.

Jamie met my eyes, steady and sure. "Yes," he said. "I have every faith in you."

Something warm bloomed inside me again. Despite the break in our partnership, I had the feeling something new was growing too.

It was only a tiny seedling—but I held on to it, nonetheless.

CHAPTER THIRTY-FIVE

The road to Oxford stretched ahead of me, dark and slick with rain, the white lines blurring whenever my eyes tried to close for more than a heartbeat.

Part of me wanted—desperately—to turn around.

Ethel was gone. Steven was gone. That should have been enough for one night, for one lifetime. My instincts screamed that I should be home, hovering over the cottage, waiting for the phone to ring, pacing the kitchen floor until dawn if I had to.

But there was nothing I could do right now.

The police had taken over. Officers were watching the cottage in case the ransom instructions arrived. Jamie had promised they'd trace any call, any message, the moment it came in. I'd been told—firmly—not to interfere.

Ironically, it helped that Steven was an internationally wanted fugitive. If this had been just a missing cat, no one would have mobilized so many resources. No Interpol. No late-night calls. No unmarked cars outside my home.

My children were inside that cottage with Emerald,

and with the police so invested in catching Steven if he turned up there, I felt they were protected.

Otherwise, the thought of my kids alone would have compelled me to turn around and go home.

Maggie might not have taken Ethel. But her interest in my cottage still gnawed at me. Ethel's warning echoed in my head, as clear as when Audrey had repeated it to me: *Don't let her in.*

A shiver ran down my spine when I thought about the protection sigils scratched into the old floorboards. And I still thought Maggie was involved with Drake's disappearance. With Hatherleigh. With everything that had happened at the inn.

The inn was Gina and Emerald's home, and I had to help them. They had been ridiculed by the press, turned into even more of outsiders, implicated in whatever dark thing had happened there. Hatherleigh's involvement, the mirror, the sigils—everything we'd learned since— screamed danger. Hatherleigh had taken advantage of Emerald to gain knowledge of and access to the inn; he would use it somehow. Drake's disappearance was just the beginning, and whatever he or Maggie—or both of them —had planned, I needed to make sure it wouldn't happen.

I was in a unique position to find out more about Hatherleigh and his plans tonight, and I had to use that opportunity.

The invitation sat on the passenger seat beside me: a torn scrap of notebook paper, creased and smudged, the address scrawled in uneven ink. I unfolded it again at a red light, reading the address for the fifth time.

It directed me to a service entrance near Broad Street.

I parked where the GPS gave up, in a narrow side street that smelled faintly of damp stone and old leaves. Oxford at night felt older somehow, as if the centuries pressed closer once the tourists and students went to bed. I tucked the scrap of paper into my coat pocket and followed the directions on foot, past locked doors and blank stone walls, until I found it: an unmarked metal door set into the side of a building.

There was no sign. No handle. Just a small, dark camera eye embedded in the stone.

I hesitated, heart thudding, then knocked.

For a moment, nothing happened. Then a panel slid open just enough for someone to look out. I couldn't see their face—only a glinting eye.

"Yes?" a voice said.

My mouth went dry. "I—" I swallowed. "The password is…*speculum.*"

The panel closed. Locks shifted. The door opened inward with a low groan, releasing a breath of air that smelled of wax and dust and something older.

I let my long dark hair fall into my face and just nodded in the direction of the person guarding the door without really looking at them. My heart thudded against my chest, half expecting them to realize I was an impostor.

But they didn't stop me as I moved down the short, narrow corridor lit by wall sconces.

Stone steps spiraled down into darkness.

I descended slowly, every nerve screaming. The sound of the city vanished behind me, replaced by the soft echo of my own footsteps. The passage widened at the bottom into a low, vaulted space—an underground chamber that might once have been part of the Bodleian library's vast underbelly, where books had been stored and ferried through tunnels long since sealed off from public access.

Thick candles lined the walls, their flames bending strangely, as if drawn toward the center of the room. A chalk sigil had been drawn on the stone floor—intricate, looping, incomplete in a way that made my eyes itch when I tried to follow its lines.

Figures stood in a loose circle around it.

I couldn't see their faces clearly. Just silhouettes. Coats. Scarves. Hands folded or clasped too tightly.

"You made it."

I flinched.

Yellow-Teeth Girl stepped out of the shadows beside me, her curls even more unruly in the candlelight, her eyes bright with something I couldn't read.

"Oh—Yell—" I stopped myself, heat rising to my face. "I mean—what's your name, by the way?"

She smiled. "Naomi."

"Nice to meet you properly, Naomi. I'm Liv," I said automatically, before it occurred to me that I might have been better off with an alias.

But she said, "I know," and I realized she must have learned more about me than I'd thought when she'd come to my rescue during my near arrest for allegedly stalking Mabel Scarboro. Now I was glad I'd used my real name— otherwise, she might have wondered what I was playing at.

"There's a more formal part first," Naomi whispered, nodding toward the circle. "Alaric gives a little speech. History, purpose, all that. Afterward, we mingle." Her smile widened. "I can introduce you to him then. I told him about you, and he's very eager to meet you."

My stomach lurched. "Can't wait," I croaked.

With my amber eyes, dark hair, and curvy build, I didn't look like Emerald, so Alaric wouldn't see a resemblance. But he would ask me questions—and I was terrible at lying.

The moment he heard that I was from Fairwyck, suspicion would spark.

As the candles dimmed and someone began to speak at the far end of the chamber, I stuck my hands into my coat pockets to stop them from shaking. The murmuring died away as someone stepped into the center of the circle.

He was tall—taller than I'd expected—and moved with deliberate, almost ceremonial calm. A long robe hung from his shoulders, heavy black wool edged with a thin line of dull silver thread. The hood was drawn low, shadowing his face, so all I could see was the suggestion of a strong nose, the pale line of his chin.

Alaric Hatherleigh.

No one announced him. They didn't need to. The room seemed to tighten around his presence, the candle flames dipping as if acknowledging him.

He raised one hand, and silence settled completely.

"Friends," he said, his voice carrying easily through the underground chamber. Cultured. Warm. The sort of voice that belonged behind a lectern—or on the radio. "We meet again at the threshold."

A ripple of recognition moved through the circle. A few people bowed their heads.

"In the eleventh century," Hatherleigh continued, "a group of scholars—monks, physicians, astrologers, translators—began to question a dangerous assumption." He smiled faintly. "That the world of the living was sealed."

He gestured to the sigil beneath his feet.

"They called themselves *Ordo Limina Mortis*—the Order of the Threshold of Death. They were accused of necromancy, but they were misunderstood."

My ears pricked up. Maggie was a necromancer. Naturally, this would be something she'd be interested in—it was about her gift.

Hatherleigh continued. "They were *liminarii*. Students of the in-between. For centuries, this order has existed under many names. In Latin. In Norman French. In English barely recognizable to modern ears. But its purpose has never changed."

He took a step closer to the chalk sigil.

"We are the inheritors of the Ordo Limina Mortis," he

said. "The Liminal Order. Keepers of the crossing. Students of the door that stands between the living and the dead."

My pulse quickened.

"The world forgot us," Hatherleigh went on smoothly. "Or chose to dismiss us as superstition, as folklore, as dangerous nonsense best left buried." A faint smile crept into his voice. "But buried things have a way of returning."

A few people chuckled softly. Uneasily.

"Centuries ago," he said, "the Order had a sacred meeting place. A powerful place, much more powerful than this one, where many ley lines converge and the rituals are fed with the right energy. We have been searching for it."

He paused, letting the moment stretch.

"And now we have found it."

The chalk lines at his feet seemed brighter now, almost shimmering in the candlelight.

"Thanks to the tireless work of one of our own," he continued, "the sacred space of the Order—where our predecessors gathered for centuries—has been rediscovered. Prepared. Claimed once more. A sacrifice has been made in our name."

An image of Dr. Malcolm Drake flashed before my inner eye—the earnest ghost hunter, devoted to his work.

My stomach twisted.

Even though I couldn't confirm it right now, I had the strong sense that I had just solved the mystery of his disappearance.

A sacrifice.

"My little disciple," Hatherleigh continued, his tone almost fond, "has done what others could not. She stands even now at the heart of it. Guarding it. Readying it."

Little disciple.

The words scraped against my nerves.

Maggie didn't fit that description. She was short, yes—

but little, in presence or in will, she was not. And she was older than Hatherleigh, sharper, in a way that didn't lend itself to discipleship.

"Our clever plan is coming to fruition," he said. "This place will soon be ours. And it's ready for us to use as we must. There, we can achieve what we have been destined to fail at so far. We have the door to the dead. It is ready and open for us. Under our control."

A low murmur of approval swept the room.

As if on cue, the candles flared—just slightly—and for the first time, Hatherleigh lifted his head.

Light caught his face.

The hood fell back enough for me to see him clearly.

And the world lurched.

I knew that face.

Sharp cheekbones. Dark, intelligent eyes. A mouth that looked kind until you noticed how rarely it truly smiled.

He looked straight at me.

For a heartbeat—just one—it felt as if the entire room vanished, leaving only the two of us staring across the chalk lines and candlelight.

Recognition flickered in his eyes.

Not surprise.

Interest.

My breath locked in my chest.

I stumbled back a step, heart hammering so violently I was sure someone must hear it.

He knew me too.

And I knew something else.

I had to get out of there.

Fast.

CHAPTER THIRTY-SIX

I turned and ran back the way I'd come.

Down the corridor. Up the stairwell. The last few steps to the service door.

There was nobody guarding it now. The person who'd let me in must have joined the meeting. Latecomers wouldn't be admitted.

My trembling hands fumbled with the latch, and I thought I heard footsteps approaching.

The door finally burst open, and I rushed out into the cold night air.

I didn't bother to make sure it closed properly behind me—I just ran. I legged it back to the alley where I'd parked my car. I was suddenly glad I hadn't found a spot closer to the service entrance. This way, I'd put distance between myself and anyone who might try to follow.

Maybe I'd only imagined it.

Hatherleigh might not have bothered interrupting the meeting to come after me.

But he had seen me. That much was certain.

Recognition had flickered in his eyes.

How well he knew me—and my connection to Emerald and the inn—I couldn't say.

It wasn't as if we'd ever really met.

I remembered seeing Alaric Hatherleigh the first time —that first jolt of recognition—in a dream.

The dream where Steven chased me through the inn, interspersed with Gina's tarot reading. The King of Pentacles had appeared, and at the time I'd been sure the card stood for Steven. But in subsequent readings, Gina had drawn the Seven of Swords for him. He'd even left that card behind in the inn, like his own little *fuck you* note.

Deception.

And oh boy, did that fit Steven to a tee.

But the King of Pentacles?

In my dream—surreal as it had been—the King had a face.

At the time, it had seemed random. I hadn't attached any meaning to it. There were all sorts of tarot decks, after all—Gina had been showing the children different ones. Some were stylized, some startlingly realistic. It hadn't struck me as strange then.

But it was Alaric's face. The sharp cheekbones, the aristocratic nose, the smile that wasn't really one—unmistakable.

The realization sent a chill through me.

It made sense in more ways than one. The King of Pentacles was also known as the King of Coins—and coins had been depicted prominently on the card. At the time, I'd assumed they symbolized money, wealth, Steven's obsession with success.

Upright, the card represented a generous, grounded leader. Someone who built security and stability.

Reversed?

Greed. Control. Corruption.

This was Alaric Hatherleigh.

It was strange that my subconscious had given me this clue so early on—before I'd understood what was really happening around the inn.

Back then, I'd only heard his name. I'd only seen the coin with the sigil he'd dropped in the library.

The King of Coins.

Gina had told me that Seven dreams were special. I'd balked at the idea of yet another gift. I didn't want to be a seer too—I had enough on my plate as a ghost photographer, thank you very much.

But Gina had warned me that my abilities encompassed more than that. She'd hinted at it during the memory regression sessions—when I'd been able to slow down and manipulate time inside a memory, and a ghost had slipped me a vital clue.

The camera wasn't my gift.

It was just a tool.

A medium.

Still…I didn't believe the tarot card had been a vision plucked out of nowhere. Alaric had recognized me too. That meant we'd crossed paths in real life before.

All my intuition had done was put his face where it belonged.

As I sped through Oxford, my mind raced.

Where had I seen him?

The answer hit me just before Witney.

I took the next exit off the A40 and found myself in a little village with the impossibly cute name of Ducklington. I pulled into a deserted car park and killed the engine.

My heart hammering, I dug my camera out of my bag and flicked through the recent images.

I reached the photos from the night of the book club meeting—just before Steven had turned up on my doorstep.

Esme and I had walked home from the library, joking

about ghosts. I'd taken pictures to prove there weren't any lurking nearby.

There had been a presence in one of the shots. Someone half-hidden behind a building. The face had been indistinct, but something about it had felt familiar.

Later, I realized it had been Steven. Watching me. Following me. Not a ghost at all.

Something similar had happened at the graveyard. I'd thought I'd seen Steven then too, and for a moment I hadn't known who was living and who wasn't.

Ghosts appeared in my photographs—never to the naked eye, only through the lens. In images, they looked like real people.

And if a real person happened to be nearby when I took a picture—someone I hadn't noticed—it would be easy to mistake them for a ghost afterward.

And there he was.

The only figure beneath the awning.

I'd thought it was the ghost of a monk.

Now I recognized the robe instantly.

It was the same one Alaric Hatherleigh had worn at the meeting.

And the face—

The face I'd seen on the tarot card.

The face I'd seen tonight.

The man in the picture hadn't been a ghost at all.

He hadn't been benign.

Alaric must have been watching Emerald. Watching the library. Listening, perhaps.

He'd followed me.

All this time, Alaric Hatherleigh had been a peripheral figure. Mysterious. Elusive. Someone we'd felt rather than seen. He'd sought the ley-line nexus. He'd used Emerald to find the map. He'd been connected to Drake's disappearance.

But he'd never shown up at the inn.

Or so we'd thought.

Even Emerald hadn't spoken much about him at first.

And yet—

He'd been there.

Hiding in the shadows.

All along.

As I drove home through the night, one thought wouldn't let go of me. If he'd been watching us without being seen…

What else had we missed?

What else was right in front of us—

And invisible?

CHAPTER THIRTY-SEVEN

I wanted nothing more than to go home. Make sure the children and the cottage were all right. Find out whether the police had made any progress in their investigation—whether they were any closer to finding Steven.

And Ethel.

And then go to bed.

Holy cow, I wanted nothing more than to go to bed.

But after what I'd learned tonight, a restless urgency burned inside me, overriding everything else. I felt compelled to do something I should have done days ago—something I'd been too cowardly to face.

So I drove straight to the inn.

Entering through the main entrance, beneath the sign with the bloated salmon, almost felt familiar now. The charged atmosphere in the tavern certainly did. But the haunted ambience—no, that was something I never got used to. It still chilled me to the bone, raised the hairs on my arms, made the back of my neck prickle.

The floorboards creaked as I climbed the stairs. My

body felt thick and uncooperative, as though I were wading through syrup, and I wasn't sure I'd make it to the door at the top.

When I finally reached it, I had to stop and catch my breath before pushing it open.

I stood alone in the upstairs hallway, my camera hanging from my neck, its familiar weight the only thing keeping me anchored.

For a moment, I listened to the silence that wasn't really silence at all. Wood groaning. Mice rustling. Pipes gurgling.

Ghosts hovering.

I turned toward the open door of Drake's room and caught a flash of myself in the mirror.

Hadn't I covered it with a coat?

There wasn't one now. I hadn't noticed that earlier, when we'd been searching for Steven. Maybe someone had removed it during the chaos.

My eyes burned. My arms felt unbearably heavy. Still, I raised the camera.

"If you're here," I murmured into the darkness, my voice barely more than a breath, "please. I need you to tell me what happened to Drake."

I lifted the camera and pressed the shutter.

The flash burst white against the dark.

When I looked at the screen, my stomach clenched.

The ghosts were there—several of them, faint and indistinct, gathered in the corners farthest from the mirror. Their forms blurred at the edges, faces turned deliberately away, just as before.

But something was different.

Across the surface of the mirror, pale markings shimmered, as if someone had breathed onto the glass and traced symbols into the fog with a finger.

I frowned and stepped closer, taking close-ups of the mirror.

The markings were still there in the new photos, glowing faintly on the display.

The writing wasn't English. It wasn't Latin, or anything I recognized from Emerald's books. The symbols looped and crossed in unfamiliar ways.

"What is that?" I whispered.

I took another photograph.

And another.

The ghosts were closer now, edging toward the mirror. I could see their faces clearly—a child clutching a candle, a knight in armor, a maid with a crooked neck.

They pointed.

At the mirror.

My pulse quickened.

"I knew it," I said softly. "This is the door. Drake went through it. That's what you're telling me, right? The door to the dead."

Alaric Hatherleigh's words echoed in my mind.

A sacrifice.

"Who's responsible?" I asked. "Can you tell me? Who made Drake go through the mirror?"

I took more pictures.

The ghosts didn't approach the mirror any closer—perhaps they didn't dare. They also didn't change what they were doing.

They just kept pointing.

I exhaled shakily and scrubbed a hand over my face. "Great," I muttered. "Very helpful."

I lowered the camera, suddenly overwhelmed by the sheer weight of the day—Mabel Scarboro, Oxford, the research at the library, the intervention, Ethel's disappearance, Steven gone, the ritual, Hatherleigh.

Everything pulling at me from every direction.

"I'm too tired for riddles," I whispered. "I really am."

"Liv?"

I nearly jumped out of my skin.

I spun around, the camera swinging wildly. "Jesus—Emerald!"

She stood a few steps behind me, hair loose, cardigan pulled tight around herself. Her face was pale, her eyes sharp with concern.

"I heard a noise," she said quietly. "Thought someone was breaking in. What are you doing up here?"

I let out a breath that felt like it came from somewhere deep in my bones. "I'm…finally asking the ghosts," I said, gesturing weakly toward the mirror. "Or trying to."

She glanced past me, then back again. "And?"

"And they're not telling me anything I didn't already suspect," I said, rubbing my temples. "Drake disappeared through the mirror. The door to the dead. After everything we've learned, it's obvious."

I blinked. "Wait. You were supposed to go to the cottage with the children."

"I know," she sighed. "Audrey refused to leave. Said her dad disappeared here, and she didn't want to abandon him. Blake went with Lucy to stay at the cottage. I knew you wouldn't want it empty—in case someone got in touch about Ethel."

"The police should have it covered," I said, yawning so widely it nearly cracked my jaw. "Still—glad someone's there."

"Come on," Emerald said gently. "You look exhausted. We can talk more comfortably in the parlor. You can tell me about Oxford."

I didn't have the energy left to protest, even though I hadn't learned everything I'd hoped to. I barely made it to the parlor before sinking onto the chaise like a stone.

Emerald sat opposite me, watching my face closely. "So —did you meet Alaric?" she asked. "What did he say?" She leaned forward, brimming with eager anticipation.

I started telling her about the meeting place. About the Ordo Limina Mortis. About the ritual circle, the candles, the speech. My words slowed, thickened. My eyelids kept fluttering shut against my will.

Before I could get to the part where I'd realized I'd seen Alaric before, sleep dragged me under.

～

I KNEW I WAS DREAMING.

I was back in the upstairs corridor of the inn. The air shimmered faintly, as if reality itself were slightly out of focus. The mirror loomed before me, larger than it should have been, its surface dull and opaque.

One of the ghosts stood beside me.

For once, it didn't turn away.

She was a young woman, dressed in clothes from another century, her expression calm and patient. The maid with the crooked neck. It had been broken long ago, her head perpetually tilted at an unnatural angle.

She didn't speak.

She simply gestured toward the mirror.

The strange writing was there again, smeared across the glass.

"I don't understand it," I said, frustration rising even here. "I don't know what it says."

Then the ghost pointed—not at the mirror, but behind me.

I turned.

Leaning against the wall was another mirror. Smaller. Plain. Unremarkable.

My breath caught.

"No," I whispered. "You can't mean—"

She nodded.

Moving as though I were underwater, I lifted the second mirror and held it in front of the first.

The moment the reflective surfaces aligned, something shifted.

The writing changed.

The symbols straightened. Reversed. Resolved themselves into letters I could finally read.

But I didn't.

Instead, I woke up to cheerful British voices.

Disoriented, I blinked and looked around.

My gaze snagged on a tumble of blond hair.

I sat up with a start.

"Audrey!"

My daughter was perched sideways on an armchair, knees pulled up, staring at the television. She didn't turn around.

I took in my surroundings, still fuzzy with sleep.

I was in Gina's parlor—which, incidentally, I hadn't even known had a TV. It must have been hidden inside one of the cabinets.

Or was I still dreaming?

At that moment, Gina bustled into the room, carrying a tray.

"Oh good, you're awake," she said brightly. "I brought breakfast."

I brushed my hair out of my face and rubbed my eyes. "Good morning," I yawned. "Are you all right, honey?" I asked Audrey.

She didn't look back at me—but at least she shrugged.

A reaction. That was progress.

Gina poured me a cup of tea. I was grateful for the warmth, though what I really needed was strong coffee. I still felt oddly detached from my own body, as if I hadn't fully returned.

"…famously known as the *Inn of Doom*," a voice on the TV cut through my fog.

I frowned and focused.

Morning television. The same grinning hosts as the other day, cheerfully holding up tabloids again.

On the screen was a particularly unflattering photo of Gina on the front page of the *Sun*, headlined: TAROT HAG OF THE HAUNTED INN.

I groaned. Maybe I was still dreaming. I could only hope.

"…and Dr. Drake still hasn't been found," the orange-faced host continued. "He hasn't come forward. According to a poll we conducted yesterday, the British public agrees that police should really take another look at the inn owner, Gina Seven."

I sank back into the cushions. Surely this couldn't be real.

"Not just Gina Seven," the male host chimed in. "But the entire Seven family. Interesting details about Gina's niece have come to light—and Dr. Drake's disappearance just might have something to do with it."

I choked on my tea, staring at the screen with bulging eyes.

Gina's niece?

Surely they couldn't mean—

"Yes," the female host said, her smile fixed and artificial. "Liv Grantham fled the USA after her husband, Steven Grantham, conned millions out of unsuspecting investors with a massive Ponzi scheme—dubbed by the FBI as the Con Job of the Century. Rumors have it Netflix is already producing a documentary."

Audrey had gotten up from her chair.

Gina was still pouring tea into her cup, even though it was overflowing.

I only noticed it out of the corner of my eye; I couldn't get any words out to comment on it.

The male host—with teeth far too white to be trustworthy—held up *The National Herald*.

PONZI-SCHEME CON MAN VANISHES IN HAUNTED INN

"Turn that off!" I screamed, frantically searching for the remote.

Audrey turned toward me, tears filling her eyes. "They don't mean Dad, do they, Mom? They said his name."

I finally spotted the remote on the coffee table and stabbed at the buttons at random.

"Oh, honey," I said softly. "I'm afraid so."

Audrey crossed the room in two quick steps and launched herself into my arms. The remote slipped from my fingers and clattered onto the floor.

I didn't care. I wrapped my arms around her, holding her tight.

I knew I'd made mistakes in the way I'd handled everything with Steven—although I'd done the best I could under the circumstances. But as long as Audrey still came to me when she was upset, still let me comfort her, things weren't beyond repair. We would find our way through this.

My eyes flicked back to the screen.

I hadn't turned it off—I'd just switched channels. Thankfully, it wasn't another morning show. No doubt Steven's crimes, and our connection to them, were being dissected everywhere by now. Someone at the police station had wasted no time feeding information to the press.

This channel, however, was showing a repeat episode of *Ghost Hunter UK*. Given the scandal and Drake's disappearance, it made grim sense. A ratings boost.

Gina seemed to recover from her shock then, finally noticing the mess she'd made.

"Oh dear," she murmured, setting the teapot down at last. "Let me get a cloth—and I really ought to make fresh toast. It's completely soaked."

"It's all right, you don't have to—" I began, but she was already bustling out of the room.

I sighed, stroking Audrey's hair, my gaze drifting back to the screen.

Dr. Malcolm Drake was delivering his closing monologue. As always, he laid out a rational explanation grounded in historical research—then gently undercut it with something that refused to be explained away. He ended, as he always did, by suggesting that the world was larger, stranger, and far more mysterious than reason alone allowed.

He looked every inch the charismatic professor in his waistcoat, unruly gray hair catching the light. His eyes twinkled as the camera moved in close for his final words.

A sacrifice.

Hatherleigh's voice echoed in my mind, and my chest tightened with pity.

Drake had been nothing but a pawn in a far darker game.

The end credits began to roll to the familiar *Ghost Hunter UK* theme. I stared at the screen, trying to think. Trying to find a way—any way—to stop Alaric Hatherleigh.

Then a name caught my eye.

I gasped. Every muscle in my body went rigid.

Audrey pulled back slightly. "What is it, Mom?"

I pointed at the screen, but no sound came out.

The credits continued to roll. The name was already gone.

But I'd seen it.

I hadn't imagined it.

No—absolutely not.

Historical advisor: Lucy Seven.

CHAPTER THIRTY-EIGHT

Gina came back into the parlor with fresh toast.

"Where is everyone else?" I stuttered, still staring at the screen, even though the credits had ended and the next show had already started. "Emerald? Lucy? Maggie?"

"Emerald is at the library," Gina said, wiping spilled tea from the table. "She had to go to work—it's open Saturday mornings, remember? Lucy is with Blake at your cottage."

"Oh. Yes. I remember," I said, adrenaline flooding my system.

I got to my feet. "I should go there. Check on them," I added nervously, my thoughts running in frantic circles. Blake, Audrey, and Emerald had all insisted that Lucy was a good person. Apparently, even Beltane the cat agreed. She couldn't have anything to do with this—could she? And if she did, she wouldn't be doing any harm in my home. She couldn't be a danger there. After all, Ethel had warned Audrey about Maggie, not her daughter…

"…Maggie is here—she just got up," I caught only the

tail end of Gina's explanation, having tuned out for a moment.

"Did someone want me?"

Maggie entered the parlor.

"Um…" I said, looking at her with uncertainty. She wore elegant wide-legged trousers, a crisp, impeccably tailored white blouse, and an expensive Hermès silk scarf. Her dark curls were piled atop her head, revealing beautiful pearl earrings that swung gently as she moved.

Alaric Hatherleigh's words from the previous night echoed in my mind—*my little disciple*. No. It didn't fit Maggie at all. But it did fit someone else.

"Do I have something on my face?" Maggie asked, an amused glint in her coal-black eyes.

I shook my head. "Maggie," I said, "I just read the strangest thing on TV. They were showing an episode of *Ghost Hunter UK*, and in the end credits I saw Lucy's name. Lucy Seven. Historical advisor."

"Why, yes," Maggie said, sounding genuinely surprised. "Didn't you know? Lucy consults for the production company that makes Dr. Drake's show. That's how we met. She introduced me to him. We connected over our mutual love of rare books."

"No. No, I didn't know." My thoughts spun wildly, trying to align this new information with everything else. I'd never thought to ask Lucy about her work. She was in her thirties, but for some reason I'd always thought of her as someone who still lived with her mother—dependent, sheltered, without much of a life of her own. She had an old-fashioned air about her, like the unmarried female relative in a Victorian novel. I hadn't expected her to be an expert in anything. "So…Lucy is an expert in history?"

Maggie, who had taken a seat at the table, picked up an empty cup and poured herself tea. "Yes. She has a doctorate in medieval history."

More alarm bells began clanging in my head, drowning out my own voice. "And where did she study?"

"Oxford," Maggie said, dropping a sugar cube into her tea in a casual, offhand way.

I gasped.

She paused mid-stir, watching me closely. "Why?"

"Well…it's just that…Oxford." I forced a laugh. "That's very impressive, isn't it?"

Maggie sniffed, taking a sip. "I suppose. Lucy is clever enough. What you must understand about my daughter, however, is that knowledge is just knowledge to her. She collects it. Catalogs it. Passes it on. All very theoretical. She has no desire—or aptitude—for practical application. For effecting change. For doing something."

I would have liked to tell Maggie right then that she was probably very wrong.

Maggie was a smart woman who missed very little—but she had a blind spot when it came to her daughter.

Lucy could very well be the mastermind behind an operation seeking precisely that, the practical application of arcane knowledge.

I didn't have time to debate it now.

If I was right, then the person who had sacrificed Dr. Drake in a dark ritual, who had dragged my relatives and their inn into scandal and danger, who was so adept at subterfuge that everyone saw her as harmless, was with my child right now. In my home. The very place that was supposed to be protected.

We'd thought that protection was meant to keep Maggie out.

But what if Audrey had misunderstood Ethel?

She'd never finished that conversation before Ethel was taken.

I forced myself to stay calm—both to avoid alarming

anyone and because I had no idea how I'd even begin to explain myself.

"I really ought to go home now," I said.

I glanced uncertainly at Audrey. I didn't want to be separated from her—but if what I suspected was true, I didn't want her anywhere near Lucy.

"Can I stay here, Mom?" Audrey asked, neatly solving the problem for me. "I want to be here in case Dad—"

"Sure," I said quickly, then left after a hasty round of goodbyes.

I sped home. A car was parked close to my driveway; the man inside had to be a police officer. That calmed me a little—I was glad they'd kept their promise. At the same time, I doubted Lucy would let herself be deterred by his presence, whatever her plan was.

I let myself into the cottage.

"Blake?" I called.

No answer.

Then I saw the note on the kitchen table, and my heart skipped a beat.

Was this a follow-up ransom note? If so, how had the police missed someone dropping it off?

I pulled my phone from my bag to check for missed calls or messages—only to realize the battery was dead.

My pulse spiked. Anything could have happened, and I wouldn't have known.

Before plugging the phone in, I grabbed the note, heart hammering in my chest.

It was Blake's handwriting.

Lucy and I have gone to the library. Love, Blake.

I exhaled slowly in relief.

Nothing about Ethel. And Blake was with Emerald— someone I trusted completely. Whatever Lucy might have been planning, my child wasn't alone with her.

I ran upstairs and plugged in my phone.

While it charged, I took a quick shower, brushed my teeth, and changed into clean clothes. Hair still wet and not bothering with makeup, I unplugged the phone and checked my messages. There were only a few from Jamie, *Are you okay?*–type messages. I skimmed them, then called him.

"Any news?" I said instead of a greeting.

"Good morning," Jamie replied. "No. Nothing yet. How are you holding up?"

"I'm home now. I spent the night at Gina's, but Lucy and Blake were here. I saw your guy outside, watching the cottage. You're tapping my phone, right? So we couldn't have missed Steven getting in touch about the exchange?"

"Right," Jamie said. "Don't worry. You haven't missed anything."

"But isn't that strange?" I asked, pacing my small bedroom. "Why wouldn't he have contacted me yet?"

"Sometimes blackmailers wait," Jamie said. "They want to give the victim time to scrape the money together —then they set a very short window for the exchange, so there's no time for interference."

"So this is…normal?" I asked, biting my nail.

"What's normal about a husband kidnapping his wife's cat—who is actually her reincarnated aunt?" Jamie said dryly.

I didn't laugh. "I'm so worried about her."

"I know," he said softly. "But one thing we do know about Steven: He wants money. That fifty grand. He will be in touch."

"Yes," I said. "You're right."

He asked about the Oxford meeting—whether I'd learned anything useful—but I didn't want to get into it.

"I don't know yet," I said vaguely. "I didn't stay long. I might have found something, but I need to confirm it. I'm heading over to Emerald now to talk it through."

We hung up.

I went downstairs and made a thermos of coffee, drinking some while the rest was still dripping through.

The caffeine must have kicked my exhausted brain into gear, because suddenly I remembered.

The dream.

The photographs I'd taken the night before.

I'd planned to show them to Emerald, to ask whether she recognized the language on the mirror—maybe something from her research.

But now I realized I might not need to ask her at all.

I took the memory card from my camera and plugged it into my laptop on the coffee table. I downloaded the latest images and pulled up the close-up of the mirror.

A quick internet search led me to a simple image-editing program. I installed it, uploaded the photograph, and clicked through a few options.

In my dream, the ghost had shown me what to do— hold another mirror up to the writing to read it. The message had been reversed, written from the other side.

The program did the same thing.

I inverted the image.

Just like in the dream, the letters straightened, resolved, became readable. I'd woken up before my dreaming mind could process them.

Now they were right there on the screen.

Clear as day.

I stared at the words, unable to breathe.

WE ARE IN HERE.

GET US OUT.

CHAPTER THIRTY-NINE

I raced to the library.

When I skittered through the door—hair still wet, coat unbuttoned, bag hanging from one shoulder—shouting, "Emerald!" a number of people in the downstairs area turned to look at me with open curiosity.

I flushed. I'd forgotten the library was open to the public this morning.

Quite a few citizens appeared to be taking advantage of that on a cold, drizzly November day. The downstairs area was open-plan, housing the children's books and a small play area, so there were several kids there as well.

A mother pulled her children closer, as if she needed to protect them from me, shaking her head disapprovingly.

I didn't have time to care.

"Emerald?" I called again.

Two elderly women standing by the magazine rack next to the reception desk whispered to each other. I caught the word *con man*, and remembered—with a sick lurch—that I was notorious now.

The patrons' reactions weren't just because of my loud entrance or rumpled appearance.

Oh well…I had bigger problems.

Thankfully, my cousin appeared, murmuring apologies to the other patrons and pulling me into her office.

"What happened?" she asked. "Are you okay?" Concern shone in her big green eyes.

"I didn't see Lucy and Blake," I said, instead of answering. "Are they upstairs somewhere?" I shrugged off my coat and dumped it onto a chair.

Emerald frowned. "Lucy and Blake? They aren't in the library."

"Blake left me a note—said they'd be here." I paced, biting my thumbnail—or what remained of it.

"No, I haven't seen them," Emerald said. "Maybe they stopped somewhere else first and plan to come by later…" She broke off, studying me. "What's going on? You seem really agitated."

That was an understatement. I didn't even know where to begin.

"Hang on," I said. I fished my phone out of my bag and called Blake. It went straight to voicemail, as if they had no reception wherever they were. I forced myself not to panic.

With shaking fingers, I typed a text.

Where are you? I'm at the library—you said you'd be here. Call me!

I tossed the phone onto Emerald's desk, where it landed on a pile of old maps, stacks of books, and sheaves of notebook paper.

"First of all," I said, "I think Lucy is involved with Hatherleigh. I think she orchestrated the whole thing—and that she came to the inn to do the work of Hatherleigh's circle."

Emerald stared at me as if I'd finally lost my mind. "Liv, I really don't think so."

"Did you know she studied history at Oxford?" I shot

back. "That's where she met Hatherleigh, I'll bet. She's a historical advisor for the company that produces *Ghost Hunter UK*. That's how she knew Dr. Drake. That's how Maggie met him."

Emerald's mouth fell open. "Lucy never said."

"Well, she never says much about herself, does she?" I said. "She's so good at reading people—knowing their feelings, manipulating emotions even. She's an empath, probably far more skilled than we realize—and her own mother doesn't seem to know anything about it. No wonder she's managed to convince everyone she's…mild. Benign. Nice."

Emerald shook her head slowly. "I can't believe it. Lucy?"

I told my cousin about the meeting the night before—everything I hadn't managed to tell her because I'd fallen asleep. I didn't remember exactly what I had reported, tired as I had been, so I probably repeated myself.

"Alaric said he wants to resurrect an old order," I said. "The Ordo Limina Mortis. It existed centuries ago, then went dormant. But it once had a powerful meeting place—"

"Yes, yes, yes," Emerald interrupted, jumping up from her chair. "I actually looked that up." She began rummaging through her notes. "Where is it…. Ah. Yes. The Order had different names over the centuries. I didn't connect them before, but once you told me last night, I found the references immediately this morning."

She was breathless now, words tumbling over each other.

"It's always the same core idea," she said. "Always the same obsession."

She jabbed a finger at a circled line.

"Limen. Threshold. Doorway. Crossing."

I bit my nail again.

"It's not about raising the dead," Emerald continued.

"Not really. They were obsessed with access. With reaching across the boundary. Early on, it reads like a spiritual inquiry—but later it becomes clear. It's about opening doors. Literally opening them. Controlling them. Controlling what comes through."

"Yes," I said impatiently. "Hatherleigh said something similar. That it wasn't crude necromancy. But to me, that makes it worse. They want to use it. Use the power."

Emerald nodded, murmuring to herself as she jotted things down, then shuffled her papers again.

"Emerald, listen," I said sharply. "Never mind what the Order did in the past. What matters is what they're doing now."

She froze.

"They found the power nexus again," I said. "The inn. They found the mirror the Order used before—everything the Ordo Limina Mortis and its successors built, everything that was mercifully buried. They put it all together."

I met her eyes.

"And Lucy is at the center of it."

Emerald looked up slowly, staring at me. "I still can't believe Lucy—"

"Alaric called her his little disciple," I said. "The one who's there now, guarding the place. Getting everything ready for them. The door is there. It's open. And a sacrifice has been made."

My voice dropped.

"That was Drake, Em. Drake was the sacrifice."

Emerald furrowed her brow. "What—"

"She must have pushed him through the mirror," I said. "Or convinced him to go through it. To open the door. But I don't think it worked the way they expected. Or maybe they're still waiting for something."

I shook my head. "I don't know. But it's clever—terrifyingly clever. The inn belongs to Gina. You and she live there. If Hatherleigh had come asking questions himself, you'd have been suspicious. Even if he was courting you."

Emerald's face went red.

"It would have taken him a very long time to gain your trust," I went on. "Enough trust for you to invite him to the inn, to let him roam freely and do whatever he wanted—if you and Gina ever would have let him at all. So… Enter Dr. Malcolm Drake."

Emerald's eyes widened.

"Gina adored him," I said. "Of course she would let him film an episode of his show at the inn. It gave Lucy the perfect way in—through her mother, who had been trying to reconnect with her estranged sister for a while. And with Maggie's big personality dominating every room, Lucy could easily stay on the periphery. No one would notice her. No one would suspect she was pulling the strings."

I shook my head. "Drake was fascinated by the paranormal. He was receptive to Hatherleigh's research. Lucy probably gave him the book. Suggested he try this ritual or that one. Maybe hinted that something like the mirror was there. That's why he hid its discovery from his production team. The way he filmed his episodes—it was the perfect setup. Lucy probably didn't even have to do much. Drake opened the door himself. Went through the mirror. Became the sacrifice."

Emerald had gone very still.

"After that, Lucy and Hatherleigh only had to wait things out," I continued. "The police got involved. The press caught wind of it. But Lucy stayed right there, close to the center of things. Monitoring. Controlling."

I rubbed my forehead. "Who knows what their plan is exactly, but I wouldn't be surprised if Hatherleigh—or someone acting on his behalf—eventually makes Gina an offer for the inn. She's being hounded by the press. It's already unbearable. If someone came along with the right sum of money…she might feel she had no choice but to sell the Inn of Doom."

"Mother would never—" Emerald began.

"*We* know that," I interrupted gently. "Lucy didn't know Gina back then. Maybe she's realized it by now, but I think that was the original plan. Hatherleigh and the resurrected Order would own the inn. They'd have free rein over the power nexus. They could perform their rituals at the heart of it, undisturbed."

I hesitated, then added quietly, "And Lucy is very good at waiting. At staying ready. At pivoting."

I pulled a face. "She did it with Steven."

Emerald frowned. "Steven?"

"When I hid him at the inn," I said. "Gina told me Lucy went to him. Brought him cake. Sat with him. Talked to him." I swallowed. "It wouldn't surprise me if—"

I couldn't finish the sentence.

"Steven?" Emerald said incredulously. "What do you mean? Steven kidnapped Ethel and disappeared—"

"I'm not so sure anymore," I said quietly. "I just spoke to Jamie. There's been no contact from the kidnapper. No instructions. No pressure. If Steven was really just after the money, wouldn't he have reached out by now? Don't you think that's strange?"

I grabbed my phone from the table. I'd emailed myself the image earlier.

"I took photos in the inn last night," I said. "There was strange writing on the mirror."

I showed her the picture and explained what I'd seen, the dream, and how I'd inverted the image.

"*We are in here*," I whispered. "*We*, Emerald." Tears spilled over. "I mean, it could be the dead. We, the dead. But I don't think so. It's Drake. He went through the mirror. He's trapped on the other side. He could write on it from there. Why would he include random dead people?"

I shook my head. "It makes much more sense that the we includes the only other person who vanished without a trace from the inn recently, doesn't it?"

"Oh my god," Emerald breathed.

She came around the desk and wrapped her arms around me.

I sagged against her, sobbing now. "What if Audrey was right all along? What if Steven didn't betray us again —what if something terrible happened to him?" My voice broke. "How would we even get someone back from beyond the door? And—and if that's true, then who took Ethel?"

I could barely get the words out. "I think Lucy is responsible," I whispered. "And Blake is with her. And I don't know where they are."

I couldn't speak anymore.

Emerald murmured soothing things, rubbing my back, trying to calm me—but then there was a knock at the door.

A patron, wanting to check out their books.

"I'll be right back," Emerald said softly.

I nodded, wiping my face.

She dealt with the patron while I forced myself to breathe, to pull myself together. By the time she returned, I'd stopped crying.

"I sent everyone home and closed the library," Emerald said. "This is more important. We need to figure out what's going on."

"I agree," I said, grabbing my coat and my bag. "You need to gather everything you have on the sigils. On Hatherleigh's rituals."

I met her eyes.

"Then we're going to the inn. I have a plan."

CHAPTER FORTY

Back in the inn parlor, we sat in a loose circle: Gina perched on the arm of a chair, Maggie standing near the window with her arms folded, Emerald surrounded by books and notes spread across the coffee table, Audrey tucked close to my side on the chaise longue. The fire had been lit, and the flames cast restless shadows across the already too-busy wallpaper.

I told them everything.

About the writing on the mirror. About the dream. About the inversion—the words written from the other side.

We are in here. Get us out.

No one interrupted me. Not even Maggie.

I didn't like that she was here. I didn't fully trust her. But I needed her.

When I finished, Emerald rubbed her hands over her face slowly, then looked up at me. "If you're right," she said carefully, "then the mirror isn't a summoning device. It's a liminal field. A threshold that was forced open and… left unattended."

"Like a door wedged open with a stone," Gina said quietly. "Anyone could wander through. Or get stuck."

Maggie scoffed softly. "Or walk through of their own free will."

I didn't rise to her bait.

Emerald glanced at her. "You don't think Drake was pushed?"

"I think Drake was curious," Maggie replied. "And arrogant. A dangerous combination. He may have believed he was special. Chosen."

"That's what cult leaders tell people," I said.

Maggie's eyes flashed. "And sometimes," she said coolly, "people want to believe it."

"Now, now," Gina said gently. "You're wrong about Dr. Drake. He was earnestly interested in paranormal research —he was probably excited to finally find something real. He was careless."

"Whatever drove Dr. Drake, I don't really care," I said. "He got caught up in it. I'm certain. He's a pawn. Alaric called someone his *little disciple*," I went on. "Someone who prepared the site. Guarded it. Readied it."

Maggie laughed outright. "I still can't believe you think that was Lucy." She shook her head. "Liv, my daughter is many things, but she's not capable of orchestrating something like this. She's sensitive. Scholarly. She lives in her head."

"And you don't see her," I said softly.

The room went still.

Gina cleared her throat gently. "Whatever Lucy's role is—or isn't—we can deal with that later. Right now, two people need rescuing."

Audrey's fingers tightened on the fabric of my sleeve. "Dad didn't abandon us again," she said fiercely. "I told you. I knew it."

I turned to her. "You were right," I said. "I'm so sorry I didn't believe you sooner."

She looked up at me with absolute certainty. "You can get him back."

It wasn't a question.

Emerald studied me for a long moment. "Liv," she said slowly, "what you're suggesting—going into the mirror—that…that's not what the texts suggest. No one ever got the idea to intentionally cross. The rituals are about control. About directing energy from the outside."

"I know," I said.

My heart was pounding now, but underneath the fear was something else. Recognition.

"I don't think this is something that can be done from the outside," I continued. "The Order got it wrong. They always tried to command from beyond the threshold."

I swallowed. "But thresholds aren't meant to be ruled. They're meant to be crossed. I think Lucy understood this, which is why she sent Drake through. To see what would happen."

Gina nodded, but Emerald shook her head.

"Liv," she said, "clearly Drake—and possibly Steven—crossed. They can't come back. What makes you think *you* can?"

I took a breath. "You always said the camera is just a tool for me to communicate with ghosts. Communication is my real gift. The photograph creates a liminal space, where time and meaning blur. But it also creates distance—I needed that because I couldn't fully trust my gift, trust myself. Dreams, memories, mirrors—that's where I get messages from the spirits. They're all liminal spaces. It's where I belong. Hatherleigh has dedicated his life to resurrecting an order of liminal men. He sought the right rituals, the right space, the right tools…" I paused. "Well, he didn't know that all he needed was me. Someone like me."

I hesitated, then added, "Maybe he did have an inkling. Naomi—who also seems to be gifted—told me Hatherleigh is very interested in women with the sight. Maybe that's what he hoped to find in you too, Emerald. To use you for…something. But your gift is a different one."

"And so he used me for something else," Emerald said bitterly. "For information. But Liv—if what you're saying is true, Hatherleigh can never know."

"I know," I said. "That's why we need to act fast." I drew a breath. "I got a message from Blake. She's in Oxford. Said Lucy wanted to show her the Bodleian—that's the library she mentioned in her note. Claimed it would cheer her up and distract her from worrying about Ethel. Lucy isn't going to hurt Blake—not now. She thinks she's in control of everything. But she won't stay away from the inn much longer. So we need to do this *now*."

I turned to Maggie. "You studied the books from the hidden chamber. Emerald researched the sigils and Hatherleigh's texts—I believe together you can set up a ritual that will help me cross through the mirror and return."

Maggie's eyes sparkled with interest. She was clearly up for the challenge.

But Emerald shook her head. "We need more time to do this properly. We can't just—"

Audrey interrupted her. "Mom can do this. She can do anything."

Gina reached out and covered my hand with hers. "She's right," she said. "If anyone can do this, it's you, Liv."

Emerald exhaled slowly. "I don't like it," she admitted. "But…if everyone is sure—and if you think you know what you're doing, Liv…I'm on board."

I stood, my legs trembling. I wasn't sure what I was

doing. I was completely relying on my intuition. But I knew it was finally time to trust my gift.

"Okay," I said. "Let's go next door and set everything up."

~

THE SIGILS WERE DRAWN ON THE FLOOR, CHALK LINES overlapping and intersecting like a map of something only half remembered. Maggie and Emerald stood on either side of the circle, murmuring chants from Alaric Hatherleigh's book, their voices low and rhythmic, Latin folding into something older, harsher, the words grating at me the longer the chanting went on.

Candles burned at the cardinal points. The air smelled of wax, dust, and old stone.

I moved in front of the mirror.

And nothing happened.

I turned around.

Audrey was curled up on Drake's old cot in the corridor, Beltane tucked into the crook of her arm, purring softly. Gina sat beside her, one hand resting protectively on my daughter's knee. Audrey wouldn't agree to stay next door, and I'd wanted her as far away from the mirror as possible. Now it looked as though I needn't have worried.

Audrey smiled at me encouragingly. "You can do it, Mom."

Gina nodded, calm and certain, as if this were already a foregone conclusion.

I was grateful for their unwavering support—but doubt was creeping in now, cold and insidious.

I looked over at Maggie. She was leafing through one of the books from the hidden chamber, her brows drawn together in a tight knot. For a moment, the thought crossed my mind that she was sabotaging us. But then she sighed softly, an embarrassed sound, and turned a page back, as if hoping she'd missed something.

It was the first time she didn't look self-possessed. The first time she looked…out of her depth.

Emerald looked no better. "I don't understand," she said, frustration bleeding through her carefully controlled tone. "This should work. Drake crossed without help. Steven too. I thought you'd just need a nudge." She gestured helplessly at the sigils, the notes, the stacks of books. "We have everything. The theory. The rites."

Something she'd said snagged in my mind.

Without quite knowing why, I reached for my camera.

I unscrewed the lens cap and lifted it, my hands steadying the moment the familiar weight settled against my palms. I took photographs of the corners of the room.

They were all there.

The knight, his armor scarred and dripping with water. The shadow man in the tricorn hat, his pistol gleaming as he turned away. The child with the candle. The maid with the crooked neck.

And others—more than I'd ever seen before. A man clutching a trumpet. A woman with a shorn head and hollow eyes. An ancient figure with a long white beard that faded into mist.

They were closer now. Watching.

I lowered the camera and looked at Emerald and Maggie, bent over their research.

"Can you clear the room?" I asked quietly. "I have an idea."

Maggie opened her mouth, clearly ready to argue, but Emerald spoke first. "Of course. We'll go into the corridor with Audrey and my mother."

No one wanted me alone with the mirror. I understood that.

After a moment, I nodded.

It didn't matter if they watched. Gone were the days when I felt self-conscious about my gift. And besides—this might not work at all.

Once I was alone, the inn felt different. Quieter. As if it were holding its breath.

I turned to the ghosts.

"I know you're afraid of the mirror," I said softly. "I think it pulls at you. Some of you have been dragged into it, haven't they?"

The temperature dropped. Just a fraction—but unmistakable.

Fear crept into the air like damp fog.

"I think the mirror is a threshold for spirits," I went on. "But two living people crossed it. And I don't think they crossed alone."

The dread thickened, pressing against my chest. Grief trembled through the room, a low, almost inaudible hum.

"I need to cross too," I said. "To help them come back. And maybe—maybe help those of you who were taken as well. I can't promise anything. But I need your help."

My voice wavered.

"One of you has to come with me."

Silence.

Then—something else. Fragile. Trembling.

Hope.

It fluttered through the room, gentle as a moth's wing.

I could have been imagining that too, of course.

And then I felt it.

A touch.

I flinched—but instinct took over. I opened my hand, fingers closing gently around a much smaller one.

A child's hand.

"Hello," I whispered.

In the mirror, a tiny flame flickered.

The child with the candle stepped forward.

Before doubt could take hold, before fear could root me to the floor, the child tugged gently—and the mirror gave way.

There was no shattering. No resistance.

Just cold.

Wet, clinging fog wrapped around me as I stepped through, the air thick as breath held underwater. The child's hand slipped from mine.

I turned, searching blindly.

Nothing.

No mirror. No room. No light.

Only endless gray, swallowing sound and shape alike.

Panic surged, sharp and immediate.

I tried to scream, but my throat locked tight.

What had I done?

I was trapped.

Inside the mirror.

CHAPTER FORTY-ONE

I finally managed to force words out of my throat.

"Hey—little ghost, come back!"

I couldn't feel anything. Or anyone.

"Drake? Steven? Little ghost?" I called again and again.

The fog swallowed my words whole.

No answer.

The silence pressed in on me, heavy and suffocating. I felt utterly alone. Why had I thought I could do this? What made me believe I could cross a liminal space and return?

Maybe I was capable of doing it—maybe that was my nature—but until very recently, I hadn't even dared to photograph ghosts. And ever since I'd begun to embrace my gift again, the camera had been my crutch.

The camera.

As always, it hung around my neck.

I grabbed my Nikon with shaking hands and began to take pictures.

At first, the display showed nothing but dense white fog, textureless and endless. Then—on the edge of one image—I caught a flicker of flame.

I stepped closer and took another photo.

There he was. My little guide. The child with the candle.

But he wasn't by himself.

He stood pressed against the side of a woman dressed in the simple clothing of a bygone era, her garments matching his. She was crying and smiling at the same time, her face radiant with relief. For the first time, the child's face was clear in one of my photographs—and I realized he was a boy. A happy, bright little boy.

The reunion pierced straight through me. For a moment, I forgot where I was. Forgot the fog. Forgot my fear.

Then, at the edge of another photograph, I saw a different figure.

I raised the camera again, heart hammering, and took more pictures.

Another ghost. Then another.

I knew the Ordo Limina Mortis—and those who followed in their wake, Hatherleigh included—were seeking the dead. They wanted to summon them through the mirror, siphon their energy, use that to amplify their power.

But what I was seeing didn't look like an army of the dead.

They looked like…ghosts.

The ghosts from the inn.

As that thought took hold, one of my photos revealed something else.

A gilded edge. A glint of reflected light.

I frowned, shifting my position slightly—though orientation in the fog was nearly impossible.

More photographs confirmed it.

I had captured the mirror.

I moved closer, snapping pictures, staring at the display.

I should have been able to see my own reflection in the glass. Instead, I could see straight through it.

On the screen were my relatives.

Emerald, tense with worry.

Audrey, hopeful.

Maggie, alert and curious.

Gina, calm, serene, unshaken.

Relief flooded me so suddenly, my knees nearly buckled.

Something tugged at me from the direction of the mirror. A gentle pull, insistent but not forceful.

I could get out. I knew it. They were my anchors. If I followed them, I could return.

Then I hesitated.

Drake and Steven were still here.

I had come for them.

I hadn't found them yet—and who knew how far this fog extended? They could have wandered anywhere.

But if I stepped away from the mirror, I might not find it again.

"Hey," I called softly. "Little ghost. My guide."

My voice shook. "Can you help me again? I want to bring you and your mother back through the mirror—but first I need to find the living humans who are trapped here. Can you find them? Can you bring them to me?"

I took another photograph.

In one image, the boy and the woman stood beside me.

In the next, they were walking away together, hand in hand, fading into the fog.

I couldn't be sure they were helping me—but I chose to trust them.

I stayed where I was, waiting.

This place—this no-man's land—felt endless. I couldn't tell how far it stretched or whether it led anywhere else. The land of the dead? Heaven? Hell?

I didn't think so.

This felt like an antechamber. A threshold that didn't open onto anything at all.

The ghosts were trapped here.

The message echoed in my mind.

We are in here.

We.

I had been so sure Drake had written it. So certain that it meant Steven was with him—that Drake wouldn't have included a multitude of dead.

Now I wasn't sure anymore.

I couldn't see the mirror with my naked eye. How would Drake and Steven have found it? How would they even know where to write?

The message must have come from the ghosts after all.

A chill slid down my spine.

Had I been wrong about Steven?

I thought of Audrey—of the devastation she'd already endured—and my chest tightened painfully. I couldn't bear to return without her father. Not again.

Drake, at least. I had to bring back Dr. Drake.

If my ghostly helpers could find him.

Time stretched. The fog seeped through my clothes, my skin, into my bones. My teeth began to chatter.

To distract myself, I raised the camera again.

That's when I saw it.

The ghosts I'd glimpsed earlier—every one of them— were gathered around me now.

Watching.

Waiting.

My mouth went dry.

They wanted to go back.

All of them.

A terrible thought took shape.

What if this had been their plan all along? What if this

—luring me across the threshold—had been their only hope? Had they written the message simply to draw me here?

So I could guide them back out?

But… They were only congregating around the mirror because I was here.

Before that, they must have been wandering aimlessly, stumbling through the fog without direction. Maybe they couldn't see the mirror either—couldn't see their exit.

The thought hit me like ice water.

Then who had written the message?

Not Drake.

Not Steven.

No one from this side.

The ghosts of the inn had tricked me. They had lured me here, used my hope and desperation to free their own.

The realization nearly crushed me.

I was seconds away from giving up—turning my back on this place and stepping through the glass alone, back into the warm, solid world of the living. Back to my children. Back to safety.

Then I heard a sound.

From the other direction.

"Liv?"

My breath caught.

I knew that voice.

"Steven?" I craned my neck, trying to locate the sound through the shifting fog.

Every instinct screamed at me to run toward it—but I forced myself to stay where I was. I lifted the camera with trembling hands and took a photograph.

And there he was.

The child with the candle.

His mother.

Steven.

And slumped against Steven's side—

Dr. Malcolm Drake.

The *Ghost Hunter UK* presenter looked like a shadow of himself: pale, gaunt, barely conscious. Not surprising. He'd been trapped here for days.

"Steven!" I shouted, waving.

"Oh my god, Liv," he said, close enough now that I could see him with my naked eyes through the thinning fog. Tears streamed down his face. "I'm so glad to see you."

He staggered toward me, one arm supporting Drake. "I felt something pulling me," he said hoarsely. "I thought I was losing my mind. But there was nothing I could do—I had to go with it. I've been desperate to follow something ever since getting sucked into that dreadful mirror."

He let out a broken laugh. "I figured I had nothing left to lose."

He tried to hug me with one arm.

"Is he all right?" I asked, nodding at Drake.

Steven shook his head. "He was better when I first found him. Well enough to talk. But he's getting worse. Much worse."

"We're getting you out of here," I said, my voice firm despite the fear curling in my stomach.

"We couldn't find a way out," Steven whispered. "I think the mirror's a trap. And now you're stuck here too."

"Don't worry," I said. "I can do this. Look."

I raised my camera, aimed it toward where I knew the mirror was, and pressed the shutter.

Steven stared at the screen, stunned. "You—you're a godsend," he sobbed. "An angel."

"Hardly," I said. "But I am a Seven. And I have a gift."

For the first time, I didn't feel self-conscious saying it. Not to Steven. Not to anyone. If Fairwyck—or the entire country, given the media frenzy—had a problem with that, they could deal with it. I had my people. That was enough.

"Come on," I said, taking Steven's hand. "Hold on to Drake."

I hesitated, then added, "And…I don't want to freak you out, but we have a few more passengers. The ghosts. They're all coming with us."

Steven gave a shaky laugh. "Ghosts don't scare me anymore. After this? Nothing will. Not even prison. I don't care. Just—please—take me back."

"All right," I said, raising my voice into the fog. "Everyone who wants to leave—hold on to me."

The air shifted. Cold fingers brushed my arms, my shoulders, my back.

I turned toward the mirror, suddenly acutely aware of my pounding heart.

What if this didn't work?

Being able to see the mirror didn't necessarily mean I could pass through it.

I lifted the camera once more and took another photograph—then locked my gaze on the screen.

Audrey's face stared back at me. Hopeful. Fierce. Unwavering.

My anchor.

A calm certainty settled over me.

I stepped forward.

The glass gave way like cool mist.

Steven, Drake, and a whole barrage of specters surged through with me, the sensation disorienting and overwhelming. We stumbled out together, collapsing onto the floor of the room in a tangled heap of bodies and fading forms.

Audrey was there in an instant.

"Oh my god," I gasped, clutching her. "Audrey, I'm so glad you were—"

"Stop right there."

The voice was cold. Male. Controlled.

My head snapped up.

Alaric Hatherleigh stood framed in the open doorway to the corridor.

And he was holding a knife to Emerald's throat.

CHAPTER FORTY-TWO

Hatherleigh stood behind Emerald, one arm hooked tightly across her chest, the silver blade hovering just in front of her throat. He looked at me without flinching.

Lucy stepped around him.

"Bravo," she said lightly. "I wouldn't have thought you had it in you."

She turned to Hatherleigh. "Dr. Drake isn't well. He needs medical attention."

"I couldn't care less," Hatherleigh replied calmly. "He was a sacrifice. He should have remained on the other side—an offering to whatever rules the domain of the dead. Living people aren't meant to come back. They certainly aren't meant to step back and forth through the mirror as they please."

His gaze fixed on me. "What are you?"

"I told you—she's a cousin of mine," Lucy said, unconcerned.

"Where is Blake?" I asked. We were all in danger, but even now—especially now—I had to know where my other child was.

Blake had been with Lucy. And I couldn't see her here.

"They're fine," Lucy said. "Don't worry. They must have noticed something while we were in Oxford—picked up on a thought, an intention. I wanted to bring them to Alaric. They have such potential." She shrugged. "But I must have slipped. Thought something that made them suspicious. They said they needed the loo and never came back."

She chuckled. "We assumed Blake would come here, warn you. So Alaric and I came straight away. Blake and I took the train to Oxford—likely Blake is taking one back too. We were faster in Alaric's car."

Her smile widened. "Little did we know you didn't need Blake at all. You figured it out on your own, didn't you?"

"Um…yes," I said faintly, trying to cope with this overwhelming situation, even though I was still reeling from what had just happened.

Steven was lowering Dr. Drake to the floor, clearly exhausted himself. Audrey knelt beside them, arms wrapped around her father. Drake stirred weakly.

"You're right," I followed up quickly, seizing the moment. "Drake needs medical attention. Please—let them go to the hospital. I'll answer all your questions. Just let Emerald go."

My eyes flicked back to the blade at her throat.

Hatherleigh gave a humorless laugh. "I can't allow Drake to go to a hospital. You've seen the news. His reappearance will cause a media frenzy."

"Yes," I said. "At the hospital. All eyes will be on Drake. That buys you time. Time here. With the mirror."

Hatherleigh opened his mouth—then stopped.

Lucy tilted her head. "It's not a bad idea," she said. "We've already diverted the reporters elsewhere." She glanced at me. "We took a leaf out of Blake's book. When

I spoke to Steven yesterday, he rather proudly told me about their little trick."

She turned back to Hatherleigh. "Drake's return will be the perfect distraction. Police, reporters…they'll rush to the hospital."

Hatherleigh considered it. Then nodded. "Fine. The men can go to the hospital. Your aunt can drive them." He jerked his head toward Gina.

"I'm going too," Audrey said, lifting her chin and fixing Hatherleigh with a fierce stare.

"Whatever," he said. "But if you want your mother to remain unharmed, make sure your father gets there immediately. Leave your phones here, everyone."

Audrey helped Steven to his feet. Together, Steven and Gina lifted Drake, who was conscious now, though barely.

"Emerald should go too," I said. "Let her help them. You have me. I'm the one you want. I can tell you everything about the mirror—how it works."

Hatherleigh laughed. "I'm not letting lovely Emerald go. She'll stay right where she is."

Lucy nodded. "Yes. Liv is a wily one. I'd wager she already has something planned. A hostage keeps her cooperative."

I glared at her, but relief flooded me as Audrey and the others made their way out.

I tried to give Emerald a reassuring look. She was pale. Terrified.

Then something struck me.

"Where is Maggie?" I asked.

Lucy shrugged. "My mother bolted when we arrived. I'm not worried. She won't go to the police. Protecting her own interests always comes first. Implicating her daughter wouldn't serve her reputation."

She giggled. "Still—it must have been quite a shock for her. Realizing she's underestimated me all my life. When she ran past, I saw it in her eyes. Surprise. And…perhaps a little pride."

The thought seemed to light Lucy from within, giving her plain face an almost unsettling beauty.

I understood, on some level, why she'd done it. Maggie had never valued Lucy's gift. Had dismissed her sensitivity as weakness. Not useful, the way Maggie's own power was.

So Lucy had turned empathy into leverage. Observation into control. She'd learned to soothe, to read, to manipulate—quietly, invisibly.

Hatherleigh had seen her potential.

And she had used that.

Whatever her reasons, Lucy had orchestrated all of this. Drake's disappearance. Steven's entrapment. My children's suffering.

Hatherleigh might believe he was in control.

But Lucy had always been the mind behind it all.

Still, Hatherleigh was still very much in control in one sense, as he reminded me that very moment.

The knife hovered at Emerald's throat as he pushed her farther into the room, coming closer to me.

"You're going to tell me—right now—how you managed to cross over and come back," he said evenly, "or Emerald here is going to pay for your stubbornness."

The terror in Emerald's green eyes threatened to shatter my composure, but I forced myself to breathe.

"I think you're wrong about the mirror," I said as calmly as I could. "About all of it. This isn't a door to the dead. You haven't opened that at all. It's just a door to somewhere. An in-between place where the ghosts of the inn got trapped."

Hatherleigh scoffed, shaking his head violently.

"It draws ghosts to it—yes, you're right about that," I went on. "But it isn't doing what it was designed to do. Not what the Ordo Limina Mortis hoped it would do. Not what you hoped it would do."

"You're wrong," Hatherleigh snapped. "This is the place. I finally found it. The Order met here centuries ago. They knew it too."

"Then why didn't they succeed?" I asked. "They performed rituals. They wrote books. They regrouped again and again—now under you. But never for long. Because they always failed here."

"You're trying to trick me," Hatherleigh shouted.

"But that's what I've been trying to tell you, Alaric," Lucy said gently. "I had the same suspicion as Liv. That's why I sent that despicable husband of hers into the mirror —to further test it."

When Hatherleigh shot her an enraged look, she continued smoothly. "I performed the rituals myself. Used the sigils. Followed every instruction precisely. There are no spirits coming through from the other side. No entities we can draw power from. No amplification."

"No!" Hatherleigh barked. "Everything is in place. The ley lines converge here. This must be it."

"Actually—" Emerald said quietly.

So quietly that Hatherleigh almost didn't hear her.

Lucy lifted a hand. "What is it, Emerald?"

"I think you may be wrong," Emerald said, her voice steadier now. "About the power nexus. About this being the strongest convergence."

Hatherleigh dismissed her with a sharp laugh. "You gave me the book yourself. The map. The Order knew about this place for centuries."

"The Order read the map incorrectly," Emerald said. "And the mistake was copied. *Paths of the Ancestors* was written centuries later—it inherited the error."

My stomach clenched. Was this true—or was Emerald bluffing brilliantly?

"You're lying," Hatherleigh said, jerking the hand that held the knife.

The blade nicked Emerald's skin. A thin red line appeared at her throat.

I flinched.

Emerald didn't.

"I'm not lying," she said. "It's in the research. I can show you. My notes are right here."

She gestured to the stacks of papers, books, and maps scattered across the room.

Hatherleigh laughed harshly. "You just want to get away from the knife, you clever little minx. I represent the Ordo Limina Mortis. I've studied them most of my adult life. I'm in possession of their knowledge. I *know* this—not you witches."

But Lucy was already moving.

"Where?" she asked, scanning the maps.

"Remember the map we looked at together, Liv?" Emerald said. "I assumed the Salmon Lands marker indicated the inn. But I was wrong. Just as you suspected—*Salmon*, in its many forms, appears all over the map."

I stepped closer.

"The power nexus is somewhere else."

Lucy handed me a blown-up photograph of the area. I recognized the map Emerald had shown me at the library.

"I want you to turn the ley-lines map around," Emerald said.

"Around?" I asked.

"One hundred and eighty degrees."

I did as she said and placed it over the old vellum map.

The landmarks aligned.

The river's original course was slightly off, a mirror image of what we'd originally thought. But the distance between the river and the convergence point remained identical.

"Oh," Lucy breathed. "Oh my god."

"Everyone read it backward," she said slowly.

"This is ridiculous," Hatherleigh scoffed, though doubt flickered in his eyes.

"No," Lucy said. "It's true. The inn is powerful—powerful enough for the mirror, for the ghosts, for whatever the Order originally built. But the true nexus is elsewhere."

"Let me see!" Hatherleigh demanded.

We brought the maps closer.

"No…" he muttered. "No. It can't be…"

Then something shifted in him.

"But I can fix this," he said feverishly. "I can move the mirror. The books. The ritual. Everything. I just need to transport it to the real site."

In his agitation, he didn't notice Emerald slipping free.

The knife fell to the floor.

Hatherleigh lunged for the maps. "Give it to me. Where is the true location?"

I stepped back instinctively, my focus no longer on convincing him—but on getting Emerald out of danger.

So I didn't really see what was happening until it was already too late.

With the map clutched in his hand, Hatherleigh must have stepped too close to the mirror.

In the blink of an eye, he was gone.

Vanished into the glass.

For what felt like minutes, no one spoke. We simply stared at the spot where he had been, the mirror now dull and unassuming once more.

Emerald was the first to find her voice. "Wh-what just happened?"

I had a growing, prickling suspicion. I lifted my camera and took a few photographs.

On the screen, I could see them huddled together in

the far corner of the room—the maid with the crooked neck, the child and his mother, the shadow man, the man with the trumpet, others who had once been trapped beyond the mirror.

There were so many of them. Too many to count.

But one was missing.

"The knight," I said quietly. "The knight in armor."

"What do you mean?" Lucy asked. "That sounds like one of Aunt Gina's tarot cards."

I sucked in a sharp breath. "Yes. That's exactly it. Gina drew that card for you, Emerald. The Knight of Cups. She told me about it. She thought it meant that your new boyfriend—Alaric—would turn out to be your knight in shining armor."

I shook my head slowly. "She was wrong. That's why she didn't foresee Hatherleigh's betrayal."

Emerald frowned. "Then what does it mean?"

"Another knight saved you," I said. "This one." I gestured vaguely toward the empty space in the photograph. "The ghost who has been haunting the inn the longest. I think he sacrificed himself."

"Sacrificed himself for what?" Emerald asked. "I was already safe from Hatherleigh."

"For the moment," I said. "But this was a greater sacrifice."

I took a breath, trying to put it into words.

"The ghosts are drawn to the mirror against their will. They try to resist, but some don't succeed. They get pulled into the space beyond it and trapped there. This isn't the true power nexus—but it is still a place of convergence. Potent enough for the Order to open something." I swallowed. "Not the door they wanted. Just…a door."

Lucy listened, rapt.

"Living people can't cross on their own," I continued. "Drake was pulled in accidentally, guided—or dragged—

by a ghost. Steven too, I think, though Lucy clearly nudged something along." I glanced at her. "When I crossed, I couldn't do it alone either. A friendly ghost guided me in—and came back out with me. Just like the others."

I hesitated. "At least, I hope none stayed behind."

"Oh," Lucy breathed suddenly. "I get it. The knight took Hatherleigh in."

"Yes," I said. "He must have sacrificed himself so that Hatherleigh would cross."

Emerald nodded slowly. "I'm relieved Alaric can't harm anyone anymore. Though…it's still awful. Being trapped there. I shouldn't wish that on anyone. Not even him."

She paused. "But why would the ghosts do that?"

"Revenge," Lucy said softly, her eyes alight with fascination.

"Yes," I agreed. "I think so too. Hatherleigh aligned himself with the Order—he even said he represented them. And the Order is responsible for centuries of suffering for the ghosts."

Lucy frowned. "What a shame he took the map with him, though. Now we'll never know where the real power nexus is."

I said nothing.

Because I did know.

I had recognized it the moment the maps aligned.

Another place marked with Salmon.

Salmonhus.

Though I had never heard it called that.

I had only ever known it as Ethel's cottage.

My home.

CHAPTER FORTY-THREE

We weren't quite too late.

Maggie was already at the cottage.

She had shoved my furniture aside with ruthless efficiency, as if the room itself were an inconvenience. The rug was rolled up. The table dragged into a corner. Sigils—freshly painted, still tacky—spiraled across the floor around the hearth. Candles stood in careful constellations, some lit, some waiting. Bowls of herbs, chalk, old coins, bones. All the paraphernalia of a ritual that had been planned for years.

But she hadn't begun.

She was still hunched over her books, muttering to herself, turning pages, cross-referencing passages.

Ironically, she possessed the very flaw she had always accused her daughter of: endless study, endless preparation, action postponed until she found the perfect solution in her books.

"You can't stop me," she shouted the moment Lucy, Emerald, and I stepped inside. Her voice echoed harshly off the bare walls. "I'm finally here, and I'm not leaving again. This cottage is mine. Rightfully mine."

She jabbed a finger at the hearth. "I should have been the keeper of the Seven power. Me. I should have guarded this place. Instead, they banished me. Exiled me for one mistake."

Her eyes burned. "One mistake made when I was young. Trying to raise the ancestors. Trying to draw on their power. I shouldn't have been punished for ambition."

Lucy stared at her mother, aghast. "You knew?" she breathed. "You knew all this time that this is the power nexus? That this is where the ley lines converge?"

Maggie sneered. "Of course I knew."

Lucy's voice trembled—not with fear, but with fury. "Then why didn't you tell me? Why did you never tell me?"

Maggie turned on her. "Because I had so much hope for you when you were born. I hoped you'd become the next keeper, take over Ethel's place in the family. But I realized very early on that I was wrong." Her gaze was merciless. "You weren't suitable. You were too soft. Too inward. Useless."

Lucy flinched—just barely.

"Why would I share the greatest secret of our lineage with someone like you?" Maggie went on. "Not even Gina knew. Only Ethel—and our mother. I overheard a conversation between them. That's how I found out. I wasn't supposed to, but I did. It was an epiphany."

Her voice sharpened. "I knew I could only come into my full power by using the untapped energy in this hearth. Look at these silly protection sigils."

She stomped on them.

"Protecting this threshold and carefully guarding it, being content with whatever power seeps through? We should open this door instead. I knew it then—when I tried and was banished by my own mother for it—and I knew it even more certainly later, when I discovered this was the most powerful ley-line convergence, quite accidentally, in an old book."

She laughed.

"I raised the author's shadow to read the map, and unlike all of you fools, I deciphered it correctly. When Ethel died, I knew my time had finally come. I was the only one fit to take over. I knew I'd have to grovel, make nice with Gina, but I was sure she would come around. Persistence paid off."

Her mouth twisted. "Except now Ethel is a bloody cat. Thanks for removing her from the cottage, by the way, Lucy. The only useful thing you've ever done."

There were a dozen things I wanted to ask, a dozen revelations colliding in my head—but one cut through the noise.

"You took Ethel?" I said, staring at Lucy. "Why? And where is she?"

Lucy waved a hand dismissively. "Relax. I didn't hurt her. I needed her gone so you'd assume Steven had taken her. So you'd go to the police. So his disappearance would have a neat, rational explanation."

She smiled, smoothing her blouse. "It worked beautifully. Quite a spectacle, really."

My stomach churned. "You wanted the world to know I'd been hiding Steven. You wanted the scandal. You wanted to humiliate Gina and Emerald—drive us out of Fairwyck—so the inn could be sold to Hatherleigh."

Lucy pouted. "I already had a real estate agent lined up. But honestly? I'm rather glad that damp, drafty, haunted monstrosity turned out to be unnecessary."

She looked around my cottage with open satisfaction. "This place suits me much better. Mother is right. It's ours now."

She flicked her wrist. "You can go."

I shook my head, trying to catch up. Her sudden

change in demeanor was disorienting. "But I thought Hatherleigh—"

"Hatherleigh was a means to an end," Lucy cut in smoothly. "We shared an interest. Resurrecting the Liminal Order. The difference is"—her smile sharpened— "he never understood that *I* was the Order."

She laughed softly. "He underestimated me. Just like everyone else."

Her eyes gleamed. "Did you know the Seven lineage began as part of the Ordo Limina Mortis? Of course you didn't. The Sevens split off early—too squeamish about controlling the dead. Decided their role was to guard liminal spaces instead. What a waste of potential."

Maggie looked up from her book, startled. "You knew that?"

Lucy inclined her head. "You told me once. When I was very small. You thought I wouldn't remember." Her smile was almost tender. "Back when you still believed in me."

She stepped closer to her mother. "Now you see you were wrong. You need me. You always did. And despite everything…" She spread her hands. "I forgive you."

Maggie stared at her, genuinely bewildered.

I had no idea what Maggie might have said next, because at that moment, the police stormed the cottage.

"Police! Steven Grantham!" voices shouted, the front door banged open, boots thundered across my floorboards.

Feet trampled over the painted sigils as the cottage filled with uniforms. I spotted Jamie—and DI Farrow— among them.

"He's not here!" I shouted over the noise. "But she is." I pointed at Maggie. "She broke in and vandalized my property."

Farrow shot me a look that said we'd unpack that later, but Jamie was already pulling out his handcuffs.

"This is my home!" Maggie shrieked. "I live here. This place belongs to me!"

To everyone else in the room, she sounded unhinged. To herself, perfectly reasonable.

Then the chaos escalated.

Steven appeared in the doorway, Audrey at his side, and Gina just behind them.

"Stand back," Steven said calmly, lifting his hands before anyone asked. "I'm turning myself in."

Several officers surged forward anyway. Steven didn't resist. Audrey stood rigidly still, pale but composed—too composed, as if she'd been prepared for this moment.

"It's okay," Steven said as the cuffs snapped shut. "Like I told you on the phone. I'm here voluntarily."

The room seemed to exhale.

Steven craned his neck, scanning the crowd. "Ah. There she is."

He nodded toward Lucy.

"That's the woman I mentioned," he said mildly. "The one who rented the cottage next door. She hid me there after Liv threw me out."

Farrow followed his gaze. "That woman?"

Lucy stared at him, stunned. "What?"

"I'm ashamed to say," Steven went on, with a rueful shrug, "that I took advantage of her feelings for me. Lonely type. Thought it was a romance. She was only too happy to help."

Lucy opened her mouth. Closed it again.

"You're Lucy Seven?" Farrow asked, already scrolling on his phone.

"Yes, but—"

"Yes," Farrow said, without looking up. "I just got word from my colleagues at the station. Records confirm you rented the neighboring property."

"That's where she hid me," Steven continued. "But

things got…odd. Locked doors. Strange behavior. And then I realized she'd locked another guy in the spare room."

Lucy let out a strangled sound.

"Dr. Malcom Drake," Steven said. "Got him to the hospital. When I figured out what was going on, I thought it best to get out. I wanted to see my daughter one last time and then"—he shrugged—"do the right thing. That's why I called DI Farrow from the hospital, told him where he could apprehend me."

Lucy laughed.

Not hysterically. Not in panic. A soft, incredulous laugh.

"You can't possibly believe him," she said, her voice warm, soothing. "A convicted fraudster spinning one last story to save his skin."

She turned to Farrow, her tone gentle, reasonable. Inviting.

I felt it then—the subtle pressure, like a hand brushing across my thoughts. A suggestion of doubt. Of sympathy.

"He's desperate," Lucy continued. "And I'm conve-nient. Check my credentials. My work. My reputation. I didn't imprison anyone."

Her gaze slid to me, sharp beneath the softness. "Liv knows how…imaginative things can become in this family."

For a heartbeat, the room wavered.

Then Farrow looked at her.

Really looked.

And nothing happened.

Lucy frowned—just slightly.

She tried again. I felt it like a ripple this time, faint but insistent. A tug at emotions that never came.

Under different circumstances, I might have pitied her.

Trying to influence DI Farrow's feelings must be like trying to squeeze water from a stone.

Farrow didn't look at Steven. He didn't look at me. He looked at Lucy.

"Ms. Seven," he said evenly, "you're not being arrested on his word."

Lucy's smile twitched.

"You're being arrested because you rented a property under false pretenses, concealed a missing person, and your movements place you at three locations we've been trying to connect for days."

He lifted his phone slightly. "It appears that you're very good at convincing people you're harmless, but facts don't lie."

Lucy stared at him, genuine surprise flashing across her face. For the first time, she looked…caught off guard.

Off to the side, Maggie laughed—a harsh, brittle sound.

"I've been patient all my adult life," she said loudly, straightening as officers approached her. "If you think I'm giving up on this cottage, you're severely mistaken."

She turned her glare on me. "You'd better watch your back, Liv. That cat won't live forever."

Audrey stepped forward before I could stop her.

"Didn't you know," she said coolly, "that cats have nine lives, Aunt Maggie?"

The room stilled.

I put an arm around my daughter's shoulders.

"Yep," I said. "And you're going to have a very long wait. Because we'll be here."

I looked Maggie straight in the eye.

"And we're not going anywhere."

CHAPTER FORTY-FOUR

Audrey tugged at my arm while the police were still busy carting our relatives away.

"You have to come next door, Mom."

I told Farrow where I'd be and followed Audrey outside, Gina and Emerald close behind me. The air felt different out here—cooler, clearer—like I could finally draw a full breath again.

At Esme's cottage, the door flew open before we even knocked.

Blake stood there.

And in Blake's arms—

"Ethel!" I sobbed.

The marmalade cat blinked serenely at me, profoundly unimpressed by the emotional collapse unfolding around her.

"Oh thank god," Gina breathed.

Ethel wriggled, indignant, then allowed herself to be passed into my arms. She was warm. Solid. Real.

I laughed and cried at the same time, burying my face in her fur.

"Tell her," Audrey urged. "Tell Mom."

Blake nodded, breathless. "Okay. So. Lucy took me to Oxford. The Bodleian. Said it would distract me." They swallowed. "She was lecturing. I was sketching—just impressions of the place—and then suddenly I was drawing something else."

"What?" I asked.

"The cottage," Blake said simply. "The one next door. In my head. And Ethel. In a cage."

My grip tightened on the cat.

"I made an excuse. Ran. Took a taxi, then a train. Used your spare key—the one you keep for cleaning." Blake let out a shaky laugh. "And there she was."

Ethel flicked her tail, as if to say *of course I was.*

"I was about to bring her straight back," Blake continued, "when I saw Maggie circling the cottage, trying to find a way in. So I waited, then crossed into Esme's garden instead. Luckily she and Anthony were home and let me hide. I tried calling everyone. Finally Gina answered— from the hospital."

Gina nodded. "Drake was being admitted."

I frowned. "I thought you'd given your phones up when Hatherleigh let you go?"

"Oh, well. That Hatherleigh chap thought an old woman like me was just going to be compliant and do as he asked." Gina waved a hand. "I gave him Emerald's phone instead. I saw it lying on top of her notes."

"That's when Dad came up with the plan," Audrey said quietly.

I sank into a chair, clutching the cat, overwhelmed.

Lucy really had rented the cottage.

To hide Ethel.

To manipulate us all.

She had grand plans—just like her mother's. To

consolidate the Seven powers under her control. But she had failed.

Gina would never forgive her sister. Maggie and Lucy would not be welcome at the inn—or at the cottage—ever again.

And Gina and Emerald still had decisions to make: about the old inn, the ghosts, the mirror with Alaric Hatherleigh now trapped inside it, and all the remnants of the Ordo Limina Mortis.

We would stand by them every step of the way.

But first—there was Steven.

He had turned himself in. There were statements to give, questions to answer. The investigation would stretch on for months. And I had a long list of relationships to repair—some strained by fear, some by silence, some by my own lies.

Still.

If I could find it in myself to forgive Steven—even cautiously, even conditionally—then maybe there was hope for forgiveness elsewhere too.

THAT NIGHT, A BONE-DEEP EXHAUSTION SENT ME INTO something like a coma the moment my head hit the pillow. The day after blurred into a visit to the police station, paperwork, phone calls, and long conversations with friends and family.

Now it was evening. The kids were asleep, and I finally had a moment to myself.

For the first time since I'd moved back, there was a proper fire burning in the hearth.

Jamie had shown me how to build it properly—how to stack the logs so the flame would take, how to feed it without smothering it. The cottage felt warmer. More settled. Like home.

On the coffee table lay the newspaper. I'd been folding it, unfolding it, reading it, rereading it, and folding it again all day.

Steven's letter had been printed in full. It had been his idea to come clean to the world.

I picked it up one last time and read it to Ethel, who was curled up on the couch next to me.

To Whom It May Concern,

My name is Steven Grantham.

I am writing this letter of my own free will, without coercion, and with the full understanding that what I am about to admit will have legal consequences. I accept those consequences.

I am responsible for orchestrating and sustaining a fraudulent investment scheme over a period of several years. What began as an attempt to conceal losses evolved into a deliberate deception. I misrep-resented returns, falsified documents, and knowingly solicited funds under false pretenses. I understand that my actions caused severe financial and emotional harm to many people. There is no justification for that.

When the scheme began to collapse, it did so faster than I had imagined possible. It was not one mistake, but dozens—small deci-sions made in panic, each one intended to buy time. I moved money through offshore accounts and shell companies, telling myself these measures were temporary. They were not. They only deepened the damage.

As scrutiny increased, I believed—wrongly—that if I stayed, every asset would be frozen immediately, and my family would be left with nothing. I told myself that running was a way to protect them. In truth, I was protecting myself: my reputation, my pride, and my fear of facing what I had done.

When investigators closed in, I fled.

I abandoned my wife and children without explanation, leaving them to carry the weight of my crimes in my absence. That is the failure I regret most—not the loss of status or wealth, but the harm I caused the people who trusted me most.

During this period, I lived under false names and relied on resources that were never truly secure. I also entered into a personal relationship that further compromised my position.

Her name was Marissa. She was my secretary.

We had an affair—brief, ill-judged, and entirely my responsibility. I ended it. She did not. Marissa was aware of the existence of certain accounts and funds I had moved. When the situation deteriorated, she threatened to expose everything unless I took her with me. She claimed she was owed compensation.

For a time, I agreed.

Eventually, she stole from me—emptying one of the accounts she still had access to. Not the largest, but enough to disappear. She vanished somewhere between Lisbon and Tangier under a new name and passport. I did not report the theft. I could not bring myself to explain how stolen money had been stolen again.

That loss left me with nothing but the consequences I had been trying to outrun.

I came to Fairwyck, knowing that my presence would only complicate matters for my family. I told my wife that I had nowhere to go, and while that wasn't true in a material sense—I had the money to hide out in a hotel room or a rented property—it was true in a philosophical one. I didn't want to go anywhere else. I told myself I was seeking redemption. In reality, I was seeking refuge—from the law, from accountability, and from myself.

I now understand that redemption does not come from hiding, delaying, or bargaining. It comes from truth.

I am prepared to cooperate fully with authorities, provide access to all remaining records and accounts within my control, and assist in any investigation related to my actions. I no longer wish to evade responsibility.

To my wife, Liv:

I know words cannot repair what I broke. I betrayed your trust long before I ever left. I placed you in an impossible position—forced to protect our children while carrying secrets that were never yours to bear. You were right to doubt me. You were right to demand honesty. I'm sorry that I gave it too late.

To Blake and Audrey:

You deserved a father who chose courage over comfort and truth over fear. I failed you in ways that may take a lifetime to fully understand. Please know that every step I take now is guided by the hope that one day you may see this letter not as another excuse—but as the moment I finally stopped running.

I do not ask for forgiveness.

I only ask that you do not give up on yourselves because of my mistakes.

Whatever happens next, I accept it.

Steven Grantham

By the time I reached the end, my hands were shaking —not with anger, not even with grief, but with the strange, fragile relief of closure.

Ethel had edged closer, her warm, solid body pressed against my side. Her eyes were closed, and she was gently snoring.

I couldn't help laughing. "Put you to sleep, did it?" I

said drily. "Well, then maybe it's time to change the subject to something that actually interests you."

I stroked her marmalade fur. "The keeper of the Seven power, is it?"

Ethel opened one eye.

"I think," I said softly, "you and I finally have a lot to talk about."

~

To be continued...

Don't miss the release of the next GHOST PHOTOGRAPHER MYSTERY and sign up for my newsletter on felicitygreenauthor.com.

You'll receive a free book, NO REST FOR THE WICKED WITCH, and get access to free short stories and bonus scenes. I'll also introduce you to my SCOTTISH WITCHES MYSTERY series, starting with book 1 THE WITCH CLUB.

Thank you for reading CLICK, CURSE, CORPSE, the third GHOST PHOTOGRAPHER MYSTERY. I hope you enjoyed reading it as much as I loved writing it. If you did, I would greatly appreciate a review on Amazon or your favorite store or book review site. Reviews are crucial for authors as well as for readers who are looking for their next book—even just a line or two are so helpful. Thanks!

I love to chat with my readers, so if you'd like to contact me, visit felicitygreenauthor.com.

Happy reading!
Felicity Green